BLAZE WYNDHAM

BERTRICE SMALL

BLAZE WYNDHAM

NEW AMERICAN LIBRARY

New American Library
Published by New American Library, a division of
Penguin Group (USA) Inc., 375 Hudson Street,
New York, New York 10014, U.S.A.
Penguin Books Ltd, 80 Strand,
London WC2R 0RL, England
Penguin Books Australia Ltd, 250 Camberwell Road,
Camberwell, Victoria 3124, Australia
Penguin Books Canada Ltd, 10 Alcorn Avenue,
Toronto, Ontario, Canada M4V 3B2
Penguin Books (N.Z.) Ltd, Cnr Rosedale and Airborne Roads,
Albany, Auckland 1310, New Zealand

Penguin Books Ltd, Registered Offices:
80 Strand, London WC2R 0RL, England

Published by New American Library, a division of Penguin Group (USA) Inc.
Previously published in New American Library hardcover and Onyx mass market editions.

First New American Library Trade Paperback Printing, May 2003
10 9 8 7 6 5 4 3 2 1

 REGISTERED TRADEMARK—MARCA REGISTRADA

New American Library Trade Paperback ISBN: 0-451-20865-X

The Library of Congress has catalogued the hardcover edition of this title as follows:

Small, Bertrice.
Blaze Wyndham.

I. Title.
PS3569.M28B57   1988   813'.54   88-1659

Set in Goudy
Designed by Leonard Telesca

Printed in the United States of America

*To my good friend and former secretary, Donna Tumelo,
of Wilmington, North Carolina. Thanks, kiddo!*

THE PLAYERS

THE MORGANS OF ASHBY HALL

Sir Robert—the lord of the manor
Lady Rosemary—his wife

THEIR CHILDREN

Blaze—the eldest
Bliss and Blythe—the eldest set of twins
Delight—the next eldest
Larke and Linnette—the second set of twins
Vanora—the seventh daughter
Gavin and Glenna—the third set of twins
Henry and Thomas—the fourth set of twins

THE WYNDHAM FAMILY OF RIVERSEDGE AND RIVERSIDE

Lord Edmund Wyndham—the third Earl of Langford, and family head
Lady Dorothy Wyndham—his elder half-sister
Sir Richard Wyndham—her husband, and distant cousin
Anthony Wyndham—Edmund's heir, his half-sister's son
Henriette Wyndham—a cousin, half-French

THE OTHERS

Old Ada—the Morgan family's nursemaid
Heartha—Blaze's tiring woman
Owen FitzHugh—the Earl of Marwood, a friend of the Wyndhams'
Lord Nicholas Kingsley—a friend of the Wyndhams'
Cormac O'Brian—the Lord of Killaloe

THE ROYAL COURT

Henry VIII—King of England, reigned 1509–1547
Catherine of Aragon—his wife
Cardinal Wolsey—the primate of England
Mistress Anne Boleyn—a daughter of Sir Thomas Boleyn
Mistress Jane Seymour—of Wolf Hall
Princess Mary—the king's only legitimate child
Sir John Marlowe—a gentleman of the court
Lady Adela Marlowe—his wife
Will Somers—the king's fool
Father Jorge de Atheca—the queen's confessor

Prologue

ASHBY HALL

July 1521

"There is no way," said Lord Morgan hopelessly. "There is simply no way in which I can dower eight daughters. What can the future possibly hold for them under such circumstances? God curse the day my sweet darlings ever saw the light!" His shoulders slumped with despair.

"Oh, my love, say it not!" protested his wife, and catching his hands in hers she looked up into his face with tear-filled blue-gray eyes. "It is all my fault, Robert! If *only* Gavin had been born first instead of last we should not have this problem. Yet I would not wish our girls away! Surely we can find the means to dower one, and then perhaps she may help her sisters to obtain husbands. We may be poor, but our daughters are beautiful. I know that counts for something with men!"

Robert Morgan sighed sadly. Then he put a comforting arm about his pretty wife. How could he explain to her that it would take a miracle to scrape together enough to dower their eldest? That whatever dowry he might manage to assemble would not be enough to gain them an available great name? That most great names were betrothed in the cradle to other great names? That only a daughter successfully placed at court would have the opportunity to help her sisters fish for their own husbands? That those men must be so captivated by the beauty of each of the Morgan sisters as to render their lack of a dowry meaningless? How could he explain all of this to his sweet wife? How could he tell her that their daughters' great beauty was as much a liability as a blessing? Only their poverty and the remoteness of his hall had kept his girls innocent; had kept them from being tempted into a less-than-honorable place in the world.

His dear Rosemary would know naught of such things. A rural squire's daughter, she had been born and bred in the country. Indeed in her whole lifetime she had never traveled any farther than the nearby town of Hereford. She was a good wife, a good mother, a good chatelaine, a good woman. Her only real fault had been the abundance of daughters that she had produced. Yet in the sixteen years she had been his wife she had never lost a child, nor had she ceased trying to give him an heir, nor did she complain unreasonably. He considered himself fortunate in his marriage.

Bending down, he kissed the top of his wife's ash-blond head. "I must think more on this, sweeting. Leave me to myself now," he said, and Rosemary Morgan, with a cheerful little smile, dutifully departed her husband's presence convinced that he would make it all right, as he always did.

Lord Morgan gazed out through the leaded-paned windows of his small library. Ashby was a beautiful estate. It was rich in fertile land, but the land must be kept whole for his five-year-old son and heir, Gavin. There had been Morgans on this land since before King William, and it was unthinkable that any of it be sold. Still, he might not have that choice if he were to successfully marry off his daughters. No matter if a woman wed God or man, she must have some portion to bring to the marriage.

Once there had been great flocks of woolly sheep grazing upon Ashby's pastureland. It had been from those sheep that the family had earned its small wealth. They had never been a powerful family, but they had been comfortable. They dowered their daughters respectably, sent well-equipped sons to fight England's wars, had even produced a bishop for the church, and they paid their taxes.

Twelve years ago, however, an epidemic had wiped out their flocks. Two years afterward the smaller, newly reestablished flocks had suffered a similar fate. Every bit of the modest family fortune had gone into that second flock, and it too had been lost. There had been no time to rebuild their former prosperity.

Since then Lord Morgan had waged a never-ending battle to earn enough monies to pay his taxes, to feed his family and his people. That he was successful was a tribute to his stubborn determination that he should not lose his lands. Now as he looked out over his rolling fields, he seriously considered the possibility of selling, or at least giving, some acreage to each of his daughters as a dowry. Then he shook his head. What suitor of worth would accept such a pittance, for he could not give away too much of his son's inheritance. Still, he could not let his girls go to men of lesser birth; yet, would they be better off husbandless under the circumstances? The whole situation was utterly hopeless, and he felt as caught as an animal in a poacher's trap.

A gentle rapping upon the library door shook him from his unhappy thoughts. "Come in," he called, and the door opened to reveal one of the house servants.

"There is a rider come, m'lord. He wishes to speak with you."

Lord Morgan nodded. "Send him in then," he replied, and the servant turned, nodding to a shadowed figure behind him. Robert Morgan hid a small smile at the thought that his was certainly no grand house with grand manners.

"Lord Morgan?" An upper servant in orange-tawny and gold livery stood before him.

"I am Lord Morgan."

"My master, Lord Edmund Wyndham, is an hour from Ashby, and begs leave to call upon you. I am to bring your reply."

Robert Morgan was somewhat startled. Edmund Wyndham was the Earl of Langford, a wealthy and somewhat mysterious figure. What would such a man want with him? Still, he could not be inhospitable. "I shall be honored to receive your master, the earl," he told the liveried servant.

The advance rider bowed most courteously to him, and turning, left the room.

Lord Morgan impatiently yanked the tapestried bellpull that hung by the fireplace. "Fetch your mistress quickly," he told the answering servant. "We are to receive a visit," he told his wife moments later, "from the Earl of Langford. He will arrive in less than an hour." He awaited her reaction.

"Is he to stay to dinner?" fretted Lady Rosemary. "Blessed Holy Mother, I pray not! There is neither meat, nor game, nor fish. We were to have soup. I gave Cook permission to kill that stringy old hen who no longer lays. Soup and bread, Robert! What kind of fare is that to serve any guest, let alone an earl?"

He smiled. "There was nothing said about the earl staying for a meal. Just that he wished to stop and call upon me. There is a cask of malmsey left in the cellar from better days that you can tap. Do we have any small biscuits?"

She nodded, her expression brightening.

"Good," he said. "That will be hospitality enough, my love, for such an unexpected visitor."

"You must change your linen, my lord," she chided him. "There is a stain upon your shirt front. 'Tis not proper to receive a guest thusly."

"Immediately," he agreed.

They each hurried off in separate directions. Lady Rosemary to her wifely duties, Lord Robert to change his clothing. When he returned downstairs once more he was wearing his best black brocaded doublet, a garment that saw little use, and was consequently still in good condition; a clean, natural-colored linen shirt with a ruffle at both the neck and the wrists; black velvet haut-de-chausses, scarlet-and-black-striped stockings, and square-toed black shoes. A heavy silver neckchain with a garnet-studded medallion lay upon the rich fabric of his doublet. It was Lord Morgan's only valuable piece of jewelry other than the red-gold family ring with the cat's-eye beryl that he wore on his left hand, and the simple gold betrothal band that his wife had gifted him with so long ago.

"You are still the handsomest man I know," declared Rosemary Morgan to her husband as he descended the staircase from their bedchamber.

He smiled at her. "And you, madam, are as lovely as the day I first saw you."

"I am older," she protested.

"Are you? I had not noticed," he said gallantly.

She colored prettily, and said softly, "I love you, Rob. I always have, and I always will."

For a moment they stood staring at one another. Then, hearing through the open front door the sounds of horses coming up the gravel drive, he took her by the arm and led her outside so they might greet their noble guest.

Edmund Wyndham's brown eyes missed nothing as he made his way up the winding drive. The land was fertile, but badly underutilized. He could easily see where the woodland had encroached and was continuing to do so upon the pastureland. The cottages, although in decent repair, had an air of sadness about them, and the children playing before them were ragged and looked ill-nourished. Still, they seemed lively enough, and the faces that peered from the cottage doors were friendly and curious. Lord Morgan might be a poor man, but he was obviously a good master.

Ahead of him he could see his host standing before the doorway of the attractive stone house that was his home. Beside him was a petite, beautiful woman in a wine-colored silk dress, its long divided overskirt showing a pretty cream-colored petticoat embroidered with tiny black and gold thread flowers. Her blond hair, parted in the center, was only partly covered by a close-fitting golden caul. The lady of the manor, undoubtedly, thought Lord Wyndham, was dressed in her very best. He smiled. The attractiveness of the couple before him boded well.

Drawing his mount to a halt before the doorway of Ashby, he dismounted with an easy grace, and turning said, "Lord Morgan? I am Edmund Wyndham. I thank you for receiving me on such short notice."

"Although we have not met before, sir, you are most welcome to Ashby. May I present my wife, the lady Rosemary."

Edmund Wyndham bowed over Lady Morgan's hand, his lips touching the back of her palm just briefly. "Madam, it is my honor," he said.

She curtsied. "I, too, welcome you to Ashby, my lord." The voice was sweet, if slightly countrified, he thought.

"Come into the house, my lord," said Robert Morgan. His eyes worriedly swept over the earl's escort. There were at least a dozen men.

Edmund Wyndham saw the furtive look, and said easily, "If my men might be allowed to water their horses, sir, they can await me here."

"They will be thirsty themselves, my lord," said Lady Morgan. "I will have the servants bring them cider. I regret I cannot offer them wine, but our cellar is small."

The earl smiled at her, and Rosemary Morgan felt a tingle right down to her toes. "Water would have satisfied them, I assure you, madam. Your sweet cider will be a treat. I thank you for your hospitality." He turned then and followed his host into the house.

Giving the attending servant quick orders, she hurried after them. Having settled both men in her husband's library with the malmsey wine and sweet wafer biscuits, she turned to go.

It was then the earl suggested, "Perhaps, my lord, you would like your good lady to remain. What I have come to discuss concerns you both."

Lord Morgan nodded to his wife, and she seated herself upon a stool by his side. "Say on then, my lord," he said.

"I was married," the earl began, "for eighteen years to Lady Catherine de Haven. Thirteen months ago my wife died. We were childless. Although I have an heir in the presence of my sister's eldest son, I am but thirty-five years of age, and there is still time for me to father a son of my own. I understand that you are the parents of eight daughters, and so, hoping that one or more of them are of marriageable age, I have come to you seeking a wife."

Robert Morgan heard his wife's tiny gasp, and he wondered that his own jaw did not gape in surprise at the earl's words. Instead he heard himself saying coolly, "I should be honored to have my family joined with yours, my lord, and daughters to marry off I have aplenty, but though my name be old, and my estates respectable, I am a poor man. Only today my wife and I have spoken on the difficulties involved in dowering one child, let alone eight. I could offer but a tiny bit of land for a dower portion. Certainly a man of your standing expects a wealthy woman to wive. I cannot deceive you, Lord Wyndham. As much as it would please me to see one of my girls your countess, I do not have the means to compete in such a rich marriage mart. I thank you nonetheless for considering our family."

"I was quite well aware before my coming to Ashby of your circumstances, sir," said the earl. "Gold, lands, and standing I have in abundance. What I lack is children. What I need is a son, and for my son's mother I would have a strong and healthy wife. My Cathy was a gentle soul. We were betrothed in the cradle. She was her father's only surviving child. His lands, which were not entailed, matched my father's lands. It was considered a good match. We knew each other all of our lives. Like Queen Catherine herself, my own Catherine suffered miscarriage and stillbirths over the otherwise happy years of our union. She died giving birth to the only one of our children to survive outside of her womb. Alas, but our son followed his mother within hours of her own death, and was buried in her arms."

The earl's voice wavered for a brief moment, and he ducked his head to hide his pain, then continued onward. "It is told me, sir, that Lady Rosemary has never suffered the loss of a child either before or after its birth. Surely a daughter of such a healthy woman would herself also be healthy. That is why I come to you, Lord Morgan. That is why I would have one of your daughters to wive. Do you have a marriageable daughter at this time?"

"I have three, my lord earl, and a fourth I suspect who is also not far from womanhood, but again I tell you I know not how I can dower one daughter, let alone eight."

"Are those daughters fit, sir?"

"They have never had a sick day in their lives, any one of them. Indeed it is miraculous, for my otherwise healthy young son snivels and wheezes his way through each winter even as I do."

"Pick whichever of your daughters you would, my lord Morgan. I care not as long as she is old enough to bear children, and does not squint. Keep your lands for your son: I will have your daughter without a dowry. As part of her marriage portion from me I will settle upon each of her sisters a dowry of her own, enabling you to make decent betrothals for them all. My bride will be treated like a queen, and shall lack for nothing that she may desire. This I swear to you upon the soul of my own dead Catherine."

Rosemary Morgan pressed a hand to her mouth to suppress her cry. She could not believe what she had just heard, for it was a miracle, and surely the answer to their prayers. Her gray-blue eyes wide, she looked up at her husband. He was pale with the shock of the earl's speech. She watched for what seemed like forever as he struggled to regain a mastery of himself.

Lord Morgan finally drew in a deep breath, and expelling it noisily as if to clear his head, he said, "I would, of course, choose my eldest daughter to be wed first. She will be sixteen on the last day of November. Her name is Blaze."

"An unusual name," remarked the earl.

"All of our daughters have unusual names," said Lady Morgan, now recovering from her initial surprise. "I am afraid poor Father John disapproves most highly. In order to have my own way I have had to baptize each of my girls with a saint's name first. As they have all been christened *Mary*, they are known as I would have them known."

The earl chuckled. "Is your daughter Blaze as determined, madam, as you are? I would hope that her name is not indicative of her temperament."

"Blaze is a good child, sir, but I would be honest with you," said Lady Morgan. "She is no milk-and-water lass. None of my girls are."

"And what are their names?" he queried her.

"After Blaze come Bliss and Blythe, our fourteen-year-old twins. Then there is Delight. She is thirteen, and still somewhat of a scamp. Our second set of twins, Larke and Linnette, are nine. Vanora is seven, and Gavin and his sister Glenna are five."

The earl smiled once again at Lord and Lady Morgan. "I envy you that fine family. Particularly your small son," he said.

"There were times when even I despaired of seeing him born," Robert Morgan admitted candidly.

"But he *was* born!" the earl replied. "With a young and healthy wife, so shall my son be born too! It is settled then, sir? Will you have me as a son-in-law?"

"I will, and gladly, though it shames me I can send my daughter to you with naught but the clothes upon her back. Still, I will swallow my pride for her sake, and for the sake of my other girls. I love them, and I want them happy!"

The two men arose simultaneously and shook hands.

"Will you stay to dinner then, and meet Blaze?" Lord Morgan asked.

His wife cast anguished eyes to the heavens. Holy Mary! Sweet Saint Anne! Did Rob not remember that dinner was but soup and bread? Let the earl decline, and I will make a trip to Hereford Cathedral to light candles in your honor, she silently vowed.

"I regret I cannot, sir," replied Lord Wyndham. "It is twelve miles cross-country to my home. I must be there before dark. Today is my sister's birthday. I have planned an entertainment in her honor. The wedding contracts will be drawn up and sent to you. Whatever you desire changed, change. Then return the signed contracts to me. The banns shall be immediately posted. I will return on the thirtieth of September for the celebration of my marriage to your daughter."

"A moment, my lord," said Lady Morgan. Rising from her stool, she moved gracefully across the room to a long library table upon which was a rectangular box of dark wood banded in silver. Opening the box revealed a set of miniatures. Drawing the first one out, she turned and held it out to him. "Our elderly relative, Master Peter, amuses himself by painting miniatures of the children each spring. This is his latest rendering of Blaze. I thought, perhaps, that you would like to have it, my lord."

Accepting her offering, he gazed down into the proud little face in the miniature. His mind was still so full of Cathy that he had not even considered until this moment what his new wife might look like. It had not mattered to him as long as she was healthy, and fulfilled her chief wifely duty, which was to produce his heirs.

The face before him, however, was a beautiful one. A fair and perfect heart with well-spaced oval-shaped eyes of a violet-blue edged with thick dark gold lashes. Her nose was just slightly retroussé. The mouth small, yet full and pouting. It was the sort of mouth a man would not tire of kissing, he thought, if the sensuality of her lips proved truth, not lie. Her hair, parted in the middle, was a rich golden chestnut in color. It hung soft and loose about her lovely face.

Raising his eyes from the charming miniature, he said, "Madam, I asked for a wife. You offer me a treasure. I am overwhelmed, and grateful."

"I hope," said Rosemary Morgan with a little smile, "that you will say all those charming things to my daughter. She has never been courted. It would be a shame for her to miss such a wonderful part of life."

"I do not think," he answered her, "that it will be hard to say such things to Blaze. Her loveliness quite takes my breath away."

"Be patient with her, my lord. She is young, but she is strong in both body and mind. Nonetheless she will prove worth the trouble, I promise you."

Edmund Wyndham nodded. "My hobby is cultivating roses, madam. Roses are fussy creatures that need a great deal of loving concern in order to bring forth perfect blooms. You have given me a perfect rose, and I swear to you that I shall treasure it with my very life, and cultivate it with the utmost care." Then taking her hand up, he kissed it in farewell, and departed the library in the company of Robert Morgan.

Lady Rosemary watched her husband escort the earl from their house, the two men speaking in quiet tones that she could no longer distinguish. She looked down at her hand as if she expected to find it had changed. Then she laughed softly at herself. She was behaving exactly like a young girl, but the Earl of Langford had had that effect upon her. In a way she almost envied her daughter. Then she sobered. Blaze had absolutely no idea of how fortunate she was!

Lady Morgan hurried from the library and up the staircase to the children's quarters, where she found Old Ada, the children's nursemaid, with her three youngest. "Where is Mistress Blaze?" Lady Morgan demanded of the servant.

Old Ada's sharp eyes considered her mistress's request. She thought a moment. "Larke and Linnette, they be in the kitchens with Cook, or maybe in the pasture ogling those two new colts that was just born."

Lady Morgan sighed and waited. Old Ada knew just about everything that went on at Ashby, but she was elderly now and it was necessary to wait upon her memory.

The old lady pondered further. "Now, Delight, she be trailing after the two busy B's, and they was with Mistress Blaze."

"Where, Ada?"

"Running about barefoot in the fields and forest, no doubt," came the disapproving reply. " 'Tis no way, I'm thinking, for marriageable girls to behave, but then who is to marry them, poor lasses? Who is to marry our sweet little beauties?" She rocked back and forth upon her chair, the tears suddenly running down her withered face.

Lady Morgan left the children's rooms, descending back down into the main hallway of her house. She was the possessor of the most wonderful and exciting news! She wanted to tell Blaze of her great good fortune. Where was the flibbertigibbet? Running barefoot like some peasant wench, no doubt! I didn't chastise her enough, she thought. Then Rosemary Morgan laughed. Had they not raised—indeed were still raising— their children with a greater sense of freedom than most? Theirs was no formal society. They had never expected that their children would marry into important families, but now things were changing. The girls, of course, all had nice manners, and their housewifely skills were above reproach. Still, they would need to know more than she had previously taught them. Blaze, in particular, as she would be wed within two months to a wealthy and important man.

Lady Morgan went to the open door of the house. Her husband, having bid farewell to Lord Wyndham, was disappearing in the direction of the stables. The earl and his troop were riding away back down the driveway. Anxiously she scanned the landscape for a sight or sign of her wayward daughters. To her annoyance there were none.

"God's foot!" she swore softly beneath her breath, startling even herself, for she was not a woman to use such language. Still, it was irritating to be the possessor of such marvelous news, yet not be able to tell it. She bit her lip in vexation. Damn Blaze! She could not shout for her, as Edmund Wyndham was yet within hearing distance. With a sigh and a grumble of annoyance Lady Morgan turned back into her house, slamming the door behind her in her immense frustration.

Part One

❧

ASHBY HALL

Summer 1521

Chapter 1

The four girls, well hidden behind the shrubbery on the far side of the driveway that faced Ashby Hall, had a fine view of the elegant visitor although they could hear nothing that was said between him and their father.

"*Who is he*, do you think?" wondered Bliss Morgan, tossing her blond hair back from her face as she spoke.

"He is most divinely handsome even if he is old," noted her identical twin sister. Blythe's daffodil-colored hair seemed always perfectly coiffed.

"Maybe he's a suitor come for one of us," said Delight Morgan in a hopeful tone. Her deep blue eyes, so like their father's, sparkled with eager anticipation.

"Ohh, Dee, don't be so foolish!" Bliss snapped at the younger girl irritably, causing her face to fall. "Look at the man! His clothes are of the very best materials, and that gold chain around his neck is worth enough to dower us all quite respectably. None of us has so much as a dried pea for a portion. Without a dowry we've little hope of making any kind of a decent marriage. We'll be lucky if we end up as farmers' wives."

"Aye," echoed her twin mournfully. "We're all doomed to spinsterhood or worse. Not even the church will have us."

"Do you really want to go to the church, Blythe?" drawled the eldest of them in an amused tone, more than any aware of her sister's worldly penchants.

"You know I don't, Blaze! I want to be married and have children," replied Blythe somewhat indignantly.

"What you mean is that you want to be wed to a *rich* man, little sister," said Blaze, her tone somewhat cynical.

"It is just as easy to love a rich man as a poor one," Bliss pointed out instantly, defending her sibling. "We are poor, and I do not like it at all. I think I should enjoy being rich."

"There is little chance of that," Blaze retorted with a rueful laugh. "Look at us, sisters! Look at us in our linen skirts that are too short for us now, and our way-too-tight bodices. When did any of us ever have something new to wear?" She sighed almost bitterly.

"Delight's bodice isn't too tight," snipped Bliss, "but then she's still a baby yet and not ready for a suitor even if one did come along."

"Old Ada says my womanhood is close upon me," Delight hissed spiritedly at her elder.

"The old woman always knows too," Blythe said grudgingly. "So then there are four of us ready for marriage. To what purpose? Ahh, how sad to have naught!"

"We have each other," Blaze replied, recovering from her bout of self-pity first.

The four pairs of eyes met. Then Bliss smiled a smile that transformed her thin little face into an extremely beautiful face.

"Aye, we have each other, 'tis true, Blaze, and what would we do without us?" She smiled at her sisters, saying thoughtfully, "I should still like to know, however, just who the gentleman is. My curiosity is burning to learn why such a distinguished fellow would pay our father a call."

"There's time to learn all you need to know later," said Blaze, "but right now there's a late cherry tree I've found on the edge of the orchards that's full with sweet cherries that can be ours for the picking. We'd best hurry before the birds get them all, little sisters!" She turned and started off. The three younger girls followed in her wake.

The Morgan sisters had learned the lessons of frugality early in life. Poverty had taught them that nothing was to be wasted. When they finally returned to their home in late afternoon their willow baskets were filled to overflowing with the cherries that Blaze had so fortunately found for them. Hurrying to the kitchens, they put aprons on over their gowns, washed the fruit carefully in the worn stone sinks, and then set about pitting them, putting aside any bruised cherries to stew for their supper. When seven-year-old Vanora wandered into the kitchens she was put to work pounding a small sugar loaf to a fine powder.

"Let's candy some of the cherries," suggested Delight. "They always taste especially good just before Lent begins."

Blaze nodded in agreement, and smiling, the older three put some of the sweet fruit aside. The rest was equally divided. One half to go into the syrup pot, where it would be boiled down into a sweet thick syrup. The remainder of the cherries would be used for jelly.

"Stop stuffing your face with our cherries, Vanora, or I shall smack you," Bliss threatened as she caught the younger child in the act.

Vanora's sharp little face was covered with the evidence of her crime. Not the least intimidated by her elder sibling, she unwisely stuck out her pink tongue at Bliss, who immediately retaliated, reaching out to pull the child's hair. Vanora howled with outrage, her earsplitting shrieks setting the maidservants agog and bringing her mother running. Vanora sobbed noisily, more outraged than hurt. She looked slyly from beneath her wet eyelashes to see what effect her outrageous behavior was having upon the others as Lady Morgan demanded to know why Vanora was carrying on so.

Vanora hiccuped dramatically, but in the moment in which she drew breath preparatory to leveling an accusation at Bliss, Blaze spoke up.

"She has pounded her finger instead of the sugar loaf, Mama." Blaze put an apparently loving arm about her younger sister's narrow little shoulders and squeezed her hard. "Do stop raging, Vanora sweeting. I know it hurts, for many a time I have pounded my fingers too."

Vanora sobbed. Looking up into her eldest sister's face, she saw the stern warning in Blaze's eyes. Immediately she ceased her wailing. Blaze was her favorite sister, but Vanora knew the danger of getting on her bad side.

"There now," said Blaze sweetly, "that's better. Return to your task, Vanora, for without the sugar we shall not be able to preserve these luscious cherries. Yours is the most important task." With a final sniffle Vanora obeyed. Turning to her mother, Blaze said, "I found a late bloomer in the orchards. We managed to get to the cherries before the birds did, Mama. I've never known a cherry to bloom so late. It's a good month out of season."

"Nature is not always predictable," replied Lady Morgan. "How fortunate, Blaze, that you found the tree, and how good of you to so quickly rally your sisters to pick the fruit, but, dearest child, I have news. *Wonderful news!*"

"Does it have to do with that gorgeous man who was speaking with our father outside the house earlier?" Delight burst out.

"You saw Lord Wyndham then?" her mother asked.

"We were all hiding behind the hedge, Mama. Since you didn't call us, we did not think you wanted us, and went on to the orchard," said Delight truthfully.

Lady Morgan smiled at her fourth daughter. Delight was quite incapable of telling an untruth. Blaze she had known to tell white lies to protect the feelings of others. As for her first set of twins, both Bliss and Blythe lied so easily that they often believed what they said to be truth, for there was no real malice in either of them.

"Lord Edmund Wyndham is the Earl of Langford," Lady Morgan continued. "He was widowed over a year ago, and is without children. He has chosen Blaze to be his next wife. Is that not incredible news, my daughters?"

"I told you so! I told you so!" Delight danced around the kitchens to the amusement of the cook and the maidservants.

Rosemary Morgan smiled, then looked anxiously toward her eldest child. Blaze appeared stunned.

"Holy Blessed Mother! *An earl!* You are to marry an earl, Blaze!" gasped Bliss enviously. "He's even handsome!"

"You are going to be a countess," Blythe squealed excitedly, clapping her hands. "Lady Mary Blaze Wyndham, the Countess of Langford! Ohhh, why are you so lucky?!"

"*Lucky?*" Blaze whispered. "Am I lucky?" She drew a deep breath. Her voice was stronger now as, facing her mother, she demanded, "Why does this man want to marry with *me*? How can I marry anyone? You have fretted often enough, Mama, that there is no dowry for us." Blaze's violet-blue eyes were filled with unspoken questions.

The kitchens had grown deathly still, only the crackle of the flames in the fireplaces breaking the silence. Looking about her, Lady Morgan saw the avid curiosity of her servants, and clamped her lips in a thin disapproving line. There was nothing wrong with them knowing that Blaze was to wed, but the details were not their business.

"Is there no work to be done here?" she asked sternly, looking at the cook and her helpers. "I smell something burning. Have we so much in this household that we can afford to waste it? Girls, get back to your cherries! Blaze, you are to come with me!" Lady Morgan swept regally from the kitchens, her eldest daughter quickly following.

They did not stop in the Great Hall, for Rosemary Morgan wanted no gossiping servants to overhear what she was going to tell her daughter. The details were not even Blaze's business, though she would tell the troublesome chit. It was parents' duty to arrange suitable matches for their children. Even despite their poverty, kind providence had this day provided them with more than enough good fortune for all of the girls. She led her eldest child to the privacy of the bedchamber she shared with her husband. Together they sat upon the edge of the great bed where Blaze and all her siblings had been conceived.

Rosemary Morgan took her daughter's face into her hands and stared at Blaze a long moment before releasing her. The girl was lovely, of that there was no doubt. "You are a very lucky girl," she began, "*and* you will make a memorable Countess of Langford if you are clever."

"*Why me?*" demanded Blaze. "How can you possibly pay him a dowry of any kind, let alone the kind of dowry it must take to marry an earl?"

"He will have you without a dowry," Lady Morgan replied.

"*Why?*" The word was sharp. The tone suspicious.

"Edmund Wyndham was married for eighteen years to a woman who, like our poor Queen Catherine, could not produce a child. At least the king has our Princess Mary, but the Earl of Langford's only child died shortly after its birth. A birth which killed its mother. He is a wealthy man, Blaze, but he wants children. He already has an heir in the person of his nephew, but he wants his own son. You surely understand that.

"Somewhere, he did not say where, he learned of our family. Of the fact that all my children are living. That they are strong and healthy. Even knowing that we could not afford a dowry, he came to us, and offered to take you for his wife without one. He believes that you can produce healthy children for him even as I have produced them for your father."

"So the great earl comes to Ashby to buy himself a blooded brood mare, does he? I will not marry him, Mother! I may be poor, but I have my pride. I should sooner be condemned to spinsterhood! How dare this man think that he can buy me? What arrogance!"

"Nay, Blaze, he is not arrogant! He came as a supplicant, and he treated your father with elegance and dignity. His coming is like a miracle. It is your duty as a child of this family to accept gratefully the wonderful opportunity that has been offered you. Do you not see how fortunate you are?"

"I do not see, Mama. Let this earl marry one of the others. Both Blythe and Bliss would kill for such an *opportunity*," Blaze said scornfully.

"You are the eldest," stressed her mother. "It is fitting that you be matched first. Besides, Blythe and Bliss are a full year younger than you are. The earl is a mature man, and you are the perfect age both to wed him and to begin bearing his children."

"No!" said Blaze stubbornly.

Lady Morgan drew a deep breath to still her rising temper. The girl is impossible, she thought. I certainly named her well. "You are not the only one involved in this, Blaze," she told her difficult daughter. "As part of your marriage settlement the earl has agreed to respectably dower your sisters so that they too may find good husbands."

"Then I am to be a sacrificial lamb!" Blaze burst out angrily.

Lady Morgan's temper could no longer be contained, and quickly spilled over. "Blaze," she said, standing up and placing harsh hands upon her daughter's slender shoulders, "you will go to the chapel at once! Pray to the Blessed Mother for her forgiveness. Your sin of selfishness, pride, and disobedience to parental will I will not tolerate! May Our Lady's good, kind heart along with her prayers help cleanse you of these unruly thoughts. Hopefully you will realize how fortunate you are to have been chosen to wed Lord Wyndham. Mayhap you will even allow yourself to consider your younger sisters. To appreciate the fact that their futures rest, may God have mercy on us all, in your two selfish hands!"

"Ohh, that is unfair of you, Mama! To put the responsibility of my sisters' welfare upon me, and me alone!" Blaze cried defiantly.

"I will not argue further with you, daughter," said Lady Morgan. "Go to the chapel this minute!"

Blaze ran from the room, her heart pounding with her anger and her frustration. Deliberately ignoring her mother's orders, she hurried back to the kitchens, stopping halfway down the narrow stone steps to look upon her sisters. Bliss and Blythe were busily overseeing the others, for Larke and Linnette had joined them. The elder set of twins were so beautiful, Blaze thought sadly. It was not right that they be condemned to living their lives here at Ashby without husbands and children of their own. They had only a few years left in which to find husbands. Some would have claimed they were already past their prime. Blaze could not remember ever seeing anyone who could match her sisters' beauty. They were identical in features but for a tiny beauty mark. On Bliss the dainty mark was located just above the left corner of her mouth, but on Blythe it was above the right corner. Each had pale daffodil-blond hair and sapphire-blue eyes. Their faces, like their eldest sister's, were heart-shaped with slender little turned-up noses and generous mouths. Their pleasingly curved eyebrows and long sweeping eyelashes were dark enough to show against their fair skins, and did not need the artifice of charcoal. Theirs was a delicate beauty, yet their rosy cheeks bespoke of good health that could not be denied.

The only other blond amongst their siblings was Vanora, whose hair had a silvery gilt look to it. With her dark blue eyes, which in certain light seemed almost black, the little girl, despite a face still round with baby fat, promised to one day be a great beauty. So did their littlest sister, Glenna, with her chestnut-red hair and their mother's gray-blue eyes.

The rest of the Morgan children were dark-haired. Glenna's twin brother, Gavin, was his father's image with his blue eyes and dark chestnut-brown hair. Winsome Delight with identical coloring. The second set of twins, Lark and Linnette, with their dark brown hair and violet-blue eyes so like her own. What future did any of them have without gold, and how could their father provide it with his sheep destroyed? He had never been able to recover financially from that second destruction of his flocks.

With a silent sigh Blaze retraced her steps back up the kitchen stairs to the main floor of the house. Moving with almost reluctant feet, she entered the family's little chapel. Kneeling at her own little prie-dieu, she gazed up at the statue of Saint Mary, and felt her conscience prick sharply at her pride. The sweet and patient face of the stone saint seemed to reproach her for her rebellious thoughts.

What is wrong with you? demanded her conscience. *An attractive and wealthy man wishes to wed with you. Why do you behave so wickedly?*

Because I want to be loved for me, myself, answered her pride. *This man wants me because I can be a healthy brood mare and give him sons. What does he care of me? He did not even stay long enough to greet me!*

What nonsense! returned her conscience. *There is but one reason for the sacrament of marriage. You have been taught it. The purpose of marriage is to have children.*

I would be loved! her pride cried.

Love, said her conscience, *will come later as you get to know one another. Love, and respect.*

I must be loved, her pride whimpered.

Your parents love one another, her conscience reminded her. *Why should it be any different for you?*

My parents knew one another before their marriage, her pride reminded her conscience.

An unusual situation, her conscience retorted. *Marriages are arranged by parents in their offspring's best interests. Your mother is right! You are incredibly fortunate that this man is willing to have you without a dowry, and what of the sisters you profess to love? Are they not entitled to some measure of happiness? This man has generously offered to dower them so they, too, may find husbands. Are these the actions of a wicked man? Your parents are content. Why can you not be?*

"But where is the love?" Blaze whispered to herself.

It will come, said her conscience. *It is bound to come. You will find love, but more important, you will have the satisfaction of knowing that you have, by humbling your overproud spirit and being a good Christian daughter, helped your seven sisters to their own happiness. How can you refuse the earl's suit?*

"I cannot," Blaze said softly, a tear of self-pity rolling down her face. "Oh, Blessed Mother of Christ, forgive me my disobedience. Help me to be more thoughtful of others," she prayed. A hand dropped upon her shoulder. Startled, Blaze looked up to see her father. Hastily crossing herself, she arose. "Oh, Papa, I have made Mama very angry," she confessed, flinging herself into his arms.

Robert Morgan's arms enfolded his eldest child against him. "I know," he said gravely, thanking heaven that she could not see the laughter in his eyes. Blaze had never been the easiest of his children. She required a special touch. His wonderful Rosemary! The best of mothers, and so good with all the others, yet she could never quite understand that Blaze needed more than the others. "Your mother tells me that you have refused to accept our decision in this matter of a husband for you. Is this so?"

"I will marry the earl, Papa," Blaze said softly. "How can I scorn such a generous offer?"

"You cannot," answered Lord Morgan quietly. He set her back so they might look at one another. "You must trust me in this, Blaze, as you have always trusted me. Lord Wyndham is more than suitable. If the truth were spoken, my dearest, it would say that you are marrying up, for indeed you are. I had not met the man before today, but I have never heard ill spoken of him. His manner is firm and kindly. It is obvious that he loved his first wife despite her inability to give him children, and that he truly mourned her death. I believe he will love you too, Blaze. I believe that you will learn to love him. He will be a good husband. His generosity to you, not to mention to your sisters, speaks well of him. Not only will the dowries he is providing for your sisters aid them in finding husbands, but his connection to them by your marriage will aid us even more. Can you be content to have faith in my decision, my child?"

Blaze nodded. "I did not mean to be so difficult, Papa, it is just that I never thought . . . never expected that I should be wed to so great a lord. I believed if I wed at all it would be to some younger son with no more than I, if that. Is the earl's home very far from Ashby?"

"RiversEdge is approximately a half-day's ride from Ashby unless one goes directly across the fields, which the earl did today. His sister was celebrating her birthday, and he wished to be there. It is this sister whose eldest son is the earl's current heir."

"They cannot be happy that the earl is remarrying," said Blaze wisely.

"It is not their decision," replied Lord Morgan, and taking his daughter's hand, he led her from the chapel. Together they walked down the corridor into the Great Hall of Ashby where Robert Morgan drew Blaze down next to him onto a settle by the fireplace. "The Langford earldom goes back to King Henry V, my child. The first earl saved that king's life at the Battle of Agincourt, and was rewarded with a greater title than he already possessed. He was only sixteen at the time. The Wyndhams are long-lived. Lord Edmund's grandfather lived to be seventy-five years of age, and his father was past seventy when he perished in an epidemic."

"The earl was his father's only son?" Blaze inquired.

"Surviving son, my dear, and only offspring of the second earl's third wife. The family seems to have been racked with difficulties in the matter of producing a strong male line. Now in his thirties and without a direct heir, the earl is very anxious. I'm sure you can see that. As you are an intelligent girl, Blaze, I am equally certain that you understand the earl's position."

"He might have at least stayed long enough to meet me," she answered him irritably.

Lord Morgan smiled at his daughter's annoyance. Although he understood why the earl had departed once an arrangement was struck between them, he also understood why Blaze felt slighted. "The earl wanted to stay, but he had planned an entertainment in his sister's honor. They are close despite the disparity in their ages. I know that loving your own sisters as you do, you can understand Lord Wyndham's motives."

"Mmmmm," Blaze considered, and her father laughed indulgently, giving her shoulder a small squeeze. She looked up at him. "What is he like?" she demanded. "Did he leave me no miniature? Did you give him one? Is he content to marry some faceless female? Does he even care?"

"He did leave the choice of a bride to your mother and me, his one proviso being that you didn't squint," chuckled Lord Morgan.

"Does he?" She bristled.

"No, Blaze, he does not. He is very well-favored. Tall and fair-skinned with dark brown hair and fine brown-gold eyes. You will find him as pleasant to look upon as he will find you, my dear."

"When are we to be married, Papa?"

"The thirtieth of September," he replied.

"*So soon?* I had thought I should have at least until next spring!" she said.

"The first banns will be cried this Sunday, Blaze."

"It is barely two months, Papa!"

"The earl has been widowed over a year, my child. He wants a wife now, not several months hence," Lord Morgan said.

"There is too much to do, Papa! It cannot be done in such a short time!"

"What is there to do?" he questioned her.

"I have no clothing that would be suitable for a bride, let alone a Countess of Langford! Even if Mama and my sisters had the fabrics, we could not sew enough for my trousseau in such a short time."

"Your trousseau is being made at RiversEdge, Blaze. Everything, including your wedding gown, will be provided for you. The earl has promised to send some of these things ahead of time so you will not be embarrassed before his family when you arrive at your new home."

"My dower chest! It is but half-filled, Papa! How can I arrive at Rivers-Edge with an empty dower chest?"

"We will take linens from your sisters' chests," said Lady Morgan, entering the hall to join her husband and eldest child.

"Indeed our two chests alone are filled to overflowing," said Bliss, who with her twin had followed their mother. "You sew much too slowly, Blaze. If you had another five years you could not fill your dower chest."

"But what you have done is beautiful," Blythe said in an effort to soften her twin's sharp words, but Blaze was used to Bliss and took no offense.

"Blythe and I will embroider the B and the E upon the bed linens," said Bliss. "We shall intertwine them within a heart."

"I will help," replied Blaze.

"No!" cried Bliss. "You are slower than cold honey, and your pokiness will only drive me to madness. We can have them done in a trice."

"But if you empty your chests to fill mine, what will you do?" Blaze worried.

"Do not fret, sister," answered Blythe. "We need not empty our dower chests to fill yours. We shall this winter easily replenish what we give. It rather pleases me to think that a little bit of us will go with you to your new home."

Blaze arose and hugged her younger sibling. "I like the idea that a little bit of you will be with me too. I suddenly realize that I am going to be alone for the very first time in my life."

"*Alone?*" Bliss scoffed. "You are to be the mistress of a great house, sister! You will have a husband, and if you do your duty by him, you will quickly have a houseful of children. Can you call yourself alone amid the bevy of servants and retainers you are certain to have? Gracious, Blaze, you are a strange girl."

Blaze laughed at her sharp-tongued sister. "I am not certain that I shall know how to handle such a 'bevy'," she teased, and then she grew serious. "It is my family I shall miss, Bliss, for though we be poor in worldly goods, we are rich in our love for one another."

"I should sooner be rich in more practical ways," grumbled Bliss with total candor.

"Then once I am settled as Lord Wyndham's wife I shall have to see what I can do to provide you with a suitable husband. Suitable," she amended, "meaning rich!"

"And for Blythe also," Bliss said, protective as always of her twin.

"For Blythe also," Blaze agreed.

"It can be no idle promise that you make, my dear," said Lady Morgan. "Your sisters will indeed need your help and influence in finding husbands. As each of them weds, they in turn will help those remaining. This miracle of a match that has happened so suddenly to you is the answer to all of our prayers. The Earl of Langford is a most kind and generous man. If you make but the slightest effort to please him, you will be, I know, the happiest of women. He has sworn to us that you will be treated like a queen. When you give him an heir, Blaze, I suspect there is nothing within his power that cannot be yours." She looked nervously at her daughter, wondering if the rebellion Blaze had exhibited earlier was still upon her.

Knowing that her mother needed the reassurance, Blaze said dutifully, "I shall indeed endeavor to be a good wife to the earl, Mama, and as I love children, I want my own every bit as eagerly as does Lord Wyndham."

Lady Morgan looked relieved. "Oh, my dear," she said, "I knew if you but thought things through you would see the wisdom of our decision." Hugging her daughter, she finished somewhat tearily, "I am so happy for you!"

"Madam," protested her husband, "you will have this entire household of females in hysterics quite shortly if I do not remove our eldest from your sphere of influence. Run upstairs, Blaze, and change into your riding skirt. There are more practical things a good chatelaine should know. As your father, I feel it is my duty to present the male side of the coin. Hurry now!"

Gratefully Blaze escaped the Great Hall of Ashby, her mother, and her sisters. She sped up the stairs to the small room she shared with Bliss and Blythe. Quickly she removed her everyday skirt and bodice, replacing them with a clean white shirt and a somewhat worn but sturdy dark velvet riding skirt. Whatever the skirt's color had once been, the material had faded long since into an undistinguishable hue. From a corner she drew out her riding boots and pulled them on, wincing at the fact that they pinched her toes, which were now longer than when the boots had been made five years ago. Still, they had a comfortable familiarity about them. As she stood, however, it suddenly dawned on her that Lord Wyndham would probably have new boots made for her. New boots, and a riding skirt of deep blue velvet with a matching bodice, and a hat with a white plume! For a moment she closed her eyes, envisioning herself in such finery, and decided that she liked the picture. There were certain advantages to marriage with a wealthy man that she had not considered. How Bliss would chide her for that oversight.

She hurried back down the staircase, out the front door to where her father was already mounted waiting. A stableboy boosted her into her own saddle, and father and daughter moved off from the house at a leisurely pace. They rode in silence for a time, but once they gained the narrow path across the estate through the fields, Lord Morgan asked his daughter, "How do you really feel about this marriage, Blaze?"

"Would my feelings really make a difference, Papa? I must marry, must I not? And is not this match indeed a miracle as Mama says?"

"If I believed that marriage to Lord Wyndham were a bad thing for you, Blaze, I should not have agreed to the earl's proposal. It is true that you must marry, and that this match is indeed an incredible piece of good fortune for us all. I would help you come to terms with yourself, however, my daughter. I do want you to be happy."

"I am frightened," said Blaze, "but of what, I am not certain. I hate the thought of leaving Ashby. Yet, as Bliss reminds me, I am to be mistress of a great house. I cannot help but wonder if it is as beautiful as here. Whether I will grow to love it. What if I do not? I do no know this man I am to marry. He does not know me either. What if we do not like each other? I understand his reasons for wanting another wife, yet if those are his only reasons, can he learn to care for me, and I him? It is all very difficult and confusing, Papa.

"One moment I am excited, for I never aspired to such a match. Indeed I fully expected to end up with Squire Greene's younger son if they would have a dowerless girl. I suspected in my case that they might, for the squire is an ambitious man. I could see him weighing the thought of sharing grandchildren with a baron of the realm each time our families met." She chuckled throatily, and Robert Morgan joined her laughter.

"Yet in another moment," Blaze continued, "there is a part of me, Papa, that resents the Earl of Langford's arrogance in arriving here with scant notice to demand one of your fertile daughters to wive."

Robert Morgan nodded his understanding of his daughter's feelings, then said, "He meant no disrespect, Blaze. Of that I am certain. Wealthy and powerful men look at these things differently. They come to the point quickly with little shilly-shallying. Time for them is a commodity to be husbanded as carefully as their gold. Lord Wyndham knew our position. He knew that as the father of eight daughters I would want to wed them to this family's best advantage. He also knew that we had little if any financial wherewithal. The advantage was really his, Blaze. Yet at no time did he make me feel a beggar at his gates. If there is any of the arrogance in him that you accuse him of, I have not seen it."

"How old is he, Papa?"

"He will be thirty-five in August," came the reply.

"That is very old, Papa."

Robert Morgan did not know whether he felt like laughing or weeping at his eldest child's remark. He was but forty. From Blaze's standpoint, however, he realized that thirty-five must look ancient. She would be sixteen on the last day of November. Still, such disparity in ages between a man and his wife was not unusual. Especially as women were apt to die younger due to the rigors of childbirth, and men were quite likely to remarry. A man, particularly a childless man or one with only daughters, would want a fecund female, not an older woman with little chance of birthing a son.

A small cough from his daughter reminded him that she needed further reassurance.

"Lord Wyndham is quite in his prime, Blaze. I expect that you will find him a vigorous lover." He glanced over at her, and saw that his words had brought a deep blush to her cheeks. He chuckled wickedly.

"*Papa!*" she scolded him, and kicked her mount into a canter.

For a moment he watched her go, the sky-blue ribbon that held her lovely golden-brown hair falling away, and her tresses streaming out in the summer's breeze. Lord Wyndham was going to be very surprised to learn that he had gotten himself quite a bargain in Blaze Morgan. Perhaps Rosemary was correct when she said that their daughters' beauty must count for something. For a moment Robert Morgan's eyes narrowed in thought. Blaze's marriage. Her new position. The dowries for his other girls. All would enable him to rebuild Ashby, even improve it. The alliances he would contract for his daughters could help him to obtain an heiress for Gavin. He was going to be very careful in the matches he made. Now he could afford to be choosy.

"*Papa!*" Blaze had stopped her headlong flight and was now calling him.

Robert Morgan waved his hand at her and grinned. "I am coming, Blaze," he shouted. "I will race you to the lake!" Kicking his stallion into a gallop, he raced after his daughter, who, hearing his words, had already sent her own horse into flight.

Chapter 2

"You place us in a difficult position, sir," said Robert Morgan. There was no mistaking the irritation in his voice.

Anthony Wyndham flushed, but he held his ground. "The matter is as hard for me, sir, as it is for you, but I am only following Edmund's—my uncle's—orders."

"My daughter is a sensitive girl," Lord Morgan protested. "She has never even met the earl. Finding herself promised in marriage to a stranger has taken some getting used to for her. Yet knowing that she would meet her betrothed before the wedding within the bosom of her family has helped her to come to terms with this match. Now you tell me that you have come to wed Blaze by proxy for your uncle, and that you will escort her back to him at RiversEdge. I like it not, sir!"

"I have already explained to you, my lord, why my uncle has sent me to ask this of you. You and your family are invited to come back to Rivers-Edge with me for the second ceremony."

Lord Morgan slammed his fist into the palm of his other hand. "We cannot leave Ashby right now, sir! It is the harvest season. All hands, even our fine white noble ones, are needed here on this estate if my people and I are to survive the winter."

Anthony Wyndham's manner softened. He knew the position that Lord Morgan was in, for his uncle had been more than frank with him. Only four years separated the two men, and having been raised together, they were more like brothers than uncle and nephew. "My uncle's people need to see the ceremony of his new marriage. They need the hope that it offers them. Surely you understand this, my lord."

"Rob." Rosemary Morgan spoke quietly. "It is certainly very disappointing for us not to have the full pomp of Blaze's wedding, but I know that you would not endanger the match in your chagrin." She smiled encouragingly at her husband.

Anthony Wyndham thought to himself as he watched her that if the daughter was as lovely as the mother, then his uncle was certainly a fortunate man. Lady Morgan was a radiant beauty.

"I know," she continued softly to her husband, "that Blaze is your especial pet, but with our large brood there will be weddings aplenty. Those weddings cannot, however, take place unless this one does." It was a gentle warning that even Anthony Wyndham understood.

Lord Morgan gave a soft groan of defeat. "You are right, my love," he said, and looking up, pierced the earl's nephew with a half-angry gaze. "*When?*" he demanded.

"Tomorrow, my lord. I must bring the bride to RiversEdge as quickly as I can."

"Blaze's dower chest is in complete readiness," said Lady Morgan, forestalling the new outburst she saw brewing in her husband's blue eyes. "The proxy ceremony can take place first thing in the morning. It is better that our daughter not dwell upon this sudden change, although she will certainly be distressed."

Anthony Wyndham's relief was openly visible. "I have brought with me a maidservant of my uncle's to be a traveling companion to his betrothed wife. Her name is Heartha. She has with her the bridal garments and other clothing for the lady Blaze."

"I shall go and fetch my daughter," said Lady Morgan. "I shall allow you to tell her of these changes, Master Anthony, for I believe you can do it better than either my husband or myself." Rising from her seat, Rosemary Morgan hurried out.

Lord Morgan snorted. Then he grinned broadly at his guest. "You do understand that my wife believes that if you tell Blaze, she will not cause a scene."

"Your daughter is hot-tempered?" Anthony Wyndham's light-colored eyes showed mild curiosity.

"You will soon judge for yourself, sir," replied Lord Morgan with a small chuckle. "Of course there is the possibility that my daughter will remember her manners." Then he laughed aloud.

Anthony Wyndham suddenly looked distinctly uncomfortable. He had not wanted this particular commission, but Edmund had insisted, and they were best friends.

"I cannot," he had said, "leave RiversEdge now. I believe the worst to be over, but if I left our people at this point it would dishearten them. Go to Ashby Hall and bring back my bride, Tony. I know it may distress her to have our wedding plans changed so abruptly, but we need Blaze here at RiversEdge now!"

"Master Anthony, I present my daughter Blaze to you." Robert Morgan's voice pierced Anthony Wyndham's thoughts.

Focusing his light blue eyes, he looked down upon the most exquisite creature he had ever beheld. A pair of violet-blue eyes set within a perfect heart of a face which was framed in a halo of golden-brown hair looked curiously back. It was all he could do to keep himself from reaching out and touching her. He felt tongue-tied as he struggled to speak, his own voice sounding hollow in his ears. "I bring you greetings from your betrothed husband, lady."

"I welcome you to Ashby, Master Anthony." Her voice was clear and musical in tone.

"Master Anthony has some exciting news for you, Blaze," said Lady Morgan, gently prompting him. "Pray be seated, as it will take some telling. Your father and I, already being informed, will now return to our tasks." Rosemary Morgan took her surprised husband by the hand and walked from the room.

Seating herself in a tapestry-backed chair, Blaze looked up at Anthony Wyndham, wondering if her betrothed husband were as handsome as this man. His coal-black hair and clear, light blue eyes with their thick sooty lashes were a startling contrast to his very fair skin. *No.* Papa had said that the earl had brown eyes.

"What is it you wish to tell me, sir?" she queried Anthony. "Has your uncle changed his mind about acquiring another wife?"

"Nay, lady! He is most eager for your arrival, which is why I have come. There has been a severe summer sickness amongst the children at RiversEdge. Several previously healthy younglings died. That tragedy was almost immediately followed by a freak storm with fierce lightning. It attacked the estate without warning. There was no time to bring the stock in from the pastures. One huge bolt of lightning struck in a field with such ferocity that it set the trees afire and killed an entire flock of sheep that had been grazing in that particular meadow. The terrible and hellish sound of it was heard for miles around.

"The people of RiversEdge are demoralized by these frightening events. The old goodwives are prattling about bad fortune visiting us because of my uncle's lack of a wife and children. Then two nights ago Edmund gave an outdoor fete to cheer his people's spirits and reassure them. Shortly after sunset a fireball was seen shooting across the heavens, thereby giving rise to more tidings of doom.

"My uncle has therefore decided that he cannot leave his estates at this time. Nonetheless he does not seek to postpone your nuptials. Rather he would use this marriage for a good omen. He has sent me to act as his proxy. We will wed immediately, and I will bring you back to RiversEdge, where Edmund hopes that a formal celebration of your marriage will encourage and cheer your people. As my uncle's wife, it will be your duty to see to such matters."

Surprised by this sudden change in her wedding plans, and outraged by his last words to her, Blaze stamped her foot. Then, standing up, she said angrily, "I am more aware than you, sir, of a wife's duties! How dare you seek to preach them to me? I regret the trials that have been visited upon RiversEdge, but I find this change of plans unseemly. I will, however, abide by my lord's wishes in this matter. When will the proxy ceremony take place?"

He was astounded by her anger, but decided it was but caused by her disappointment. "Tomorrow," he answered her.

"Tomorrow?" she shrieked. Her head was beginning to throb.

"My uncle wants you at RiversEdge before the week's end, lady." He was not certain how to deal with this outraged child-woman who was about to be his aunt. Had she been his betrothed wife he would have found himself torn between kissing her and spanking her.

Blaze drew a deep breath to still her anger. She could not ever remember having been so furious. The earl was most considerate of his people, and very eager for himself, but what of her?

"You will like RiversEdge," Anthony said in an attempt to placate her. "It is a fitting setting for such a beautiful jewel of a woman as you are."

"I do not think you have the right to speak to me in such an intimate fashion, sir," she said stiffly. "Remember that I am to be your uncle's wife, and in future, address me with the respect due my station." She almost gasped with surprise at her own words. Why on earth was she behaving this way?

"No disrespect was meant, madam," he said coolly, thinking that though she be beautiful she was prudish. He pitied his uncle now, for gentle Cathy had been a warm and vibrant woman.

"Is there anything else you would tell me, sir?" Blaze demanded. When he shook his head in the negative, she curtsied, saying as she left the room, "Then I shall bid you a good day, sir."

It took every ounce of self-control she possessed to walk from the room with what she hoped was a regal stance. Her heart was hammering violently within her chest. She was angry, and excited, and afraid all at once. She was certain that her legs were wobbling even if her backbone was stiff and straight. As she closed the door behind her she broke into a run, fleeing up the staircase to her bedchamber so she might have a few moments to regain her composure before she must face her family. It was not to be. All her sisters, but for baby Glenna, were crowded into the room awaiting her.

"*Well?*" demanded Bliss. "Who is he? He's got a full dozen men-at-arms wearing the Langford livery with him. There's even a female servant who came with them, and is closeted with Old Ada now. They are unpacking the most gorgeous clothing I have ever seen!"

"Am I allowed no privacy in my own chamber?" Blaze grumbled.

"Not until you tell!" replied Delight mischievously.

"We're all dying of curiosity," said Blythe in her sweet, soft voice.

"Oh, very well," muttered Blaze. "There are no secrets in this house anyway. You'll all know soon enough. *He* is Master Anthony Wyndham, the earl's nephew."

"*He* is gorgeous," remarked thirteen-year-old Delight with an exaggerated sigh that caused her younger siblings to giggle.

"No future," said the practical Bliss. "Blaze is bound to have a dozen sons if the earl does his duty by her."

"It won't change the fact that he's gorgeous, as Delight says, even if he is poor," said Blythe with a twinkle. "Besides, he cannot be too poor."

"Time enough for gorgeous men after we've all married rich men," Bliss replied, dismissing Anthony Wyndham's prospects. "Why is he here? Your wedding is not for another fortnight."

"My wedding is tomorrow," Blaze said irritably, plumping herself into the middle of their big bed, and going on to explain to her astounded sisters the whys and wherefores of the change.

"Why, 'tis outrageous!" sputtered Bliss when her elder sister had finished with her explanations. "A woman may have more than one wedding in her lifetime if she is widowed, but there is only one *first* wedding. It is like only being able to lose your virginity once! It is special!"

" 'Twas to be no great affair, Bliss," Blaze offered logically, trying to reason away her own disappointment. "The most important thing for me was that my family would be there, and you all will be."

"But we have not yet met Lord Wyndham!" wailed Blythe. "You will marry a man that none of us even knows! It frightens me to even think on it."

"Don't be such a goose," Bliss scolded her twin. "The only one who has to know the earl is Blaze, and she will soon enough. Perhaps your wedding was not to be a great affair, sister, but there was to have been a small celebration. Now you must be wed first thing tomorrow morning. Then be bundled off to RiversEdge without so much as a bridescake and wine. A girl's wedding day is important to her, but I suppose the earl would not have stopped to consider that. How dreary of him!"

"I was angry too when I first learned of these changes in our plans," admitted Blaze, "but as I reconsider Master Anthony's words I realize that it is rather flattering that the earl should feel my presence can cheer his people. No one has ever before thought me useful for anything."

"I think it very romantic that the earl cannot live another day without his bride." Delight sighed. "I would love a man to feel that way about me." Her deep blue eyes grew dreamy with the thought.

Bliss opened her mouth to make a scathing retort, but instead shrieked, "Ouch!" as a frowning Blythe with uncharacteristic spirit pinched her arm.

"Will we ever see you again, Blaze?" asked Vanora, her baby-round face with its almost black eyes worried.

Blaze leaned forward, brushing a lock of Vanora's pale silvery-gold hair back from her forehead. "Of course you will see me, Vana. As soon as I am settled you may come for a visit to RiversEdge. I am certain that my husband will permit it."

Vanora smiled with relief.

"We will miss you," Larke and Linnette chorused. They often spoke in unison. Although frequently scolded about it, they could not seem to break the habit.

"I will miss you also," Blaze replied, "but RiversEdge is only twelve miles from Ashby as the crow flies."

"As none of us will be flying crows, however," said Bliss sharply, "it will be a half-day's ride across the fields, or almost a full day going around on proper roads."

"Mistress Blaze," quavered the voice of Old Ada as she hobbled into the room. "There is someone here from yer betrothed to meet ye." She glowered at the other girls. "Get ye gone, ye chattering group of flibber-tigibbets!" she scolded them. " 'Tis the bride's business I've come about. There's no room here for all ye! Shoo!"

Giggling at the old woman's pretended ferocity, the Morgan sisters trooped out, leaving their eldest sibling with Ada. Behind the nursemaid stood a small, plump woman with a merry countenance, whose bright eyes twinkled at the girls as they passed her.

"This be Heartha," said Old Ada. "She be sent to wait on ye, and she has brought ye beautiful things."

"My lord has sent you a gown that you may wear tomorrow, and clothing for travel, my lady. He hopes it will please you. May I show you?" Heartha asked.

"Please," replied Blaze. "My younger sisters said the items you were showing Ada were beautiful."

"Curiosity killed the cat," muttered the old lady.

Heartha smiled broadly, showing large horse teeth. "Those garments was for them, my lady. The earl knew that your sisters would want to look especially nice even for a proxy wedding. He understood that the suddenness would perhaps leave them without proper garments ready. Ada"—Heartha turned to the old nursemaid—"would you have the young ladies try on their gowns? If any alterations be needed, they had best start now if they are to be ready tomorrow."

"Aye, aye, and yer right," Old Ada agreed, and without another word to Blaze she hobbled off to find her other charges.

Heartha laid the garments she carried upon Blaze's bed. With quick movements she separated them, placing matching pieces together so that her new mistress might see everything. "His lordship thought you might wear this tomorrow, my lady." Heartha pointed to an exquisite skirt and matching bodice of cream-colored velvet with a matching silk underskirt. The underskirt and the bodice were both embroidered in gold-thread daisies with delicate long stems and fernlike leaves. The wide bell sleeves were turned back at their lower edge to show their silken lining. It was a simple but totally beautiful gown.

"There's stockings, and velvet shoes to go with the gown, my lady, and the earl sent you these trinkets to wear with it." She handed Blaze a flat black leather box.

Stunned by the most beautiful dress she had ever seen in her entire life, Blaze automatically opened the box and looked down. "Blessed Mother!" she gasped. "These are for me?" Nestled within the box upon a bed of black velvet was a double strand of perfectly matched pink pearls from which hung a heart carved from a single piece of rose coral and set within a frame of white gold studded with tiny diamonds. The necklace was so lovely that Blaze almost missed the fat round pink pearls hanging from diamond studs that were meant for her ears. Tears welled up within her violet-blue eyes. She had never possessed anything like these jewels in her entire life. Even her mother had nothing as fine. She felt almost guilty.

Seeing her tears, Heartha nodded to herself. "The earl will be pleased to know that he has made you happy, my lady," she said.

Blaze looked up. "These are surely the finest jewels in the world," she said.

"Nay, my lady! Wait until you see what belongs to a Countess of Langford. There are chests of glittering stones and pearls that would buy a kingdom. They will all be yours!"

"I wouldn't know what to do with them," said Blaze honestly.

Heartha chuckled. "You'll learn quick enough, my lady. The earl's sister will see to that. She's a proud one, Lady Dorothy, but she's got a good heart."

"Did you know Lady Catherine?" Blaze asked curiously.

"Aye, I was her tiring woman the last five years of her life after her old Nan passed on. She was a kind lady, but driven in her desire to give the earl a child. Not that he ever reproached her with it."

"Does it disturb you to now serve me?" Blaze wondered.

"Lord bless me, child," said Heartha, momentarily forgetting her place, "life is a constant cycle of life and death. One just naturally follows the other. You weren't responsible for Lady Catherine's death. The good folk at RiversEdge are happy with this new marriage of the earl's. They await your coming eagerly. Now that I've seen your fine family I know that you'll give us the heir we so desperately want for RiversEdge."

"Is Master Anthony not my husband's heir?"

"Master Anthony's always known his uncle would one day have sons of his own. He's never really expected to inherit from the earl. He'll inherit from his own father. Riverside is his real home. Its lands match those of the earl, although it is much smaller. His uncle always jokes about Master Anthony's firstborn daughter marrying his firstborn son."

"Master Anthony is married?"

"Nay. It isn't easy for a man lacking in means to find himself a wife, begging your pardon, my lady. Master Anthony has a nice little home, and a small income. He's no great catch like his uncle, and he seems to be in no hurry either. Time enough for him, says I."

Blaze laughed. She liked the jolly outspoken woman that Lord Wyndham had sent to be her servant. Heartha's easygoing manner, while not perhaps the most proper, had certainly put her new mistress at her ease. I wonder, thought Blaze, if the earl knew she would? Was this stranger she was to wed possibly sensitive to her needs after all? It was something to consider, especially as by this time tomorrow she would be meeting her husband for the first time.

"The earl also sent you a riding outfit, my lady," said Heartha's voice, penetrating Blaze's thoughts.

"Ohh," she cried, and her delight was evident. "Blue velvet! Dark blue velvet! I have always dreamed of having a riding skirt and jacket like this! How could he have known?" Her eyes swept over the swatch of rich velvet that made up the skirt down to its hem, where a pair of black leather boots stood upon the floor. "Ohhhh," Blaze sighed, and immediately sat down upon the edge of the bed, kicking off a shoe so she might try on a boot. Reverently her hands caressed the supple leather as she fitted her slender foot into the boot and slowly drew it up her leg. The fit was a perfect one. "Is the earl a magician," she asked Heartha, "that he could know the size of my foot?"

Heartha chuckled. What a sweet and ingenuous little creature the earl's bride was, but then Edmund Wyndham had always had good luck. The girl's sweetness, however, was a good omen. "Think, my lady," Heartha said in answer to Blaze's bemused question. "In all the bridal preparations, was not your foot measured? I think it was, for all those measurements were delivered to my lord several weeks ago. The village cobbler has been busy at work ever since on all manner of shoes and boots for you."

Suddenly Blaze found herself weeping. "It is not right," she said, "that I should have so much, and my family so little!"

Heartha put comforting arms about the girl, saying, "Why, bless me, child, you must not feel that way. Now that you are to be the earl's wife you will be able to aid your family. The earl has much wealth, but he would give it all for what your father has. A son. Give my master that son, and neither you nor yours will ever lack for anything, I'm thinking." She gave Blaze a hard hug, saying, "Let me help you to try on your new riding outfit, that you may show your mother and sisters what a fine lady you now are."

As Blaze pirouetted shortly afterward for her mother and her siblings, Rosemary Morgan looked approvingly upon the relationship she saw beginning to form between her eldest child and the tiring woman. A loyal body servant was important to a young woman going to a new home.

The family was somewhat subdued at the evening meal. The reality of Blaze's imminent departure was suddenly upon them. They also found themselves put off by the rare presence of a stranger in their family unit. As for Anthony Wyndham, he was both fascinated and enchanted by this family with whom his uncle was allying himself. Lord and Lady Morgan were to his eye both attractive and intelligent. The daughters were beautiful and, he suspected, in a less tense situation, charming, fun-loving girls.

As for the heir to Ashby Hall, young Gavin Morgan was not in the least subdued by his sisters' unusual quiet. It was rare that he and his twin sister, Glenna, were allowed in the hall for a meal. Gavin was a sturdy little boy with dark brown hair and his father's features. He chattered away quite unconcerned with his family's guest, telling Anthony about his dog, who had just last week whelped a litter of six fine puppies, showing off his rudimentary Latin, and, to his parents' relief, being a general delight.

"How my uncle would love a fine lad like Gavin," said Master Anthony softly to Lady Morgan.

"I am certain that my daughter will be able to oblige him, sir," came the mischievous reply. Lady Morgan could not help but smile a smile that quickly faded with her daughter's sudden harsh words.

"I realize, my lord," snapped Blaze, "that the earl weds with me only for what he hopes will be my fertility, but it would indeed be nice if for just a brief time I were allowed to believe I possessed other charms that might entice him!"

"*Blaze!*"

"What, Mama? Should I apologize to Master Anthony for being so indelicate? Very well then! Forgive me, sir, for discussing my fertility so openly, but everyone else seems to be doing it." She stood abruptly, and without even asking her parents' leave, walked swiftly from the hall.

"It must be bridal nerves," said Lady Morgan weakly, and then she stared fiercely at her next three daughters, who had had the temerity to giggle. Her husband's sudden fit of coughing did not help matters. It would be better, she thought, to send all of her children from the Great Hall before Master Anthony received the wrong impression, if he had not already received it. Perhaps amid an adult quiet, and with a goblet of good malmsey, her husband could repair any damage Blaze's sharp words had caused. She signaled discreetly to Old Ada, who came forward to shepherd her charges from the hall.

While the nursemaid saw to the littlest of the Morgan children, the elder six crowded into the chamber shared by Blaze and the eldest twins. They found their eldest sister lying upon the bed staring up at the beamed ceiling. She wore only her chemise.

"Go away," she muttered. "I need to sleep."

"Nay," said Blythe. "This is the last night of our lives that we shall all share together as maidens. Tomorrow night you will become a woman. It will never be the same again for us. You are the first, Blaze. After you we will all be wed, and go away from Ashby. In a way it is the end of child-hood for us all. Let us stay and talk as we have on so many nights before this one."

"Oh, please, yes!" said Larke and Linnette.

Blaze sat up and gazed at the eager faces about her. Her heart melted within her. She felt the tears pricking at the back of her eyelids. She loved her sisters, every one of them! She was going to miss them terribly. Oh, yes, she would see them again, but it would not be the same thing as living with them. Blythe was correct. It was the end of their childhood.

Blaze smiled. "Make yourselves comfortable," she said, and then laughed as they all once again plumped themselves onto the bed that she shared with the twins. "What shall we talk about?" she asked them.

"Let's talk about what it's like to become a woman," said Delight, a shiver running down her little spine. "After all, Blaze, tomorrow is your wedding, and tomorrow evening will be your wedding night."

"How would I know about such things, you silly goose?" responded the bride-to-be.

"You've got some idea," retorted Delight, offended at having been called a silly goose. "We've all seen the animals in the fields when the male mounts the female."

"I cannot believe that people behave *that* way," said Blaze.

"Then how do they behave? Hasn't Mother said *anything* to you about it?"

The eldest sibling shook her head.

Bliss laughed aloud. "Of course Mama hasn't said anything to any of us. She's so busy running the house, and worrying about Papa and his wor-ries about Ashby, that it has probably never occurred to her. Undoubtedly she meant to speak with Blaze just before her marriage, but with the sud-denness of today's developments, it has, I think, flown from her mind."

"I know how men use women."

The sisters turned to look at seven-year-old Vanora, who sat directly in their midst, her dark eyes bright.

"How could you know such things?" scoffed Bliss. "If you persist in telling lies, Vana, I shall smack you!"

"I watch from the stable loft when the serving men use the serving women. I've even seen Papa, though not often, go at one of the milk-maids," Vanora said smugly. "Do you want to know how they do it, or not? And if you smack me, Bliss, *I'll never tell!*"

The bedchamber grew very silent, and six pairs of curious eyes turned upon Vanora.

"*Well?*" demanded Bliss, her sapphire-blue eyes narrowing danger-ously. "Are you going to tell us or not?" Her fingers itched with their de-sire to wipe the self-satisfied smile from her younger sister's face.

Vanora was relishing the moment that gave her a superiority over her elder sisters, but even in her victory she knew the limits to which she might drive them, particularly the sharp-tongued Bliss. She drew a deep breath. "Men," she began, "have long things between their legs just like the animals. They are not, of course, as big as the stallions', but they are larger than Papa's hunting dogs'. *Much larger,*" she said with a heavy em-phasis.

"Ohhh," whispered Larke and Linnette, their small mouths making perfect O's at this revelation.

"Are they long and red like the animals'?" queried Delight. She was genuinely interested, for like her sisters, she would one day face this mys-tery. The key to overcoming fear, she knew, was a complete knowledge and understanding of what you were to face.

"It's hard to see too much detail from the hayloft in the stables and barns," admitted Vanora, "but it appears to me that only the tip of the man's thing is a purplish red."

"Get on with it!" hissed Bliss.

"Aye," said Blaze, "I would know how the act is done if I am expected to do it tomorrow. Ohh, why did Mama not explain this to me? The earl will think me a perfect fool, although I do not expect virgins should have too much knowledge in these matters."

"But we should know what is going on," said Blythe. "Girls should really be taught what they should know in these matters. Say on, Vana. Though Bliss will not admit it, we are *all* dying of curiosity."

"Sometimes the men kiss and cuddle the women. They seem to like to feel their titties, and slip a hand between the women's legs. The women appear to like this, for they giggle and sigh and encourage the men onward. I've even seen some of the women fondle the men," con-tinued Vanora. "After a while this play ceases. There doesn't seem to be any set period of time. With some it's longer, and with others shorter. Finally the man will lay the woman upon her back, climb atop her, take his thing from his drawers, and stick it between her legs up into her belly."

"I don't believe you!" said Bliss furiously. "You have made it all up just to get our attention!"

"I do not care if you believe me or not," retorted Vanora spiritedly, " 'tis true! They call it fucking. The servants are always doing it in the barns. Just hide yourself in the haylofts, and you will see that I speak the truth!"

"You say you've seen Papa doing it with a milkmaid?" Bliss demanded. *When?*"

"I've only seen Papa twice and both times it has been when Mama was ill," came the answer.

"Do the women seem to like it, Vana?" asked Blaze.

"Aye, they do, but for the life of me I do not know why. It seems a silly way to have fun. The men bounce up and down on the women, who bounce right back at them. They moan and groan, and kiss and lick at each other. It certainly does not look to me like anything that I would want to do," finished Vanora.

Larke and Linnette nodded their heads in unison, agreeing with their younger sister.

"Sometimes," admitted Delight, "I think about what it would be like to have a man make love to me."

"Humph!" snorted Bliss derisively.

"What of you, Blaze?" said Blythe. "It is, after all, you who are to be wed tomorrow. Have you thought of the earl's loving you?"

"Until my betrothal I rarely thought of a man in that way," said Blaze honestly. "There was no point to it. I did not know if I would ever marry, and who was there to even court us here at Ashby? Since my betrothal I have tried to think of what it will be like as Edmund Wyndham's wife. Alas, the man is faceless to me! I try to dream of him, for it seems that I should, but it is hard when I do not know the man. I am afraid to make him something that he might not be, for then my disappointment would be hard to bear."

"Do you think he is as handsome as his nephew?" wondered Blythe. "Do you think there is a family resemblance?"

"I hope not! I find Master Anthony arrogant and impossible," said Blaze furiously.

"*What's this?*" pounced Bliss.

"*This*, as you put it, is nothing," responded Blaze. "I simply do not like Master Anthony."

"Why?" demanded Bliss. "You haven't known the man long enough to either like or dislike him."

Blaze pondered a moment. "I don't know why," she finally answered, "but he irritates me. I can only hope that his uncle is nothing like him, and that we will not have to see too much of him at RiversEdge."

"That may not be possible," warned Blythe. "From what that Heartha told Old Ada, the two men are but four years apart in age. They were raised together by your husband-to-be's half-sister, Master Anthony's mother. They are more like brothers, and very close. You had best hide your dislike, sister. Your husband-to-be and his nephew are friends as well as relations."

"I can mask my feelings, Blythe. Later, when the children come, Master Anthony will be of less importance to my husband. My lord will have his own family and his nephew will no longer matter to him that much."

"What's this? What's this?" Old Ada's grizzled head popped around the door. "Why are ye not abed, my chicks? There is a wedding to be celebrated on the morrow, and ye'll not look yer best, any of ye, if ye don't get yer sleep. To bed with all of ye!" she scolded fondly as she chased Delight, Vanora, and the second set of twins from the little chamber.

The room had grown chilly with the night. Bliss and Blythe quickly undressed down to their chemises while Blaze pulled back the covers. The three sisters climbed into their bed, pressing together for warmth.

"It will seem strange tomorrow night without you, Blaze," said Blythe.

"Take Delight in with you," came the reply. "She's nearer in age to you both than she is to Vanora and the other twins. Mother will probably want to separate Glenna from Gavin now that she has the room. As the only boy, he really ought to have his own chamber. If Glenna goes in with Vanora, Larke, and Linnette, it will really be too crowded for Delight. She would be thrilled if you would ask her to join you, Bliss." Blaze knew that Blythe was more generous of heart, and would gladly have Delight share their chamber now that she was apprised of the situation.

"Oh, let the little brat join us," said Bliss grudgingly. "As I sleep in the middle, I shall freeze to death this winter unless I have another body beside me." She put her back to Blaze. "I'll tell her in the morning," she finished, and then with her usual habit dropped off almost immediately to sleep.

"She is going to miss you more than she will admit, Blaze," said Blythe softly in the darkness.

"I know, and I will miss her too."

The room grew quiet once more. Soon Blaze heard Blythe's even breathing, and knew that she had fallen asleep also. It was all so familiar and safe, but tomorrow she would be torn from the haven of security that she had known all her life. She would begin a new life with a stranger in a strange place. Blaze considered. She wasn't really frightened, for she knew her parents would not have allowed this marriage if they were not certain that Lord Wyndham was a good and decent man. She understood the logic for this sudden change in plans, for a proxy marriage ceremony and a swift return to RiversEdge. Logic always prevailed. Yet deep within her burned a small flame of angry resentment. She knew she had no choice but to trust the judgment of the Earl of Langford in the matter of his people's welfare. Still, she could not help but think he might have left RiversEdge for one day. Was one day so very much?

Blaze turned onto her side. Tomorrow should have been the most memorable day in her life. It was her wedding day, and now it was spoilt! Instead of a day of feasting and joy, it would be a hurried affair. She would leave almost immediately after the ceremony. Her mother had taken her aside earlier when she had gone to show her the beautiful clothing that the earl had sent for her.

"You must take the long way around to RiversEdge, for you will be passing through several villages belonging to the Langford earldom, and it is necessary that the villagers see you," said Rosemary Morgan to her eldest child. "Therefore there can be no feasting following the marriage ceremony. A health will be drunk to you and your husband, you will change your clothes, and you will depart." She put motherly arms about her daughter. "Oh, my dear, I am so sorry, for poor though we may be, I had intended that this most special of days in your life be more festive. Somehow it does not seem fair. Yet when I think of the fine marriage you are making, I realize that I must put my own concerns aside."

Well, thought Blaze sleepily, whatever I may feel about the matter, the die is cast, and it is out of my hands. I will be wed tomorrow in a proxy ceremony whether I like it or not, *and* I shall go off to meet my husband.

Her husband! What was he like? Would he be kind to her? Would he ever love her? Would she learn to love him? Would it be as little Vana had said? Surely the earl would be gentle with her, taking into account her virginity. She wanted to imagine what it would be like to be loved by him, but it was so hard trying to picture it in her ignorance. Vana, of course, had shed some light on the mysteries between a man and a woman, but one could not be certain if the nobility did it the same way as the lower classes. I shall know soon enough, she considered, and with a great effort put her busy and nervous mind on the business of sleep.

It seemed she slept not at all. Then suddenly she was being shaken awake by her sisters, even the tiny red-haired Glenna. With hugs and laughter they drew her into the land of the awakened, pelting her with asters, and Mary's Gold, and purple-and-white Michaelmas daisies.

"Wake up, sleepyhead!" they cried together. "It is your wedding day!"

Blaze couldn't help but weep a little, for once more she realized that this was the last time that they would all be together like this. To her surprise her sisters became weepy too, even Bliss, who muttered irritably, "All of our lives we have dreamed of wedding days. Now that the first of us is to go, we sob and carry on like babies. I do not understand it!"

Lady Morgan and Old Ada arrived accompanied by several maidservants who carried a tub and the buckets and jars of hot water necessary to fill it. The bed that the three sisters shared was pushed into a corner of the small room so the tub might be set up.

"Heartha will help you to bathe and dress," said Rosemary Morgan to her eldest child when the others had been shooed from the chamber and they were alone. "There is something, however, that I must discuss with you beforehand. It is the way of a man with a woman. It is not necessary nor would it be appropriate for you to have too great a knowledge, but you should know what to expect, Blaze. As for the rest, the earl will instruct you as pleases him, which is as it should be. Do you understand?"

"Yes, Mama," Blaze said dutifully, hoping her mother's explanations would clear up the several unanswered questions she had due to Vana's discourse of yesterday. Lady Morgan, however, seemed disinclined to go into too great detail regarding the relationship between a husband and wife. One thing Blaze did learn to her relief was that all couples, no matter their social standing, performed the act in approximately the same fashion.

"You need not be afraid," said Lady Morgan, "although it will seem a bit awkward and strange to you in the beginning. Oh, yes! I must not forget to tell you that the first time your husband's manhood penetrates into your body it will hurt you. It is only the first time, though, and it is due to the barrier to your maidenhead, which he will pierce, thereby ending your state of virginity. Now, dear child, I shall leave you to the kindly ministrations of the good Heartha. You are a good daughter, Blaze, for all your high-spiritedness. I know you will make us proud in your new life as the Countess of Langford." Then, giving her eldest a quick hug and a peck on the cheek, Lady Morgan departed the room.

Heartha came, and wisely sensing the bride's pensive mood, refrained from chatter. Removing the girl's chemise, she helped her into the small tub, bathed her, and washed her hair. Rubbing her down with linen cloths, the tiring woman noted the girl's well-shaped limbs, the broad span between her hipbones, so unlike poor Lady Catherine's, and the girl's small round breasts. It was a body much more suited to childbearing than the late countess's had been. Wrapping Blaze in a large rough towel, Heartha carefully removed the snarls from her long wet hair, then brushed it until all the excess water was gone from it.

"Now, my lady," she said, "let me sit you by the window. If I spread your hair out over the sill, it will soon be dry in that lovely September sun."

While Blaze sat quietly, almost dreamily, her lovely golden-brown hair blowing in the gentle breeze of early morning, Heartha moved busily about the room, laying out the silk stockings and other undergarments that the bride would be wearing. The door opened to admit a serving woman who carried the bridal gown.

The time seemed to pass in a haze after that. It was as if her body were merely a vehicle from which she peered out at what was going on around her. She could hear her sisters exclaiming with delight as they donned their own gowns. Only the tiniest of alterations had been needed upon the beautiful velvet dresses that Edmund Wyndham had so thoughtfully provided for his sisters-in-law-to-be.

Sky-blue for Bliss and Blythe. Scarlet for Delight. Rose-pink for Larke and Linnette. Peach for Vanora, who had almost swooned with pleasure over the first gown she had ever owned that had not been handed down to her. For five-year-old Glenna with her chestnut-red hair there was a gown of dark green velvet. Nor had Gavin, her twin, been forgotten. He strutted about quite proudly in a black velvet suit with the first pair of breeches he had ever owned.

"Ohh, my lady, you are the most beautiful bride I have ever seen!" exclaimed Heartha. "I only wisht there was a glass here that you might see yourself in, but no matter. There's a lovely pier glass in your apartments at RiversEdge. Tomorrow you will wear this gown once more for our people to see. You can see yourself in it then."

Lady Morgan entered the room. "Good, my dearest, you are ready. Your sisters have made you this wreath of Michaelmas daisies for your head." She placed the flowery little circlet of white and yellow atop Blaze's soft hair, which was loose and unbound, testifying to her virgin state.

Together, Lord and Lady Morgan led their eldest child into the family chapel. It was overcrowded with Blaze's family, the servants, and major tenants belonging to Ashby. Just below the carved oak altar with its beautifully embroidered white linen cloth stood Father John, a man of middle years with receding sandy hair and light blue eyes that peered myopically in the candlelight of the room. With the priest stood Anthony Wyndham, who would act as proxy for his uncle, the earl. The proxy bridegroom was garbed in black velvet.

Blaze was now so benumbed by the last twenty-four hours that the wedding ceremony was more like a dream to her. Blindly she spoke her part when requested to, staring down almost in bewilderment when Master Anthony shoved a heavy band of Irish red-gold carved round with hearts and flowers upon her hand. She somehow managed to stumble through the Mass that followed. The host upon her tongue melted away like a sugar drop; then her mouth was suddenly dry. It was not like any wedding day she had ever imagined.

Finally it was over. Master Anthony led her out of the chapel. For the first time in over an hour Blaze was able to draw a deep breath. Almost instantly her head cleared. Within the chapel with its flickering beeswax tapers and heavy clouds of exotic incense her chest had felt constricted.

"You are quite pale," he said quietly. "Are you all right?"

Blaze nodded. "A wedding, even such a hurried, proxy affair as this one, is apt to be overwhelming for the bride. I could not breathe, but I am fine now."

He led her into the Great Hall. Her family and the others came behind them. There her father raised his goblet to her, as did all the others within the hall.

"A health to my daughter Blaze," Lord Morgan said. "Long life! Happiness! And many sons to my beloved first child, the Countess of Langford!"

"Long life! Happiness! Many children! And God bless her, the Countess of Langford!" came the echoed reply from the guests in the hall.

Her health and that of the absent bridegroom were drunk. Then Blaze was hurried from the Great Hall back to her own chamber. There Heartha helped her to remove the lovely wedding gown, redressing her in the dark blue velvet skirt and matching bodice with its pearl-and-gold embroidery. Blaze's new boots felt wonderful upon her feet. There was more than enough room for her big toe, which was overlarge. Heartha fitted a small flat bonnet with a jaunty white feather upon her lady's head, handing her a pair of white leather riding gloves embroidered with gold and pearls, as was the bodice of her gown.

"Now, there's a coach if you gets tired, my lady," Heartha said. "No need to exhaust yourself before we gets to RiversEdge."

Below, her family had gathered to bid her farewell. Gently she hugged Gavin and Glenna. "Take good care of that gown," she cautioned Vanora. "Remember that Glenna can wear it when you've outgrown it. I will see you have another. I promise."

"I want one the color of your riding outfit," said Vanora boldly. "Dark blue should suit me well."

"We shall miss you, dearest Blaze," chorused Larke and Linnette. "Come home and visit when you can."

"I will," she promised, kissing them upon their rosy cheeks.

Delight flung herself at Blaze, hugging her eldest sister hard. "Who will protect me from Bliss now?" she wondered aloud. "Did you know that they have asked me to share their chamber with them? I'm moving in tonight."

"Blythe will protect you, though you really need her not. You have always been able to outrun Bliss and her temper," laughed Blaze, "and aye, I knew, for it was Bliss's idea."

"*It was?*" Delight was astounded. "Perhaps I am too hard on her."

"Be patient with her," warned Blaze, giving Delight a final hug. "Do not allow your quick tongue to overrule your common sense."

Bliss and Blythe stood before her. They were absolutely gorgeous in their sky-blue velvet gowns, which were trimmed with seed pearls. Certainly they were meant for greater marriages than could have been obtained for them before her own marriage to Edmund Wyndham. "You are beautiful," she said. "I promise to seek the best husbands for you, but any man seeing you as you look today would offer his all to wed with either of you."

"Be happy, dearest," said Blythe, kissing her elder sibling upon the cheek. "I know that you will do your best for us all."

"Fine words," grumbled Bliss. "Fine words, but we shall see. Only time will tell the true tale for us." Then her sapphire-blue eyes welled with tears which, to Bliss's mortification, spilled over and ran down her cheeks. "God's foot!" she swore softly as her scandalized mother rolled her own eyes heavenward.

"Ohh, Bliss," said Blaze, trying hard not to laugh. "You have offered me the nicest parting of all. I shall miss you so very much!"

"Forgive me, my lady, but we must go," Anthony Wyndham intruded.

Blaze shot him an unfriendly look. "I must bid my parents farewell, sir. You will wait upon me, like it or no." She turned to her mother. The two hugged, and in that instant Blaze knew how very much she loved her mother.

"Now, try to remember all I have taught you, my child," Lady Rosemary began.

"Indeed she will! Indeed she will," said Lord Morgan, understanding Anthony's impatience. Grasping his eldest child by the shoulders, he turned her about. Giving her a loud kiss upon the cheek, he then gently pushed her out the door of the hall to where the horses were waiting. Before she realized what was happening, Blaze found herself being boosted into her saddle.

"But, Papa!" she protested.

"You are a married woman now, Blaze. We love you. We bid you Godspeed, but if you linger much longer your mother and sisters will begin weeping and wailing. Besides, we must get back to the fields, for Master Garth says it will rain within another day or two. You know it is impossible to harvest and store wet grain. Go home to your husband, daughter."

She understood her father better than even he realized. A soft smile touched Blaze's lips. "Farewell, Papa," she said quietly. "I love you." Then, kicking her horse, she moved off away from her family, away from Ashby, away from everything she had ever known; toward a new identity *and* a new life.

Part Two

RiversEdge

Autumn 1521–January 1525

Chapter 3

$\mathcal{I}$n her entire life Blaze had never ridden more than a few miles from Ashby Hall. Within an hour the landmarks well known to her disappeared, and the countryside became unfamiliar. Her childhood home was located within clear sight of the Malvern Hills on the east side of the River Wye. They traveled northwest, for RiversEdge was set upon the west bank of the Wye with a view of the Black Mountains. The land was overripe and lush in the September sunshine; the green pastures with their grazing cattle and sheep giving way to greener fields of ripening hops and golden fields of ripening grain. The road wound through ancient orchards of apples ready for the harvest, whose fragrance perfumed the air to the point of excess.

It was a peaceful land. There was little serious need for the escort of armed men who accompanied them other than the fact that they did the bride honor. Blaze had been given a lovely white mare to ride. Master Anthony rode beside her upon a dappled gray stallion with Heartha behind them upon a fat brown pony. Their pace was easy, but not leisurely, for they had some seventeen miles to go using the roads between Ashby and RiversEdge. They would ford the Wye some four miles below their destination.

The sun was at its zenith when to Blaze's relief Anthony Wyndham called a halt to their journey. She was starving, as the marriage ceremony had been in the early morning. She had not eaten before the Mass. After her health had been drunk in the Great Hall she had been dressed and hustled off. No one had thought to offer her some food before her departure on a day's ride to her new home.

Easing himself gracefully from his saddle, Anthony walked over to Blaze's mount. Lifting her down, he felt her stiffen as his fingers tightened about her narrow waist.

She moved away from him as quickly as possible, saying as she did, "I am ravenous, sir. I hope this halt is so we may eat. I am certain the Ashby cook has not let you get away without providing food for our journey."

"The halt is mainly for the benefit of the horses and so that the men may relieve themselves, madam," he said wickedly, enjoying the deep blush that reddened her cheeks.

"Ohh, you are insufferable!" she cried.

"Perhaps you would like to relieve yourself," he said, continuing his gibing. "We will not stop again until we reach RiversEdge."

"Cease your teasing, Master Anthony!" said Heartha, who had managed to dismount her pony by herself. "Ohh, he's got a wicked reputation for such behavior, my lady. Pay him no mind. There's a lovely spot over there by those trees for you to rest and eat. Poor lamb," she rattled on, "ye've had naught to eat today, have ye? Well, the Ashby cook did pack a fine basket, which is in the coach. As for you, Master Anthony, 'twill be up to the countess as to whether you gets anything to eat or not." She led Blaze to the spot she had so quickly located. A small narrow brook not clearly visible from the road tumbled over its rocky bed just past the trees where Heartha ensconced her mistress.

"Oh, how lovely," said Blaze as she knelt down to bathe her face and hands in the crystal cold water. Then, spreading her skirts, she sat down, her back against a tree.

Heartha, who had gone to the coach to fetch the basket of food, now hurried back with it. Blaze motioned her servant to sit, and together they rummaged through the contents. Within the basket were two loaves of freshly baked bread, each loaf carefully wrapped in a linen napkin with a small slab of marble that had been heated to keep the bread warm, which it still was. There was a small pat of butter, and a wedge of hard yellow cheese. There was a broiled rabbit which had been cut into several pieces, a little plum cake, several apples, a few pears, and a small corked bottle of sweet golden wine.

"Eat!" Blaze encouraged her tiring woman as she tore into a loaf of bread, spread it generously with the butter, and topped it with a slice of cheese she cut off the wedge with her own knife. "Ummmm," she said happily, and reaching for the wine bottle uncorked it. Heartha held out a cup, which Blaze filled while chewing happily upon the bread and cheese. Swallowing, she reached for the cup and quaffed down a deep swallow. "Oh, that tastes so good! Heartha, eat something yourself. I can't finish this all."

"What of Master Anthony, my lady?"

Blaze looked toward the road where Anthony Wyndham stood amongst his men speaking while they appeared to be eating something. "What are the men eating, Heartha?"

"They carry wine and bread with them, my lady."

"Does Lord Anthony have a ration?"

"I do not know, my lady. I believe he expected to dine with you."

Blaze frowned. "I cannot let him go hungry as he leads our party," she said. "Take him some food then, Heartha."

" 'Twould be unkind before the men, my lady," Heartha gently advised her young mistress. "You should really ask him to join you."

Blaze's pretty mouth made a moue of annoyance, but she nodded to her servant. "Very well, then, Heartha. Ask him to join me."

Anthony came, silently determined not to offend this prickly new *aunt* of his. That Blaze seemed to dislike him was evident to him, although he did not really know why, for their acquaintance was much too short for her to have formed an opinion. Perhaps because he was Edmund's heir right now she resented him. Proprietary little witch, he thought, amused. He hoped that once she found he was not really a threat she would like him better. They were a small family, and they should be close, for a close family was a strong family. It was time, he suddenly realized, that he choose himself a wife. Perhaps one of the other fetching Morgan sisters would do him. Gentle Blythe was a possibility, or perhaps the merry Delight.

Reaching Blaze, he was his most charming. "Thank you, my lady, for offering to share your meal with me. May I sit?"

She nodded regally, motioning with her hand to a place opposite her. Then, handing him a napkin with buttered bread, cheese, and the haunch of a rabbit, she said, "Eat, Master Anthony."

His fine white teeth tore into the meat, and quickly he stripped the bone clean. Fascinated, Blaze handed him another piece of the rabbit, which disappeared as swiftly, to be followed by the bread. Blaze nibbled daintily upon a single piece of meat, her appetite having been eased by the bread and cheese.

"Wine, sir?" she offered him as with her nodded permission he helped himself to more bread and cheese.

"I've some of my own, thank you, madam, and there is, I think, just enough for you. I would not deprive you."

There was little other conversation between them. Blaze broke the plum cake into three pieces, sharing it with Anthony and Heartha. When she had devoured the sweet, a particular favorite of hers, she ate both an apple and a pear. As nervous as she was about getting to RiversEdge—and they were already halfway there—she felt at ease for this break in their journey.

Anthony Wyndham wiped his hands upon the napkin, and arose saying, "We will be on our way shortly, my lady. Forgive my lack of delicacy, but this really is the last opportunity you will have before we resume our journey to, ah, attend to, ah, personal matters for yourself." Then, before she might reply, he turned and hurried off.

"He is right, my lady, and nothing's more uncomfortable than riding along when one has to . . . well, you know, my lady," put in Heartha.

"Aye," said Blaze with a grin, "I know, but 'tis still very annoying to have to be constantly reminded, as if I were a child, Heartha. Keep watch for me now."

They continued upon their journey, and soon they could see the River Wye before them stretching its silvery self in the warm, golden midafternoon sunlight. When they finally reached its banks a ferryman was awaiting to transport them across the water.

"Is this the bride then?" he asked Anthony frankly.

"Aye, Rumford, this is your new mistress, the Countess of Langford. Madam, may I present to you the keeper of the Michaelschurch ferry, Master Rumford."

Blaze smiled at the weathered man. "I've never crossed a river before," she said. "It cannot be an easy task to bring the boat safely to the shore each time, Rumford."

"Aye, m'lady, and a child could do it," the ferryman replied modestly, pulling his cap from his head and bobbing politely. "I've been the boatman for his lordship since my father grew too old for it, and I've three sons to carry on after me. 'Tis Rumford business to guide the boats, and yer not to worry, for the old Wye is as smooth as glass today. 'Twill be no more than a glide across a millpond."

The ferryman was true to his word, and three trips saw them all safely across the river and on the other side.

"You're now on Langford land," said Master Anthony. "There are two roads to RiversEdge from here. The more direct one runs along the river, and the house is but three miles away. If you are not too tired, Edmund wanted you to go the long way around, which will take you through two of his villages before you reach RiversEdge. I was to leave it up to you."

Blaze stretched in her saddle. More than anything she wanted to reach her journey's end and have a hot tub. She had never ridden so far in her life. She was both tired and sore. Still, it was important that she get off on the right foot with her husband. He wanted her to do this. "We'll visit the villages," she said quietly.

"Good girl!" he approved, and though his patronizing tone annoyed her, she was relieved to have her judgment confirmed.

Afterward she was glad that she had done it. The warmth of her welcome and the obvious approval of the villagers in Michaelschurch cheered her, giving her courage for what was to come. They poured from their houses smiling and greeting her with friendly words. A small girl rushed up to her mare to press a hastily made bouquet of Mary's Gold and asters into her hand. She smiled down at the child, calling her thanks, and received a host of, "God bless yer ladyship," from the little lass's family. Her welcome in the second village was even warmer, and her cheeks grew pink as she overheard several groups of goodwives loudly approving her form as a good one for successful childbearing.

"They mean well," Master Anthony said, "and though they do not wish to embarrass you, they are anxious that my uncle have an heir of his loins."

"I understand," said Blaze tightly. "Is that not the purpose of this marriage? Has it not been drummed into my head for the last two months?" She smiled and waved at the last of the villagers as they passed by them by moving out onto the open road again.

"Edmund is a good man," Anthony ventured. "I hope you will learn to love one another. I believe that love is important to a marriage."

"Did my lord love his first wife?"

"Aye, he loved Cathy. They had known each other since they were children."

Blaze grew silent. If he loved his first wife, was he capable of loving her? Oh, she hoped so! She did not know what love between a man and a woman was, but she knew that she wanted to feel that most fabled and desired of emotions. To think of going through life without knowing that emotion was very frightening.

Then suddenly Anthony said, "Look! There is RiversEdge."

They had climbed to the top of a hill, and below them, the River Wye, its eastern boundary, RiversEdge was placed like a fine jewel within a parklike setting. Its well-tended gardens were abloom with early-autumn color. The house was built in the shape of an H to honor the king who had elevated the Wyndhams to their earldom. It was of dark redbrick, its walls embraced by shiny green ivy. From the gray slate roof at least half a dozen chimneys soared. Blaze could see the busy daily activity about the house as they descended the hill, and her heart began to beat quite quickly.

She dared not look for fear of what she might see. What if she were disappointed in him? What if he were disappointed in her? Of its own volition her mare came to a stop. Strong hands reached up and clamped themselves around her waist, lifting her from her mount's back and setting her firmly upon the ground.

The thumb and forefinger of an elegant hand caught her chin and tilted her head up. She found herself staring into a pair of the warmest and kindest brown eyes she had ever seen. The most beautiful voice she had ever heard—a deep and caressing voice—said, "Welcome home, Blaze Wyndham. I am your husband, Edmund." The eyes twinkled down at her. "I am most anxious to know if I meet with your approval, madam."

"Oh, yes, my lord!" she burst out, the relief in her voice very evident. Then she blushed, realizing how her words must sound to him, but Edmund Wyndham laughed.

"It only dawned upon me this morning as I awoke that although I had been most happy to carry away from Ashby a miniature of you, you had no possible idea of what I might look like because I thoughtlessly neglected to send you a miniature. I hope you will forgive me, Blaze. I promise I shall make up for that neglect if you will but let me."

Again she blushed. Did his words hold a deeper meaning than they appeared to, or was she simply imagining it? Seeing her confusion, Edmund Wyndham tucked her small hand within the safety of his, and led his bride into the house. She was very charming, he thought. He realized that he was surprised by her complete innocence, but then, should he be? His single visit to Ashby had told him the complete and utter isolation of the Morgans' life.

As for Blaze, she was greatly relieved to have a moment to recover her poise. She could not yet believe her good fortune. When she had hidden with her sisters behind that hedge at Ashby and spied upon Lord Wyndham and her father, she had not really been able to see him, nor had it even mattered at the time. Then she had learned her fate, and she could not for the life of her remember any of the earl's features. Now she was delighted to discover that she was married to an extremely handsome man. How envious Bliss would be if she but knew!

She must write to her sisters! Write and tell them that her husband was as tall as Lord Anthony. That his hair was a dark brown, and that his eyes were the warm color of sherry wine. Curiously she gazed down at the hand holding hers. It was not an overly big hand, but large, the fingers long with well-shaped almost square nails. He was dressed in black velvet with a doublet that was heavily encrusted with jewels. The dark fabric made his fair skin even fairer.

He led her into the Great Hall of RiversEdge, a marvelous room with a soaring ceiling and carved beams that were gilded with a scrolled design. There were four huge fireplaces, all burning fragrant cherry wood, and beautiful windows which lined both sides of the hall high up. Through those windows that faced west could be seen the beginning of sunset. The high board was carved beautifully of golden oak. Behind it, centered, were two thronelike high-backed chairs. The room was filled with servants.

"I know how tired you must be, Blaze," the beautiful voice said in a low, intimate tone meant just for her, "but can you compose yourself just enough to greet your servants, my dear?"

"Yes, my lord," she answered him softly, thinking: If you asked me to fly to the moon right at this minute, I believe that I could. Was there another man alive so thoughtful and kind? She had been so afraid that he would be like his arrogant and mocking nephew.

The next few minutes passed, and it was as if she were within her own body looking out at all that happened about her. She greeted all of the house servants and the headmen of the outdoor hierarchy graciously, smiling, and with a kind word for each. Her mother, she thought, would have been proud of her, for she hid her real feelings well. All she wanted to do was to be alone with this man with the marvelous voice. To learn more about him, to please him. Yet she stood straight, doing her duty as the new Countess of Langford, until the last servant had gone his or her way.

"That was well done," the earl approved, to her intense delight, when they were once more alone in the Great Hall. "You are tired, I can see. Let me take you to your apartments, my dear. When you have bathed and are comfortable, I have arranged for us to have supper within your chambers if that pleases you."

"Oh, yes, I should like that very much," Blaze told him. "It was just about this time yesterday afternoon that I learned I was to come to you today. It has all happened so quickly that I can scarcely believe that I am here myself."

Edmund Wyndham smiled at her ingenuousness. "I realize," he said, "that having our wedding date changed so precipitously must have been a shock, but I am certain that Tony explained to you and your parents the pressing reasons for it. You came through Michaelschurch and Wyeton, and you could see yourself the happiness that your arrival has generated. The events of this summer have frightened my people. There were those old and superstitious goodwives who claimed that someone had put the evil eye upon Langford, her master, and its people. It was necessary that I counteract such rumors as quickly as possible. I would not have stolen your wedding day from you except for those circumstances. I shall make it up to you, however, Blaze Wyndham. That I promise you."

They had walked from the Great Hall while he was speaking, and he had led her up a wide staircase and down a wide hallway that was lined with windows on one side. Stopping before a dark oak door and turning the brass handle on the door, the earl flung it wide. Then to her complete surprise he picked her up and carried her over the threshold into the room. When he placed her back upon her feet Blaze was not quite certain that she was going to be able to stand, for her legs were suddenly wobbly.

"I will leave you in Heartha's capable hands," he said quietly. "When you are ready to receive me, you have but to send for me." Taking her by the shoulders, he placed a gentle kiss upon her brow, and turning, left her.

Blaze stood there rooted to the floor, staring at the door which had closed behind him. She should get down on her knees and thank the Blessed Mother for providing her with such a wonderful and kind husband. She almost laughed aloud to think of how reticent she had been about this marriage. Ohh, if only he would love her! she thought. She believed she was already falling in love with him.

"My lady." Heartha lightly touched her shoulder.

Blaze looked up and laughed softly. "I think I have been moonstruck," she said in gentle self-mockery.

"We all want you to feel that way about *him*," said the tiring woman quietly. "He is such a good man, my lady, yet his luck these last few years has not been good. We all believe that you will bring him good fortune as well as healthy children. Come now, your bath is ready for you."

For the first time since she had entered the house, Blaze concentrated upon her surroundings. The receiving room in which she stood was paneled in linenfold paneling. Upon the well-polished wide board floors was a beautiful red-and-blue wool carpet such as she had never seen. At Ashby the hall floor was covered with herbs and rushes, and the bedchamber floors were bare except in deep winter, when they had sheepskins upon the cold boards. The lead-paned casement windows were hung with French-blue velvet draperies. The furniture was carved and polished oak, and upon a long table was a pottery bowl filled with pink roses. A cheerful fire burned in the fireplace.

Blaze had never seen such a lovely room, but she had scarce time to admire it, for Heartha was leading her into her bedchamber. Blaze's mouth made a small O as she viewed this second room. Like the receiving room, the bedchamber walls were linenfold panels and the windows velvet-draped. The great oak bedstead was also hung with the soft blue velvet. The bedchamber had a fireplace too that even now warmed the room. There were several carved oak chests about the chamber, and small tables set on either side of the bed. Upon each was a silver candlestick with a pure beeswax taper.

"The garderobe and your dressing room are through here," said Heartha, pointing to a paneled door.

Blaze was stunned. Her parents' bedchamber wasn't this big. "Was this Lady Catherine's room?" she asked her servant.

"Of course, my lady. By tradition this is the countess's apartment, but my lord has had it redecorated for you. In Lady Catherine's time the hangings were crimson, for 'twas her favorite color, and it suited her; but come, my lady, your tub will grow chill if we do not hurry."

Blaze looked to see a huge oak tub sitting before the fireplace. From it arose a fragrant steam. Their tub at home was half the size, but it seemed that everything here was larger. She allowed Heartha to undress her and bathe her. The tub water was oily and smelt of violets. When she was dry Heartha came forward to dress her in a cream-colored silk chamber robe. As she fastened the last of the small pearl buttons, Blaze glanced through the windows and saw that night had fallen. Heartha drew her over to the pier glass so she might see herself.

"Are you not beautiful, my lady?" the tiring woman said. "You cannot fail but please his lordship."

It was then that Blaze realized that it was her wedding night. There had been no time to think today. So much had happened. Now suddenly she was to be faced by a bridegroom anxious to claim his rights, and equally eager to sire a child upon her. She gazed into the mirror and because she was no fool she saw a face and form created to tempt the strongest man. She saw a girl who stood no taller than five feet, three inches and whose clinging robe with its deep V neckline offered an enticing view of firm young breasts. Her brown-gold hair was loose and fluffy about her face, and poured down her back as soft as the silk against which it lay. She trembled, then started nervously at the knock upon the door.

A pretty maidservant popped her head around the door, saying, "Excuse me, m'lady, but Cook wants to know if you are ready for supper to be served."

Before she might reply, Heartha did so for her. "Of course she's ready, lass! Send the footmen quickly to remove that tub before his lordship comes. Hurry up now, girl!"

Blaze watched in amazement as the footmen, eyes politely averted, hurried into the room to remove the tub, while through the door between her receiving room and her bedchamber she could see the maidservants setting up a table with snow-white linen and a silver candelabrum.

"Shall I send for his lordship now, my lady?" Heartha asked.

For a moment she hesitated, but then Blaze nodded. She had no excuse for denying him. It would certainly cause a scandal should she do so. She kept trying to remember what it was her mother had told her, but it kept getting mixed up with what her little sister had seen and reported upon to them all. She was becoming more frightened as each moment passed.

How could she give herself to this stranger, no matter how kindly he was? She wanted to know him better. Right now she knew nothing of him but his name. She didn't even know his birthdate, or if he liked music, or what his favorite food was. Suddenly she realized she was alone, and when a door well hidden in her bedroom paneling swung open, she almost screamed in her fright. Edmund Wyndham stepped into the room. He was wearing a quilted gown of dark green velvet.

"Blaze, what is it? You look positively terrified," he said, his voice rich with concern.

"I . . . I did n-not expect y-y-you to en-enter quite that w-way," she managed to stammer.

"The door connects my bedchamber with yours," he explained. "It is not necessary that our comings and goings be public knowledge."

"Oh." Did she look as great a fool as she felt?

He moved to take her hand in his, leading her into the other room, where their supper awaited them at the table before the fireplace.

"You must be quite hungry," the earl said. "Tony told me that you stopped only briefly just after the noon hour for a small repast that your cook at Ashby packed. You will find the cook here at RiversEdge an artist of the first rank. Was your journey a pleasant one?"

"Aye, my lord, it was. The countryside is so beautiful between Ashby and RiversEdge. I have never seen it before, nor the river this far north."

He smiled, and seated her at their supper table. "Tonight," the earl said, "I shall serve you, my lady." He walked to the sideboard, and taking a plate, filled it, pausing before each covered dish to consider before lifting the lid from it. When he set her plate before her, Blaze saw that she had a slice of delicate pink salmon set upon a bed of cress, a slice of breast and the wing of a capon that had been prepared with lemon-ginger sauce, a baby lamb chop, and some pale leafy greens that had been braised in white wine. There was a hot loaf upon the table, a silver crock of sweet butter, and two cheeses—a hard, sharp golden one and a soft French Brie with which Blaze was unfamiliar.

The earl had filled two plates for himself. Upon one were at least a dozen open shells containing raw oysters, and upon the other was a large slab of beef, the leg and thigh of the capon, three chops, and some of the braised lettuce. Before sitting, Edmund Wyndham poured a fruity, dark red wine into the chased-silver goblets by each place. Seating himself opposite her, he cut two slices from the loaf and gave her one.

"Have you ever been away from Ashby, Blaze?" he asked her.

"Nay, my lord. No more than a few miles. On my twelfth birthday I asked to go to Hereford to see the cathedral. The trip was planned, but alas my younger sisters all came down with some complaint of the belly and running bowels, so we never went." She shrugged, and bit into the capon wing.

The earl wolfed down his oysters, then said, "When you are settled and comfortable here at RiversEdge, perhaps you would like to have your sisters for a visit."

"Ohh, yes, my lord!" Her very look lightened, and he suddenly realized that she was afraid. "Ohh, I should like that very much! I miss them already. We never thought to be separated from one another even in marriage, for of course none of us ever thought to make such a fine marriage." Her words tumbled out hurriedly as her lovely violet-blue eyes looked directly at him, rendering him breathless with her beauty. "How can I thank you for your kindness, my lord?" she continued. "You have become a fairy godfather to us all by first making me your wife and then dowering my sisters so that they might make good matches also. I shall endeavor to be the best of wives to you, my lord, and surely God will bless us with the sons you desire!"

Fairy godfather! He almost winced at her earnest words. For almost two months he had stared at her miniature, but the reality was far better than he could have ever anticipated, surpassing the painted image by far. He didn't want to be her fairy godfather. He wanted to be her lover. She was the most tempting creature he had ever seen, and already he desired her. Instead he said in a calm and grave tone, "I am certain you will be a perfect wife, Blaze, and that we will have a houseful of children, some of whom will be sons."

They ate, and when they had pushed back their plates he noticed that her plate was still half full, though her goblet was empty. There was an apple tart upon the sideboard along with a bowl of clotted cream. Rising, he removed their dinner plates to that sideboard, and served them each a slice of the tart, placing cream upon their table. That, he noted, she ate. When they had finished and she had wiped the crumbs from her mouth, he arose. Coming around the table, he drew her up, slipping his arm about her waist.

Blaze stiffened. She knew she should not, but she simply could not help it. Anxiously she bit her lower lip, her gaze now averted from his. She could feel her heart beginning to beat more rapidly within her chest. He is my husband, she thought desperately. I must acquiesce to his every demand. I must please him. I cannot give way to childish fears. I am a wife now. She trembled against him.

"You are afraid," he said quietly. It was a statement.

"Aye," she whispered, hating her cowardice.

He tipped her little face up so he might look at her, and bending his own head, touched her lips with his. They were cold and stiff, and at his touch she began to shake uncontrollably. He was surprised, but following his instincts, he held her in his protective embrace. "You are a virgin," he said. Another statement. "It is natural for you to be afraid. Has your mother told you what to expect?"

Mutely she nodded, hiding her head again from his direct glance.

There was more to this, he realized, than just a virgin fearful of her first sexual encounter. "You must not be afraid of me, Blaze," he said in a calm voice. "I want you to tell me why you are frightened. You must not worry about the fact that I am your husband, and think that you owe me any loyalty. I would have the truth from you, my dear. Truth between a husband and a wife is the cornerstone of a strong and happy marriage. Look at me now, sweetheart, and speak."

She raised her face to his, and her wonderful eyes looked into his. "I know that you will think me foolish, my lord, and I pray you not be angered by my words. I know that women wed with men that they do not know; and I know they are expected to bed with them immediately, but it is not my way. I do not know you. I know that you would have a son, for that is the purpose of our union. It has been pounded into me by my family for weeks, *and* by your nephew both yesterday and as we rode from Ashby this day.

"Still, I am uncomfortable with the notion. I am happy and honored to have been chosen to be your wife. I swear to do my best to give you a son, but you, sir, have stolen my courtship from me. I would have it of you before you have my maidenhead! Perhaps you will not ever learn to love me, but I want more between us than sacred bonds and children. I already have evidence of your kindness. If you would just give me a little time until we could at least become friends. Is that so very much to ask?" she pleaded of him.

To court his own wife. It was a fascinating and piquant idea, and strangely one that was not displeasing to him. He had grown up with his first wife. Their marriage had simply been the end result of a long friendship and practical necessity. Although he found that he already lusted after this charming stranger who was now his wife, he was a man of delicacy. The thought of bedding her so impersonally was, now that she had pointed it out, beginning to seem highly unattractive to him.

Gently he grazed a knuckle over her right cheekbone, and then he said slowly, "What you say has merit, Blaze. I would very much enjoy paying you court. Passion between a man and a woman should be mutually enjoyable. Tell me, though: for how long is this courtship to go on?"

"Will we both not know the right time to end it, my lord?" she answered him.

"Why, Blaze," he said with a smile, "what a wise little creature you are. Very well then, I will agree to your proposal. I shall court you with all the skill of my years and experience. Then when the right moment comes we will be united in the true sense of a man and his wife. First, however, I would teach you how to kiss."

"I have never kissed a man before," she admitted.

"It is painfully evident," he teased. "Your lips were as cold as ice toward me, and worse, as stiff as untanned leather."

"Perhaps," she returned with spirit, "now that I do not feel so threatened by you I will do better. Shall we try?" Closing her eyes so that her thick dark gold lashes fanned out across her cheeks, she raised her heart-shaped face to him, pursing her lips adorably.

He almost laughed aloud at her artlessness. Damn, but she was sweet! He bent to kiss her, this time finding her more compliant within his arms. Her lips softened beneath his, as smooth and delicate as a rose petal, parting slightly with some deep and primitive instinct as he increased the pressure of his mouth upon hers. Finally he drew away reluctantly and quite intoxicated with the fresh innocence of her. He was almost dizzy with her kiss.

"Is that better, my lord?" she asked him demurely. Her own heart was pounding violently. Her belly was doing flip-flops, and although she knew he could not know it, she could not quite focus her eyes clearly for a moment or two.

More experienced, he managed to regain his equilibrium quicker, and he laughed to cover his own surprise. "*Much* better, madam. You are an apt pupil. I think you will make great progress under my expert tutelage."

Recovered slightly herself now, Blaze twinkled back at her husband. "I think, sir," she said, "that you are probably a master of the art."

He caught her two hands in his, and raising them to his lips, kissed them. "I do not think, Blaze, that it will be hard to love you."

Her eyes widened with this flattery, and she thought silently to herself, although she was too shy to say it: Neither, my lord, do I think it will be hard to love you.

"I know you are tired," he told her. "Let me call Heartha to ready you for your bed." He brushed her cheek with his lips. "Sleep well and safe, Blaze Wyndham." Then he left her.

She was almost sorry to see him go, for she had enjoyed their meal together, and his company. Still, she was relieved to be left her maiden state for at least the time being.

While Blaze pondered her mixed feelings within the privacy of her bedchamber, her husband descended the main staircase of his house to the Great Hall of RiversEdge. There he found Anthony sprawled in a tapestry-backed chair by the fire enjoying a goblet of his best Rhenish. Edmund poured himself a matching goblet and joined his relative.

"What, uncle? Not upstairs enjoying the favors of that tasty little sweetmeat I brought you?" Anthony grinned lecherously.

"My many years have taught me, nephew, that a man cannot force a horse to water, nor an unwilling woman to his will," was the droll reply.

"*She refused you?*" The younger man sat up, looking aghast. "She is your wife, and you her lord."

Edmund Wyndham laughed. "Have you ever known me to force a woman, Tony? She is young, frightened, and a virgin. Until several hours ago she didn't even know what I looked like. She wants to be courted."

"*Courted?*"

"Aye, courted."

"But you're already wed!"

"Because a man is married doesn't mean he should cease to court his wife. I must live with Blaze until death parts us, which I trust will not be for many years. How we begin will determine the course of our lives together. Should I destroy our chance for happiness to satisfy a moment's lust? God and his Blessed Mother forbid it! Blaze wants a little time to know me, and she is right. I intend giving it to her." He drank deeply from the goblet.

"I do not understand you, Edmund. You mourned Cathy a full year, during which time you did not to my knowledge lie with any woman. You then immediately sought for a new wife. You even hurried the wedding day in order to soothe the nerves of your people. I still do not believe you have had a woman. Now this lovely creature is wed with you, and you will not lie with her because it does not suit her. Will you not spoil her with such indulgence, and lead her to believe that it is she who wears the breeches in this family?"

"You do not understand women, Tony. Blaze is here, and that is the important thing for my people. Whether I bed her tonight, or few weeks hence, will make no difference to anyone but ourselves. You have never had a serious relationship with a woman in your life. You do not comprehend that a wife cannot be treated like a common whore. Blaze would get to know me before she gives herself to me. She has denied me nothing, but rather pleaded her case quite well."

"God's foot! You're already besotted with the little creature, but let me warn you, Edmund, that I have seen a side of your bride that I hope you will not soon see. She has quite a temper for such a small thing."

"Aye, I expect that she does, for most women do. Did she turn that temper upon you when you lectured her about her duties to produce an heir for me?" His brown eyes were twinkling with amusement.

"*She told you that?*" Anthony was surprised.

"Aye, she told me. She was very outraged, for it seems that everyone has been preaching to her of her duty toward me since our betrothal became official. She was willing to take such instructions from her family and her priest, but I'm afraid she did not consider it your place, Tony. I should like to see her in anger!" He chuckled.

"I'm going home," said Anthony, disgusted. "There's a moon to light my way, and I suppose I had best see Mother before tomorrow. She will be mightily curious about my new *aunt*."

"Tell Doro that Blaze and I will receive Father Martin's blessing before our people upon the church steps at eleven o'clock tomorrow morning. I would like her there. Will your father be well enough to come?"

"If it does not rain or grow damp, he should be fine," said Anthony. "How I dread the coming winter! I have never seen Father so crippled up as he was last winter. Yet he is so brave. He rarely complains."

"Your father is not a young man any longer. He is close to sixty, Tony, and he has never been strong of limb. I am surprised that he has survived this long. It is a tribute to Dorothy's determination, for she has loved your father her whole life. That's the kind of love I would have develop between myself and Blaze. Can you understand that?"

Anthony Wyndham arose from his chair. "Aye, Edmund, I think I can."

"You should really think about seeking a wife yourself now, Tony. You are your father's only heir, and in a position to make a good match."

"I thought of that myself today," came the reply. "Perhaps one of my new aunt's sisters. They seem to be a comely, lively bunch of girls, and the stock is good. Aye, it would please my father to dandle grandchildren upon his knee before he dies."

The earl now arose himself, and putting an arm about his nephew, he walked with him from the hall to the main door of the house. Within minutes Anthony's horse was brought around. Mounting it, he rode off northwest along the river road to his own home of Riverside. Edmund watched him go until he was out of sight. Then he stood for a long minute in the warm September night staring up at the moon, which was almost full. Finally with a sigh he stepped back into the house, closing the door behind him, and sought his own yet lonely bed.

Chapter 4

$\mathcal{F}$or a moment after she awoke, Blaze was not certain of where she was, and then her memories of yesterday came flooding back. She was at RiversEdge. She was married and she had slept wonderfully upon the most comfortable mattress she had ever known. It seemed strange, of course, to be alone in such a big bed. It had been the first time in her entire life that she had slept alone. She stretched herself down to her toes, and then turning her head, discovered upon the pristine pillow next to her own a single red rose, its stem wrapped loosely with a length of pale blue silk ribbon embroidered with tiny pearls. Pulling the ribbon away, she discovered to her immense surprise that an oval sapphire set in a gold frame was sewn directly into the center of the strand of blue silk.

"Ohh," she gasped softly. Even she in her remote home had heard of such baubles, but she had never expected to possess one. Sitting up, she affixed the ribbon about her head, as was fashionable, and then realizing she could not see herself, she climbed from the bed and hurried over to the pier glass. Blaze turned her head this way and that in order to admire the jeweled headband.

"Good morning."

She whirled to see her husband as he came through the little door that connected their bedchambers. "Good morrow to you, sir, and thank you so very much for my gifts!"

"Which pleases you more?" he queried curiously.

She paused a moment to consider, and then laughing said, "I am not certain. I adore roses, and I think it romantic for a gentleman to gift his lady so. Yet I have never received such a lovely present as this jeweled ribbon. I'm afraid, sir, I am a greedy creature. I like them both!"

"I think greed is not in your nature, Blaze," he told her. "Beautiful things are meant for beautiful women. I am but making up for lost time. After all, I sent you no betrothal gifts."

"No gifts!" she exclaimed. "Why, my lord, you have seen to the welfare of my seven sisters. No bride ever received a more wonderful gift! It was more than enough."

How good she is, he thought, and walking the distance that separated them, he took her in his arms, holding her close. "There is something I would have you do for me, Blaze," he said.

She liked the feel of his arms about her, she decided. It was safe within his embrace. Unconsciously she rubbed her cheek against the velvet of his quilted robe. "What would you have of me, my lord?" she asked him.

"A simple boon. That you call me by my name, Blaze. Since your arrival you have not once said it. You have called me *sir* and *my lord*, but nothing else."

"I was not certain, Edmund, that it was allowed," she answered him. "My mother told me I must wait until you gave me leave before I spoke your name. She said that some men prefer that their wives call them *sir* or *my lord*."

"I lay awake last night wondering how my name would sound upon your tongue," he said.

"How extravagant your compliment, Edmund. Beware lest you turn my head."

He laughed, liking her quick mind, which could repartee with him so easily. "On more serious and mundane matters," he said. "I have come to tell you that we will receive Father Martin's blessing upon the church steps at eleven this morning. My sister, Dorothy, and her husband, Richard, will come with Tony to witness it."

"I would repeat my vows, my lord. This time with my husband, and not a proxy. Would Father Martin permit it?"

He was flattered beyond measure. "I see no reason why not. I will arrange we repeat them within the church, with my family as our witnesses, and then we shall stand upon the steps for the church's blessing. The blessing must be there, for I would please our people in this way."

Giving her a kiss, he left her. Heartha came with a tray that held soft, warm white bread and butter and honey and a carafe of sweet, watered wine. "There's to be no Mass this morning, so you may break your fast with a good conscience, my lady."

When she had eaten, she bathed her face and hands in a basin of perfumed water and vigorously cleaned her teeth. It was then the tiring woman with the aid of several giggling young maidservants began to dress her in the lovely cream velvet gown with its gold-and-pearl embroidery. The little maids grew quiet, their eyes round with pleasure at the beauty of their new mistress.

"I would wear my new ribbon," said Blaze, and Heartha affixed it atop her head, smiling to herself at her lady's unconscious preening.

The double strand of pale pink pearls with its coral heart was fastened around her neck. The diamond studs with their pearl drops were set into her ears. Her long brown-gold hair was given a final brush as her matching slippers were slipped upon her feet.

"Now come and see yourself in the pier glass," Heartha said, and taking Blaze's hand, she led her across the room. "Did I not tell you that you are beautiful?" the servant said.

Blaze stared at herself in amazement. Her mother had had a small pier glass, but as their clothing was so shabby, Blaze had never felt the need to stare at her own image. Now, seeing herself in her beautiful wedding gown, she was astonished. "Do I have other gowns like this?" she asked Heartha.

"His lordship had a complete wardrobe made for you, my lady. You have dozens of gowns and slippers, each one prettier than the other. You have petticoats, undergarments, chamber robes, and capes of wool, silk, and fur. There is nothing for which you lack. You are, after all, the Countess of Langford. His lordship might even take you to court one day."

Blaze stared into the glass as the impact of Heartha's words struck her. She was a wealthy woman. After a lifetime of poverty, although she had never really felt a lack, she found herself a rich woman. She even had jewelry! Then suddenly Edmund was beside her in the mirror, and turning her head, she looked up at him with a smile. He was garbed in black velvet, his doublet bejeweled even more lavishly than the one he had worn yesterday.

"I believe, my lord Edmund, that we make a very handsome couple," she said.

"Aye," he agreed, "we do. Do you think that means we shall have handsome sons and pretty daughters?"

She blushed, but replied, "I hope so!"

Together they descended the staircase to find awaiting them at its bottom Master Anthony, a rather formidable-looking lady, and a gentleman with a sweet smile.

"Dorothy!" the earl said in greeting, and kissed the woman upon both her rouged cheeks. Then, stepping back, he said, "May I present my wife, Lady Blaze Wyndham, the Countess of Langford. Blaze, my sister, Dorothy."

Blaze curtsied politely to Lady Wyndham, although it was really the older woman who should have curtsied to her, for Blaze held the greater rank. Still, her gentle behavior pleased her new sister-in-law.

"A pretty wench," growled the elder lady, "but then so was Catherine, for all the good it did her. Can you give this family sons, Blaze Wyndham?" she demanded.

"I believe so, madam," said Blaze, realizing quickly that Dorothy Wyndham was more bark than bite.

"Humph," she said, her dark eyes snapping, and then, "My husband, Lord Richard."

"How do you do, sir," said Blaze as she curtsied to him.

"I do well indeed, my dear," came the reply. Richard Wyndham smiled his sweet smile. "What a lovely addition you are to the family, my lady Blaze." And taking her hand he kissed it.

"If I had but known how gallant the men of this family are, sir, I should have come sooner," said Blaze with a twinkle in her violet-blue eyes.

"Even me?" teased Anthony provocatively.

"I must think about you, sir," Blaze retorted quickly.

"Be nice to your aunt, Tony," snapped his mother. "You need a wife, and she has sisters for whom you would be an eligible *parti*."

Blaze was somewhat startled. Lord Anthony to wed with one of her sisters? Which one? Certainly not sweet Blythe, and Bliss would aim higher, ambitious girl that she was. Delight? Merry little Delight? It seemed the only option, unless he chose to wait five more years for Larke or Linnette.

"Come, sweetheart," said Edmund gently, breaking her reverie and taking her by the arm. "We are due at the church shortly."

A carriage stood before the door awaiting them, for the church was located upon the road between the villages of Wyeton and Michaelschurch. The Riverside Wyndhams had their own vehicle, which Lady Dorothy, Edmund told his wife as they rode along, pretended was an accommodation for her, but in reality was for her husband, Richard, who was becoming more crippled each year. It was virtually impossible for him to ride any longer.

"Have they no other children but Lord Anthony?" Blaze asked curiously.

"Anthony had two younger brothers, Richard and Edmund, as well as a sister, Mary. He was no more than six and I ten when an epidemic struck RiversEdge and the other children were taken. Mary was only four months old. The other boys were two and four. We never understood why we were spared, for we were as sick as our siblings, but somehow we survived. My sister could not seem to conceive after that. It broke her heart, for she is a woman who loves children."

"Ahh, poor lady," said Blaze.

"She will enjoy her grandchildren if we can ever get that scamp of a nephew of mine to marry."

"Why hasn't he?"

"I do not know, except that it has never pleased him to do so. I wed with Cathy the day after my sixteenth birthday."

"When is your birthday?" Blaze demanded. "I know so little of you."

"August twenty-eighth. I have just celebrated my thirty-fifth year."

"I will be sixteen on November thirtieth," she replied. "You were married three years to Lady Catherine before I was even born."

"Nonetheless, despite my vast age, Blaze, I promise that once we are physically united I shall more than do my duty by you." Her innocent allusion that he was old enough to be her father stung him.

"*Sir!*" She blushed, and he chuckled.

The carriage drew up before the church, and the footmen hurried to lower the steps so that the earl and his countess might disembark.

"The church is called St. Michael's, which is why I had originally scheduled our wedding for its feast day at month's end," explained Edmund as he handed his wife from the coach and led her into the building.

A tall white-haired priest in his white-and-gold vestments awaited them. "Welcome, my child," he said, greeting Blaze. "I am Father Martin. I am to be your confessor should it please you."

The priest led them to just below the high altar of the church, where he allowed them to repeat the vows that Blaze had said the day before with her husband's proxy. She felt better speaking the words to, and with, Edmund. She believed that he would now feel more of a real husband to her for having said the words himself. While the priest prayed over them, Blaze glanced surreptitiously about the stone building. She had never seen such a rich-looking church. It had arched windows made of colored glass fashioned to show figures of apostles and angels. She had never seen windows like that before, and the candlesticks upon the altar were of gold!

There were several fine statues of saints, some of stone, some of wood which were painted and jeweled, including a wonderful interpretation of a militant St. Michael brandishing his gold sword. Edmund gave her hand a tiny squeeze. She gazed at him guiltily, but his warm brown eyes twinkled back at her in a conspiratorial fashion. Oh, yes! she thought. She could easily love this man.

"Now," said Father Martin, concluding the short ceremony, "the bridal couple must appear upon the church steps, where I will bless them."

As they exited the church, Blaze saw that the churchyard and the road beyond were awash with people who, upon seeing the earl and his bride, began to cheer. Father Martin smiled and held up his hands to quiet them. When it was silent once more but for the breeze and the birdsong, Blaze and Edmund knelt before the cleric upon the stone steps of the church while he blessed them in a loud voice that could be heard by even the farthest spectator. When he removed his hands from their heads and they arose to face their people, a mighty cheer burst from the throats of all those present.

"God bless the countess!" and "Long life, and an heir for Langford!" were typical of the words called to them.

The earl and his countess reentered their carriage, and, escorted by the crowds, moved once more down the road back to RiversEdge, where a great feast for all had been set up in the gardens of the house.

"I have declared this day to be a holiday," said Edmund with a smile.

Blaze smiled back at her husband. "I so wish my family could have shared this day with us," she said almost wistfully.

He took her hand in his, and turning it, kissed the inside of her wrist. "They will come when you are settled, I promise." His eyes caressed her, and she decided that she liked the turmoil that he caused with her senses.

An awninged pavilion had been set up for the wedding party upon the lawn at RiversEdge. Whole oxen, roe deer, sheep, and sides of beef were being cooked over open fires down by the river's edge. There were tables piled high with loaves of bread, wheels of golden cheeses, and willow baskets of apples and pears. There were casks of cider and ale already broached. Afterward there would be pieces of sweet bridescake for all.

At the high board there was more varied and delicate fare as well as fine wine. The bridal couple sat amid their family and the invited guests, who were mostly neighboring gentry, though none of as high a rank as Edmund Wyndham but for one, Owen FitzHugh, the Earl of Marwood.

Lord FitzHugh fastened a mischievously bold eye upon Blaze, saying as he did so, "God's foot, Edmund! Where did you find such a beauty?" He grinned winningly at her. "Madam, if you have a sister as lovely as you, I am in need of a wife. The tiresome chit to whom I have been betrothed since her birth has gone and died of a spotting sickness."

"I have seven sisters, my lord," Blaze replied, her look quite serious. "If you would but tell me your requirements, I am certain that my father could supply your needs. Would you have a maiden with golden hair, or one with dark tresses? We do have one who is a chestnut red, but alas, she is but five. You should have to wait at least eight to ten years for Glenna. All are quite sound of limb, and as breeding stock, our mother has no equal. Best of all, none squints."

Owen FitzHugh burst into laughter. "Tell me, madam," he managed to inquire between guffaws, "do they all have your way with words?"

She twinkled at him.

"Actually, Owen," put in Anthony, "my new aunt's younger sisters are all lovely, *and* there are three of marriageable age. I may take one to wive myself. What think you, aunt? You are barely married, and we have already matched two of your siblings. This marriage has already proved greatly to your advantage."

"I think, my lord FitzHugh, that you would be a most eligible husband for one of my sisters, should you be truly serious in your intent. As for you, *nephew*, you drink too much wine, *and* you talk too freely about matters which are not your affair," Blaze finished sharply.

"Ahah ha ha!" chuckled Lady Dorothy. "Here's one pretty maid not taken in by your handsome face, Tony. If her sisters are as sensible, I should be pleased to have one as a daughter-in-law." She reached over and patted Blaze's hand. "I like you, Blaze Wyndham!" she said.

"Gently, my love," Edmund admonished his bride. "You rise too quickly to Tony's bait. If you continue to give him pleasure, he will continue to tease you."

"I would certainly give him no pleasure!" she protested softly.

"Good," he replied, "for I would have you pleasure only me, sweet wife." He took her hand beneath the table, squeezing it for emphasis.

Blaze glanced up at him from beneath her thick lashes. Seeing the intensity of his gaze, she blushed a fiery pink.

The village children ran happily about the lawns. Blaze turned her eyes to them in her confusion. Beside her she heard her husband laugh softly, and the intimacy of the sound sent a shiver up her spine. She felt her breath shorten, and hoped that she wouldn't faint. A troupe of gaily clad Morris dancers arrived, having heard of the marriage celebration, and asked the earl's leave to entertain the wedding party. Since Morris dancers were considered good luck, the troupe was welcomed.

The afternoon was sunny and warm for mid-September. The dancers with their garb of bright ribbons and their tinkling bells moved gracefully, tripping through the ancient patterns, so old that their origins were lost in time. When they had finished their entertainment they were invited to join the feasting, and the earl rewarded the leader of the dancers with several silver coins. Local musicians now began to play upon the pipes, the tabor, and the drums. Anthony Wyndham and Owen FitzHugh thrilled some of the prettier village girls by dancing the country dances with them. By late afternoon, with the casks running low and the sun beginning to disappear behind the hills, it was deemed time to end the wedding celebration.

Since it was assumed that the bridal couple had slept together the night before, following the proxy ceremony, there was to be no "putting-to-bed" frolic, much to the disappointment of some of the guests.

"A lot of silly nonsense, if you ask me," said Lady Dorothy. "I remember when I married Richard how embarrassing it all was. You are fortunate to be spared, Blaze. Tell me, though I know it is early, will you be keeping Christmas here at RiversEdge? Catherine always kept a magnificent Christmas, the full twelve days."

"I should like to do that, ma'am," replied Blaze shyly. "I shall need you, however, to teach me how it is done, for I have never run a big house myself. I fear the simple customs of Ashby will not do for such a fine house of which I am now mistress."

"Why, bless me, Blaze Wyndham, I shall be delighted to guide you, though I doubt after this year you shall need me. Still, I am happy to be of use. Many of the customs here were kept in my own childhood. RiversEdge is a large house. You will want to invite your family to come for the Twelve Days of Christmas." Lady Dorothy was beaming with gratification that her brother's young bride would ask her aid.

"That was nicely done," approved Edmund several minutes after his sister and her family departed for their own home.

"I do need her help," Blaze replied candidly. "Though I would bring a part of myself to this family, I would not ignore the conventions that have been a part of RiversEdge since before my coming."

"What an interesting little creature you are, Blaze. You have a charming innocence, yet you have wisdom beyond your years."

"You flatter me, my lord. I have but a modicum of common sense. It is nothing more."

He smiled at her modesty. "Did you like our neighbors?" he asked her.

"Very much. Is the Earl of Marwood really looking for a bride, or did he simply seek to flatter me?"

"It is as he said. He was betrothed for twelve years to a young woman his late parents chose. She died last spring."

"Would he be an eligible *parti* for one of my sisters?"

"Absolutely! He is twenty-five years old. His title is ancient, though both his estates and his fortune are small. The dowry I have settled upon each of your sisters would be more than adequate for such a match. Have you a bride in mind for him?"

"I do not know him well enough to choose, but I think either Bliss or Blythe would suit. May we invite Owen FitzHugh for the Twelve Days of Christmas, my lord?"

"Aye. He would like that. He has no family left, and it is lonely for him. He spends little time on his estates, but usually follows the court."

"I am surprised then that he has not found a wife amongst the ladies of the court," Blaze remarked.

"There are many women at court, my sweet innocent, but those who are free are usually not the sort of women a man would take to wive. You would not know about such things, however."

The passing days slipped into weeks. It was an unusually mild and golden autumn. Blaze rode over the estates owned by her husband, and was somewhat taken aback by the vastness of the Earl of Langford's lands. He possessed enormous flocks of sheep and cattle. His orchards stretched as far as the eye could see. There was a large forest whose hunting rights were the Wyndham family's by grant of royal charter. There were nine villages belonging to the earl, including the two through which Blaze had passed on her wedding day. More than ever she became aware of the responsibility upon her to produce an heir for her husband. She had never in her life imagined that such holdings or wealth could belong to one person. It was a maturing thought.

Edmund Wyndham courted his young wife with a skill that only a man of experience could. There was not a morning that she did not open her eyes but to find some trinket or other token of his favor upon her pillow. Though he normally spent a great deal of time monitoring the running of his estates, Edmund temporarily put aside most of his personal responsibilities in order to spend the time with Blaze.

He found her an interesting young girl with a good mind and an eager intelligence that readily learned all he was willing to teach her. She could read and write. She had been taught simple mathematics, and church Latin. It was actually more than he had expected in a girl who had been raised so simply in a backwater such as Ashby. She had a small lute upon which she could play. Her voice was clear and sweet. Finding that she had an ear for languages, he began to broaden her Latin, and added Greek and French to her curriculum.

Their lives became a pleasant routine that ended before the fireplace in her receiving room each evening. There they sprawled upon a carpet before the warm blaze while he taught her the history of their country in story form. She had known very little of it, and she loved to hear his rich voice speaking to her of kings and queens, knights and maidens fair; battles in England, France, and the Holy Land; courtly love and tournaments.

Blaze was most intrigued by the current ruling family, the Tudors. She loved the tale of how Princess Elizabeth of York and Henry of Lancaster had wed, thus ending the Wars of the Roses and bringing peace back to England once more. She wept at the plight of poor Queen Catherine, the current king's wife, who could only produce one living child, her daughter, Princess Mary. Now it was rumored that after many years of marriage the king wished to put his wife aside.

"How can he do that?" Blaze demanded of Edmund one evening.

"There is precedent for such things," he answered her.

"But she is his wife in the eyes of both God and man, my lord!"

"Henry is King of England, Blaze, and he must have a son. Catherine of Aragon cannot seem to produce a living son, and is now, if the rumors be true, past childbearing. Other Christian queens have, with the church's blessing, stepped aside. Some have founded their own religious orders. Others have simply retired to some quiet spot and been honored for their selflessness to both their lord and their country.

"The queen, in my opinion, is a prideful and stubborn woman. King Henry should not have wed with her in the first place. She was his brother's widow, and had not the old king who ruled then been so greedy to gain her dowry, she would have been long gone back to Spain. Old King Henry, the present king's father, amassed great wealth in his time. When Prince Arthur died, only half of Catherine of Aragon's dowry had been paid. The old king thought to gain the other half by betrothing the widow to his younger son, the new heir, our present King Henry.

"The Spanish king, Ferdinand, was as greedy as our old king. An English prince had already, he believed, tasted of his young heifer's milk, and without the whole dowry. He saw no reason to keep his bargain with England to pay the full dowry. The English were not threatening to return Catherine, and were even betrothing her to the young Henry despite the fact that she was almost six years his senior.

"The old king stubbornly refused to give up his belief that the dowry would be paid. It is said that once it was, he intended returning Catherine to Spain and betrothing his heir to a French princess. The Spanish dowry was, after all, agreed upon for the match between Prince Arthur and Princess Catherine, not Henry and Catherine. There would have been no dishonor involved in the act."

"Do kings not believe in morality, sir? To have gained the whole dowry and then returned the princess would have been a terrible thing!" protested Blaze.

"A king's morality is generally suited to his own desires, my sweet," said Edmund with a smile. It pleased him that she reasoned so well. He would have to add logic to her schedule of learning.

"Why, if his father really didn't want him to marry the Spanish princess, did King Henry do it?" asked Blaze curiously.

"It is likely that the old king shared nothing of his plans with Henry. You see, Blaze, he was totally unprepared for Prince Arthur's death. His elder son was his pride and joy. Queen Elizabeth's too. She died a year after his death in childbed, but some said it was actually grief that killed her. The old king was never really the same after their deaths. He did not think a great deal of his younger son whom he intended for the church, and he preferred to keep the reins of government in his own hands.

"Finally, upon his deathbed old King Henry realized that King Ferdinand had outsmarted him. The rest of the dowry would never be paid. Had he managed to live long enough, I believe that he would have sent the Spanish princess packing, but alas, the old king died before he might correct the situation. The new king, our King Henry, was eighteen then. He was, and is, a tall, handsome man. The Spanish princess was a petite woman with red-gold hair and a pretty, youthful face. The king had admired her ever since he was a boy. He was not so much in love with Catherine as he was in love with love. Before anyone might convince him otherwise, he wed with her.

"There are some who say that her incapacity to birth a living son, and the fact that the two boys who did live past birth, but died soon afterward, is God's sentence upon the king for taking his brother's wife as his own wife. Those are judgments I prefer not to make, but I do believe that the queen should now step aside and allow the king to contract another, hopefully more fruitful marriage. The fault lies with the queen's inability and not the king's. That much is plain."

"Is it, my lord? How so? Both the king and the queen are responsible for the child's initial creation. Why should the whole blame be placed upon the poor queen?"

"It is obviously the queen, Blaze, for the king has a healthy living son by another lady."

"But if he is wed to the queen, how can that be?" she demanded.

For a moment Edmund Wyndham was completely and totally startled. That she was innocent he knew, but he had never suspected the scope of her naiveté to be that wide. "Men," he said quietly, "even married men, occasionally find amusement and solace in the beds of women other than their wives, Blaze. If a man is particularly loyal to a woman other than his wife, she is called his mistress."

"Have you ever had a mistress?" she asked him artlessly.

"No."

"You never made love with any other woman but your first wife?"

"I did not say *that*, my sweet," he replied, his voice edged with laughter. Reaching out with an arm, he drew her near. "You ask far too many questions for a wife," he teased, his eyes growing warm with something she did not understand.

Blaze's breath grew short. Her heart skipped several beats as her belly knotted and unknotted. He put his mouth upon hers, and she felt her lips immediately soften as the pressure of his kiss grew. His kisses had the most mesmerizing effect upon her, despite the fact that they had been kissing for several weeks now.

He laid her back upon the carpet, and looking up at him, she managed to say, "But if I do not ask questions, how will I learn, my lord?"

He ran a gentle finger over her kiss-swollen lips. "I will teach you everything that you need to know, my sweet. I have spent so much time these past weeks on Greek and French and history that I have neglected a far more enjoyable part of your education." His graceful fingers swiftly undid the six little pearl buttons that ran down her pale blue silk chamber robe from the V neckline as, leaning over her, he put an arm about her shoulders. His other hand slid swiftly beneath the loose silk, caressing her breast for the very first time.

She gasped, and for a moment thought that her heart would burst through her chest. To her surprise, Blaze found that she was not frightened. Indeed she found his touch to be most pleasurable. With a soft little murmur she pressed up against his hand, feeling as she did that her nipple had hardened, sensing a rough spot in his palm with her delicate flesh. This action caused him to groan as if wounded, and unable to help himself, he forcefully tore away the delicate fabric of her chamber robe, baring her to the waist.

"*Edmund!*"

For a moment he was beyond reason. He covered the soft and sensitive flesh of her tender virgin breasts with his kisses, reveling in the sweet freshness of her skin and the delicate fragrance that clung to it. He seemed unable to satisfy some deep and primitive longing that was possessing him.

The shredding of the silk, the touch of his warm lips upon her skin, had set her senses reeling wildly. Some instinctive carnal knowledge told her that this was desire. *Her husband desired her.* If only he would love her a little, she thought sadly. If it were not just his longing for an heir. His mouth closed over one of her nipples, and he drew sharply on the sentient little crest. It was that small act that caused Blaze to cry out again.

"*Edmund!* Ohh, my lord!" She struggled slightly beneath him, seeking to escape the rather frightening passion he had unleashed with his lips upon her responsive flesh.

He wanted her! Dear God, how he wanted her! He wanted to rip away the remainder of the silk that hid her from him. He wanted to cover her body with his and plunge the weapon of his manhood deep into her warmth. His temples throbbed with his longing, but the tone of her sweet voice penetrated his consciousness, even if the words did not. Christos! She was his wife, and his by right, but she was also yet a virgin. He could do nothing that would destroy that fragile and wonderful relationship that they had spent the last two months building.

Reluctantly he raised his head from her breasts to see her half-frightened and questioning look. "Oh, Blaze," he said softly, "I beg your pardon if I have frightened you, but surely you must know that you tempt me beyond reason. I could no longer contain myself, or my desire for you."

"I did not know until a minute ago that you did desire me, my lord," she said somewhat breathlessly. "I do not find it unpleasing, Edmund. Indeed it is most pleasurable."

"Can it be," he said hopefully, "that you are ready to become my wife in the fullest sense?"

For the briefest moment he saw fear leap into her violet-blue eyes. "Not yet," she whispered. "Please, not yet, my lord!"

Gently he kissed her trembling lips, and his hand smoothed softly over her breasts. "Not until you desire it, my sweet. Only then. I want you eager for your initiation into love, not frightened."

Reaching up, she touched his face with her fingers, and caressed it. "I think, perhaps, that I am beginning to love you, my lord," she said. For a brief second her eyes met his. Then, blushing, she shyly looked away.

In the days that followed, the deepening desire between them escalated. He now felt free to catch her in his loving embrace, giving his hands license to roam at their will, and indeed she encouraged him in his passion. For the first time they lay together, though fully clothed, upon her bed. His kisses and caresses were like heady wine to her. Catching her small hand in his, he led it below his doublet, and Blaze felt for the first time the hardness of a man. Tremulously she let her fingers close around him. Then when he felt her fear easing, he encouraged her to stroke him.

"It gives you pleasure?" she asked softly.

He nodded, his eyes smoky with longing.

The next morning he hunted in his forest with his nephew, and his mood was subdued.

"So, you have not yet breached the virgin walls," mocked Tony. "If you do not do so soon, *uncle*, I fear for your sanity. You cannot produce an heir unless you do. How you have refrained from taking the toothsome little wench is truly beyond me."

Edmund sent his nephew a black look. "Have all the village girls grown wise to you then, Tony, that you lack amusement and must concern yourself with my marital state?"

"Ahhh," laughed Anthony Wyndham, "so you have *not* deflowered her! Your lance is ready, but her sheath is yet closed to you. Take her and be done with it, Edmund. She makes a fool of you! You are her husband, and her lord. It is what you want! Your wishes are what matter, not hers!"

"Nay, my nephew, it is you who are the fool! Cease your banter now, for I have no wish to discuss my private life with a stripling who knows naught!"

Anthony rolled his eyes mockingly, but quieted his tongue. He had never seen Edmund quite like this. Was it possible that his uncle was falling in love with his bride? The thought disturbed him, though he knew not why. When Edmund spurred his horse ahead, Anthony followed him into the deep forest. The morning was unusually warm for late November, and he could already feel a trickle of sweat slipping down from his neck. He loosened his shirt.

They hunted for most of the day, but though the dogs flushed several rabbits and game birds, they found no deer. They finally exited the forest in late afternoon at a fork in the road near a point equidistant from both RiversEdge and Anthony's home of Riverside.

"You're not asking me home to supper?" teased Tony.

"Nay, I'm not!" came the surly reply. A rumble of distant thunder seemed to punctuate the earl's point as he turned his stallion and cantered off with his men and dogs behind him, leaving his surprised nephew alone in the middle of the road.

Chapter 5

Blaze disliked thunderstorms. She strove to hide her nervousness, relieved to see her husband's return. Edmund was not aware of her fears, for she took great pains to hide what she now considered a childish anxiety. It had been a dry autumn. The rain that had fallen had done so quietly. Today's unnatural heat seemed to have unleashed an aberrant violence in the weather that followed.

The distant thunder grew in intensity as it drew nearer to RiversEdge. The sky beyond the hills bloomed and faded with bursts of an unearthly pearly light. Blaze was subdued throughout the evening meal. Edmund quietly thoughtful, unaware of her edginess. He was in no mood for an evening of kissing and cuddling that would lead him nowhere. Tony's gibes had stung him harder than he was willing to admit. For the first time since his first wife had died he considered tumbling some serving wench, and looking about the room, his eye lit upon the buxom maidservant now adding logs to one of the fireplaces. His sherry-brown eyes narrowed speculatively. God, how Tony would mock him! He needed more time to think before he made a total fool of himself.

"Go to bed, my sweet," he ordered the surprised Blaze.

She arose obediently, and curtsying to him, left the hall on trembling legs. Why had he chosen tonight of all nights to leave her completely alone? It was ridiculous that she have this fear, but she would master it this night if it killed her. Determined, she marched upstairs to her apartments.

"Prepare my tub," she ordered Heartha and her staff.

"Shall I draw the draperies, my lady?" asked the tiring woman.

Blaze hesitated a moment, then said, "Nay, I would watch the progress of the storm."

She bathed amid a fragrant cloud of sweet violets while outside the night grew pitch black but for the shattering lightning, which was always followed by crashes of thunder.

The young maidservants skittered nervously about the room preparing their mistress's bed, setting out her pale pink silk nightrail with its matching beribboned nightcap, carefully banking the fire in the bedchamber fireplace so that a sudden gust of wind would not encourage it to unruliness. Heartha helped Blaze from her tub, quickly drying her off. The silky night garment was slipped over her head, and slithered noiselessly to her ankles. Lovingly the tiring woman brushed her lady's long brown-gold hair as the tub was dragged from the bedchamber by the serving maids into the receiving chamber, where the footmen were waiting to take it away.

Heartha tied the nightcap's ribbons beneath Blaze's chin, and helped her into bed. "Would you like me or one of the other girls to stay with you on the trundle, my lady? The storm is something fierce, and it ain't peaked yet, I'm thinking."

"Nay," said Blaze bravely with a nonchalance she was absolutely not feeling. "The storm bothers me not. Good night, Heartha."

Heartha curtsied, and with a final pat to the down coverlet hurried from the room, saying, "Sleep well, my lady."

Sleep? She was never going to sleep with all that booming and flashing going on outside her windows. She snuggled deeper into the bed, wishing that she had allowed her servants to draw the draperies. Then she would have had only the thunder to contend with. The wind began to moan and keen around the house. A fierce little gust hissed down her chimney, teasing the fire, which leapt at it, sending eerie shadows to mottle the walls of the room. Blaze shivered, suddenly remembering Old Ada's stories of the ghosts and ghoulies that rode upon the roiling back of storms such as this one.

"I will not be afraid," she whispered aloud to herself, and the very sound of her own voice was somehow comforting.

The night seemed to grow blacker, and the storm now began to mount in its intensity until the very house itself seemed caught directly dead center in the midst of the maelstrom. Blaze's good intentions dissolved amid a roar of thunder that actually shook the house to its foundations, which, coupled with a ferocious crack of lightning that struck one of the chimneys upon the roof directly above her, sent a rattle of bricks cascading down and over the slate roof above her windows.

Terrified, she began to scream. Peal after peal of pure, unadulterated terror. Despite the great noise of the storm, her frightened cries sounded throughout the upper floor of the house. Almost immediately the connecting door between her bedchamber and her husband's burst open as the earl dashed into the room.

"*Blaze!* What is it, my sweet? What has alarmed you so? Is it a nightmare, my darling?" Edmund was at her bedside, gathering her into his arms. The sweet fragrance of her bath oil made his head reel with desire.

"Th-the s-storm! I h-hate th-thunderstorms!" she sobbed piteously into the fine linen of his nightshirt, for he had not taken the time to put on his dressing gown.

"Why did you not ask one of the maids to stay with you then?" he asked practically.

"It . . . it's ch-childish to f-fear th-thunderstorms!" she wept wildly, shivering as another boom sounded overhead. "I . . . I did not want you to th-think that I was s-so fainthearted as t-to f-fear a little th-thunderstorm!"

Little thunderstorm? He would have laughed, had her terror not been so real. It was a horrendous storm. One of the worst he had ever known. Her warm, wet tears had soaked his nightshirt through at the shoulder where her face was hidden. She was yet trembling. His hand reached out to stroke her honey-colored hair in a soothing gesture as the thunder crashed once more outside the windows.

"Do you want me to stay with you?" he asked her, thinking as he did that she was the sweetest armful of female that he had ever held.

"Aye, my lord."

Gently he set her back against the feather pillows, catching her gaze with his. Her eyes were like rain-washed crystal violets, and her mouth was quivering with seductive innocence.

"I cannot guarantee my behavior, Blaze. Do you understand what I am saying? I must be completely candid with you about that, my sweet." His look was a serious one.

She caught at her lower lip in consternation, her small even white teeth worrying the pink flesh. "You would make love to me?" she said low.

A small smile played at the corners of his mouth. "You would quickly forget the storm, I promise you," was his answer. "If you prefer, however, I will leave you, my sweet," he finished.

Again Blaze paused to consider her plight, but another fierce shattering of thunder that rattled the windows sent her hurtling back into her husband's arms again. Desperately she clung to him, her soft breasts pressing against his chest. In that single moment Edmund Wyndham's good intentions dissolved. He was a mortal man, not a high-minded knight from some ancient world of courtly love. Blaze was his wife, and he yearned desperately for her. Tony was right! She was his! By God, he would have her, and no more of this nonsense! With a groan of longing he pulled his nightshirt off, tangled his hands into her hair, tipped her head back, and finding her mouth, he kissed her.

His passion surprised her. They had kissed and cuddled these many weeks past, but he had never kissed her as he was kissing her now. It was a demanding kiss that seared her tender lips, forcing them open that his tongue might pillage within the fragrant cave of her mouth. Their tongues met for the first time, and she shuddered with the sensuousness of the new feeling. Warm velvet stroked warm velvet. Her entire body felt weak with the sensation, yet she strained to answer his hunger.

There were no more words left between them now. Edmund kissed her until she moaned pleadingly at him to cease, and so instead his hot mouth sought a path down her satiny throat. Strong fingers shredded the blossom-pink silk of her night garment, yanking the fabric away that he might gaze upon her innocence lit golden by the pale firelight. With another groan he buried his face deep in the valley between her virgin breasts, branding the flesh above her wildly beating heart with another kiss.

Fingers reached out to tease at the nipple of one breast. His touch was almost a relief, she thought, so charged with tension was her whole body. Yet she was not afraid. Nay! There was no fear of what was to come in her mind, for she loved him. In her budding passion she dared to admit it to herself. She had known it almost from the beginning. *She loved her husband!* What she knew now was that she wanted him to love her. Raising his head, he then lowered it over the little nipple he had been fingering. Shyly Blaze reached out to stroke his dark brown hair. His mouth tugged hungrily upon her flesh, and she whimpered softly. His teeth scored the nipple gently, sending a thrill of pure longing down to her very toes. Fiercely she kneaded the shapely back of his neck.

His other hand began to smooth itself in seductive circles over the sensitive tight skin of her belly, moving ever downward until it slid across one silken thigh. Blaze murmured with open pleasure. His touch was mesmerizing, and she was frankly enjoying it. Playfully his fingers pushed between her closed legs once, twice, remaining the third time to press lightly against her nether lips, which to Blaze's surprise were moist, and encouraged the invading digits forward between them. She gasped when her thighs fell apart seemingly of their own volition.

Edmund raised his head from her lovely breast. "No, my sweet," he reassured her tenderly. "It's all right."

His dark head dropped to her other breast, drawing on it hard at the very same moment he pushed a single finger into her trembling body. Blaze arched against him, shocked by this invasion of her most secret self. The finger withdrew as easily as it had entered, and he pulled himself level with her once more to taste of her lips again.

"You are not afraid of me anymore, are you?" he murmured against the softness of her mouth. Playfully he nibbled upon her lower lip.

"Nay, I am not fearful," she whispered back breathily, "for I find that I love you, my lord," she finished boldly.

"*Do you indeed?*" he replied, somewhat startled by her honest admission. Then his fingers trailed tenderly back and forth over her cheekbone. "Do you indeed love me, Blaze Wyndham? Could I be so fortunate a man as to have found love twice in a single lifetime?" He kissed her lingeringly, his lips moving softly over hers. He had never wanted her more than he did at this moment, but the unspoken question shining so nakedly in her eyes needed an answer. "And if I loved you, my sweet, would it make you happy?" he asked her.

"Ohhh!" All her vulnerability was there for him to see in that soft sound. Her perfect heart of a face shone with the joy his words brought her. "*You love me?*" she asked ingenuously.

"From the moment I saw your adorable face in that miniature your mother gave me," he said, "though I have been loath to admit such feelings even to myself."

"Because of Lady Catherine?"

"Aye. I felt it somehow disloyal, but remembering the sweetness of Catherine's nature, I know she would want me to love again, and by the blessed rood, Blaze, I do love you!"

He kissed her hard, and her arms wrapped themselves about his neck, drawing them into a passionate embrace. From that moment on, the world took on a dreamlike quality for Blaze. His tongue seemed to be everywhere on her. In her mouth fencing with her own tongue, teasing at her nipples, boring into the cleft of her navel. Her hands took on a life of their own, smoothing down his back again and again, fondling the rounded curves of his firm buttocks.

She felt his weight suddenly pressing upon her, his legs, unlike his chest, delicately furred and surprisingly soft against her skin. Then she became aware of something hard, warm, and smooth pressing against the inside of her thigh. Instinctively she knew, and she wanted to touch him there. She wanted to know better the means of her destruction, for certainly once they were joined by that fierce yet fragile bridge, her girlhood would be destroyed even as she reemerged in her new incarnation as a woman.

"Let me know you *there*," she begged him, and he took her hand to let it touch his manhood, no longer covered by civilized velvet as it had been in their past encounters, but hot and taut in its natural state. Her slender fingers caressed him, sliding with a soft and graceful touch back and forth along the length of him, closing about him finally in bold embrace.

Edmund shuddered and a low groan escaped him. "Ahhhh, my sweet! Ahhhhhh!" God's mercy! He could bear no more of her trifling. Her unschooled but wonderful touch had him near to spilling his seed. As her grip relaxed, he pushed her hand away. "Enough, Blaze!" he said through gritted teeth.

"Oh, my lord, have I not pleased you? I thought you enjoyed it when I touched your manhood." There was genuine distress in her voice.

Pinioning her beneath him, he raised himself so he might look down into her face. "There are times, my sweet wife, when a man's desire for his woman overcomes all else. This is one of those times. I would have you, Blaze, and I would have you now!" he growled.

Beneath him he felt her legs part widely for him. Her beautiful face shone with her love for him. It was almost fierce in its look. "Then have me, my lord, I await you!" she cried out.

In that moment his admiration for her was almost as great as his love. What sons they would breed up together! He waited no longer, thrusting hard into her eager young body. There was but a momentary impediment to her passage, and he saw pain spring into her eyes, but she bravely pushed up against him, and he drove his weapon deeply home.

For a moment Blaze believed that she was to be torn asunder, so fierce was his passionate assault. He had battered against her maidenhead, but to her surprise it had given way fairly easily. Now he lay atop her, allowing her a moment to recover herself, and she felt the bigness of him within her passage throbbing his message of love. Then he began to move upon her, pressing deeply into her, then almost completely withdrawing himself so that she whimpered for his return, twisting beneath him, straining upward to prevent his escape. In her semiconscious state Blaze suddenly realized that here was pleasure heretofore unknown. She understood now why Vanora had been able to gain so much knowledge in their father's stables, for surely this was paradise, this conjunction between a man and a woman.

She was not even aware that her nails raked savagely down her husband's strong back, leaving in their wake bloodied welts. She did not realize that she thrashed wildly beneath Edmund, begging him over and over again to continue this incredible pleasure lest she die. Blaze soared, soared to the stars and beyond, while above her Edmund loosed his pent-up torrent in an effort to quell her raging fires, totally amazed to see his virgin bride had galloped the entire course of passion.

He rolled off her finally, and they lay together gasping with their mutual exertion. Reaching out, he caught her hand in his and squeezed it, delighted to feel her squeeze back. In a sudden flash of memory he remembered his wedding night with Catherine, and how she had wept and carried on for hours after he had claimed his husbandly rights. Despite the fact that he had loved her well, and she had tried so hard to give him children, she had never really enjoyed their coming together. She had certainly never responded to him or his lovemaking as Blaze had just done.

Almost fearfully he said, "I did not hurt you, Blaze, did I?"

She sighed lavishly. " 'Twas but momentary, my lord, and quickly forgotten, so sweet was the afterwards. Can we make love again now?"

His laughter had almost a relieved quality to it, though she did not notice. "A man needs more time to recover from love's combat than does a woman, my sweet. Give me but a little time, and we shall indeed make love again."

"Ohh, Edmund, I never knew that anything could be so very wonderful! Do you think we may have conceived a child?"

"It is possible," he said quietly. "Time will tell us that."

"We must not stop making love until we are quite certain," she replied. "I want a large family, my lord. I hope you are prepared for it."

"Madam, I will do my very best to accede to your wishes." He chuckled, amused by the seriousness of her attitude in the matter.

Suddenly he found her leaning over him, and her mouth touched his teasingly. "Are you recovered your strength yet, sir?" Her little pointed tongue snaked across his lips daringly.

To his surprise, he felt hot desire begin to roil within his loins. God's nightshirt! She was making him feel like a stripling of eighteen again!

"Love me, my lord Edmund," she murmured, and he could see the smoky desire filling her eyes.

Reaching up, he caressed a plump young breast, and she whimpered softly. His eyes narrowed speculatively, and then filled with pleasure as he realized that in taking her virginity he had unleashed an incredible pent-up well of passion within his sweet wife. She was like a young mare come into her first season, and he would have to be a strong stallion to satisfy her longings. It was not an unpleasant thought. Rolling her over beneath him, he kissed her almost cruelly, crushing her soft lips with his, yet feeling her respond with a wildness he hadn't even known could exist in a woman. There was no time for niceties, for he found himself hard and eager for her, and as for Blaze, she was as eager, her newly opened passage wet and hungry for him. With an almost pained cry he drove into her!

At various intervals throughout the rest of the night they made fierce and passionate love, until finally in the first pearly light of dawn they slept, tangled together in pure and utter exhaustion. Heartha, entering her mistress's chamber at the usual hour, gaped with wide eyes upon the scene, and then with a broad smile splitting her face, backed from the room to hurry off so she might spread the good news that the young countess was no longer a virgin. That an heir to the earldom was now but a simple matter of time!

In the days that followed, Blaze and Edmund's deepening passion for one another became openly obvious to all. They could not bear to be away from one another for too long a time. They touched constantly, and their languishing looks at one another were, in Heartha's pithy opinion, "like to set the hayricks afire." They spent the long autumn nights behind closed doors, and did not arise until the sun was well past the horizon. If Blaze did not conceive a child immediately, it was not from want of trying.

Family was forgotten in their newly born love, and Lady Dorothy, arriving early one mid-November afternoon to discuss the Christmas celebration at RiversEdge with her brother's wife, was vastly amused, and secretly delighted, to be told that the earl and his wife were "resting" in milady's bedchamber. With a rich chuckle and all the tact of a seasoned diplomat, Lady Dorothy withdrew, leaving a message that she had called and would return on the morrow.

Anthony Wyndham was not so amused, and his irritation with both Blaze and Edmund puzzled him. Why should he care that his uncle and new aunt were in love, were obviously striving to create an heir for Langford? He had never coveted Edmund's holding, believing it but a matter of time before an heir was born. He had been as disappointed as Edmund and Catherine had been when their deeply cherished hopes were dashed time and time again. He had been equally pleased when Edmund had remarried, even if he did not believe Blaze the right bride, for God only knew the earldom of Langford with all its wealth could have brought an heiress, and not this poverty-stricken little girl of English and Welsh heritage with only her fertile mother to recommend her.

Arriving at RiversEdge late one morning, he rode into the stableyard to find it deserted. Undoubtedly the grooms and stablemen were all out exercising the horses. Dismounting, he walked his own sweating animal about for a few minutes to cool him down, and then led him into the semidarkened stables to tether him in an empty stall. As he dumped a small measure of grain into the bin for his horse he heard the distinct sound of a woman's laughter in the rear of the building. It was followed by a man's deeper laughter. Curious, he moved silently toward the sound to catch the servants who would amuse themselves on their master's time. Perhaps he would tumble the guilty wench himself as the price for his si- lence. He grinned wolfishly as he approached the stall from which dis- tinct sounds of loving combat were now emitting. Perhaps it was that great creature with the big breasts who hefted logs so easily into the fire- places of the Great Hall. Anthony licked his lips in anticipation, and peeped over the side of the stall.

To his immense shock, he saw not a pair of miscreant servants, but his uncle sprawled over the half-clothed body of his wife, pumping valiantly away upon her. For a moment he stood frozen and staring down at the erotic living tableau. Blaze had long legs for a petite woman, and she wore black knitted stockings gartered with rosettes set just below the tops of her white, white thighs. Her skirts were about her waist, and her bodice was wide open, revealing two plump, round creamy breasts, each topped by a bright cherry of a nipple. Her eyes were closed, the lids almost mauve in color. Her head was thrown back, her mouth open to emit soft moans of obvious pleasure. Her honey-colored hair was totally undone.

"Ahhhhh, sweetheart! Ahhhhh!" groaned Edmund in his ecstasy.

"Ohhh, my darling, yes! Yes! Yes!" Blaze cried in return.

Galvanized by the sound of their voices, Anthony recovered himself and slipped shaken from the stables. For the briefest of moments he had, as he watched the couple, imagined himself in Edmund's place. Thought of what it would be like to plunge himself deep into Blaze's eager sweet- ness. For the tiniest heartbeat he had envied Edmund, and he wanted to yank him off the writhing woman beneath him and take his place. With that admission came the horrifying realization that he desired his uncle's wife. *He wanted Blaze for his own!*

Anthony Wyndham closed his eyes, anguished. Was he in love with Blaze, or had the blatant sensuousness of the scene merely aroused his own lusts so that they fastened upon Edmund's bride? He did not honestly know. I have got to take a wife of my own, he thought desperately. If I do not find myself a bride and settle down to the business of having my own family, I shall never really be happy. Automatically he walked toward the house and was admitted entry.

"My lord and my lady are out riding," said the majordomo. "They are expected back soon, Master Anthony, if you would care to await them."

He nodded blindly, and was led into the library, where a warm applewood fire burned. Throwing himself into a chair, he accepted the goblet of Rhenish that the attending footman handed him before leaving him to his thoughts. God's foot! She was so lovely! So damnably lovely! Even now the reminiscence left him burning with desire, and he was ashamed. Blaze was a respectable woman who had never offered him the slightest encouragement. She was in love with her husband, who was not just his uncle, but the best friend he had in all the world. What kind of a man coveted his best friend's wife? The very thought made him almost physically ill.

Abruptly he stood up. He had to leave. He had to go before they even knew that he was here. How could he face them, having seen what he had seen in the darkened stable, and feeling as he now did? Before he could stop himself, the memory slammed into him again. The shaft of sunlight filled with dancing dust, the golden beam grazing her bare knee only to bury itself in the straw upon which she lay. The rustle of that straw. The groans of pleasure from Edmund, coupled with the little cries of rapture that issued forth from Blaze's straining throat.

"Tony!" Edmund had entered his library unheard or unseen by his nephew. "By the rood, you are deep in thought, man! What brings you to RiversEdge?"

For a moment Anthony could not focus his eyes, but when he did he felt almost a sense of physical pain, for his uncle's face shone with such happiness that the younger man's guilt assailed him sorely.

"Tony? Is anything amiss?" Edmund had noticed his nephew's discomfort.

Quickly Anthony regained control of himself, and said, "Nay, Edmund, nothing is wrong. Mother sent me over because she would invite you to my birthday celebration on the thirtieth. Will you and Blaze come?"

"November the thirtieth? Good Lord, Tony!" the earl exploded. "That is Blaze's birthday too! She will be sixteen. Had you not reminded me, I should have forgotten all about it. My mind is otherwise occupied these days. Nay, we will not come to Riverside. It is you who must come here. I must plan a surprise fete for my bride! What can I give her? I know! I shall send for some of her sisters to come! Is that not a wonderful idea? She misses her family greatly, you know."

"Aye, 'twould be a fine gift, Edmund," Anthony answered low.

"Give you a chance to look over Blaze's sisters and consider whether one of them might not make you a suitable wife. You're past thirty, nephew! I'm but four years your senior, and I'm already on my second wife, while you've had none," teased Edmund. "Believe me, Tony, a pretty young wife is a wonderful thing! I've never been happier!"

"So," Anthony said in what he hoped was his formerly mocking banter, "you have at long last breached your bride's maiden defenses. It took you long enough, uncle."

"Ahhhh," chortled Edmund, "but she was well worth the wait, nephew! Catherine, may God assoil her sweet soul, was never enthusiastic about our coupling, though she did it gladly enough to gain us children. Blaze, however, is a different story. Never have I known such passion in a woman! The little witch is nigh to wearing me out, Tony! No wonder Lord Morgan spawned himself nine children. These things are inherited, and certainly the mother is as passionate as the daughter. You would not do badly to take one of Blaze's sisters for your own. Your nights would be spent in paradise, I assure you!"

"I shall certainly consider it," replied Anthony dryly, "and I shall pass your message on to my mother about surprising my aunt."

Anthony returned to his own home to find his mother thoroughly approved her brother's idea of surprising his bride with a fete on her sixteenth birthday.

"Blaze's birthday is more important than yours," she told her startled son. Then she smiled archly. "I like the idea of Edmund's asking his sisters-in-law to come. It will give us an opportunity to look them over to see which one would be a suitable wife for you, Tony."

"I do not think Edmund will ask all of the Morgan sisters this time. Besides, only two or three of them are old enough to marry. Have you considered the possibility, Mother, that none will suit me?" Anthony teased his parent.

"Nonsense," bristled Lady Wyndham. "They are bound to be pretty, which is an advantage. They all have respectable dowries, thanks to Edmund, and other than that, all you want is a healthy, strong young breeder, my lad. You need only pick the one who is most amiable to you. It is quite simple."

"Nay, Mother, it is not. I would have love both from and for my wife," he answered her.

"God's foot, Tony! You sound like a moonstruck virgin," snapped his mother, "and that I know you are not!"

"Do you not love my father?" he demanded.

"Of course I love your father, but it is a love that came and grew after our marriage. You know that Edmund and I have different mothers. Mine, God assoil her, was as plain as a pikestaff, and so am I! Your grandfather was not a man to waste gold needlessly, and he quickly saw that not even a great dowry would gain me a great marriage. On the other hand, his younger brother's heir was willing to have me for what your grandfather considered a more reasonable dowry. So I was wed to your father, who is a kind and good man whom I have grown to love and respect over the years.

"A marriage, Tony, must be worked at to succeed. You choose a good girl from a good family with a decent portion with whom you can get on, and then you strive to make your happiness. That is the way it has always been. What is this foolishness you prattle about *love?* Love will come if you seek it, but it comes after a match, certainly not before!"

He did not argue with her, for it would have done him no good. How could he explain to his mother that he was already in love? In love with Edmund's wife. Or was it love? Perhaps his mother was right after all. Perhaps love came after a marriage, and not before. Certainly it had been that way with Edmund and Blaze. He would keep from RiversEdge until the thirtieth, for it would give his emotions time to cool. Then with a clear mind and conscience he would attend Blaze's birthday fete prepared to choose one of her sisters for his wife.

He was surprised, however, to discover some ten days later that life did not always go as smoothly as one planned. Arriving at RiversEdge with his parents, he found that he was not the only eligible male invited to the feast. Owen FitzHugh, the Earl of Marwood, was already there. So was Lord Nicholas Kingsley of Kirkwood. Bliss, Blythe, and Delight Morgan had already arrived to surprise their eldest sister.

Lady Dorothy hummed her approval beneath her breath. "As pretty a trio of pigeons as I've ever seen," she said with a smile at both her husband and her son. "Any one of the three will do, my lad, but you had best move quickly. Nick Kingsley and Owen FitzHugh will not stand tongue-tied and idle with such quarry about, and both are wife hunting I am told."

"Which one would you prefer, Mother?" he teased her.

"The older the better for breeding purposes," she returned, not one whit put out by his sarcasm.

Her husband chuckled. "He may not have the choice, my love," noted Lord Richard. "See how one of the twins stalks poor Marwood, and the other, Kingsley is clearly smitten with her. I think Lord Morgan will soon find himself short several daughters."

Lord Wyndham of Riverside was a perceptive man, as his wife well knew, and looking more closely, she was distressed. Bliss Morgan had clearly set her sights upon Owen FitzHugh, and was flirting with him in a most charmingly outrageous manner. The Earl of Marwood, who spent most of his time at the king's court, was both amused and enchanted by her, for although she was bold, her innocence was clearly apparent.

Her identical twin was obviously the opposite side of the coin, and where Bliss was forward, Blythe was shyer. This character trait was evidently most appealing to Nicholas Kingsley, who had a bemused and besotted look upon his face as he hovered about Blythe like a moth about a candle.

"Doro! Richard! Nephew! Welcome to my wife's birthday fete," said Edmund Wyndham, coming forward with Blaze. They were both smiling, and Anthony felt a momentary pain in his chest.

Blaze curtsied prettily to the gentlemen, but then caught at her sister-in-law's hand to draw her forward. "Come and meet my sisters, Doro! Edmund has brought them to RiversEdge to surprise me! Was that not the most wonderful birthday gift?!"

"Surely he has given you something else as well," the good lady commented with a twinkle in her eye.

"Ohh, yes! My lord is the most generous of husbands, and you shall see his generosity tonight. Sapphires, Doro! The most beautiful necklace and earbobs of blue sapphires with just the merest hint of violet in them. Edmund says they reminded him of my eyes."

"My brother waxes poetic these days," chuckled Lady Dorothy.

The earl flushed at his elder sister's words, much to her great amusement. "Do not tease me, Doro," he said pleadingly. "I cannot help it if I am in love with this minx."

Dorothy Wyndham reached out with her free hand and gently touched her brother's cheek. "You deserve to be happy, dearest," she said quietly before she was drawn off by Blaze, who hurried her away across the room to meet her siblings.

The elder Lady Wyndham openly assessed the trio presented to her. The twins, who had turned fifteen earlier in the month, were both exquisite beauties. Though identical, she quickly found that the key to identifying them correctly was in their countenances. The indomitable Bliss had a sharpness of expression that was missing in the sweeter look of gentle Blythe. No honey-tongued miss, this one, thought Lady Dorothy. It was well she had set her sights upon Owen FitzHugh, for Bliss would be at constant sword's point with Anthony, his mother could easily see. As for the other twin, Lady Dorothy could see she was too soft a creature for Tony. He would be bored within a week.

Her glance turned to the youngest of the trio. "And who, my dear Blaze, is this pretty wench?" she demanded with a toothy smile.

"This is Delight," replied Blaze with a smile. "She is my parents' fourth-born."

Lady Dorothy assessed Delight openly, and decided that she was a pretty girl with her dark brown curls, and her deep blue eyes. "And how old are you, my child?" she asked Delight.

"I will be fourteen June seventh next," came the pert reply. "My womanhood is upon me, and I am ready to wed."

"*Delight!*" shrieked her scandalized elder sisters.

" 'Pon my soul!" laughed Lady Dorothy. "You are most frank, child."

"I think Master Anthony is the handsomest man in the whole world," sighed Delight.

"Do you indeed?" His mother smiled. "Well, I shall tell you a secret, Delight. I think Anthony is the handsomest man in the world too. He does not take after me a bit, thank heaven! He is all Wyndham."

"Why is he not wed then?" was Delight's query, much to her sisters' chagrin.

"He has not found the right girl yet," was the reply.

"Delight, there is a smudge of dirt upon your left cheek, and your hair is now in disarray because of your romp with the puppies. Go and repair your coiffure and wash your face," ordered Blaze. "Mother would be so shocked."

With a quick curtsy to her sister and Lady Dorothy, the young girl hurried off.

"You must forgive her," said Blaze. "It is her first time away from home, and she has always had the habit of saying exactly what comes into her head."

"A most embarrassing habit," said Bliss tartly, and Lady Dorothy decided for good and all that Bliss Morgan would be a most unsuitable daughter-in-law.

"Delight did not mean to be rude, madam," said Blythe. "I believe she harbors a secret tenderness for Lord Anthony. She is but nearly come to womanhood, and like most girls in her state, apt to be overly romantic."

"I find her a charming child, as are you, my dear," replied Lady Dorothy, deliberately leaving out Bliss, who, though wise to the slight done her, was obviously not in the least put out by it.

That evening Lady Dorothy could see most clearly how the wind blew with regard to her matchmaking. A marvelous feast was held in the Great Hall of RiversEdge. All the gentry within the region had been invited to celebrate the young countess's sixteenth birthday. Many eligible young men crowded about the Morgan sisters, who were gowned and bejeweled to befit their natural beauty.

Blaze wore a gown of violet-colored velvet, its heavily embroidered underskirt encrusted with gold, pearls, and crystal beads. The square neckline of the gown was low, and her lovely round breasts swelled dangerously above the fabric. The bell-like sleeves were sewn with gold threads and pearls. She wore her birthday gift from her husband—a magnificent necklace and matching earbobs of violet-blue sapphires set in rich gold. Lady Dorothy was pleased to see, despite a coterie of admirers, that Blaze had eyes only for her husband, who could not resist reaching out occasionally and touching his bride's pretty curls.

The twins were garbed in a rich-looking midnight-blue velvet whose lighter blue underskirts were embroidered in silver threads and seed pearls. When the sisters had been invited to RiversEdge they had been told that new wardrobes awaited them so they need bring nothing but themselves. In their wildest imaginations they had not dreamed that such luxuries as Edmund Wyndham provided for them could exist. Bliss and Blythe's lovely yellow-blond hair was held back with silver ribbons, and about their necks were strands of fine pearls interspersed with pink crystal beads.

As for Delight Morgan, she could barely contain her excitement, for her very grown-up gown was a deep ruby-red velvet whose red silk underskirt was embroidered in black silk threads. Red velvet ribbons contained her luxuriant dark chestnut curls, and about her slender little neck and in her ears sparkled garnets of the first quality. Though the twins teased her about her lack of a bosom, her happiness could not be deflated. Her blue eyes followed Anthony Wyndham wherever he went, although the gentleman knew it not. Nor could he know of her innocent prayers to the Blessed Mother that he fall in love with her. She would have been heartbroken to know that he thought of her only as a charming child.

After the feasting was over, the tables in the Great Hall were pushed aside, and there was dancing. The other gentlemen soon found themselves cut out with regard to the twins by milords FitzHugh and Kingsley. Soon, however, in the general merriment and drinking that went on, no one even noticed that Bliss and Blythe were absent from the company. Blythe, her small hand tucked through Lord Kingsley's arm, walked quietly with him in the picture gallery of RiversEdge. Their low conversation could not be overheard by anyone, but had there been anyone there to view the scene, Nicholas Kingsley's open and complete adoration of the girl with whom he walked was easily discernible upon his homely face. Blythe did not seem in the least distressed by her companion's plain features. Rather she seemed to hang upon his every word.

As for Bliss, she found herself suddenly in a rather deserted alcove at one end of the Great Hall, where, though she could easily hear the sound of gaiety from her eldest sister's birthday celebration, neither she nor her companion could be seen. Owen FitzHugh towered over her, a wolfish look upon his very handsome, somewhat sharp features. He grinned down at her, and Bliss, looking back up at him, had to force herself not to shiver.

"Well, puss, here we are," the Earl of Marwood said quietly.

"Indeed, sir, and why are we here?" she countered bravely.

"So I might kiss you, pretty puss. You have the most adorable mouth, but then that is obvious, and you have undoubtedly been told it a hundred times or more," he said.

"Nay, sir, I have not," Bliss answered him. "My sisters and I lead quiet, indeed almost solitary lives at Ashby." Her look was cool, but her heart was hammering with excitement. So this was flirting!

"You have not been courted before?" His look was disbelieving.

"*Are you then courting me, sir?*" Her sapphire-blue eyes feigned surprise.

He pinioned her gently against the stone wall of the alcove, saying as he did, "Mayhap, so give me a kiss then, puss," but Bliss managed to duck away from his faulty aim.

"*Sir!*" Her tone was one of outrage. "Our parents have warned us of such lechery as yours. My kisses are saved for he who weds me, and are not to be given lightly or carelessly to any who ask! Release me this instant!"

"Are you telling me that you have never been kissed, Mistress Morgan?" His dark eyes searched her beautiful face for the truth. She was the most exquisite creature he had ever beheld, and he knew even as he trifled with her that he must have her for his own. He would have to spend the rest of his life guarding her virtue from others, lest he find himself cuckolded. Such beauty as Bliss Morgan's led only to trouble, yet even acknowledging this truth, he could never let another man have her.

"Nay, my lord earl," said Bliss sweetly, sensing her victory, "I have never been kissed by any man but my father. You seek my kisses, do you not? What value do you place upon them, then?" The prey had become the predator.

Owen FitzHugh was not so easily led by his lust, however. He grinned wickedly at her and drawled, "I must sample your wares, Mistress Morgan, before I can place a price upon them."

"Innocence once given, sir, cannot be restored," she replied. "Do you take me for a fool that I should allow you to have for naught that which is my greatest treasure?"

"It is not your virginity I seek at this moment, pretty puss, just a kiss," he mocked her.

"My first kiss," Bliss said pridefully, blushing at his bold words.

"A first kiss is sweet for its innocence, and honors the recipient," he told her bluntly, "but as kisses go, a maiden's first efforts are usually childish, and 'tis somewhat like kissing a mackerel with its lack of passion."

"Ohhhhhhh!" Both Bliss's look and tone were of pure outrage, and furiously she hit at Owen FitzHugh with closed fists.

It was exactly the opportunity he sought. Catching her wrists in his strong grasp he forced her arms to her sides while pressing her body with his against the dark stone wall of the alcove. There was no way in which she could escape him, and there at his leisure he took her first kiss, moving his mouth sensuously over hers until with a helpless little moan Bliss's lips parted beneath his.

"Now, puss," he murmured against her quivering mouth, "that's over and done with, and I will teach you how to *really* kiss. You had best learn to please me, Bliss, for know now that you'll never kiss another as long as I have breath in my body!"

Bliss felt wild exultation pouring through her. She had never ever suspected that passion could be so wonderfully exciting as it was proving to be. The moment he had first looked at her earlier today she had known that he was the man for her, and now, her mouth dry with longing, Bliss looked up at Owen FitzHugh, and said but two words. "Teach me!" But before he might comply, a warning voice interrupted them.

"I cannot allow you to compromise my young sister-in-law, Owen," said Edmund Wyndham.

Releasing Bliss, the Earl of Marwood turned to face his host. "I intend escorting Bliss home to ask her father's permission for her hand in marriage, Edmund."

The Earl of Langford nodded. "You will have company then in Nick Kingsley, who it seems has fallen under the spell of Mistress Blythe, and intends a similar mission."

"Ohh, how wonderful!" cried Bliss, clapping her hands together with joy. "It would have been so awful if Blythe and I did not find happiness together. I could not have left her alone, but now she will have a husband also! Ohh, come, my lord! Hurry! I would be the first to wish my twin happy!" Catching at his hand, she dragged him impatiently from their rendezvous back down the hall.

"Blythe will want to be the first to wish us happy as well!" she finished, while behind her Edmund chuckled.

"Does that mean what I think it means?" said Dorothy Wyndham coming up to stand beside her brother. "Is Marwood offering for her?"

"Aye," he answered her. "And Kingsley has declared himself for Blythe."

"God's foot!" swore Dorothy Wyndham. "I had hoped to have one of them for Tony."

"Neither would have suited Tony," replied her brother.

She nodded. "You are right, but yet with all of Blaze's sisters there must be one that would suit my son. I suppose we must settle for Delight."

"Delight is naught but a child, Doro!" the earl exclaimed.

"She says her womanhood is upon her, and can I doubt her word? Besides she already adores Tony, which is all to the good."

"Whatever Delight may say, she is not yet a woman. The child has no breasts, Doro, and is yet tiny. Were she a woman her bosom would be swelling and she would gain height. She is near, but not yet ready for marriage. Tony will have to seek elsewhere for a wife, I fear."

"Every eligible girl for miles is either wed, or betrothed, or too young," complained his sister. "There is not even an available widow! Tony's lack of interest in finding a wife to date is now hampering him. I do not know what we can do, Edmund. Perhaps he should go to court to seek a wife."

"The court is no place right now to find a respectable wife, but mayhap he will meet someone with a sister or daughter who needs a husband. Aye, Doro. Send him to court after Twelfth Night. His future could possibly be awaiting him there. God only knows there is nothing here for him."

Chapter 6

❦

*B*laze's birthday fete over, her sisters departed for home the following day looking greatly forward to their return a week before Christmas, when they would come with their entire family. Bliss and Blythe were glowing with happiness, and despite the cold weather rode proudly beside their intended husbands. Within the coach Delight huddled morosely. She had never felt more gloomy in her entire life. Blaze was radiantly happy in her marriage. The twins had both found love at first sight. Delight knew that their father would heartily approve of both Lord Kingsley and the Earl of Marwood. The spring would see those weddings celebrated at Ashby.

Delight sighed as a great wash of self-pity engulfed her. She would be fourteen next June, and she was practically a woman. She was just as ready to be wed as were her three older sisters. Why could no one else see it? Why could not Anthony Wyndham see it? His mother liked her, she knew, and Lady Dorothy wanted her son married. Why could not that good lady realize that Delight Morgan was the perfect choice for Anthony Wyndham?

The tears flowed unchecked down Delight's pretty face, and she was glad that Bliss and Blythe were riding outside the carriage. How they would mock her. Only her brother-in-law, Edmund, understood the true depth of her feelings about Anthony. He had taken her upon his knee last night when she had been feeling so despondent, and said to her that the man who wed with her one day would be most fortunate. Then he told her that Tony would be going to court to find a wife after Twelfth Night. When she had wept into his velvet-clad shoulder he had comforted her with sweetmeats and said Tony was not worthy of her. *But he was!*

She cried all the harder with the memory, realizing suddenly that she felt simply awful. Her head hurt. She felt nauseous, and her belly was cramping dreadfully. Miserable, she curled herself into a tight ball and attempted to sleep. She was secretly pleased when upon arriving home at Ashby her woeful state took immediate precedence over the twins' news. Her mother hurried her off to Old Ada, who upon undressing Delight discovered the reason for the girl's misery.

"Look, my lady! Look! Did I not say that Delight's womanhood was upon her? And here is her first flux! I am never wrong!" the old woman crowed, pleased. She took the young girl's bloodstained petticoats and handed them to a serving wench. "Take these to the laundress, Mab!"

Delight almost shouted with her joy at this turn of events. She felt suddenly better. Now they could not say she was too young for marriage! Now she had a chance with Anthony Wyndham, and come Christmastide she would make her move. She stood quietly while Old Ada bathed her, and her mother explained the proper ways a woman in her condition cared for herself. Fed warm mulled wine and tucked into bed with a flannel-wrapped hot brick at her feet, Delight drifted off into a pleasant dream.

On the eighteenth of December the entire Morgan family along with a few especially chosen servants descended upon RiversEdge.

"I hope we will not be crowding them out," fretted Lady Rosemary, who had no real idea of the size of the house which her eldest daughter now managed. "The whole family seems like a great deal of people to me, especially now that Bliss and Blythe are betrothed and their fiancés will be there. Lord Kingsley's widowed mother has been invited too. I do hope she will like Blythe."

"I am certain," Lord Robert soothed his wife, "that Blaze is in full control of the situation. She would not have asked us all had she not the room. As for old Lady Kingsley, I am certain that she will love Blythe as we all do."

Still Rosemary Morgan fretted until, finally gaining her first glimpse of RiversEdge, her pretty mouth fell open in amazement. " 'Tis a palace!" she gasped, for although she had never seen a palace, she was certain that one must be as gorgeous as was this house.

"Nay, just a great house," her husband replied with more aplomb than he was feeling. He had seen somewhat more than his wife in his lifetime, but although he would not let her know it, even he was surprised by the magnificent house that was now his daughter's home.

The carriages carrying Lord Morgan, his family, and his servants rolled onward down the hill road from the village and into the large courtyard of

RiversEdge. As the Morgans and their retainers stepped from their vehicles, they found themselves warmly greeted by both Blaze and Edmund, who had hurried from the house at the first sounds of their arrival and as quickly drew them inside, where all the many fireplaces were blazing merrily.

"We've only asked the immediate family, and those about to be," apologized Edmund. "I hope it will not be too dull a time for you, *belle mère*."

"Nay, my lord, I like family best on these occasions," said Rosemary Morgan, her quick eye counting over twenty people excluding servants within the Great Hall.

Blaze had waited until her sisters' arrival to decorate the house, and so the following morning while the men went out upon their first hunt for the Christmas boar, the women hurried off to seek and cut the greens. When the men returned that night unsuccessful in their quest, they found the women had not been at all unsuccessful during their day. RiversEdge was garlanded with evergreens, holly, boxwood, laurel, and bay. Each room was fragrant with sweet smelling pine, and Christmas candles, which were representative of the Star of Bethlehem, had been placed upon the mantels and sideboards and any other flat surface that would contain them.

Anthony Wyndham was unanimously appointed the Lord of Misrule over the festivities, and he immediately ordered a game of blindman's buff. Even Blaze was encouraged by her husband to join in, which she did with much relish, and was soon as tousled as the rest of her guests. Delight deliberately allowed herself to be caught by Anthony, and when asked what forfeit she would pay, boldly said, "A kiss!" Recognizing his victim by both her size and voice, Tony turned his head just slightly at the proper moment, and to her vast disappointment, Delight found her lips making contact with his cheek, which was not at all the way she had planned it. Before she might protest, however, she found herself blindfolded, and *It*.

On the twenty-first of December, which was the Feast of Saint Thomas, they entertained parties of children from each of the Langford estate's nine villages, who came a-wassailing into the Great Hall of RiversEdge.

> *Wassail, wassail, through the town,*
> *If you've got any apples, throw them down;*
> *If you've got no apples, money will do;*
> *The jug is white and the ale is brown,*
> *This is the best house in the town! . . .*

piped the enthusiastic young voices to their master and mistress and all their assembled guests. Each child was rewarded with a small silver penny, and Lord Robert and his wife marveled to themselves at their son-in-law's great generosity.

The twenty-third of December finally saw the gentlemen hunters successful, and a great boar with ugly curved tusks was brought home trussed securely between two poles. Little Gavin Morgan, who was almost six, rode excitedly ahead of the hunting party as they returned, triumphantly blowing upon his hunting horn. It had been his first grown-up hunt, and he could not sleep that night for his excitement.

The twenty-fourth of December saw the Yule log cut from the trunk of a huge fallen ash, hauled in from the forest through the Great Hall, and set into the huge main fireplace, which it more than filled. Everyone in the household from the lowliest scullion to the earl himself had pushed and pulled the great Yule log to its final resting place, for it was considered good luck to do so.

It was Blaze's duty as mistress of RiversEdge to light the Yule log. Custom dictated that each year's log must be first lit with a brand from the previous year's log, which had been kept safe beneath the bed of the lady of the house. As Edmund Wyndham had not formally celebrated this holiday the year before due to his first wife's death, it was now the brand from Catherine Wyndham's last Yule log that he gave to Blaze. Their eyes met as she thrust the burning brand into the dry kindling, and she somehow felt that in completing this simple act she was truly Edmund's wife, and the Countess of Langford. Catherine Wyndham, God assoil her good soul, was now only memory.

There had been much singing and laughter, and now that the huge log burned red-gold within the Great Hall's main fireplace, all were served ale, and a merry Christmas was toasted. From the minstrel's gallery now came music. Special Yule cakes were served along with hot Christmas frumenty, which was fine hulled wheat boiled in milk and sweetened with a sugar loaf. This was a very special treat for the servants, for sugar was a precious commodity.

Shortly before midnight they departed for Saint Michael's church, reaching it just on the hour as the bells in the church tower, and all over England, joyously tolled in the Christmas. The bells celebrated not only Christ's birth but also the firm Christian belief that that birth signaled the devil's destruction. Stepping from their carriages, the earl, his family, and his guests entered the church to celebrate the first Mass of Christmas.

The night was calm and black. The stars above surely as sharp and bright as the very night of the Nativity itself. From within Saint Michael's came the pure high voices of the church's choristers, their clear tones floating to the heavens as they sang.

> *Venite adoremus, Dominum!*
> *Venite adoremus, Dominum!*

and,

> *Gloria! Gloria in excelsis Deo!*

Within the church there was barely room to move, for everyone from the eldest soul to the littlest children in the villages and outlying farms of Michaelschurch and Wyeton had come to share the Christmas Mass with the earl and his beautiful countess. Blaze did not believe that she had ever been happier than she was at this moment, her hand tucked into her husband's hand, her beloved family about her. Only one thing would make her life perfect. A child. *Next year,* she prayed. *Let me stand in your house on Christmas next with my child, O Lord!*

Returning to the house, she made certain that all her guests were comfortable before taking her own rest. "I have sent Heartha to her own bed," she told Edmund. "You will have to be my tiring woman, my lord."

"Not an unpleasant task, my sweet," he told her, turning her about so he might unlace her. Tossing her jeweled bodice aside, he slid his hands into her chemise front, cupping her round breasts within his hands. Teasingly he rubbed his thumbs over her nipples, and grinned to himself, pleased when he felt the flesh pucker beneath his touch. The softness within his hands grew taut and firm as his kisses moved from her rounded shoulder to the junction between her shoulder and neck.

"Hmmmmmmmmm," came her murmur, and arching her back, she pressed her little buttocks into his groin, rotating her hips as she did so. Feeling his length harden against her, it was Blaze's turn to smile.

"Witch!" he groaned through gritted teeth as she increased her sensuous little movements.

Blaze laughed low, and moved out of her husband's grasp. Turning about to face him, she loosened her skirts and petticoats, allowing them to slip to the floor. Stepping away from the colorful pile of fabric, she pulled her chemise over her head, and but for velvet shoes and dark knit stockings, was nude.

"Come, sir, my nightrail," she teased him.

Edmund Wyndham's dark brown eyes burned with open desire as he stared at his beautiful wife. With quick deliberate motions he tore his own garments off until he stood completely naked, his aroused state no longer hidden from her. Catching at Blaze's hand, he drew her down upon the bed.

"My footwear!" she protested.

He slipped the shoes from her feet, and then drew each stocking with its saucy garter down her pretty legs. "I'll not wait," he said. "You've roused me beyond a mortal man's capacity to wait."

"I am ready for you, my passionate lord," she whispered back, pulling his head down so they might kiss.

With a groan of despair mixed with relief he returned her kiss, all the while plunging his sword within her burning sheath. As always, she was eager for him, and just as eager to please as to be pleasured.

Blaze felt him filling her with his great throbbing desire, and she gave in almost at once to the wonderful feeling of delight that he never failed to arouse in her. Was it wrong to so enjoy this heavenly conjunction of a man and a woman? She was yet too shy to ask her mother, and besides, she suspected that it was not something a girl might easily ask her mother. She would be glad when Bliss and Blythe joined her in nuptial pleasures so she might compare notes with them, but she hoped that they would enjoy this aspect of married life as much as she did.

"Ohhh!" she cried softly, reaching her first peak. "Ohhh! Ohhhh! Ohhhhhhh!" as wave upon wave overtook her. She thrust herself up gladly to meet his downward plunge. "Ohhhhhhhhhh, Edmund!" she sobbed as his hardness delved deeper and deeper into her responsive flesh. Was it never bad?

His excitement finally overcoming his control, the earl poured a libation of his love into his wife's golden cup before collapsing upon her heaving breasts. "Dear heaven, how I love you," he murmured hotly in her ear.

Surely a child must come from this, she thought sleepily when he had rolled off her and lay dozing by her side. Next Christmas! We will have a son by next Christmas, I am certain!

Christmas dinner was served late in the afternoon, and Lady Morgan was once again overwhelmed by the bounty of her daughter's kitchens. The variety of seafood so far from the sea itself was a luxury in which she happily indulged herself. The men feasted delightedly upon oysters, which were brought in oaken tubs filled with ice. Noisily they cracked the shells open, swallowing the cold creatures within whole, all the while making suggestive remarks to the ladies about the benefits of such fare.

Great platters of thin, sliced pink salmon dressed with watercress were brought, as well as platters of boiled carp, and prawns in white wine, lobster, pike, lampreys stewed in red wine with chervil, sole in a sauce of cream and Marsala wine. There was trout from their own streams broiled and served with carved lemons. Blaze's sisters were fascinated by the fruits, for they had never seen any before, and they commented on the oddity of such a pretty fruit tasting so sour.

A plum porridge was also amongst the first course. Made of a beef broth and thickened with bread crumbs, it was filled with the dried plums from which it took its name, as well as chunks of sugar loaf, currants, raisins, rare spices such as cinnamon, ginger, and nutmeg, and sweet wines. This traditional Christmas fare was greeted with delight by all the guests.

The next course offered fresh roe deer brought in by the hunters only two days before, as well as venison, a side of beef that had been packed in a blanket of rock salt and roasted, several finely cured hams, and a half-dozen legs of baby lamb roasted with garlic and rosemary. There was swan, and a pheasant, and a peacock that had been completely reconstructed with its feathers to sit upon a platter of shining gold. There were capons in lemon-ginger sauce, pies of pigeon, lark, and rabbit, and a dozen succulent geese as well as ducks that had been turned upon their spits to a crisp golden brown and set three upon a platter with a sauce of dried plums and cherries. There were bowls of lettuce cooked in white wine, and small leeks with peas, as well as loaves of fine white bread and crocks of sweet butter for all.

The highlight of the Christmas feast was the bringing in of the boar's head. By tradition the honor of carrying the beast was given to the youngest son of the house, but as there were currently no Langford heirs, Edmund had delegated this task to his brother-in-law, Gavin Morgan. Young Gavin, being but three months short of six years of age, was yet too small to bear the heavy weight of the boar's head, which had been set upon a gold platter, an apple in its mouth, garlanded and crowned with rosemary and laurel leaves. The huge salver had instead been placed upon a specially gilded and garlanded cart, which the little lad proudly pulled into the hall as all the guests rose from their places singing the traditional carol that greeted the entrance of the boar's head:

Caput apri defero,
Reddens laudes domino.
The boar's head in hand bring I,
Bedecked with bays and rosemary;
I pray you all sing merrily,
Quot estis in convivio.

"This is the best Christmas that I can ever remember," Blaze said softly to her husband.

"It is the happiest Christmas I have ever had because you are now my wife," he answered her, his dark eyes brimming with his love.

The servants cleared away the plates and platters from the main part of the meal, and the last course of sweets was brought into the hall. There was sweet Malmsey wine served along with dainty wafer-thin sugar biscuits. There were candied rosebuds, violets, and celerylike angelica, as well as tarts made from dried apples, cherries, and plums and served with thick clotted cream; rich cakes that had been soaked in honey-sweetened wines; and silken custards offered with a conserve of stewed cherries. The younger members of the family particularly enjoyed the marzipan, which had been molded into various shapes—flowers, fruits, beasts, and stars— and dusted with colored sugars.

A troupe of mummers arrived. Made up of men from the earl's two nearest villages of Michaelschurch and Wyeton, they apologized profusely to their master, for it was custom that they come on Christmas Eve. To their embarrassment and shame, they had enjoyed too much their own success and the potent cider offered them the evening before in their own villages. Before they had realized it, it was midnight and time for the Mass.

Before Edmund Wyndham might reassure the mummers, however, his wife spoke up. "Good sirs, you need feel no regrets. Your coming into our hall this blessed Christmas Day both brightens and brings honor to our feast. Perform your play, I pray you, and God bless you for it!"

Immediately the blackened faces of the mummers were wreathed in smiles. "God bless yer ladyship, and bring her a fine son by Christmas next!" they cried with one voice. Their faces were blackened, for it was believed their secret identity brought both their performance and their hosts good luck. Even those who recognized the players pretended that they did not.

Then the mummers performed their traditional Christmas play, which involved Saint George, England's patron saint, and a Turkish knight and a dragon, both of whom Saint George was called upon to vanquish. The mummers did not wear elaborate costumes, and so their acting skills were called most heavily upon to make their performance real. This particular troupe of village men was quite skilled and very believable. When Saint George, having vanquished first the dragon, was apparently mortally wounded by the wicked Turk, the fourth major character in the play, the quack doctor, made his way forward to attempt a cure upon the fallen hero. With the audience shouting its encouragement now, the quack tried first this remedy, and then that, until at last to the cheers of all he found a magic elixir which instantly restored the brave saint.

The Turk gnashed his teeth and stamped his feet as the miracle became apparent. Fiercely he menaced the loudly cheering children, who squealed, half-fearful, half-delighted, but his reign of terror was quickly over, for the newly cured hero dashed forward and overcame the Turkish knight, to the rousing cheers of the audience. All agreed that it was the best mummers performance that they had ever seen. The successful troupe was loudly praised and profusely thanked before being rewarded with a bag of silver and sent off to the kitchens for cakes and ale.

The day after Christmas they celebrated the Mass of Saint Stephen, the first Christian martyr. Afterward, as it was also Boxing Day, the special alms box in the parish church was opened by Father Martin, and the monies collected within distributed to the poor of the area. Then one of the earl's finest horses was ceremoniously "bled" to ensure the good health of all the estate's horses in the coming year.

The festivities continued throughout the whole Twelve Days of Christmas at RiversEdge. New Year's Eve saw bonfires spring up on all the surrounding hills as the bells tolled in the new year of Our Lord, 1522. On New Year's Morning the family exchanged gifts with one another. Edmund delighted Blaze with an elegant cape of rich brown velvet that was lined in rabbit's fur. The clasp that held the cape together was fashioned of gold with a large golden topaz for a button. Blaze surprised her husband with a magnificent gray stallion that had been bred by one of his neighbors and that she knew he coveted for breeding purposes.

"How on earth . . . ?" he began, and she laughed.

"Doro helped me arrange it," she replied in answer to his unspoken question.

The other gifts that they had arranged for together for their combined families were equally lavish, but it was Blythe Morgan's New Year's gift to her future mother-in-law that won the day. Lady Mary Kingsley was a devout and pious lady who, since her husband's death many years before, had devoted herself to her God. With the church's permission she had founded a small religious order, the Community of Saint Frideswide, named after the eighth-century Anglo-Saxon saint who was the patron of the city of Oxford. As Mother Superior of her small order she oversaw close to four dozen nuns whose chief duty was to minister to the poor and sick. Having learned of Lady Mary's piety, Blythe had spent the few weeks since her betrothal sewing upon an exquisite altar cloth which she presented to Nicholas's mother on New Year's Day.

"Dear child!" Lady Mary's sweet and gentle face beamed with pleasure from within its wimple. "You could not have given me a more wonderful gift! Although my son has taken overlong in finding himself a wife, God has rewarded my prayers by sending you to him. Bless you, dear Blythe!"

"Did I not tell you?" whispered Lord Robert to his wife. "Who could not love Blythe?"

Rosemary Morgan nodded in agreement with her husband's words, but then said, "It is equally well that Lord FitzHugh does not have a close relation to approve or disapprove of Bliss. Love has not lessened the sting of her tongue. I hope she will not drive her betrothed away before the marriage ceremony."

Robert Morgan chuckled. His wife was perfectly right in her observations, but watching his daughter with the Earl of Marwood had convinced him that only death would drive Owen FitzHugh from the beautiful girl's side. The young man was completely besotted by her, and Bliss was more than well aware of his hapless state. Lord Morgan was well satisfied with this particular match. Bliss would do very well at court once she learned its unspoken rules. She would be totally in her element, as would be her twin sister, Blythe, living the life of a quiet country wife.

He looked to Blaze. Never had he seen her so radiantly content. It was obvious that she had fallen in love with her husband, and he was relieved to note it. He had worried himself that Edmund Wyndham's deep involvement with his first wife might make Blaze naught but a means to an heir. The match had been too good to refuse, particularly in his woeful financial state, but his conscience had pricked him sorely even as he had sent his daughter off to a husband she had never even met. Everything was working out exactly as he had hoped it would. Blaze was happy, and his next two daughters would be wed in the spring after Eastertide to men of good families. At this moment in time Robert Morgan felt expansively content, and taking his wife's hand in his, he smiled at her.

The Twelve Days of Christmas ended with Twelfth Night on the fifth day of January. A final feast was held that evening with all declaring afterward that they would not be able to eat again until Candlemas. This last night of the Christmas season seemed to bring out particularly riotous behavior amongst all. Anthony Wyndham, in his last hours as the Lord of Misrule, called for a game of Hot Cockles. Nicholas Kingsley was chosen to be *It* first. Carefully Blythe tied the blindfold about his eyes and when asked, Lord Kingsley swore that he could see nothing. He was spun about, and then holding out his hands, palms upward, he cried, "Hot cockles! Hot!" There was much giggling and scuffling to his ears, and then his hands were slapped hard.

"Guess! Guess!" cried the other players as they danced about him.

"Owen, 'tis you!" said Lord Kingsley.

"Damn! How could you tell?" grumbled Owen FitzHugh as he removed his friend's blindfold.

"Your signet ring, man. I could feel it on your right hand when you slapped me," was the reply.

Owen FitzHugh was blindfolded, spun about, and then called out in his turn, "Hot cockles! Hot!" Almost immediately he was slapped upon his upturned palms. "Bliss!" he chortled, for the hands had been dainty and feminine to his touch.

"Nay, my lord, 'twas not I." Bliss laughed. "Once I have slapped you, you will never doubt who it is if I slap again!"

"Then Blaze!"

"Nay, my lord," came her voice. "Not I!"

"Three wrong guesses, and you must pay a forfeit," came Tony's voice.

The hands had been definitely female. He considered who had been playing the game. All the sisters were. No help there. He did not think it would be Blythe, for that would be too easy. "Delight!" he said. It had to be Delight.

There came a chorus of "nays," and the blindfold was removed.

"Well?" he demanded. "Who was it then?"

" 'Twas us, my lord Owen," chorused Larke and Linnette, giggling mischievously at him. "We each slapped a hand."

"Forfeit! Forfeit! He must pay a forfeit!" cried the other players.

Anthony Wyndham nodded his agreement, and then his face grew sober as he appeared to consider the matter. Slowly a devilish grin replaced his serious demeanor and he said, "His forfeit is that I shall kiss Mistress Bliss!"

"Nay!" shouted the Earl of Marwood furiously, his handsome face red with its outrage. " 'Twas not fair to be tagged by two!"

"Pay the forfeit! Pay the forfeit!" the other players cried.

"Have I no say in this?" demanded Bliss, who was looking particularly beautiful this evening in an apple-green gown.

"And what say you, Mistress Bliss?" demanded the Lord of Misrule.

"I say I am willing to pay my lord's forfeit, for he tells me often enough that his kisses are the finest in the world. How am I to know whether he speaks true if I have naught with which to compare them?" Her sapphire-blue eyes were twinkling with mischief.

Before Owen FitzHugh might protest further, Anthony Wyndham caught the obviously willing Bliss Morgan to him and kissed her most thoroughly. When he released her she was blushing rosily. "Now," laughed Tony, "you have the means of comparison, mistress, but I am too much the gentleman to ask you which one of us pleases you best!"

"Why, my lord Owen, of course," replied Bliss promptly. "You did not make my toes curl as he does, sir!"

With a pleased grin, the Earl of Marwood put a proprietary arm about his betrothed wife's waist. "If you are a good fellow, Tony, I shall one day tell you the secret of making a lass's toes curl," he teased his friend smugly.

The game continued with much merriment, to be followed by dancing, and then a game of Hunt the Slipper. The feasting had begun in early afternoon, and now as the sunset hour approached, the Earl and Countess of Langford escorted their guests outdoors and into the orchards, where the fruit-tree wassailing was about to take place. A huge bowl of apple-cider wassail was brought forth, and amid the bright bonfires that had been lit by the earl's farmers, a toast was drunk to the trees, and then that which remained within the great bowl was sprinkled upon the fruit trees to ensure their fertility in the coming growing season.

> *Here's to thee, old apple tree!*
> *Whence thou mayst bud,*
> *Whence thou mayst blow,*
> *And whence thou mayst bear apples enow!*
> *Hats full!*
> *Caps full!*
> *And my pocket full too!*
> *Hurrah! Hurrah! Hurrah!*

sang the assembled throng.

The sun had now set, and the western sky was as vibrant as only a winter sky can be. Across the horizon a narrow bank of deep-purple clouds lay, their tops lit red-orange, their bottoms lit gold. The evening star was crystal blue in the evening sky as they returned to the house to finish their celebration.

A simple supper was now served, and there was more dancing as the musicians in the minstrel's gallery plied their instruments. The younger guests played hide-and-seek and blindman's buff, but the young lovers were strangely absent. Delight, to her great pleasure, managed to get Anthony to dance with her twice, but to her equally deep disappointment he did not seem to take her seriously, and she simply didn't know what to do. How could she tell him of her womanly status without seeming bold?— and she was certain that he would not like a bold woman. Could he not see the change? Even Bliss admitted that Delight was finally gaining a bosom. Finally Old Ada came, and the little children were taken to their beds. Shortly afterward the other guests began drifting to their own bed-chambers, for they would be leaving RiversEdge on the morrow for their own homes.

In their hidden alcove, Bliss Morgan pouted her well-kissed lips at her betrothed husband. "I do not see why you must return to court now, Owen," she complained at him prettily.

"Anthony will need a proper introduction, Bliss, if he is to be success-ful at court. To be successful at court one must find favor with the king as I have, but to find favor with the king requires gaining his attention, which only someone who has already found favor with the king can help to do." He laughed. "It is really not as complicated as it sounds."

"I find your explanation long-winded, but not incomprehensible," Bliss replied tartly. "Why must you go now? Cannot Anthony wait? He has done well enough all these years without going to court."

"Bliss, be patient. Once Lent begins all the festivities normally associ-ated with the court come to a halt until after Easter is celebrated. Would you have Tony lose the next several months while I dance attendance upon you? We will be wed shortly after Easter in April. Is that not soon enough for us to be together, my love? Of course if you would wed with me now without all the fuss of a large celebration, we might go to court together."

Bliss stamped her little foot. "Nay, sir! You will not do me out of my wedding as Edmund did Blaze!"

"Your sister's lack of a large wedding does not seem to have spoilt her happiness in any way," noted Owen FitzHugh dryly.

"Oh, go to your precious court!" snapped Bliss. "But sow your wild oats well and quickly, my lord, for once you are wed to me I shall scratch the eyes of any female who dares to set cow eyes upon you!"

Owen FitzHugh laughed. "Why, bless me, sweetheart, you are jealous."

"Go to the devil!" she hissed at him.

"Only if you'll promise to come with me." He laughed, kissing the tip of her adorable nose.

Bliss stuck out her tongue at him, and then she laughed too. "We are surely two of a kind, my lord," she admitted with surprising candor.

He nodded. "I think you are correct, my beautiful Bliss. We will do very well together. Of that I am quite certain. Now, my quick-tempered betrothed wife, seek your bed, for I am not of a mind to play kiss and cuddle with you this night."

Bliss's blue eyes widened in genuine surprise. "What, sir, does our arguing stir your blood to passion then?"

Owen FitzHugh pulled the girl hard against him, and looked down into her face. "You have much to learn, Bliss, and I will enjoy teaching you as much as I suspect you will enjoy learning from me. Aye, sweetheart! Arguing with you does rouse my passions, and that has never happened to me before with any woman. Right now I want you very much, but I will deny myself the pleasures of passion with you until you are formally wed with me."

"A betrothal ceremony such as we have had is almost as binding, my lord," she whispered up at him, and her mouth was tempting beyond all.

"Nay, my fiery Bliss, you will not lure me with your adorable wiles. In our bedchamber, sweetheart, I will be the master!"

"Only until I learn the ways of love!" she replied fiercely at him. "Then, my lord, we will be equals, or we will not be at all!"

"Do not toy with me, Bliss." He smoldered dangerously at her as she pressed her breasts against his chest to give emphasis to her words.

With a quick movement Bliss removed herself from his embrace. "Good night, my lord," she said sweetly. "Sleep well!" Then she was gone from the alcove, and he was left standing there for a surprised minute, his manhood angry and hard.

With a smothered curse he stepped from their hidden place to go after her. He would catch her, and he would kiss her into mewling submission. What nonsense did she spout about equality in the bedchamber? A man was master in his own house. Certainly she knew that. Looking about, he discovered that Bliss was nowhere in sight. A grin suddenly creased his handsome face. The little witch! She spoke her nonsense but to arouse his passions even more. God's foot! She played with him like a fisherman with a trout. She did it, of course, to keep his interest hot, clever witch! He suspected, however, that even after their marriage Bliss would not be a dull woman to live with. Rubbing his aching member ruefully, he hurried off to find his lonely bed, for he and Tony had the beginnings of a long journey ahead of them tomorrow.

When the morning came Blaze seemed to be everywhere overseeing to her guests' various departures. Lady Mary Kingsley protested the comfort of one of the earl's coaches that was to take her back to St. Frideswide's.

" 'Tis not necessary, my child. My convent is but five miles on the other side of the river. The day is pleasant, and not too cold. I should enjoy the walk."

"Were it May, Reverend Mother, I should not disagree with you, but 'tis January. Though the day be fair, I sense a storm coming. Take the coach to please me."

Lady Mary did not argue further, and was shortly gone. The coach from Riverside arrived to take the lesser Wyndhams back home. Lord Richard had not been well over the holiday, and had sadly kept mostly to his room. Now his manservant aided the crippled gentleman to his coach as Lady Dorothy fretted and fussed.

"Is it wise for Tony to leave them now?" Blaze asked her husband.

"He does his father no good in staying. Richard would have him wed. Tony pleases his father best by going off to court with Owen. If my sister's husband is meant to die now, he will die whether his son be here or not," answered Edmund fatalistically.

Delight Morgan watched sadly as Anthony Wyndham rode off with Owen FitzHugh. They would escort the lesser Wyndhams home, and then go on to court from there. The handsome Earl of Marwood kissed Bliss quite thoroughly, to her deep satisfaction, as he bid her goodbye, but there was no especial farewell for little Delight, who bravely held back her tears of disappointment. She had tried so hard to attract Anthony's attentions, but he didn't even know she was alive.

Lord Kingsley intended to return to Ashby with the Morgans for a visit. Other than his mother he was alone in the world, and his small estate was well run even without him. Blythe was radiant with her happiness, for she had truly fallen in love with the kind and homely young man who was to be her husband. He had become her whole world even as she had become his, for Nicholas Kingsley could still not believe his good fortune in having this exquisite young beauty for a betrothed wife.

Blaze was not unhappy to see the several coaches belonging to her husband making their way from the house and down the river road to the ferry crossing. She had enjoyed her family's visit, but now she was eager to be alone with Edmund once more. It seemed that she had not had him really to herself for close to a month. She looked forward to the long winter months of isolation, and snuggled against him as she happily waved her family off.

As if he sensed her mood, he said, "Are you as glad as I am to be alone once more, my sweet?"

She giggled. "Aye! I am! How awful that must sound, but as much as I love them, I am happy to see them go."

"Shall we ride today? 'Tis warm for January, and we'll not see many fine days like this until spring."

"Aye, my love, let us ride," she agreed with him.

Within the hour they had changed into the proper clothing, and rode out across the winter landscape. There was a springlike feel to the day, but no breeze. Only the sheerest of gauzelike clouds broke the bright blue of the sky, and the sun was warm upon their backs. The trees stood leafless and quiet, but looking closely, one could see carefully protected fat buds upon the branches that silently foretold of the rich spring to come. Two gray-brown rabbits nibbled on a tiny patch of greenery that had been revived by the warmth of the day, and in a field on the forest's edge a small flock of red deer browsed. Edmund and Blaze did not speak for long periods of time, the calm beauty of the morning absorbing them completely. High in a tree a squirrel chattered a warning, and gazing skyward, Blaze could see a red kite circling as it sought for its breakfast.

She had grown to love this land in the few months since she had come to RiversEdge. It was a beautiful land, and she felt a strange pride in knowing that the son she bore one day would inherit Edmund's earldom and all the traditions that went with being a Wyndham lord. That she had been chosen to be Edmund's wife still amazed her, and she smiled, thinking that a year ago she had not even known his name. She had been nothing more than the eldest daughter of an impoverished baronet with no dowry and no hope for a future. What a difference twelve months could make!

"Why do you smile?" he asked her.

"I was thinking on how fortunate I am," she replied honestly. "I was thinking of January but a year ago when my future was so uncertain. Now my future is no longer unsure, for I am your wife, and I shall mother our children, and we shall live to grow old together!"

"Ah, my sweet," he answered her, "you are yet too young to know that nothing is ever certain. Times change. People change."

"No," Blaze said in her innocence. "We will never change."

"We will grow old. Age is change," he told her.

"But our love will not change, Edmund! If our love for one another does not change, then no matter the years that pass, we shall remain as always. We shall not change."

He found her logic interesting. "May God see it so, my sweet," he said quietly, and he signaled her to turn her horse for home.

The remainder of January was cold but pleasant. In February, however, winter returned to remind them that it had not yet finished with the land. The snows came, and soon great drifts covered the estate. It grew so cold that the river froze solid, forcing old Rumford, the ferryman, and his sons to sit idle in their cottage. To Blaze's delight they rode one frigid sunny day for several miles upon the river itself. Blaze had never imagined such a thing possible, and Edmund found himself both amused and refreshed by her enthusiasm. He thought once again as he had so many times since she had come to RiversEdge that she made him feel like a lad of twenty again. When in her excitement she rode directly up the center of the river away from him, he felt great fear, for he realized he could not have borne the pain of her loss.

On the last day of February Richard Wyndham died quietly in his sleep. Lady Dorothy, though prepared for her husband's demise, nonetheless mourned him deeply, but in the letter she sent to her son at court, she cautioned him not to spoil his chances with the king by returning to be with her. She did not, she stated bluntly, need him hovering about her as if she were some fragile flower. Knowing his mother wanted her time to grieve alone so she might come to terms with her loss, Tony sent his mother's servant back home with the message that he would honor her request.

With March came rain, and wind, and mud. There was no one who did not look forward to Easter, and the end of fasting. Blaze was beginning to hate the smell of cooking fish, and only the thought of her sisters' upcoming nuptials could cheer her.

Bliss and Blythe had decided to marry on the same day, thus saving their father the expense of two separate weddings. As Father John could find nothing in canonical law to forbid the marriage sacrament being performed for two siblings at the same time, he had agreed to it. Edmund had suggested to Blaze that the twins be wed at RiversEdge, but she disagreed with him.

"You are kind, my lord, to offer," she said, "but you must understand that my father swallowed his pride for the sake of his children when he allowed you to have me without a suitable dowry; and again when he allowed you to settle dowries upon my sisters as part of your settlement upon me. The people of Ashby were robbed of our wedding. My father would not take their pleasure from them a second time. Even my dear and ambitious Bliss would agree with me on this, Edmund."

She was right, he realized, and he marveled that one so young and lacking in worldly experience could be so wise.

The rains continued into April, leaving the roads mired in thick mud, and although the countryside grew lush with new green, and flowers sprang up upon the hillsides, Blaze despaired. Her sisters' wedding day was fixed for the last day in April. Would the rains never cease? Though it was but cloudy the day that they left RiversEdge for Ashby, the Wye was swollen with an excess of both melting snows from its northern tip and the spring rains. It took both Rumford and his eldest son to keep the small ferry from being caught up in the whirling waters and swept away.

Pale of visage, Blaze clung nervously to her husband as the boat bobbed across the river. Her color did not return quickly as they rode, and he began to fear for her, but she laughed weakly.

"The bouncing but distressed my belly, sir. Sadly the jogging of my horse helps not, but I will be all right when we get to Ashby," she told him.

Ashby! Blaze looked down upon her ancestral home for the first time in seven months, and tears filled her eyes. It had never looked so beautiful to her eyes, and as much as she loved RiversEdge, there would always be a place in her heart for Ashby. To her delight the sun was beginning to peep out from behind the clouds for the first time in over a week. It was a good omen for the impending marriages that would be celebrated on the morrow. It would be so good to see her family again.

"Your color has returned," the earl noted to his wife.

"It is the excitement of being here," she answered him. "I am so glad for Bliss and Blythe. I want them to be as happy as we are, my darling! Had it not been for you, neither would have met her husband. You are the most wonderful man in the world, Edmund Wyndham!"

"Madam, you will turn my head for certain." He chuckled as they rode up before the house.

The Morgan family poured from their home to welcome Blaze and her husband. Quickly their escort was sent off to be settled, and the earl and his countess brought inside for refreshments. Though Blaze refused the food offered her, she gratefully drank a small goblet of sweet red wine.

Rosemary Morgan with a sharp maternal eye noted this, and drew her eldest daughter aside. "Are you breeding?" she demanded without any preamble. "When was your last flux? Do you have any strange cravings? Has your belly been distressed at all these last weeks?"

"At the end of February, Mama." Blaze felt like a small girl again in her mother's presence, which annoyed her somewhat.

"Then you're breeding," said Lady Rosemary matter-of-factly. "What of the rest?"

"My belly has been distressed more than is usual for me," admitted Blaze, "and I found that I could not eat the fish as Lent drew to a close. I have no craving that would be considered odd, however."

"It is too early for that, but you *are* breeding," repeated the older woman. She smiled at her daughter. "In these matters I am expert. One day you will be too. Have you told your husband yet?"

Blaze shook her head. "I was not certain, and had I even suggested it, Edmund would not have let me come. He would have remembered poor Lady Catherine and all her sickness. I am not like his first wife in any way, Mama. I am strong, and I will bear my lord strong sons. I would not have missed the twins' wedding for anything in the world!"

Lady Rosemary frowned. "Blaze," she said, "you are a Wyndham, and your first duty is to the Wyndhams, not to the Morgans. We are now your second loyalty, but your first must always be to the family whose name you carry, and whose sons you will bear. If you have endangered your child by your willful actions, you will never forgive yourself, but," she finished, seeing her daughter's distressed and contrite look, "I do not believe you have, for you are very much like me in form. You will carry your babes to term."

"When, Mama, do you think my child is due?"

"Depending upon when Edmund's seed took root within your womb, sometime just before the year's end, I should suspect. There were times when I knew exactly when your father and I had created a child, but not with the first. That is an instinct that comes with experience."

"A *child*," Blaze whispered softly, and then quick tears filled her lovely violet-blue eyes. "Oh, Mama! I feel so blest!"

Rosemary Morgan put her arms about her eldest daughter. "You are, Blaze, for to be chosen to bear life is the greatest gift of all. Remember that in the future when you think to allow your own personal desires to overrule your common sense. Now, let us rejoin the others, lest the gentlemen miss us and think something amiss," she said with a smile. "Nothing must spoil your sisters' wedding!"

Chapter 7

⟡

*B*liss and Blythe Morgan were married on the last day of April in the year 1522. After weeks of rain the day dawned fair and remained that way. Father John conducted the marriage ceremony in Ashby's small church, St. Hilda's. The wedding party walked the short distance down the tree-lined lane from the house. The Ashby folk standing along the lane were treated to a fine view of the two brides, and cheered them mightily as, skirts held up to keep them from the mud, they tripped by.

The twins were gowned identically in dresses of heavy cream-colored satin brocade whose bodices were sewn with tiny pearls and gold thread, as were the sleeves and underskirts. Their lovely blond hair was unbound, attesting to their maiden state, and upon each head was a garland of white roses whose centers were a pinkish-gold. Each carried a nosegay of white violets tied with gold ribbons. There was only one difference between the two. Bliss, about her slender neck, wore a rope of perfectly matched pearls from which hung a gold pendant in the shape of a heart studded with pearls and tiny diamonds. Blythe had a strand of small pearls and garnets. Their necklets were gifts from their grooms.

The ceremony uniting the two couples was held in the open upon the church steps so that all might see, for St. Hilda's was not a large building. Then the bridal party entered into the church for a Mass, to emerge an hour later to the cheering throng. Before returning back down the lane to the house, Lord Morgan ceremoniously invited all to join with them in the wedding feast. Tables had been placed upon the lawn, with a high board for the gentry being set upon a dais beneath a red silk awning.

There was food aplenty, and as the day grew warmer, Lord Morgan's goodly supply of ale was sorely drained. Musicians with their drums, tabors, and pipes played accompaniment to the lively dances being performed upon the green grass. Two bridecakes were served, and the village maidens nibbled but a taste, secreting the rest in their pockets to dream upon this night. It was said that the man a girl dreamed of upon a bit of bridal cake would be her true love.

The evening came and torches were lit, for the music and dancing showed no signs of abating. Lord Morgan's ale supply was as yet holding out, and few were of a mind to go home, for the night was clear with a bright, almost full moon, and the air still pleasant. Finally, with the sunset at least three hours past, it was deemed time to put the brides and their grooms to bed. Bridal chambers had been arranged in the room that had been shared by the twins and their sisters, and in the house's only guest chamber. Since the rooms were next to one another there was not too great a difficulty in preparing both girls at the same time, although there was much scurrying back and forth between the two bedchambers.

Bliss flushed with excitement. She looked eagerly forward to her deflowering, although deep within her there lurked the tiniest fear. Still, her mother had given them both a dry lecture on a wife's duties several weeks before, so they knew what was expected of them. It seemed that Vanora's tales were fairly accurate, but it was not until Blaze spoke with the twins that Bliss felt entirely at ease.

"Lovemaking is wonderful!" she had enthused to them the evening before.

"Tell, tell!" demanded the twins. They were alone but for Blaze, having firmly ejected their other sisters from the discussion.

"It is really impossible to describe," Blaze said. "You must be involved to really understand."

"There must be something that you can tell us," said Bliss irritably. "The first time! What was it like the first time?"

Blaze laughed softly. "Edmund and I did not celebrate our wedding night for several weeks after our wedding," she confessed.

"Ohhh!" Blythe's eyes were round with surprise.

Bliss, as ever, was more direct. "How could you bear to wait?" she demanded. "I know nothing of what lovemaking is, and yet I am so hot to be with Owen that I cannot sleep at night, and worse, I ache with a longing that I don't even understand."

"You know Owen, and Blythe knows her Nicholas. Do you forget that I had never even laid eyes upon Edmund until the day I became his wife? How could I desire a man whose face I would not even recognize? When I voiced my fears to him, he understood, and took the time to woo me before consummating our marriage. I think I fell in love with him because of his kindness and patience.

"You ask me about the first time, Bliss. The feelings that Edmund generated in me were wonderful. I do not have the words to explain, but you will understand tomorrow night when you become one with your husbands. One thing, though. Has Mother bothered to tell you that your first encounter with passion may give you a momentary bite of pain?"

"Nay," said Bliss, speaking for them both.

"It comes with the piercing of the maidenhead by your husband. For me 'twas but a momentary prick, and afterward there is never again any pain. I thought you should know."

That thought was the only thing that disturbed Bliss's great anticipation of her wedding night. Now, sitting up in bed, gowned in an innocent-looking white silk nightrail, her lace-trimmed nightcap with its silk ribbons tied beneath her chin, she awaited Owen FitzHugh. About her the women giggled and chattered as they dashed back and forth between her and Blythe, who she assumed was in a similar condition now in the next room.

Then she heard the raucous shouts and loud laughter of the men, and Bliss's heartbeat quickened. The bedchamber door was flung open, and Owen FitzHugh, in a white silk nightshirt, was pushed into the room. With astounding agility the Earl of Marwood whirled about, and slamming the door on his escort, shot the bolt home. For a moment there was a mighty pounding upon the door that Bliss thought surely would shatter the portal, but it held.

"Owen," she heard a voice call. "We've not yet drunk the caudle cup."

"Drink it without me," Owen FitzHugh called back. "I've a more pleasant task ahead of me, and I'll waste no more time getting to it!"

There was much laughter from the other side of the door, and then a chorus of "Good night then, my lord and my lady," followed by a semiquiet as the revelers moved next door with the other bridegroom to see him safely bedded. Bliss clutched the bedcovers to her breasts in momentary panic.

Owen FitzHugh turned about and grinned at his wife. "Well now, puss, and here we are at last." He walked over to the bed, and in one swift motion pulled his nightshirt off, flinging it aside.

Bliss gasped with shock, but she was far too curious to even avert her eyes. She had never imagined a man's body could look so . . . so . . . so interesting. Her sapphire-blue eyes traveled across the width of his shoulders and down his chest which was furred with dark, curly hair. Dropping her glance lower, Bliss's gaze widened, and she whispered, "Ohhhhh!"

The Earl of Marwood chuckled, knowing full well the cause of her exclamation. "Come, puss," he said, drawing her up and from the bed. "You've seen my goods, now let me see yours." With gentle hands he untied her dainty nightcap and dropped it to the floor.

She was not afraid, Bliss thought, as, undoing the ribbons upon her nightrail, she shrugged it off. Nay, she was not afraid of him, for she loved him. Raising her eyes to meet his, she said, "Well, my lord, and do I meet with your approval as well as you meet with mine?"

Owen stared, both bedazzled and astounded. Bliss was not only fair of face, she had the loveliest form he had ever beheld upon any woman. Her skin was like cream. Her limbs rounded and shapely. Her breasts high and pointed. She turned for him slowly, and he groaned softly as he felt his desire stirring wildly.

"Come, sir, have you lost your tongue as well as your heart?" Bliss mocked him gently.

"God's blood, puss! Your beauty defies description, but lest you think me a poor lover, Bliss, kiss me before I expire of my longing for you!" Drawing her into his embrace, his lips met hers in a firey union.

As she tumbled headlong and heedlessly into passion, Bliss had one last thought. She hoped that Blythe was as happy at this very moment as she was. Her heart was so full that she wanted to share her joy with the whole world if she but could.

Shy Blythe. Gentle Blythe. He must not frighten her, thought Nicholas Kingsley as the revelers finally made their way from the guest bedchamber, having spent some minutes making ribald jests and drinking down a caudle cup to wish the couple good fortune and many children. Closing the door behind the guests, he locked it firmly, and joined his beautiful bride in their nuptial bed.

"You must not be afraid of me, Blythe," he began.

"I am not," she said calmly.

"Your mother has explained everything to you?"

She nodded. "And Blaze also, Nicholas."

"I will go slowly with you, my love, I promise," he said earnestly.

"If it pleases you," she answered.

"But I would please you!" he told her.

"Soon, I hope, Nicholas!" was the reply.

Startled, he could only gape at her.

Blythe took her husband's hand in hers and spoke softly. "My lord, hear me, I pray you. Blaze tells me that lovemaking is wonderful. Bliss admits to being hot to couple with Owen. Our mother has produced nine children, and despite the fact she is near forty, still smiles secret smiles at our father when she thinks no one is looking. Such things do not betoken an act to be feared, but rather to be enjoyed. I know my defloration will hurt, but afterward Blaze says it is wonderful beyond description. If we do not begin, however, I shall never know, will I? Do not think me bold, my lord, but please kiss me!"

Nicholas sighed with relief, and drawing his new wife into his arms, kissed her most thoroughly and to her complete satisfaction before going on to other and more delectable pleasures that left her equally enraptured and most delighted with him.

Blaze, however, did not stay the night at Ashby, and would not learn until afterward of her sisters' contentment with the married life. There was simply no room in the Morgans' house now for additional overnight guests, and so the Earl and Countess of Langford with their armed escort of men made their way home to RiversEdge beneath the light of the moon. The night was calm, and the moon silvered the landscape as they rode.

"You look tired, my love," the earl worried solicitously. "I must aid your father in building another wing upon Ashby. There is not enough room for us all as it is, and only two of your sisters are wed. What will happen when they are all wed, and there are grandchildren too?"

"Aye, for there will be a first grandchild before year's end, my lord," said Blaze softly.

"*What?!*" The earl looked astounded. "What is it you tell me?"

"That I am with child, my lord. I needed only for my mother to confirm my suspicions, for as I have never had a child before, I was not certain."

"My God, Blaze! You should not be riding!"

"Why ever not, my lord?"

"You might miscarry of my son, sweetheart! Do you not know that?"

"Edmund, I am well. I will not miscarry of *our* child. I am just like Mama. I will give you healthy children, I swear it! My mother rode during her confinements until she became too fat to pull herself upon her horse's back. She lost no babes, as you well know."

He shook his head. "I will not let you ride," he said in a voice that she had never heard him use to her. "Once we are home, I will give orders that you are to be forbidden the stables."

"I suppose that you think a jouncing coach is better for a woman in my condition?" she railed at him.

"Where do you plan to go that you need to ride or sit within the coach?" he asked of her.

"I had thought to visit Blythe and Nicholas, who live not far from us on the other side of the river, and what of your sister? Am I to be forbidden going to Riverside? Doro has been lonely since her husband's death. Would you imprison me because I am carrying a child?"

"Your family can come to visit you," he said stubbornly. "If you would go to see Doro, and I see no harm in it, you can take the dogcart."

"*The dogcart?!*" she shrieked at him, and the men-at-arms escorting them grinned at each other. "Am I a child that you would have me ride in the dogcart?"

"Do not distress yourself, my sweet," he begged her. "I am only thinking of your good, and that of the child. Oh, Blaze, my poor Catherine lost so many babes, and then I finally lost her. I have found love at a time when I had only hoped to find a second wife who might prove a good breeder. I love you! Yes, I desire an heir; but I would have you safe too!"

"Edmund, having a child is a normal and a natural thing. I am not some delicate creature to be wrapped in cotton wool. The lady Catherine? Was her health only poor when she was with child?"

"Nay. Catherine was always frail," he admitted.

"But I am not frail, my lord. I am strong, and I shall not be less strong because I am having our child."

"I want this child, Blaze!"

"I will give it to you, my lord earl, but you must not make me unhappy because I am carrying your babe."

"No riding! I mean it, Blaze. It is too dangerous, my sweet, and if you must be happy during this time, so must I. I cannot bear the thought of losing either of you."

"At least let me use a pony cart," she pleaded. "The dogcart is too slow. It would take me all day to get to Riverside."

He grinned. "We will consider each situation," he conceded, allowing her to believe he was willing to bargain with her.

Blaze smiled sweetly. "That is fair enough," she said, silently thinking if he meant to get around her he was sadly mistaken, but let him learn that later on, for she did not want to fight with him.

The Wye, which only the day before had been a roiling mass of currents, was tonight like a bolt of silvered cloth rolling between the dark spring-green hills. Rumford, the ferryman, brought them across the smooth, calm river while Blaze, leaning against her husband, thought that she had never seen a night as lovely as this one was. Reaching RiversEdge, she found that Heartha had waited up for her, and she was soon luxuriating in a warm bath that smelled of her favorite fragrance of sweet violets.

"Heartha, there is no soap," she complained.

"Those dim-witted girls," fussed Heartha. "I should not have let them go to bed until I was certain that they had performed their duties as I told them. I am getting old and careless. Do not fret, my lady, but enjoy your soak. I will fetch the soap, and be back before you even realize that I am gone."

Blaze closed her eyes and did as she was bidden. It was not too hard a task to relax within the deep warmth of the fragrant tub. She heard the door reopen, and said, "You were quick, Heartha. For an old woman you move like a young girl. Give me the soap." Eyes still closed she held out her hand, and was startled to have her upturned palm kissed. "Ohh!"

Edmund laughed, and without preamble climbed into the tub with his wife, handing her a cake of soap as he did so. "I sent Heartha to bed, my sweet. She is growing older, and I could see she was tired. Besides, I am expert in playing the tiring woman for my wife, am I not?"

"You have never washed me," she said, her tone thoughtful.

"You have never washed me," he replied.

"No, I have not. Shall I do so now, sir?"

His dark eyes narrowed. "Do you think you can please me, wench?"

"If I do not, my lord, then you may choose your own forfeit, and I shall gladly pay it," she answered him.

"And if you please me?" he teased her.

"Then you must pay the forfeit, sir." Dipping the sweet-scented little bar into the water, she said, "Turn about," and when he had, with some difficulty, slopping water onto the floor, she began to lather his back with long sweeping strokes.

Edmund closed his own eyes, and enjoyed the delicious sensation. Her fingers kneaded into the muscles of his shoulders, and he suddenly knew how the old gray striped tomcat who was king in his stables felt when someone took the time to pat him. He practically rumbled his contentment as his wife's hands expertly rubbed him.

"Why have we not done this before, madam?" he demanded of her.

Blaze chuckled. "I do not believe that we ever thought of it," she replied. She slid her hands beneath the water and boldly fondled his buttocks.

Edmund groaned, but the sound was not one of pain, rather it was a sound of pleasure. "Witch," he said softly, "you will kill me with your kindness."

"Turn yourself about, my lord, and try not to splash the water this time," was her reply.

When he had obeyed her command, she began to lather his chest with the sweet-scented soap. Her slender fingers delicately encircled the nipples on his chest, sending small ripples of delight down his spine. Again her hands disappeared beneath the water to slide over his belly, to caress his rampant manhood. Her heart-shaped face gave no hint of what she was thinking, although he thought he detected the corners of her mouth twitching with amusement.

"Sit back, my lord, and give me a foot," she finally said. Carefully, with serious demeanor, she washed the foot, soaping it thoroughly, thrusting a suggestive finger between each toe, then rinsing it off. The second foot was given its equal share of the same treatment, and when she had finished, Blaze said, "You are now bathed, sir, and it is my turn." Then with a little smile she handed him the little cake of soap.

He signaled her to turn about, and began by washing her back as she had washed his. When he reached her buttocks she wriggled most provocatively against his touch. He slid his hands around to cup her round wet breasts, sliding them beneath the soft flesh to gently crush it in his grasp. His thumbs reached up to tweak at her hardened nipples, and she wriggled once more against him, causing his manhood to ache most furiously. "Be still!" he growled in her ear, nipping it with his strong white teeth, then kissing away the quick pain.

"I cannot help it," she whispered at him.

"Shameless little witch," he replied, and he stood up, pulling her up with him. Turning her about, he yanked her water-slicked body against him and found her mouth.

Slowly he kissed her, letting his lips move lingeringly against her lips.

The warm water had weakened her after the long ride, and she half-sagged against his lean body. She could feel his manhood raging against her thigh as she parted her lips to receive his tongue. She was dizzy with his kisses which were like heady wine to her.

Picking her up he carried her to the bed, and together they fell upon it, heedless of the fact they had not dried themselves off. Gently he stroked her, his hand moving down her arm, smoothing over the curve of her hip. "I want to love you, Blaze," he murmured into her ear, "but I'll not harm the child."

She struggled to open her eyes, for her lids were heavy with her passion. "Mama . . . Mama says it is all right . . . until the end of June." Reaching up, she pulled his head down to her breast, and sighed as he clamped his mouth over the nipple, suckling upon her until he drove her into a frenzy of desire. "Now! Oh, please, now!" she sobbed.

"Nay, my sweet. We will take our time, and make these moments last, for soon we will not have them until after the child is born." He caressed her other breast with a tender hand before bending to suckle upon it.

With great effort Blaze struggled to master her own passion, and when she had succeeded, she felt the sweetness of his love pouring through her, and found greater satisfaction than she had ever found before in his arms. Together they reexplored each other's bodies, stroking slowly, touching with tenderness, and anticipating without haste the final pleasure to come. When at last he entered her eager body, moving with deliberate lack of haste, it was as if he were determined that they enjoy every second of their coming together.

Her breasts were swollen hard, the nipples tight. The rest of her body felt an almost painful fullness such as she had never felt. She felt the heat of his manhood as he pressed it deep inside her, to be followed by an almost aching suction as he drew back so he might thrust within her again. Her senses were reeling, and she felt suddenly weightless as she was whirled off into a golden haze of the most powerful, undiluted pleasure she had ever known in her young life. Desperately, as if she sought to keep herself from falling, she clung to her husband, her fingernails digging deeply into his shoulders as with a cry he released his tribute into her waiting body.

They immediately fell into a deep sleep, not awakening until the morning. During the next few weeks the intensity of their passion for each other seemed to grow as if the knowledge of their future abstinence drove them to desperation. Though Blaze found herself nauseous in the late afternoons, there was not, for the time being, any other outward sign of her condition.

News of her impending motherhood seemed to race upon the wind, however, though no formal announcement had been made. As the summer came, and the orchards and fields grew ripe with their crops, so Blaze ripened with her child. To forestall any argument on his wife's part, Edmund invited his sister to come and visit until after the birth. Lonely at Riverside, Dorothy Wyndham gladly agreed. Though he had not yet found himself a wife, Anthony remained at court. His new status as Lord Wyndham of Riverside had increased his chances of finding a wife, but if there was a woman who had taken his fancy, he had not yet communicated that fact to his mother or uncle.

On the sixteenth of September Blaze and Edmund celebrated the first anniversary of their marriage. Michaelmas came and went along with a particularly rainy autumn. On the last day of November the Countess of

Langford had her seventeenth birthday. She was large with child, but she bloomed with a happiness that transmitted itself to all about her. As for Edmund, he was visibly more relaxed than his sister had seen him in years, for as each month of his wife's pregnancy passed without all the symptoms and emergencies he had come to expect with poor Catherine, he began to believe even more strongly that he would at last have an heir.

So convinced was he finally of his wife's good health that he did not argue with her when Blaze announced in early autumn that Christmas would be as usual at RiversEdge. Reconsidering somewhat later, however, he was reassured by his sister that she would see Blaze did nothing to injure either herself or the child at this late date.

"Christmas without the family would be depressing, Edmund," she told him. "Besides, Rosemary Morgan will want to be with her daughter at the birth of her first grandchild. Who better could we have to help your wife than her mother, who has birthed so many children herself?"

"Blaze has been a good chatelaine from the beginning," he replied. "She will want to supervise everything, I know it!"

"She can supervise from her chair in the Great Hall, brother. Cease your fretting! Carrying a child is a condition usual to women. It is not an illness," Dorothy finished tartly.

Blaze's eyes twinkled with laughter as her sister-in-law, with whom she was fast friends despite the disparity in their ages, repeated this conversation. "Poor Edmund," she said. "I do not know who will be more relieved to have this child, he or I."

"Pah!" came the sharp reply. "Men have no idea what it is like to bear a new life beneath your heart. Only a woman can know that, my dear. I remember the joy I felt each time I carried one of Richard's children. A man's relief stems from the eventual delivery of his heir, for that child is his immortality. Men, bless them, are simple creatures, and if you fill their wants, they are usually content. Those needs are very basic. Food, clothing, shelter, women, sons, riches, and power."

Blaze laughed aloud. "Edmund does not seek power, Doro."

"Nay, not he, but there are men who do, my dear. Beware them, for they can destroy you."

"My life is here, Doro, with Edmund. I shall never leave RiversEdge but for little visits to my sisters and my parents. My world is simple, even as I would have it."

Christmastide was upon them once again, and with the Twelve Days of feasting and merrymaking came the Morgan family and all their offspring. Blythe and her husband, Nicholas Kingsley, lived just a mile upstream and across the River Wye from RiversEdge. Lord Kingsley had caused a comfortable barge to be built so he and his wife might be rowed across the water, thus making their journey an easy one, as young Lady Kingsley was almost as great with child as her elder sister. Bliss, her belly as flat as her twin's was round, arrived from court with Owen and Anthony. Her clothing was the absolute height of fashion, and she was brimming with delicious gossip that kept all the women of the family enthralled for days.

Lord Morgan and his wife arrived, and Blaze, looking closely at her mother, gasped. "Mama! You are . . ."

"I am having a baby, Blaze, even as you and Blythe. There is nothing unusual about my having a baby." She smiled at her husband. "Your father and I have made a habit of it, and the house seemed so empty with the three of you gone, and Delight is going to be visiting with Bliss and Owen this winter. I cannot remember when last I felt so very lonely. I know it is foolish of me. I am thirty-four years of age, but I seemed to need just one more baby."

"Except in your case, Mama," laughed Bliss, "it is rarely just one, but tell us, when is this sister or brother of ours to be born?"

"Sometime in late March or early April," replied Lady Rosemary.

"You have stolen my thunder, Mama," teased Blaze. "Here I, with my child's birth impending, hoped to be the center of attention this Christmas."

Rosemary Morgan laughed. "Indeed, Blaze, and you will be, for I can see that your child will not wait much longer to put in an appearance."

"By Christmas Day," said Blaze. "I remember praying last year for just such a gift from God."

Her prayer, however, was not answered. The feast of the Christ Child's birth came and went, yet Blaze's child remained firmly rooted within its mother's womb. The Countess of Langford found herself growing cranky. Gazing at Bliss across the Great Hall, she sighed deeply. How beautiful and slim her sister was. And Delight. There was another surprise. In the eight months since the twins' wedding Delight had grown taller than her three elder siblings, and had developed a beautiful bosom that even Bliss did not tease her about, being secretly jealous. At almost fifteen years Delight Morgan was promising to be a ravishing beauty within another year or so.

Larke and Linnette were now eleven and a half and Vanora would be nine in February. The elder two were coltish, and had taken to whispering behind their hands and giggling a great deal. Vanora, however, had lost her baby look. There was the hint of a young girl about her, and her boldness had not decreased one whit. She still delighted in baiting Bliss who, despite her months at court, was as yet vulnerable to her little sister's taunts. As for the youngest Morgans, Gavin and his sister, Glenna, they seemed unchanged at this time.

On the last day of the old year Blaze's child announced its impending arrival. If she had ever been grateful for her family, she was most grateful for them now, for all the old bad memories came racing back to haunt Edmund, and he feared for his young wife. She could not concentrate upon easing his fears right now. All her energies must go to bringing her child safely into the world. She was relieved to learn from Bliss that her father, Anthony, and her two brothers-in-law had taken her husband into the Great Hall and were getting him drunk.

Bliss and Blythe were also sent to the Great Hall to oversee the children, for Blythe, near her own confinement, was deemed in too delicate a condition to help with the birth. Bliss, however, wandered back and forth between the two camps bringing news to each of the others.

"I do not know why Delight cannot take care of the younger ones," she complained to her mother.

"Bliss, be fair. Delight is desperately attempting to attract Anthony's eye. Why do you think she begged to come and visit you at court this winter? He has yet to settle upon any female, and Delight is ready for marriage."

"Her flux has begun?" asked Lady Dorothy.

"A year ago," came the reply.

"Hmmmmmmmmm," considered the good lady. "Perhaps then we should help things along between those two. If no one at King Henry's court has caught his eye, and his heart, then Delight is as good a match as any, say I!"

Rosemary Morgan smiled, knowing how Lady Dorothy's words would please her fourth-born child. Delight had obstinately refused to consider any of the possible matches her parents had proposed over the past year. "We can, of course, speak on it, Doro, but first let us see to Blaze's safe delivery."

The young Countess of Langford labored lightly throughout the entire day and evening. Her labor grew harder as the night deepened, until, a few minutes before the midnight hour, she brought forth her child. In the Great Hall they heard the loud and squalling cry of the infant, and Edmund, still sober for all his in-laws' efforts, leapt to his feet. Bliss dashed from the hall, her skirts held high to prevent her from tripping. They waited, and then as the bells began to toll in the new year of Our Lord, 1523, Dorothy Wyndham appeared in the Great Hall, a swaddled bundle tucked within her arms.

Walking up to her brother, she placed the bundle into his arms, saying as she did, "My lord, your daughter. Blaze has delivered of a fine and healthy girl!"

Edmund looked down at the infant in his arms. Catherine's babes had been tiny and pale. This child was big and rosy. From her small head sprang a wealth of dark curls, and to his great surprise, he found her blue eyes were focused most distinctly upon his face. She blinked solemnly at him, and he laughed joyously. It was more than obvious that this child would live. What matter that it was a daughter, and not the desired son? They would have other babies, and there would be sons enough among them. He looked up at Doro. "Blaze?"

"Happy, but furious not to have had a boy. You must go and reassure her," came the reply, and Dorothy took her niece back from her brother's arms.

He hurried from the hall while behind him the rest of the family crowded about to get a glimpse of the newest member, passing Old Ada on his way, hearing the nursemaid saying as she went, "Bring that baby here to me at once, Lady Dorothy. Just born, and all this excitement!"

Entering his wife's bedchamber, he saw Blaze, her golden-brown hair plaited neatly into a single braid and freshly clothed in a silk nightrail, sitting up in her bed. Rosmary Morgan was just taking from her a silver goblet into which she had mixed some herbs, eggs, and wine into a strengthing posset for the new mother.

"She is gorgeous," raved Bliss of her niece. "What will you name her?"

"I do not know," said Blaze. "I had not considered that I would have a daughter. I wanted a son!"

"Her name," said Edmund, "is Nyssa. My daughter is called Nyssa."

"*Nyssa?* What does that mean?" demanded Blaze of her husband.

"Think on your Greek, sweetheart," he told her.

For a moment Blaze's brow furrowed in thought, and then she laughed as her mother and sister looked curiously to her. "Nyssa. It means a starting point!"

"Precisely, my sweet, and that is exactly what our daughter is, a starting point. She'll have brothers and sisters soon enough, my darling. For now, however, I am content. We have a healthy daughter, and you have come through your travail well. How can I be discontent under such circumstances?"

"But I prayed so hard that our first child be a son and heir," Blaze said.

"And I prayed that our first child be a healthy one that would live," he answered. "I prayed that you would live through the ordeal of childbirth. I could only remember poor Catherine, and all her weak or stillborn babes."

"Nyssa must have a Christian name or Father Martin will not baptize her," noted Blaze. "Let that name be Catherine, my lord, in memory of your first wife, if it would please you."

Rosemary Morgan smiled to herself, thinking that Blaze had always been a wise little creature. She caught Bliss's eye, her look plainly telling her second-born that she might learn a lesson from her elder sister. Then she signaled silently to Bliss that they should leave the new parents alone, and together mother and daughter slipped from the bedchamber.

Hearing the door close behind them, Edmund Wyndham bent and kissed his wife. " 'Tis the new year, my sweet, and a wonderful beginning it is indeed!"

"You are truly not disappointed, my lord?" Her eyes worriedly scanned his face.

"Nay, my sweet. I am every bit as pleased with Nyssa as I am with her beautiful mother. You have given me the best New Year's gift of all, Blaze, and so I shall give you your New Year's gift. My little manor of Greenhill belongs to you now. I have had papers drawn up transferring ownership into your name. It is yours, in your own right, to do with as you would. It generates a small but comfortable income, and that too is yours, with my thanks for giving me such a beautiful daughter."

She was astounded by such generosity. "Surely, Edmund," she said, "you meant that gift in thanks for a son, not a daughter."

"Nay, Blaze. I meant the gift in thanks for my firstborn child."

She could not believe it! She was a property owner in her own right! She had monies of her own to do with as she chose. Blaze looked up at her husband. "Thank you, my lord," she said simply.

He raised her hand to his lips and kissed it passionately. "Nay, my sweet, thank you. Thank you for Nyssa, and thank you for being my love." He arose from her bedside. "Now I think it is best that you get some rest, my love," he said, and he left her.

Blaze lay back, and found that she was suddenly filled with an overwhelming contentment. When Old Ada entered the room with the baby, she said to the nursemaid, "Bring my daughter to me, and let me see her again. There was so much fuss at her birth that I did not get a proper look at this miracle I have wrought."

"She's a bonny little thing, she is," approved Old Ada. "What will you name her?"

"Her father has named her. Her first name is Nyssa. My daughter is Lady Nyssa Catherine Wyndham." Blaze gazed down on the baby that Old Ada had just placed in her arms, and then she laughed. "There is nothing of me there at all except perhaps the eyes. She seems to be all Wyndham." The baby looked mildly back at her mother, and then she closed her eyes in sleep. Blaze felt an immediate rush of motherlove and protectively tucked the infant's swaddling blankets more closely about her. "Sleep safe, my little Nyssa," she said, and bent to place a feathery kiss upon her daughter's brow. "Who will watch over the cradle when I sleep?" she demanded of Old Ada as she gave her back the child.

"I've picked the nursemaid myself, Mistress Blaze, and I've been training her in the proper ways of caring for a baby ever since we got here. Her name is Maisie, and she is a good girl. I'll watch tonight, however. I watched over you the first night you was born, and I'll watch over little Lady Nyssa. Tomorrow is time enough for Maisie and her assistant, Polly, to take over their duties. You go to sleep now, Mistress Blaze. Sleep is what you need, and 'tis the best healer." Old Ada placed the baby carefully in its cradle, and then hobbling across the room, fluffed Blaze's pillows, and tucked the covers in about her. Returning to her place by the fire she sat down.

Blaze realized that she was indeed very tired. Her mother assured her it had not been a hard birth, but still she was tired. With a sigh of contentment she closed her eyes, and fell into an immediate sleep.

Chapter 8

꧁꧂

$\mathcal{L}$ady Nyssa Wyndham flourished and grew beneath the doting eyes of her parents. She spoke early and she walked as well, tottering about the Great Hall on her fat little legs until one day she was no longer unsteady. She had as frequent companions her uncles Henry and Thomas Morgan, who had been born three months after her birth. Blaze's twin brothers had arrived on April first, which gave the family cause to joke that God had had the last laugh on Lord Morgan, presenting him with twin sons after so many twin daughters. The child destined to be Nyssa's best friend, however, was Blythe's little daughter, Mary Rose Kingsley, who had been born nine and a half weeks after Nyssa, on February twenty-sixth.

In the late summer before Nyssa's second birthday Blaze learned that she was to have another child. The knowledge came as a great relief to her, for in the time since Nyssa's birth, Blythe had produced not only Mary Rose but also her baby brother, Robert, who had been born just this June past.

"Now you shall have a brother just like Mary Rose," Blaze told her daughter.

"I want a little sister!" Nyssa said, stamping her tiny foot.

Edmund took his child upon his lap, and Nyssa snuggled against her father, throwing her mother a very proprietary look. "Papa needs a son, Nyssa. There is time enough for Mama to have a little sister for you, but first I would have a lad," the earl said.

"You have me!" Nyssa said, as if her words solved everything.

"You cannot explain to her." Blaze smiled. "She isn't even two yet."

"I would not fret but that the estate is entailed," Edmund told her. "I could be quite happy with just Nyssa but for that. When I am gone she will need a brother to defend her and see to her marriage portion."

"This is a son I carry," Blaze said firmly. "I could not tell last time. I simply assumed that I would have a boy, but this time I know! I somehow sense it."

"Pray God," he answered her, "that you are right, else Tony inherit. Still, 'twould not be such a bad thing, for he is in the direct line, and a Wyndham on both sides."

"Edmund, you are too young to even consider such a thing," Blaze chided her husband. "I am young and healthy, and this is a son I carry. Tony will never inherit RiversEdge," she finished vehemently.

He heard the venom in her voice, and was disturbed. "Why do you dislike Anthony so much, my sweet? What has he done to offend you so?"

"Why will he not marry?" she demanded. "He has been at court over two years now, and he is certainly not a bad catch as gentlemen go. He is Lord Wyndham of Riverside. He has a pleasant estate, and a good income. I cannot believe there have not been opportunities for him to wed. Yet no one suits him. Why does he dally? Does he hope to inherit your title and estates, by chance, making him an even greater catch? Bliss says there have been any number of suitable women, both maidens and widows, dangled before him. I do not trust him. He is distressing Doro beyond all. I believe him to be a calculating and totally heartless man!"

"You are prejudiced because of Delight," Edmund said quietly.

"He broke her heart!" Blaze burst out. "I will never forgive him for it! *Never!* She tried for months to attract his love. Bliss says in the end her conduct bordered upon the pitiful. My God, Edmund! That my poor little sister should be driven to such conduct, and all over the love of a man not worthy to wipe her shoes! Owen finally sent her home when she shamed herself publicly by cornering Anthony and declaring her love for him. It almost killed her when your nephew rejected her! She has still not recovered from her heartbreak, and she may never recover from it."

"Be fair to Anthony, Blaze," Edmund chided his wife. "He never realized that Delight's passion was a serious one. He believed it the simple adoration of a young and inexperienced girl. He did not repulse her publicly. He spoke to her with kindness in private and in the presence of both Bliss and Owen. Delight is a romantic girl who had allowed herself to imagine a love affair between herself and Tony that did not exist. That was not Tony's fault. He never encouraged her, but rather thought of her as a little sister."

"He is a callous man, my lord!" Blaze's voice was tight with her anger. "Doro and my family attempted to make a match between my sister and Anthony. No others had caught his fancy, but no! My lord Wyndham of

Riverside would not have it! Delight would have made him a wonderful wife, and I hate him for breaking her heart!"

"Delight will make someone a wonderful wife," replied the earl, "but she would have been a terrible wife for Anthony."

"How can you say that?" cried Blaze.

"Delight's temperament, for all her amusing wit, is more like Blythe's. It is too soft a temperament for a man like Tony. Forced to the altar with her, he would have been bored to death within a month. He needs a wife with more spirit. One who will stand up to him even as you stand up to me, my sweet."

He was right, and in her heart of hearts she knew it, but she could not admit it to him. Perhaps one day when Delight was restored to her merry self she would, but not now. Fortunately she had not been exposed to Anthony Wyndham since Nyssa's baptism, when he and Bliss had stood as godparents to the child. My lord Wyndham of Riverside had remained at court amusing himself, and to Blaze's mind, neglecting his estates and the responsibilities entailed therein. Lady Dorothy had not seen her son in over a year, and it would have been longer had not Doro taken herself to court the summer before. She had returned saying she wasn't surprised that Tony could not find a wife. The court was full of wantons and flibbertigibbets. The queen was being disgracefully neglected by the king, whose behavior set the tone for the other members of the court. Without Queen Catherine there to set the standards of good behavior, there were none. As for the king himself, and here Dorothy Wyndham rolled her eyes heavenward, he might be a handsome young man, but she questioned his morals. There had been talk of his majesty and Mistress Blount, and his majesty and Mistress Mary Boleyn.

Because she would go no more to court, Anthony Wyndham was returning home for a visit, for he truly loved his mother. That he had chosen to come in late autumn when the hunting was good did not fail to catch Blaze's notice. The Earl of Langford chided his wife about her behavior, but Blaze, placing one hand over her belly, waved the other airily. "Fear not, my dear lord, I shall be polite to the villain."

He laughed at her. "Sometimes, my sweet, I think that I should beat you."

"But you do not, my lord," she murmured provocatively, sliding easily into his embrace and pressing against him.

He brushed her lips with his. "Perhaps I am remiss in my husbandly duties, madam," and he slipped an arm about her still-slender waist.

"You are never remiss, and I love you, my lord," Blaze said softly.

"Once again, my sweet, you have rendered me your captive," the earl replied gallantly. Then he kissed her with passion, and said as he released her, "I love you too, my beautiful and beloved wife."

Anthony Wyndham arrived home without fanfare, riding up to the front door of his uncle's great house unannounced, and with but a single servant. Dorothy Wyndham, who had been living at her childhood home since before Nyssa's birth, hurried to greet him. Her face was wreathed in smiles, and she hugged him hard and long in a shameless public show of maternal affection. "So you have come at last," she declared, her voice husky with emotion, and grinning down at her, he hugged her back.

He had not changed much, thought Blaze as she watched him entering the Great Hall with his mother. Anthony Wyndham, she decided, positively swaggered. He was as tall as Edmund was, with the same fair skin, but where Edmund's hair was a warm dark brown, Anthony's was coal black. It was obvious that the two men were closely related. Both had the same strong jawline, high cheekbones and forehead, but Edmund's eyes were brown, an inheritance from his mother. Tony's were a clear, light blue. Wyndham blue. His mouth, which she had previously thought a trifle soft, seemed to have narrowed and hardened, and there was a wary look in his eyes.

He greeted her graciously enough. "Madam, you grow more beautiful each time I see you."

"How easily the flattery trips off your tongue, my lord," she replied sweetly. "You have truly become the elegant courtier. Welcome back to RiversEdge."

He cocked a curious eyebrow, hearing the masked hostility in her voice, but then Edmund was coming into the hall, and he turned his attention to his uncle, forgetting Blaze easily. Anthony would stay at RiversEdge for the next few nights. Then he would escort his mother home, where they would remain until Anthony returned to the court after New Year's.

"Do you need a day to rest from your journey, or shall we hunt tomorrow?" asked the earl of his nephew.

"We'll hunt, of course!" Tony grinned. "I hunt at court, but 'tis a different game I seek than here at home."

"Sweet birds, I've not a doubt," chuckled the earl, "but when will you find one to suit you, and settle down to raise a family? You cannot spend your life at court amusing yourself, Tony."

A servant hovered at Lord Wyndham's elbow with a goblet of fine red wine. He quaffed half the cup thirstily, and then wiping his mouth with the back of his hand, answered, "I know, Edmund, I know! I must find a wife, and soon, but alas, when I contemplate each lass and consider spending my life with her, I find the thought distasteful. Until I meet a woman who does not affect me that way, I feel I am wisest in remaining a bachelor."

"Sometimes a man must take a chance, Tony, as I did with Blaze. I have known nothing but happiness since we wed. Would that you could have my good fortune."

"Perhaps that is what keeps me careful, Edmund. I want that kind of happiness. I cannot settle for anything less."

"Perhaps, my lord," said Blaze sharply, "you use that as an excuse to play the bull amongst the court cows. Perhaps you are really enjoying yourself too much to consider that your mother weeps for her unborn grandchildren, and your people are masterless, and Riverside lies dark and empty for want of its lord and his family!"

Lord Wyndham was surprised by her outburst, but then he laughed, replying, "Blaze Wyndham, you still have your sting as you did the day I escorted you from Ashby, a bride, home to RiversEdge. I am happy to see marriage has not changed you. You scold me harder than my own mother would. I promise you as I promise her that I shall marry as quickly as I can find the right woman."

Blaze glowered back at him. She had the distinct feeling that he was mocking her somehow, and she did not like it. Delight was better off without this big and arrogant man, and she would tell her sister that the very next time she saw her. God help the poor woman that Anthony Wyndham finally decided upon, Blaze decided.

The hunters departed early the next day, leaving shortly before the dawn, and returning just after sunset. Blaze saw that they had cold meats, bread, cheese, and wine to take with them, but they always came home hungry. Finally the night of October thirtieth the earl announced to his wife, "Tomorrow will be our last day of hunting, for Tony must go home to Riverside. He and Doro will leave after the Mass on the Feast of All Saints."

"I shall miss Doro," replied Blaze, snuggling into her husband's arms. "She is so much a part of our family now. I will be lonely without her."

"Will you not miss Tony?" he teased her, kissing her ear.

Blaze sighed. "Oh, Edmund, I know I am hard on him. I cannot seem to help it. He irritates me, and I do not know why. Aye, I do! There is an arrogance about him. It is subtle, but it is obvious to me, and 'tis like waving a red flag before a bull. That, coupled with his rejection of my sister, makes Tony anathema to me."

"He is not really arrogant, Blaze, but I know the attitude of which you speak, and I thought that only I could see it. It stems, I believe, from being the lesser Wyndham. Remember that we were raised together, yet at no time was Tony ever allowed to forget that I was one day to be the Earl of Langford while he would be simply Lord Wyndham of Riverside. Even his own mother, who raised us both, could not forget that gulf between our ranks. Remember, Doro had been born an earl's daughter. Were Tony not so truly sweet-natured, my darling, there would have been a serious breach and rivalry between us, as there was between my grandfather and his brother, who was Tony's great-grandfather."

"In all the history you have taught me, you have never told me this story," Blaze said. "I would know this family history so I may pass it on to Nyssa, and to her brother when he is born."

"My great-grandfather," Edmund began, "was Richard Wyndham, the Lord of Riverside. He had two sons, Edward and Henry, born two years apart to the day. From earliest memory the boys were adversaries and rivals, each struggling constantly to overcome the other and emerge triumphant. Of course the elder, Edward, was always given preference over the younger, Henry, as it was Edward who would one day inherit.

"Then Edward made his mark when at the age of sixteen he saved the life of King Henry, the fifth of that name, in the battle that was fought between the English and the French at Agincourt. It was immediately after the battle that the king created him Earl of Langford and awarded him the lands that are ours today. Those lands belonged to an heiress, Cecily de Bohun, to whom the king also married my grandfather. Since the bride was only three at the time, it was some years before the marriage was consummated. My father was their third son. The elder two died. One of a spotting sickness, and the other in the Holy Land fighting the infidels.

"But I digress, my sweet. When my grandfather was made Earl of Langford in his own right, his brother despaired, for how would he ever overcome his sibling now? It was my great-grandfather, Richard, who saw the solution. Riverside was not entailed upon the eldest son, and so he asked his elder son to forfeit his natural right and let him leave his estate to the younger. To this my grandfather agreed, for despite the rivalry that existed between the brothers, they loved one another, and that is how there came to be two branches of the family. The brothers remained friendly rivals their whole lives long, but there was no real animosity between them, for each had his fair portion.

"The families have always been close, and the marriage of my half-sister, Dorothy, to Anthony's father cemented the relationship for this generation. Tony and I have always spoken of wedding our children to each other one day, but now it seems as if that is not possible."

"Until Tony takes a wife it is not possible," said Blaze, and she turned onto her side, pressing herself spoon fashion against her husband, for she was more comfortable that way.

"Forget my nephew," he said, nuzzling her neck as his hand moved around her to cup her full breasts. "I'd far rather amuse myself with these sweet little apples than talk."

"Must you hunt tomorrow?" she asked him. "It was cold today, and I think it will rain soon. I do not want you catching a chill, for then we shall all catch it," she murmured sleepily, enjoying his fondling.

"Perhaps I shall tell Tony I prefer to stay at home tomorrow," Edmund said, feeling her relaxing into sleep against him.

"Hmmmmmmm," was her reply, and he smiled in the darkness.

In the morning, however, a pale lemon-colored sun shone weakly from the sky, and when the earl allowed that perhaps they should stay at home, Anthony mocked his uncle gently.

"Come, Edmund, are you growing old that you would sit by the fire with your wife rather than stalk the red deer within your forest?"

Edmund laughed, and said ruefully to his wife, "I cannot let this stripling nephew of mine put a gray beard on me yet, Blaze. I see no sign of rain. We will be back before sunset, my sweet," and bending to kiss her, he left the hall with Tony.

The day continued to glow wanly, and Blaze began to think that her husband had been right. It was All Hallows' Eve, and in a corner of the Great Hall Maisie sat telling Nyssa the very same ghost stories that Old Ada used to tell Blaze and her sisters. Nyssa's eyes were round with interest. Lady Dorothy sat working upon the tapestry of Jesus blessing the Wedding Feast at Cana that she had been working on since her son went to court. She intended it as a wedding gift for her son and the bride he finally chose, but the beautiful tapestry was nearly done.

When Blaze heard the sound of the autumn rain against the windows of the Great Hall she felt no satisfaction. If he caught an ague he would get no sympathy from her. Putting her feet up on a stool, she dozed lightly by the warm fire, only awakening when the sounds of men and horses and dogs came from outside the house. Slowly she opened her eyes and stretched.

Anthony Wyndham came into the hall. He was pale and haggard-looking. "Mother . . ." he half-sobbed, "Mother! Edmund is dead!"

Dorothy Wyndham leapt up with an agility surprising for a lady of her age. Her hands were pressed to her heart as if she were attempting to keep it from leaping out of her chest. "God have mercy, my son! Tell me that I did not hear you aright!"

Blaze struggled to her feet, and half-staggered across the hall. "Where is Edmund?" she demanded of Anthony. "Where is my husband?"

Lord Wyndham came slowly forward, and taking her hands in his said, "There is no gentle way to say this, Blaze. Edmund is dead. We were on our way home, for it had begun to rain, and Edmund said he dared not catch a chill lest you scold him. It had been a poor day's hunting, and he was teasing me that we would have been better off by your fire than being frozen for naught." Lord Wyndham's voice faltered, and he half-sobbed on, "Without any warning a stag raced out of the forest directly in front of Edmund's horse, and the dogs went wild and broke. The horse reared up suddenly, and Edmund was thrown from the beast. His neck was broken, and he died instantly. Ohh, Blaze! I am so sorry!"

For a long minute the impact of his words did not hit her, but when they did her pain was terrible. Her legs felt like jelly, and yet she somehow stood firm. For a time she did not think that she could breathe, but then she saw Anthony standing before her, the tears running down his face. A fierce black anger rose up in Blaze, and she slapped his face with all the strength that was in her.

"*You!*" she hissed furiously at him. "You are responsible for this, Anthony Wyndham! You have killed my husband as surely as if you stabbed him in the heart! *You have killed my Edmund!*" she shrieked, and then she began to beat him with clenched fists about the chest and head.

He was helpless against her terrible accusation and, unable to move, he stood there taking the punishment until finally Lady Dorothy, recovering from her initial shock, ran forward to pull Blaze away from her son. Angrily Blaze turned her fury upon her sister-in-law, lashing out at her with both her fists and her tongue, while Maisie clasped the frightened Nyssa to her ample bosom and the others in the Great Hall stood by watching in horror.

"Do not protect him, Doro! Do not protect him! He has killed my husband! He has killed Edmund!"

"Nay, Blaze," cried Lady Dorothy, dodging the blows and attempting to gather the grief-stricken younger woman into her embrace. "It was a terrible accident. *An accident!* No one is to blame." The tears were pouring down her cheeks. She had taken her infant brother from the midwife when he had been born, and his natural mother, her stepmother, had died. Though she was but twelve at the time, she had raised him as if he had been her very own son, and now he was dead. Gone from them, never to return. Dorothy Wyndham never even felt the tears that ran down her cheeks.

As the first wave of her grief began to recede, Blaze ceased the physical assault of Lady Dorothy. Her tongue, however, continued to score Anthony. "Your son is indeed to blame for my husband's death," Blaze declared. "Edmund would never have gone hunting today but that Tony teased him into it by impugning his manhood!" She whirled to face her enemy. "I could kill you for this!" she shrieked. *"I could kill you, Anthony Wyndham!"* Then suddenly she went white, and gasping as she doubled over, she clasped at her belly. "The baby! I am losing my baby! Ohhh, God curse you, Tony! God curse you!" she wept as she collapsed upon the floor.

Finally galvanized into action, the servants rushed to aid their countess. Gently they picked the fallen woman up, tenderly carrying her to her chamber to place her upon her bed. Heartha and Lady Dorothy hurried to help Blaze, pulling her bodice off, pulling her skirts off to see the stains of blood and birthing fluid upon the white fabric of her petticoats. Both women were weeping profusely at this terrible tragedy made doubly worse by the fact that the child Blaze miscarried of was indeed the son she had predicted she would bear. A tiny, perfectly formed little boy too small and too fragile to survive outside of his mother's womb after but six months in it.

Anthony, learning of it, groaned and tore at his garments in his grief. *Edmund's son!* Edmund's long-awaited heir was as dead as his father. "Blaze?" he asked his mother. "How is Blaze?"

"She will survive to bear other children for another husband," said Lady Dorothy, and then it was that she saw with shock the naked truth upon his face. "God have mercy," she whispered. "That is why you have not been able to decide upon a wife, my son. *You love her!* You are in love with your uncle's wife!"

"My uncle's widow," he said low.

"She despises you, my son."

"In time I will teach her to love me, Mother, for I have loved her since the day I first laid eyes upon her," replied Anthony Wyndham.

"God help you, Tony," said his mother. "It will take a miracle now to bring about what you so desperately desire."

"My lord earl. My *lord earl*," came the voice of the household's majordomo more insistently. "What orders would you give for Lord Edmund's body?"

For a moment Anthony Wyndham looked uncomprehendingly into

the face of the upper servant, and then it came to him that he was now the Earl of Langford. Shocked, he found he could not speak.

"Take my brother's body, and lay it out in the family chapel," said Lady Dorothy. "Then send Father Martin to me immediately."

"Very good, m'lady," replied the majordomo, backing off.

"*Anthony!* Get a hold of yourself this minute!" she said sharply to her son. "There is no help for it! You are indeed the fourth Earl of Langford, and as such it is to you that your people look. Edmund's death and the miscarriage of his son will bring great sadness to Langford and its people. You are now their leader, and as such you may grieve, but you may not show that grief, lest you distress the people even further. It is to you that Langford people will now look for guidance. A ruler must be strong, for the people are weak!"

There was a long silence, and then Anthony Wyndham raised his head. His eyes were sad, but their look was resolute. His voice when he spoke was now firm. "I'll send a messenger to Ashby. The Morgans will want to be with Blaze now in her mourning."

Lady Dorothy nodded approvingly.

In the next few days there was much coming and going at RiversEdge. Lord and Lady Morgan arrived to comfort their daughter, who lay in her bed weeping for the loss of her husband, and her son, but recovering from her miscarriage. Lady Rosemary had overruled her daughter Delight, who, seeing her eldest sister's tragedy as another opportunity to chase after Anthony Wyndham, wanted to come.

"None of you are to come," said Lady Rosemary firmly. "We must leave immediately. Delight, you will be in charge of your sisters and brothers. If Lord Anthony did not want you before he became Earl of Langford, he will not want you now," she said bluntly. "He can aspire to a much higher name, and undoubtedly he will. Now that he is the Earl of Langford, he will certainly marry when his mourning is over. I hope that, knowing this, you will decide to stop your foolishness, and accept one of the good offers we have had for you. You are, after all, sixteen and a half. Soon you will be considered too long in the tooth to be a wife. Is that what you wish? Surely you do not intend to end your days a maiden?"

Delight, Lady Rosemary found, was far easier to control than her eldest child. Blaze lay weakly within her bed, her eyes burning dark with her anger. "*He* killed Edmund," she told her parents. "If I could kill him, I would!"

"Stop this, Blaze!" said Lady Rosemary in her firmest, most maternal tone of disapproval.

"What do you know, Mama? You have lived your whole life happily at Ashby having Papa's children. You have never lost a child *or* a husband!" Blaze snarled at her mother. "Edmund would be alive today, and our son also, had not Tony goaded my husband into hunting that day. He planned to kill Edmund! I know it! He wanted Edmund's place all along, though he masked it well, the bastard!" Her voice bordered on the hysterical.

"Nay, daughter, do not allow your sorrow to blind you to the truth," said Lord Morgan in a quiet, firm tone. "Edmund wanted to hunt that day. Admit it. He grasped at the first excuse to do so. Do you really believe that Anthony was responsible for making that deer bolt from the forest directly in front of your husband's horse? There were a dozen witnesses to the incident, and Edmund's was not the only horse to shy. Unfortunately he was taken unawares, else he would have controlled his animal, for he was a fine horseman. It was an accident, Blaze. A terrible accident. It is unfair of you to blame Anthony for it. Unfair, and unkind. Edmund was Anthony's best friend. They were more brothers than uncle and nephew. He grieves too for Edmund, and as deeply as do you."

Blaze gazed mutely at her father, but Robert Morgan saw the pain she suffered, and took her into his embrace, where she wept until her eyes were burned closed with the salt of her tears. "I hate him!" she sobbed into her father's shoulder.

"Hate him if you will, Blaze, but do not blame him for something that was not his fault," replied Lord Morgan.

After two days in the family's private chapel the body of the third Earl of Langford was moved to the Church of St. Michael, where it stayed on view another day so that his people might come and pay their respects. Had the weather not been cool they would not have had the opportunity. Atop the coffin rested Edmund Wyndham's effigy, and within the closed casket, out of sight of the mourners, the earl held in tender and eternal embrace the swaddled body of his infant son, having gained in death that which he had so dearly sought in life, but had been unable to attain.

Blaze had insisted upon being present at her husband's funeral and had been carried into the church by her father. The people wept all the harder seeing their beautiful young countess, for Blaze appeared to them to be brave and noble in her terrible grief. What sons would have come from such a woman, they thought silently, and mourned all the more their double loss.

It began to snow as they exited the church, having interred Edmund Wyndham's broken body in its designated place within the family crypt. To her shock Blaze found herself alone with Anthony inside a coach.

"I *must* talk with you," he said quietly, and when she did not reply he continued. "I plan to settle Riverside and its lands upon Nyssa as her marriage portion. I know that Edmund had not yet even considered her dowry, and now it is my responsibility. As a reigning earl's daughter she would have been greatly sought-after. Her father's death would lessen her value as a bride, but that I have given her Riverside. She is now a great heiress."

"Are my daughter and I to live at Riverside?" she asked him coldly.

"Nay, Blaze, RiversEdge is your home," he replied. "You are now the dowager Countess of Langford, and nothing has changed."

"My husband and son lie in the family crypt at Michaelschurch," she said bitterly. "That has changed my life, and that of my daughter, my lord earl. I will never live at RiversEdge as long as you are there, Tony! I will take my daughter and go to Greenhill which belongs to me. Edmund gave it to me when Nyssa was born, and 'tis where we shall live!" Her pale face was resolute in its determination.

"Greenhill? You cannot live at Greenhill!" he said. "The manor house there is very old, and has not been lived in for thirty years. It is probably uninhabitable at this point."

"Then why did Edmund give it to me?" she demanded of him.

"He was giving you the manor with its lands, not a house to live in," explained Tony.

"But I will live in it," she said stubbornly.

"It is not proper for a young woman without a husband to live alone in an isolated place," he said through gritted teeth. "I will not allow you to live at Greenhill."

Her violet-blue eyes darkened in their anger and narrowed dangerously. "*You will not allow me?* Who are you to say what I may or may not do? How dare you even presume to do so, sir!"

"*Who am I?*" he repeated, and his voice was deep with his own rising anger. "I am the Earl of Langford, madam, and you as its dowager countess are my responsibility, as is your daughter, who I would remind you is Wyndham-born. It is I who will say where you may live, and *if* the Lady Nyssa Wyndham may go with you. As Earl of Langford it is my decision you remain at RiversEdge, madam, *and* because you are young and attractive, *and* because I would have a care for your reputation, my mother will remain as your chaperon. Is that quite understood, Blaze?"

"Am I to be your prisoner then?" she queried him sarcastically.

"You are the honored widow of my predecessor, madam. You and your daughter belong at RiversEdge. What would people say if you no sooner buried Edmund than you moved bag and baggage with your child to another house?"

"And if you wed, sir, what will your bride think of our presence?"

"If I wed we will then discuss possible changes," he answered.

She was the most irritating woman he had ever met, he thought. Yet he wanted to take her into his arms and comfort her, for he could see her pain over Edmund's loss.

"Let me go home to Ashby for a time," she said low. "I cannot bear the thought of Christmastide here at RiversEdge right now."

He reached out to take her little hand in his, but she drew herself back into a corner of the seat like some wounded animal.

"*Please,*" she said, and although he could not see the tears in her eyes he knew that they were there, and he was torn.

"Would you take Nyssa with you?" he asked.

"Of course," she replied. "You would not ask me to leave my child, would you? I will be with my parents. Surely you trust them to do the right thing even if you do not trust me."

"You may go," he said helplessly, for to have refused her would have been churlish, and he was desperate to gain ground with her. "I will expect you to return by Candlemas."

"Oh, please," she begged him, "let us stay until after Eastertide, my lord! I need to be with my family, and Nyssa will have her uncles for playmates."

He nodded. Distance would give her time to think, and he believed that when she did, she would realize that he had not been at fault in the matter of Edmund's death. Then, come the spring, upon her return, he would gently court her.

Bidding Lady Dorothy farewell, Blaze returned to Ashby with her parents. She would have her own apartments in the beautiful new brick wing of the house that Edmund had gifted his in-laws with just last year. It was well that he had done so, for Blaze traveled with her tiring woman, Heartha, her child, and her child's two nursemaids. She had her own groom, who looked after her white mare, and the young gray gelding Edmund had given her, and several liver-and-white spaniels who adored her, always following in her wake. Without this new wing Lady Rosemary would have been greatly put upon to house her eldest daughter and her small entourage.

After a few weeks back at Ashby Blaze realized that what her younger sister had said those three years back was true. Time had passed, and she had, of course, changed. Nothing was the same now as it had once been. She did not feel as if she belonged at Ashby, and she certainly did not belong at RiversEdge any longer. Having run her own large house, she was uncomfortable with her mother, and several times she caught herself opening her mouth to criticize something that her mother did that was not done that way at RiversEdge. She walked and she rode until the weather became simply too foul for being outdoors, which was worse, for she found that the sibling rivalry existing between her younger sisters was now beneath her.

Delight irritated her most, for all she seemed to want to talk about was the very thing that Blaze did not want to talk about. Anthony Wyndham. Larke and Linnette were sweet creatures, but their simple conversation, most of which was in unison drove her to distraction. They were so alike, she wondered if her parents would ever find husbands for them. She would have liked to spend more time with ten-and-a-half-year-old Vanora, but Vana was like a will-o'-the-wisp, never in one place for long, and leading a secret life that had caused Lady Rosemary to throw up her hands in desperation. Glenna, she hardly knew now, and Glenna was shy of her eldest sister, who in coping with her grief was not of a mind to win over the youngest of the Morgan sisters.

Blaze found herself looking forward to Christmas now, when Blythe and Bliss would come with their husbands, but a messenger arrived saying that Mary Rose and baby Rob were ill. Although in no danger, Blythe had chosen not to travel with them to Ashby. Bliss and Owen did arrive, however, bringing with them a heavy snowstorm that left the countryside blanketed in a mantle of white.

Bliss had the perfect solution to her sister's problems, and she shared the idea first with her mother.

"She will come back to court with us," Bliss said.

"Your sister is in mourning," chided her mother.

"She can mourn him as well at court as in the country, Mama. Though she says nothing, she still blames Anthony for Edmund's death which makes her residence at RiversEdge uncomfortable at best. She is bored to death here at Ashby. Can you not see it? She needs to be someplace new where she will be distracted from her grief, and where she may even find herself a new husband. Think, Mama! Blaze is the widowed Countess of Langford with a widow's generous portion *and* lands of her own. She is quite a catch, and there are plenty of suitable gentlemen at court who should be happy to have her for a wife. What can you and Papa do for her, really? As for Anthony Wyndham, he will now be far too busy finding a wife of his own, lest the Wyndhams die out. He cannot help Blaze," finished the practical Bliss.

Robert Morgan agreed that there was merit in Bliss's suggestion, and Blaze, when approached with the idea, considered a moment and then agreed, to everyone but Bliss's surprise.

"You will have to leave Nyssa, however," said Bliss. "Lodging at court is a crowded thing at best. If Owen and I did not have a small extra bedchamber at Greenwich we could not offer to house you. Heartha will have to sleep upon the trundle in your room, but there is no room for Nyssa and her entourage. I hope you understand, sister."

"Nyssa will be just fine with us," said Lady Rosemary. "Henry and Tom adore her. They have grown so used to her now that they would be lost without their little niece."

"She bullies them disgracefully," said Blaze.

"My goddaughter is a child after my own heart," remarked Bliss laughingly. "I wish we could take her with us, but the court is really no place for a child. You will come even so, won't you, Blaze?"

She considered again her quick decision. She was bored at Ashby although she tried hard not to show it. Her only other choice of a place to live was RiversEdge, and she would never live there again as long as Anthony Wyndham was Earl of Langford. Then a small smile touched the corners of her mouth. Tony had thought himself quite the fine lordling telling her that he was now in charge of her life. How magnanimous he had been when he had *permitted* her to return to her childhood home with her daughter. And ordering her back by the week after Easter! She almost laughed aloud now. She knew he would not bother with them thinking them safe at Ashby. Aye, she acknowledged to herself, Nyssa was better off here with her parents and her sibling uncles to bully and play with; but the dowager Countess of Langford was going to court, and his mighty lordship would not know it until after Easter when they did not return to RiversEdge! It would be impossible for him to interfere with her then.

"Aye, Bliss, I'll come with you, and I thank both you and Owen for the invitation as well as the lodging."

They left Ashby the second day of January, for the Earl of Marwood had promised his sovereign that they would be back in time for them to take their usual places in the king's Twelfth Night masque. Bliss, who was considered one of the most beautiful women at court, had an important role to play. She was to be *Innocence*, who would be overcome by the king's *Ardent Desire*.

Blaze had never seen a masque before, but Bliss assured her that she would love the pageantry that surrounded the king. "He is quite in his prime, being only thirty-three his last birthday. He is very, very tall, and he has the most wonderful red-blond hair, though it be thinning. His eyes! God's mercy, such eyes! They are as blue as a lake, and so deep that you could drown in them! He is learned and witty, and altogether most amiable. He is the greatest king in the world, Blaze. There is none to match our good King Harry!"

"Indeed," agreed Owen FitzHugh, "Bliss speaks the truth. You will be amazed at the wonders and delights that you find at court. I am proud to be considered among the king's friends. He is a great and noble lord. Only in his wife has he been unfortunate."

"Why is that?" Blaze asked.

"He should have never wed Catherine of Aragon, Blaze, but this, of course, you must not ever voice aloud. There is talk that he has been denied living sons because he committed a sin by taking his brother's widow to wife. Although it is not known widely yet, the king is seeking to gain a papal dissolution from his marriage to the queen so he may remarry and sire legitimate sons. Elizabeth Blount, who is now Lady Tailboys, has given the king a fine lad, young Henry Fitzroy, who is to be six this year. Mary Boleyn's baby son, Henry Carey, is also said to be the king's get. So you see, the king can sire strong sons, but not on the Spanish princess. Besides, she is now past her childbearing years, sad lady. The king deserves better, and with God's blessing he shall have it," finished Owen FitzHugh.

The Earl of Marwood's traveling coach was extremely comfortable. Well-sprung, it had real glass windows that could be raised and lowered, which was considered quite a luxury. They traveled to Greenwich, where the king was now in residence, snug and warm beneath lush fur rugs, hot bricks wrapped in flannel at their feet. The weather had turned milder on New Year's Day, and though muddy, the roads were passable.

Blaze had bid her family farewell, hugging her little daughter to her heart and promising to bring the child a present when she came again. Nyssa, who had received a surfeit of gifts just several days before upon her second birthday, was not overly impressed. Bidding her mother goodbye, she immediately turned back to her playmates. Blaze laughed weakly. "I am glad she is so self-reliant at such an early age."

The coach rumbled away from Ashby, and looking back at her family standing before the house, Blaze had a feeling of déjà-vu. Once before she had left Ashby, and she had found great love. What would she find this time? she wondered.

Part Three

❖

KING'S CHOICE

Twelfth Night 1525 –
Autumn 1525

Chapter 9

"Will I really get to meet the king?" Blaze asked her younger sister for the third time.

Bliss laughed. It seemed strange to her, but she felt more like Blaze's elder sister at this moment than a younger one. "Owen is one of the king's best friends," she said once again, as she had said thrice before. "You will get to meet the king, but I shall tell him that you are in mourning lest he want you to take part in the gaiety. You really should not, you know."

"You sound like Mama," Blaze replied, and now it was her turn to laugh. "I do not want to involve myself in the court quite yet, Bliss. Perhaps I shall never involve myself in it, but I had nowhere else to go right now. You know that."

Bliss wisely held her tongue. For one so young she was amazingly knowledgeable of human nature. As great as her sister's pain was now, it would pass in time. Bliss did not mention another husband, but she knew the ways of the world well, and of course Blaze would have to remarry eventually. What better place than the court to find a husband, and Bliss was generous enough to concede that her sister was beautiful. Perhaps not as beautiful as she was, but nonetheless lovely enough to capture many hearts.

Despite three years of marriage, however, Blaze was an innocent, Bliss thought. She would have to steer her sister carefully through the shoals of this dangerous and fascinating place, but innocents like Blaze either learned to survive quickly, or they found themselves gobbled up like so many hapless lambs. The court was greedy for pretty little girls, but if one were wise, one could survive.

The room that Bliss had so kindly supplied her with was indeed small, and while her sister and brother-in-law hurried off to practice their parts in the masque to be given tomorrow night, Blaze and Heartha settled themselves.

"I know we're lucky to have the room," grumbled Heartha, "for that Betty of your sister's tells me so often enough, but Lady Bliss didn't tell no lies when she said it was small, m'lady." She looked with jaundiced eyes about the almost square, paneled room with its one lead-paned double window and small fireplace. There was nothing in the room except a large bed with a trundle, and a single straight-backed chair. There were no hangings upon the bed, which almost took up the entire space.

"It will be fine, Heartha. It is neither RiversEdge, with all its memories, nor Ashby, where I cannot be myself any longer. This little room is now my home and yours. Let us work to make it comfortable before night-fall."

Though the tiring woman fussed that Blaze should sit quietly while she made the room presentable, Blaze would have none of it. Surprisingly the room was quite clean, and freshly swept. Together the two women hung the bed hangings, which were green velvet on natural-colored linen. Blaze had beautiful linen sheets, which she brought from a trunk, placing her fine feather bed over the straw mattress first. The sheets were scented with her favorite fragrance, sweet violets, and the bed quickly looked comfortable and inviting. Working together, the two women had the chamber quite presentable by the time Bliss and Owen returned. There were draperies upon the window, a candlestand by one side of the bed, the small trunks holding Blaze's clothing had been placed strategically, and Blaze's gowns were already hung in a small section of her sister's dressing room which had been allotted her by Betty, who was Bliss's tiring woman.

At supper they sat with Lady Adela Marlowe and her husband, Sir John. John Marlowe had a small place as a gentleman of the bedchamber, and his wife had become Bliss's best friend since her arrival at court. Adela Marlowe was a pretty girl with coal-black curls and lively brown eyes.

"We are so sorry to hear of your loss, Lady Wyndham," she said, "but you were right to come to court. It is the best place to find another husband."

Bliss choked upon a mouthful of rabbit pie, but she managed to quickly say, "Dearest Adela, Blaze has not come to find another husband."

Adela Marlowe looked disbelieving, but seeing her best friend's pleading look, she stammered, "N-no? Oh? I . . . I did not know."

"I do not plan on marrying again, Lady Marlowe," Blaze said softly. "No man could possibly take the place of my Edmund."

"N-no, no, certainly not," murmured Lady Marlowe, wondering if Lady Wyndham were mad, but Bliss later confided in her friend, much to that lady's relief.

The following day the two women showed Blaze about Greenwich. The palace had been built in the previous century and originally was called 'Bella Court. Over the years it had passed through various royal hands, becoming Pleasaunce under the ownership of Henry VI's queen, Margaret of Anjou, who paved the floors with terra-cotta tiles, and glazed all of the windows as well as adding a vestry to house her jewels, and a pier on the river for her barge. Henry VII changed the palace's name once again, this time to Greenwich Palace, and gave the stone buildings a new face of redbrick.

The palace was built around three quadrangles, which were called the Fountain, Cellar, and Tennis courts. Its main gateway stood directly opposite Queen Margaret's pier. On the land side of the palace were gardens and a hunting preserve that was enclosed. It was Henry's favorite residence, Bliss told her sister.

"How many does he have?" asked Blaze, curious, for it seemed odd to her that anyone would need more than one house, even a king.

"Well," said Bliss, "there is Westminster in the city, although since the great fire in 1512 the king has not lived there, although his bedchamber, the Painted Chamber, was untouched. There is The Tower, of course, and Baynards Castle on Thames Street, which is considered very beautiful, and is large and modern. There is Bridewell, also in London. The king built it just a few years ago, but we only sometimes stay there. Outside of the city there is Richmond, Eltham, Windsor, Woodstock in Oxfordshire, but that is just a tumbledown hunting lodge, and the court never goes there. And, of course, Greenwich."

"I still do not understand why it is necessary for him to have all those castles," said Blaze.

"He has them because he is the king, silly," laughed Bliss.

They had exchanged Twelfth Night gifts that morning, Blaze giving her brother-in-law a fine jeweled dagger with a gold hilt. For Bliss she had a pair of pearl-and-sapphire earbobs, which caused Bliss to squeal with delight, for she loved beautiful jewelry. In return she and her handsome husband gave Blaze a lovely gold-and-black enameled chain from which hung a large tear-drop pearl with a pinkish hue.

"Oh, how lovely," Blaze exclaimed. "I shall wear it tonight."

In the evening after the feasting, Bliss left her elder sister with Lady Marlowe while she hurried off to change into her costume. The king had been in the banqueting hall, but Blaze had only seen him from a distance, but he indeed seemed everything her sister said. It would be exciting to actually meet him, which she would do after the masque.

The masque was beautiful to the eye. Young pages in red velvet and cloth-of-gold suits rolled in a castle with four delicately soaring towers, all constructed of wood covered in paper of silver and gold gilt. Suddenly there was a dull boom and a puff of smoke, which, upon clearing, revealed a most fearsome dragon with green-gold scales and ruby-red eyes guarding the castle.

"Look," whispered Adela Marlowe, pointing to the four towers of the castle where had suddenly appeared within each window a beautiful woman. "They are Innocence, Charm, Wisdom, and Virtue," said Lady Marlowe. "The dragon is Gloom and Deceit."

Blaze could see that the women were clothed in beautiful glowing draped silks. Bliss in sky-blue and gold, the others in pink and silver, green and silver, and red and gold. Then from the dimness of the area set aside for the masque came four knights, each garbed in a single color. There was a gold knight that Adela murmured was the king, as well as a silver knight, a green knight and a red knight.

"They are Ardent Desire, Tender Passions, Worldly Wise, and Sweet Pleasures," said Blaze's companion, "and they must overcome Gloom and Deceit in order to gain their ladyloves."

Blaze's violet-blue eyes were wide with amazement. She had never seen any entertainment other than Morris dancers and mummers. She had not even imagined that such elegant amusement could exist. Fascinated, she watched as the mock battle was fought between the brave knights and their fearsome opponent. At one point the dragon belched flame and smoke, and she shrieked her surprise along with the rest of the audience. Finally however the great beast was overcome. From the castle emerged Innocence, Charm, Wisdom, and Virtue in their flowing garments to dance gracefully with Ardent Desire, Tender Passions, Worldly Wise, and Sweet Pleasures.

"What did you think?" demanded Lady Marlowe as the four couples danced their way off into the gloom.

"It was wonderful!" said Blaze, her face bright with her excitement. "Being in mourning, I feel almost guilty sitting here enjoying it."

"You have behaved properly," said Lady Marlowe. "You have not involved yourself, and you will not dance this evening, although from the looks that have been coming your way, I know that many gentlemen will be deeply disappointed."

"Why would gentlemen look at me?" Blaze said innocently.

Adela Marlowe laughed softly. "Dearest Blaze, I see that Bliss and I shall *really* have to keep an eye on you. For a widow you are most naive. The gentlemen of the court look at you for various and sundry reasons. For one, you are very beautiful. You are also a new face. Then, too, they are for the most part a randy bunch who see any newcomer as fair game."

Blaze blushed, understanding her new friend quite well. "I do not see the queen," she said, attempting to change the subject.

"And you will not," came the reply. "The king has sent her away, for he is angry with her, and the Princess Mary also." She lowered her voice. "The queen, you see, refuses to be reasonable regarding the king's great matter."

"I cannot help but feel sorry for her," said Blaze.

Adela Marlowe nodded. "She is a good and virtuous woman, but she is too prideful. She puts her own pride and her own interests above those of England, but what could we expect? She is, after all, a foreigner, no matter her many years in England."

Bliss rejoined them, now regowned in her dress of medium blue velvet with its pearl, silver, and rose-quartz embroidery. "Owen is bringing the king to meet you," she said excitedly, and then she adjusted Blaze's head-dress. "Ohh, I wish your gown were more festive!"

"I mourn my husband, Bliss," Blaze reminded her sister. "My gown is quite suitable."

"Indeed it is," agreed Lady Marlowe.

"I wore your lovely chain," Blaze said, trying to cheer Bliss.

"It does help," she admitted, surveying her elder sister once more. Blaze's gown of rich black velvet was virtually unadorned but for some pearl-and-gold embroidery on the bodice. Even her underskirt was plain black silk brocade. Only the delicate lace of her cream-colored chemise top and its ruffled cuffs which showed from beneath her gown relieved the severity of her look. Bliss silently mourned that Blaze's beautiful honey-colored hair was almost totally hidden beneath her charming cap, but at least the cap was heavily adorned with gold and pearls, and its flowing black silk veil shot through with bits of gold thread.

"Here he comes!" hissed Adela Marlowe, and she swept her skirts into a graceful curtsy that was echoed by her two companions.

"Sire," said Owen FitzHugh, "may I present to you my sister-in-law, Lady Blaze Wyndham, the dowager Countess of Langford."

Henry Tudor looked down on the three women. Both Bliss and the pretty Lady Marlowe were smiling up at him from their obeisance. Reaching out his big hand, he cupped the face of the third woman and tipped it up so he might see it. "Such beauty, Lady Wyndham, should not be hidden from your king," he said in a smooth, deep voice.

Blaze's eyes widened noticeably, the pupils black against the violet blue of her irises. She could not speak for a moment, and beside her Bliss almost groaned aloud. Didn't her sister realize that the king's favor was important? Henry continued to stare for a moment longer, and Blaze's cheeks grew pink with a blush which caused the king to smile.

"You are even prettier with your pink cheeks," he noted. "It is rare I see so charming and genuinely innocent a blush here at court. Welcome, Blaze Wyndham."

She finally found her tongue. "Your majesty is most gracious, and I thank you," she said.

The king raised her up, which allowed the other two women to arise also. "Owen tells me you are newly widowed. I regret that such tragedy should bring you to us, but I cannot be sorry to have such a particularly lovely woman adding luster to my court."

"My lord was killed in an accident two months ago," said Blaze softly.

"Then I cannot ask you to dance, my lady, and that saddens me, for I suspect that you dance well. On May Day, however, I shall ask you to dance, for surely by then you will allow yourself that small pleasure." His blue eyes swept over her assessingly. She was very lovely, he thought. Her skin was so very white against the black velvet of her gown. He contemplated the delights of caressing that skin, which was surely as soft as it looked. As for the pearl which hung down from her chain to nestle between her breasts, he envied it its place. In time, he cautioned himself. He could see that despite her widowhood she was indeed an innocent, but with the experience born of his royalty he hid his lust well.

She spoke once more. "I believe that if your majesty should ask me to dance with him on May Day, I could not refuse. Indeed I should consider it the greatest honor I have ever had." Then she smiled up at him, and Henry Tudor realized she was not just pretty. She was startlingly beautiful!

He smiled back at her, and then without another word he moved off. So she would consider dancing with him an honor. The king's smile broadened. He had other, far sweeter honors in store for the beautiful widowed dowager Countess of Langford.

"You have pleased him!" chortled Bliss. "God's foot, I thought you would disgrace yourself and us too when you were at first so tongue-tied with him."

"Do not be so openly ambitious for your sister, Bliss," Lord FitzHugh chided his wife. "The king understands sorrow, for he mourned his mother and his brother, Arthur, deeply. Besides, he does not like bold women. Blaze was perfect." Perhaps too perfect, the Earl of Marwood worried silently. He had been with the king for many years, and he knew all of Henry's looks, though the king thought himself a master of deceit. The king was bored for feminine amusement. Bessie Blount was no longer his lover, but rather his good friend. Pretty little Mary Boleyn had slipped into domesticity. She had never been particularly witty and quick for all her bovine charms. No, Henry was bored, and looking for a new conquest. Owen FitzHugh knew his sovereign well. The king was patient when he truly desired something. Time would tell how serious his intentions were regarding Blaze.

The winter passed quietly enough, and with the Lenten season, many of the court took the opportunity to visit their holdings, for Lent at court was dull without all the usual amusements. The Earl and Countess of Marwood and Blaze were among those who remained, however, for the king could not be left devoid of companions. Owen FitzHugh was the king's favorite tennis opponent, for despite his sovereign's royal station, the young earl played to win, which pleased the king. Henry did not always triumph in his matches with Owen FitzHugh, but he won more than he lost, and when he won, he knew it was fairly. By mid-February the weather was beginning to grow slightly milder, and the king, when not hunting or shooting at the butts, played tennis.

Evenings were spent quietly talking, playing at word games, and listening to gentle music, for frivolity was forbidden in this penitential season. Lady Wyndham was now, amid the general dearth of pretty women, obvious to all the gentlemen, and her company eagerly sought out. To those who merely desired to repartee with her, or walk with her chatting through the picture gallery, she was charming and amusing. Unfortunately, far too many of the king's gentlemen, even those with wives, sought more than the pleasure of Blaze's company, and they found to their surprise that the gentle-looking widowed countess had a fierce temper. More than one gentleman had his face slapped in attempting a kiss, and this gave rise to the rumor by those of the more vindictive and disappointed gentlemen that Lady Wyndham was a coldhearted tease. Some, however, were more graphic in their failure to breach virtue's walls.

"The little bitch is no more than a cock-tease," grumbled Thomas Seymour one evening.

"What, Tom, and have you also failed with Lady Wyndham?" mocked

Lord Arden. "You are in good company, my lad, for none of us has been able to skirt the lady's defenses."

"What you mean, gentlemen," laughed Charles Brandon, the Duke of Suffolk, who was both the king's brother-in-law and close friend, "is that none of you has been able to *lift the lady's skirts!*"

"Well punned, brother Charles," chuckled the king, "but I must reprimand you gentlemen who would seek to impugn a helpless young widow's honor."

"You would not think her so helpless had you been slapped by her, sire," complained Thomas Seymour. "By God, my ears are still ringing with the blow!"

"Cease your chatter, Seymour," hissed Lord Arden. "Have you not realized by now that the king means to have Lady Wyndham for himself?"

Seymour looked furtively to the king, but Henry Tudor had already turned away and was engaging another friend in conversation.

The weather grew milder until it seemed as if spring had simply burst suddenly upon the land. The court had moved twice over the winter, going into the city to stay first at Baynards Castle, and later moving on to Bridewell, which was but three years old. With Easter coming, however, the court returned to Henry's favorite home, Greenwich. There the grass was bright green with the season, and the lanes were lined with primroses.

With the coming of Easter, gaiety returned to court along with all those who had earlier left it. The king now took the opportunity to seek Blaze out more and more, insisting that she ride next to him in the hunt; that she walk with him in the picture gallery, where he introduced her to all of his ancestors; that she sit before the fire and play chess with him.

"My God," said Bliss excitedly to her husband one day as the king escorted Blaze off for a stroll in the palace gardens, "does this mean what I think it does?"

"Pray God it does not!" replied Owen FitzHugh fervently.

"Are you mad?" Bliss demanded of her husband. "Blaze has much more to her character than ever did Bessie Blount or that silly cow Mary Boleyn. She could be a true *maîtresse en titre*, as is the French king's mistress. If she bore him a child, so much the better, particularly if it were a son. God knows the king has done well by both Lady Tailboys and Mistress Carey. If she could but engage his heart, our fortunes would all be made! It does not hurt to be related to a king's mistress, as you well know."

Owen FitzHugh shook his head. "What you are suggesting is not in your sister's nature. Now you, my darling ambitious Bliss, would indeed do well under your sister's circumstances. Blaze, however, is not that kind of woman."

"She cannot refuse the king," said Bliss.

"No," said the Earl of Marwood sadly to his wife, "she cannot, but should it come to that, then you and I must give her all the support she will need."

"Oh, pooh!" exclaimed Bliss. "Even Blaze for all of her naiveté cannot fail to realize such a golden opportunity should it be offered to her."

The king had led Blaze into the middle of a boxwood maze in the gardens and now he teasingly asked, "Shall I leave you here, m'lady, to find your own way out?"

"I do not think I could," said Blaze with a smile. "Surely you tease me, sire."

"Knowledge has its price, m'lady, and you seek my knowledge in escaping this fair green prison. What price will you pay me?" He cocked his head, and in doing so rendered the feather in his flat velvet cap to an even jauntier angle.

She paused as if to consider his words. She had been at court long enough to know that the king was playing a game with her. She did not know whether to laugh, or whether to be frightened. Henry Tudor was very powerful. Better never to show fear, she thought, and laughed.

"Very well, my lord, what price would you put upon this great knowledge of yours, which will free me from this labyrinth?"

"An extravagant one, madam. I would have a kiss of you."

Dangerous ground, yet she could hardly refuse him. "I must pay," she said with a mock sigh, "but not until we have reached the outside, sire."

Now it was his turn to laugh. She was a clever little puss for all her virtue and modesty. "Done!" he said with a grin, and reaching out, took her small hand in his rather large paw so he might lead her from the maze. Finally he stopped and said, "Around this corner lies freedom. You must pay your tithe now, but here where we may be private and safe from prying eyes." Reaching out, he drew her into his arms.

Suddenly Blaze found she was afraid. She placed her hands upon his wide velvet-clad chest to hold him off saying as she did so, "My lord . . . please . . . I . . ."

"Hush, sweetheart," said the king gently. "I will not harm you. You have ne'er been kissed except by your late husband, I can see that; but for all your sweet virtue, madam, I mean to have your lips, so cease your useless chatter," and then the king clamped his mouth firmly over hers.

It was a passionate and demanding kiss, and far from being quickly over, as she had assumed, the king's lips lingered on hers, moving tenderly over the softness, coaxing a response from her that when it came surprised her so that she moaned low.

Cradling her with one strong arm as she fell back against him, the king loosened her laces with expert fingers and slipped his hand into her bodice to cup a breast. His thumb rubbed quickly and insistently over the sensitive little nipple which hardened beneath his sensual touch.

"*No!*" she cried, attempting to struggle. "Oh, please, no!"

"Shhhhhh, sweetheart, do not fight me," he begged her, and his head dipped so he might kiss the soft perfumed flesh of her breasts. "Ahhh, my beauty, you are so lovely. So very, very lovely!"

Using every ounce of her strength, and sobbing with defiant terror, Blaze pulled desperately away from the king, and clutching her open bodice to her heaving bosom, she turned and fled him around the last corner of the maze into the garden proper. Finding a distant spot, she quickly redid her laces as best she could, and then hurried back to Bliss's apartments. She was relieved to find herself completely alone, and slipping into her room, she sat down upon the bed and wept.

That the king would accost her surprised her totally. She was not so innocent any longer that she did not know he enjoyed dallying with the ladies, but she was not at all like Bessie Blount or Mary Boleyn. She had not sought to gain his attention, and she had believed that her virtuous demeanor, while not protecting her from other men whose behavior was apt to be gross, would have at least sent a signal to the king, who she believed must surely be the most chivalrous of gentlemen. How wrong she had been, and now what was she to do?

A knock sounded upon her door. Her heart leapt in her chest. Had he dared to follow her to her very bedchamber? Nay. Not even the king would do that. "Come in," she called, and a young page entered the room.

"His majesty requests that you attend upon him at once, my lady Wyndham," said the boy in his piping voice.

Blaze gasped. "I cannot!" The words were out before she even had the time to think.

The boy whitened, looking shocked. "Madame, for God's own mercy, do not send me back to the king with such a message. I shall be surely dismissed from my position, and I am a younger son. I can only make my way in life through my success at court!"

"Nay," said Blaze, rising. "I did not mean it. I will come with you." Poor lad, she thought. He was as much of a victim as she was. Following in his wake, she allowed him to lead her to the king's apartments, and through the royal antechamber, where half the men at court it seemed were there to witness her shame, and into the king's privy chamber. The boy, opening the door, bade her enter, and was then gone.

Turning from the windows, the king said, "Are you quite recovered now, madam?"

What could she say? He was the king. Mutely she nodded.

"I will try and go slowly for your sake, Blaze," the king said, using her name for the very first time, "but understand, madam, that I mean to have you for my own."

"Sire—" she began.

"Be silent! I have not given you my permission to speak. You have a child, do you not?"

"Aye, my lord. A daughter. Her name is Nyssa."

"Greek! Do you speak Greek, madam?"

"My husband was teaching me, sire."

"Your daughter, how old is she?" the king asked.

"She is two, sire."

"And who is the legal guardian of little Lady Nyssa and whatever fortune she may have?"

"I assume I am, sire," she answered him hesitantly.

"Nay, madam, a woman cannot hold such a position without my express permission, and for now you do not have that permission. What property does the child possess?"

"Nyssa was given a small estate with two villages and a fine house called Riverside."

"I shall have to think about a guardian, a *proper* guardian for this little heiress. She will, of course, be raised within her guardian's house as well. I am certain I can think of someone suitable."

Blaze could feel her heart hammering wildly in her chest. "Sire, you would surely not take my daughter from me?"

"A child with your daughter's value must have a suitable guardian," said the king. "A woman, particularly a disobedient woman who does not understand how she must behave with her sovereign, is certainly not a proper governor for an innocent child."

"Then appoint my parents, Lord and Lady Morgan of Ashby to be Nyssa's guardians. They have had eleven children, eight of whom are still home. My daughter is with them now!"

The king appeared to consider, and then he said, "Nay. A child with the kind of wealth your daughter possesses needs a more powerful person to oversee her upbringing. Someone with influence who has the king's favor and his ear. I must think upon it, madam, and my decision, of course, will rest upon your future behavior. Do you understand that, madam?"

"Aye, my lord, I understand," Blaze said low.

"Then come and kiss me, sweetheart, for it pains me to quarrel with you. There are far more pleasant things that we might do together, Blaze."

Slowly she walked across the room to him, and raising her head accepted his kiss.

"Open your mouth, Blaze, and receive my tongue," he ordered her, and his arms closed about her, imprisoning her within his embrace.

Obeying him, she shivered at the touch of his tongue on hers, though she sought to hide it. His tongue swept with unhurried grace about her mouth. His arm was tight about her waist, pressing her hard against him, and the scent of orris root assailed her nostrils. I am going to faint, she thought, feeling herself growing weaker in his embrace.

The king felt her sink against him, and with a swift single movement he picked her up in his arms, and seating himself in a chair by the fire which was lit to keep the damp of the river from the room, he said as he cradled her, "There, sweetheart, don't be afraid of me. I only want to love you a little."

Dear God, Blaze thought as she huddled in his lap, biting back her sobs, how mercurial he was. One moment he was threatening her, and the next he played the tender lover. Now she understood the meaning of real power, and it was a bitter lesson. Why had she not stayed safe in the country? Better to be surrounded by the pain of her happy memories than to be at Henry Tudor's mercy.

Undoing her laces, he slipped a large hand into her bodice and fondled her breasts. "How I long to see you as God fashioned you in your natural state," he said softly. "What sweet breasts you have, Blaze."

She made another effort at deterring his intent. "My lord, please, I beg of you, I am not like the others! I was raised to be chaste, and I have always been chaste."

"That, my little country girl, is more than obvious. You have been quite the talk of my gentlemen this winter for your persistent refusal to yield to their amorous intent. Tom Seymour says that you hit him so hard when he tried to steal a kiss that his head rang for days after with your blow. I, however, am not a simple gentleman of this realm. *I am the first gentleman of this realm.* Did your parents not teach you that your first duty was to your king?"

"I was taught that my first duty was to God, my lord, and what you hint at is against God's law," Blaze retorted with more spirit than she was actually feeling.

"Your first *spiritual* duty, madam, is indeed to God; but your first *temporal* duty is to me, your king," he replied, a bit surprised by the logic behind her quick reply.

There was a long period of silence between them, during which the king caressed the globes of her breasts and smoothed warm kisses upon the tender flesh of her throat. Then finally he spoke again. "Where do you reside within the palace, madam?"

"With the Earl and Countess of Marwood, sire," she answered him softly.

"I certainly cannot be seen stalking the palace corridors to seek your favors in Owen's apartments. There are those who would certainly leap to the wrong conclusions. You will be moved into your own apartments, Blaze. They are located directly above mine, and I may gain entry to them by using a small private inner staircase. People may speculate all they want, but no one will really know if or when I visit you."

"Oh, no, my lord, please! I will obey you in all things, but do not make my shame a public matter!" Blaze begged him.

"Why, sweetheart," Henry Tudor said in a kindly tone, "there is no shame in belonging to a king. I shall give orders that your apartments be refurbished at once. You shall move into them on May Day, when you will reign as Queen of Beauty and Love over all the court. Until that time I will remain a patient lover, only kissing and cuddling you, for there is a certain piquancy to abstinence."

He kept her in his lap for a few more minutes, taking his pleasure of her, and then lacing her bodice back up, he dismissed her with a gentle kiss. Blaze left the king's privy chamber, her head held high, despite her flaming cheeks, as she passed through the crowd of the king's gentlemen, who all smiled at her with knowing looks and winks.

Thomas Seymour stepped boldly before Blaze to block her way. "So, Lady Wyndham, you have saved your precious virtue for the king." He sneered.

"Better a king than a knave!" she snapped angrily, and pushing him aside, hurried from the royal apartments while behind her the room erupted into guffaws of delighted laughter.

Bliss knew! How could she know? Did everyone in the whole damned palace know of her humiliation? "Do not even speak to me," she warned her younger sister as she hurried into their apartments.

"Do not be a little fool, Blaze," replied Bliss, not one bit intimidated by her elder sibling. "My God, *you* have been singled out by the king!"

"I do not want to be singled out! And for what have I been singled out, Bliss? Are you aware that he seeks to bed me? Do you think I count it an honor to be the royal whore? Dear God, I wish I had never come to court! I wish I were safely home with my child! Why, oh why, did God take Edmund from me?" Then she burst into tears.

Bliss grasped her sister by her arms and shook her. "*Stop it!*" she commanded Blaze. "Stop it this instant! Would you rouse all of Greenwich? It would get back to the king, and he would be humiliated that the lady he has honored with his attentions finds them so odious! God's foot, Blaze! This is not some randy gentleman. This is the king we speak of, dearest."

"The king is the randiest gentleman of them all!" Blaze half-sobbed.

"You cannot refuse him, sister, and having been singled out by him, you must put on your prettiest face. No king's mistress ever wailed and wept publicly at her fate, and neither can you. Think, dearest, there are others involved in this too. If you offend the king, Blaze, his anger will not just fall upon you, but upon Owen and me as well. After all, you came to court under our protection," Bliss reasoned, leading her sister to the settle by the fire, where they sat down together. "Come, Blaze," she said more gently. "What is so terrible? The king wishes to make love to you, and he is, at least by reputation, an excellent lover. There is nothing so awful in that, is there?"

"The king is a married man, Bliss! Does that not distress you, for it certainly distresses me."

"The king has not cohabited with the queen in some time now, sister. Besides, it is not considered that a king is unfaithful to his queen if he but keeps a mistress. After all, he does not seek to set his mistress in his consort's place. The queen has politely turned a blind eye for many years to the king's pleasure. The only sins she found in Bessie Blount and Mary Boleyn were that they gave him living sons when she could not.

"The king means to do away with Catherine of Aragon one way or another, Blaze. He needs a wife who can give him sons, and he will have one. What a pity that you do not have a greater rank, sister, else you might aspire to Spanish Catherine's place."

"*Bliss!*" Blaze was horrified by her younger sister's statement.

Bliss shrugged prettily. "Well, at least you have stopped your weeping," she said practically.

"What am I to do, Bliss? Help me, sister, I beg of you!"

Bliss sighed. "Face the facts, Blaze. The king has made his intentions most clear. You have no real choice in the matter, except perhaps," she laughed, "in choosing the color of the draperies in your new apartments."

"How . . . ?" gasped Blaze.

"You are to be a king's mistress, little silly! This is not some hole-in-the-wall, havey-cavey *affaire de coeur* between a maid of honor and Sir Somebody of No Importance! Of course the king would install you in your own apartments, and quite near to him, I expect."

"Directly above him with a private inner staircase," said Blaze dryly. There was an almost macabre humor to the situation.

"Ohh," said Bliss, momentarily awed. "You will have a wonderful view of the river. We must engage you several more maidservants at once! When are you to move?"

"Do you think I want a gaggle of strange serving wenches gossiping my every kiss and sigh about the palace? Thank you, no! Heartha is all that I need," snapped Blaze.

"God's foot!" swore Bliss. "My Betty will be so envious. She has become quite ambitious since we came to court, and she has had high hopes for me, you know."

"*Bliss!* You would not be unfaithful to Owen surely?"

"Nay," laughed Bliss, shaking her head. "I could never be entirely unfaithful to my husband. Alas, I love the rogue! The king rarely considers happily married ladies anyway. He is too much the gentleman."

"What do you mean when you say you could not be *entirely* unfaithful to Owen?" demanded her elder sister.

"Welllll," allowed Bliss, "I do not object when a handsome gentleman steals a kiss or a cuddle. That is not *really* being unfaithful."

"Oh, Bliss," laughed Blaze helplessly, "I never realized until this moment how very different we really are. You are so much of the court, and I am as the king has duly noted, a little country girl."

"Has he kissed you?" Bliss was unfazed by her sister's words.

"Aye."

"Was it wonderful?"

"It was a kiss," said Blaze, trying not to remember how possessed she had really felt by his lips.

"God's foot, sister! Do not ever tell a man that he kissed you 'just a kiss.' Pretend if you must, particularly with the king. Swooning is always a fine device. It seems to give men a greater feeling of power. Has he caressed you?"

"Aye."

"*Aye? Just 'aye'? Tell me all!*" Bliss demanded.

"There is nothing to tell," said Blaze, rising from the settle. "Let me be, Bliss! I am exhausted, and I must rest. Even I, for all my country ways, know that I must appear at dinner this evening bright and smiling lest I cause more gossip than is already flying about Greenwich with regard to the king and me."

From that day onward Blaze was marked as royal property, and she was treated with sudden deference. It was that evening she noticed it first. People of great rank who had not deigned to admit her existence before were suddenly bowing, smiling, and nodding to her as she walked by. Invitations to card parties and picnics flowed into the Earl of Marwood's apartments. There was no more pretense on the king's part. His desire for Lady Wyndham was marked and quite obvious. Now she was bidden to sit by his side at the high board in the banqueting hall where he would offer her sips of wine from his own goblet, and feed her sweetmeats from his very plate.

Her behavior was perfect. Indeed, said Bliss, there had never been such an elegant royal mistress, for Blaze was charming to all, but carefully favored none. She was wise enough to know that it was unlikely the king's passion for her would last forever, and so she tried not to make enemies.

"I am not the king's mistress yet," Blaze protested to Bliss.

" 'Tis but a matter of time, and we both know it," said Bliss airily. "Do you think that after you move into your new apartments tomorrow, you will be able to so easily keep Henry Tudor at arm's length as you have been doing? He is more man than most, and I am surprised that you have kept him at bay this long. God's foot! Are you not excited? To be loved by a king! What heaven!"

What hell! thought Blaze silently. Bliss was right, of course, and after tomorrow she could not keep the king at arm's length. Tomorrow was May first and she would reign at the king's express command over the May Day festivities. Blaze Wyndham would be the royal court's Queen of Beauty and Love. Bliss had even brought her very own dressmaker down from London to fashion Blaze's gown. The woman was an artist in her own right, Blaze admitted to herself, but she detested her fawning manner. Why was it that everyone thought it such an honor to be a king's paramour? Was she wrong, and they right? Was there any wrong or right about the matter?

The first of May dawned bright and beautiful. Blaze and other young women of the court arose early according to custom to gather flowering branches and bright blossoms from the fields before the dew was off them. They would decorate Greenwich with their floral tribute. A royal-purple-and-gold-striped awninged pavilion with a raised dais had been set up upon the lawn where the Maypole had been erected. After the Mass, which everyone in the court was required to attend this morning, the festivities began.

The king was magnificently attired in a short, close-fitting doublet of spring-green silk brocade, heavily embroidered with gold threads, glittering orange citrines, and golden pearls. Should he remove his outer garment later in the afternoon, the sleeves of the doublet were slashed to show beneath the sleeves of his cream-colored silk shirt, which were all embroidered in tiny seed pearls. Over his doublet the king wore an open gown that came to his knee. It was of forest-green velvet, trimmed in a wide band of thick ermine that ran from the rounded neckline to its hem. It had wide puffed sleeves embroidered and banded in gold and pearls from beneath which the ruffled cuffs of his shirt showed. He wore haut-de-chausses of darker green, while his stockings, which accented his shapely calves, were spring green with narrow bands of gold thread for accent. His square-toed shoes were bejeweled.

His thinning red-gold hair was cut in the French fashion, straight across his forehead, and he wore a flat green bonnet upon his head that was decorated with three ostrich tips. His thick neck rose above his upper garments, and over them Henry wore several magnificent chains of gold, some with emerald squares, others studded with colored gemstones. Upon each of his fingers he wore a fine gold ring, some of which were bejeweled. His costume had been chosen to complement that of his ladylove.

Blaze's silk gown, which she wore over several silk petticoats, was of a bright spring green with a bell-shaped skirt. Its cream-colored underskirt was embroidered with daisies and primroses fashioned with gold thread, and studded with orange citrines. The entire underskirt was scattered over with small golden-hued pearls, and the sleeves of her gown were slashed even as the king's were. It was an extremely rich-looking garment and worthy of a queen. She wore a fine rope of pearls about her slender neck as well as the fine golden chain that Bliss had given her on Twelfth Night. At the king's request her hair was left long and flowing like a maiden's and unadorned but for a cream-colored silk ribbon embroidered entirely with seed pearls.

"That honey-colored hair of Lady Wyndham's is extraordinary," remarked Charles Brandon to the king. "What a pity that caps are the fashion."

Blaze danced with eleven other young women including Bliss and Lady Adela Marlowe, both of whom she had included in her party, her word being law in this matter, as she discovered to her surprise. So this was power, she thought, considering whether she enjoyed it or not. Perhaps the price was too high. Around and around the Maypole they went, weaving in and out of the intricate figure, their multicolored ribbons held high. When the Maypole was completely wrapped, each lady sought among the gentlemen for a partner with whom to dance upon the chamomile lawn. Blaze of necessity chose the king.

Together they danced first the elegant dances of the court, and then, remembering the day, the more lively country dances. The king was an excellent and tireless dancer and few could keep up with him, but Blaze easily did. For a moment she forgot her situation, and simply enjoyed the day. Soon her cheeks were flushed a delicate rose, and her laughter sounded amid the noise and music of the festivities as he lifted her high, and she laughed artlessly down into his face. Finally in fairness to the others who, at this point, could barely keep up with the king and Blaze, they ceased dancing and, taking goblets of wine from a passing servant, walked among members of the court.

Suddenly there were other men casting secretly envious glances at the lovely Lady Wyndham, despite Henry Tudor, and Blaze was chatting and laughing more easily than she ever had since coming to court. The king watched her, his lust for her growing. Her beautiful bosom was heaving as she now caught her breath. The others watched her too, some even daring to openly covet what Henry Tudor thought of as his, and it was then he realized that until he possessed her fully, she would not really be his. She was so beautiful and so innocent, his little country girl. He had to have her! He would wait no longer! God only knew he had been patient. Sometimes it was better to take command when a woman resisted. Blaze's laughter rose above the others as her sister recounted a particularly amusing anecdote, and the king's control snapped.

Grasping tightly at her hand, he pulled her away from the group, saying, "Come, madam! We have other business." He hurried her across the lawn, not caring about the surprised looks and stares of those about them. He hurried her into the palace, where he led her to his privy chamber.

"What is it, my lord?" Blaze cried, worried that she had offended him somehow, and fearful for those she loved.

Henry slammed the door to the room shut. "*What is it, madam?* I will tell you what it is. You haunt my hours both waking and sleeping! I offer you my love, and you demur! I desire you above all women, and you resist! I have been patient, madam, but I will be patient no longer! I want you for my own, and I shall have you! I shall have you here, and I shall have you now!" He yanked her into his arms and kissed her fiercely, his hard mouth bruising hers with his raging hunger.

Blaze put her hands up to fend him off once more, but the king would have none of it.

"Nay, madam! I will no more accept your reluctance! *No more!*" He half-dragged her across the room to where a long table of polished golden oak stood, and forcing her about so she faced it, he said, "Bend over, madam, and place the palms of your hands flat upon the tabletop."

"My lord, I beg of you—" she began, but he cut her abruptly off.

"Speak again without my permission, madam, except in passion, and I swear I shall give your child into Tom Seymour's keeping," he threatened. "Now do as I have bid you!"

Slowly she placed her palms upon the table, bending slightly from the waist as she did. I must not cry, she silently warned herself. Nyssa's very life may depend upon what I do. I cannot repulse him any longer, and if I displease him, my daughter will suffer.

The king reached out and lifted her heavy silk skirts with their petticoats up, and tucked them firmly into the waistband of the skirt. For what seemed an eternity there was silence as Henry contemplated her naked posterior, made all the more fetching by her tightly banded dark stockings against the creaminess of her fair skin. "Spread your legs," he ordered her. "Aye that's enough. Now bend your pretty neck, Blaze, to make your submission to your king more fully. Aye, sweetheart, very good."

She felt him unlacing her bodice, yanking roughly at the silk, then moving his hands around to her front to pull away the fabric so that her breasts tumbled forth from her gown. She muffled her gasp. The king fumbled to undo his heavily bejeweled codpiece, and his male organ, already engorged with his lust, burst forth.

Leaning over her slightly, Henry pushed her soft hair aside and kissed the back of her neck. "Do you know how very much your king desires you, sweetheart? You have made me wild with my hunger for you."

She felt him grasping her about the hips with his large hands, his fingers clutching at the soft flesh. She felt his manhood, hard and hot, probing, searching, seeking to find its way to her feminine passage, and finally successful, thrusting without preamble into her helpless flesh.

"Ahhhhhhh," groaned the king as he pushed deeply into her, "now has my bird truly found its way into your sweet little nest!" and he began to pump her vigorously with long, deliberate strokes for some minutes. When he had taken the edge from his hunger, he stopped, though he remained lodged deeply within her. Leaning over her so that his weight pressed her partly onto the table, he reached for and found her naked breasts. "How I have grown to love these little apples of yours, sweetheart," he told her playing with her nipples, pinching and pulling, and teasing until to her great shock Blaze found that her body was beginning to respond to the king's passionate lovemaking.

"Ohhhh," she whispered, surprised, feeling her hips, seemingly of their own accord, begin to press back and forth against him.

Henry chuckled, understanding her confusion. His little country girl had not known that even a chaste woman's body, skillfully loved, would respond to a man other than her husband. He began to work his own lower body in rhythm with hers, all the while continuing to play with her full breasts.

"Ohh, my lord," Blaze gasped, shamed, but unable to help herself. "Ohhh! What is this magic that you work upon me? Ohhhh!"

"Only the age-old magic of a man and a woman, sweetheart," he replied. "God's foot, you are sweet, and so very, very tight! I do not believe that my big boy has ever lodged himself in so sweet and tight a little sheath!" His movements became more furious as he worked her.

Oh, God, Blaze thought, this cannot be! It cannot! I am responding to him as I did to Edmund, yet I do not love him! I do not! Why can he make me feel this way? She was beginning to lose control of her very emotions as she had already lost control of her frail and female body. The king's huge hardness was probing her deeply, and she felt the pleasing languor of passion beginning to overtake her, catching her up in its whirling vortex. She did not even hear herself begin to whimper, nor did she realize that at her crisis she cried out the king's name.

Suddenly she found herself in his arms, weeping, and wondering if she would ever be able to understand this world which was so different in its morals and values than was hers. The king's hand soothed her loose soft hair, and he murmured softly against her ear, "There, my sweetheart, now the dreadful deed is done, and you will never be afraid of me again, will you?"

"How can this be?" Blaze asked. "How is it you can make me feel this way?" She hid her face against his broad chest, unable to look him directly in the eyes.

"My little country girl," the king explained gently, "a woman's body is like a fine instrument. Be her face fair or plain, her body is a delicate and sensitive thing. I am a skilled player of this female instrument. Perhaps the most skilled player in the world, although the French François brags that he is, the pox-ridden coxcomb! Perhaps he must brag so, for he is a great, gawking, ugly man, unlike your king." Henry continued stroking her hair. "This has been just a foretaste of my passion for you, Blaze.

Tonight I will come to you, and together we will find even greater pleasures, I promise you."

Greater pleasures? She almost swooned at his words. The dark passion she had felt with him frightened her, for it was so all-consuming. The wonderful passion she had felt with Edmund had left her feeling content and strong. With the king she felt drained, for she sensed that he wanted to possess not only her body, but her soul as well. Yet she could not flee him for her baby's sake.

"Are you recovered enough to stand straight so I may relace you, sweetheart?" the king asked her.

She nodded, and stood quietly while his fingers expertly redid her laces. Silently she walked to a small mirror framed in silver that sat upon another table, and looking in it, saw herself. She did not appear to have changed. Quickly she fluffed her hair, undoing her pearled ribbon, tying it back neatly. She caught a glimpse of him as he replaced his now flaccid male part within the confines of the bejeweled codpiece, but even now his manhood seemed extraordinarily large. She could only imagine what it had been like fully engorged. Tonight, she thought and shivered, she would learn the answer to that unsought mystery.

His hands dropped upon her shoulders, and he turned her about to face him. He was so very tall, she thought, and she felt so very small beside him. "Can you not smile a little at me, Blaze?" he asked, and for a moment she detected a small poignancy in his voice.

He is lonely, she thought, surprised. In the midst of all this great court of his, he is lonely *and* he is sad! This sudden new knowledge, despite his brutal treatment of her, made Blaze sympathetic toward the king. For a moment she had heard the echo of a boy in his voice. Making the effort, she smiled a little smile at him. "You must give me time to accustom myself to this new state of affairs, my lord," she said softly.

"Tell me I did not hurt you, sweetheart!" he cried, catching her to his great chest. "I could not help myself, Blaze! Suddenly I wanted you, and I could not wait! I am not a man who is cruel to his women. Nay, sweetheart, if I have any fault, it is that I am too softhearted towards the fair sex."

"You did not hurt me, my lord. Perhaps you frightened me at first, but you did not hurt me," she reassured him. He was vulnerable. As vulnerable as any mere man, despite his kinghood. How strange it had never occurred to her that a king for all his royalty was no more than a simple mortal. A powerful mortal, but a mortal nonetheless. It made what she had just endured, and would endure in the future, just a little bit easier to bear. "Should we not rejoin the court lest the lack of our presence be spoken about, my lord?"

"You will call me Henry in private," he said, taking her arm, and leading her forth, they rejoined the court.

"God's foot," swore Charles Brandon softly to the Duke of Norfolk as he saw them walking across the lawns, "so he's finally had a taste!"

"What makes you think it?" returned Lord Howard.

"He has suddenly become jovial, while the lady is sweetly subdued. Aye, he's had the first taste, and from the looks of him, 'twas not enough. He'll want more!"

"Now the question is," replied the Duke of Norfolk, "whether she will last as long as my lady Tailboys, or my niece Mary. And will she too give him a son? It is all to the good. Each time one of these pretty diversions gives him a boy, he becomes even more convinced of the rightness of his cause in ridding himself of his Spanish queen. If his holiness will just cooperate with us, we will soon have some nubile young princess wed to his grace, and spawning England healthy sons."

The May Day festivities continued under the benevolent rule of the court's fair Queen of Beauty and Love. There was a wrestling match, and the king challenged all comers, beating them handily. Blaze rewarded him with a laurel crown and a warm public kiss. There was a mock joust, the tips of the lances being couched carefully. Blaze and the king sat beneath the awninged pavilion sipping sweet golden wine while the combatants fought until only the Duke of Suffolk remained, emerging victorious from the fray to receive a jeweled cup from the May Queen as his reward.

"What, m'lady, no kiss to the champion?" teased the duke.

"Nay, my lord," Blaze answered quickly. "My kisses are reserved for my lord, the king, alone."

The butts were set up, and many of the men stripped their elegant gowns off so they might shoot in comfort. The king was an excellent archer, and very much enjoyed the sport. He proposed a contest, but his gentlemen laughingly declined, saying that no one could triumph over so fine an archer as Henry Tudor, and they preferred to shoot for the mere sport of it.

As afternoon slipped into evening tables were set up upon the great lawn at Greenwich, and a country-style banquet was held, to be followed by more dancing upon the green. Gradually, however, the guests began to slip away into the shadows in pairs, and the king leaning over said softly so that only Blaze might hear him, "Go now, and make yourself familiar with your new apartments, sweetheart. I will come to you soon."

She did not argue, knowing it futile, but instead arose, saying softly as she did, "Give me an hour, my lord. I would bathe first."

His nod was barely discernible, and she hurried off.

"Was she worth the wait?" murmured his brother-in-law, Charles Brandon, silkily, slipping into the seat that Blaze had just vacated.

A small smile touched the king's lips. "Aye!"

"And if, Hal, you compared her to Bessie or Mary, how would she fare?"

"She is better, brother Charles, for other than her husband she has known no man. She is as sweet as a virgin without being a virgin, yet her lack of experience holds great charm. I shall enjoy teaching her the things she obviously does not know."

"You are to be envied, Hal. Lady Wyndham is a rare little creature. I wonder how well you will like your creation, however, when you have schooled her to your satisfaction."

"She will be the closest thing to perfection as any woman can get then, Charles, *and* she will still be mine."

The Duke of Suffolk laughed, and affably raised his goblet to toast his monarch, half in admiration, half in envy. Henry accepted the toast with a boyish grin, but his mind was on his ladylove.

Despite her situation Blaze would have had to be a saint not to adore the beautiful apartment which was now hers. It was not overly large, but it was spacious and comfortable. There was a lovely Day Room with its oak-paneled walls, large leaded-paned windows that overlooked the River Thames, and a fireplace. The polished floors had wool carpets in dark blue and reds that had been given the king by a group of London merchants. The furniture was made of gracefully carved golden oak. There were porcelain bowls of fresh flowers and potpourri set about to freshen the air in the rooms, and the candles set within the silver candlesticks were of the purest beeswax.

Blaze also had a small paneled dining room with a table that could seat a dozen along with a fine sideboard. There would be times when the king would want to eat privately with her, or perhaps she or he might choose to entertain friends. There was a dressing room for Blaze's growing wardrobe, and a separate room for Heartha. Both the dining room and the tiring woman's sleeping chamber had their own fireplaces.

"Such luxury, m'lady! Never have I seen the like, even at RiversEdge," said Heartha, awed.

"Indeed, such luxury, Heartha, but at what price?" said Blaze sadly.

" 'Tis no shame to you, m'lady, that the king has chosen you for his pleasure," the tiring woman responded. "You are a widowed lady, and the queen is already put aside."

Blaze shook her head silently. Heartha had as quickly put away her country morality as had Bliss's servant, Betty. She looked about her lovely new bedchamber. The bed was extraordinarily big as it must be in order to accommodate as large a man as the king. Henry was not fat, but he was tall, and big-boned with a thick neck and limbs like tree trunks. The bed was hung with crimson velvet draperies, and the linen sheets were scented with lavender. The bedchamber walls were of oak linenfold paneling, and there was a large fireplace opposite the bed whose bedposts were carved round with vines and flowers, and quite pretty. There were matching candlestands with silver tapersticks on either side of the bed, and there was a long table before the large leaded-paned windows that overlooked the river, as well as several chairs in the room. Despite the generosity of the furnishings, there was still more than enough room within the chamber to walk about.

A large oaken tub was set up within Blaze's dressing room, and with Heartha's help she bathed herself in warm violet-scented water. Heartha dried her mistress with towels that had been heated before the fire, and then dusted her with delicate powder. She then slipped over Blaze's head a diaphanous night garment of sheerest black silk whose long skirt was a mass of narrow little pleats. The gown had long sleeves that fell to points over her hands, and a V neckline that revealed more than it concealed.

"Where did this nightrail come from?" demanded Blaze. "It is certainly not one of mine."

"It is a gift from my lady FitzHugh, mistress," replied Heartha. "She sent it this afternoon with strict instructions that you were to wear it tonight. I ain't never seen one quite like it meself."

Blaze laughed at Heartha's words. How very like Bliss to send her such a thing. "Nay, Heartha," she answered her servant, "nor have I ever seen anything like it. It looks like something that a French courtesan would wear, but no matter. If my sister thinks it proper, then who am I to say, being but a country mouse to Bliss's court cat."

" 'Tis good to hear you laugh, m'lady," said Heartha. "I know you've not been happy these last weeks." She took up a brush, and seating her mistress, began to brush her hair.

"I have decided not to fight my fate, Heartha. How can I, under these particular circumstances?" responded Blaze.

Heartha brushed her lady's hair with long strokes until it shone with warm golden-brown lights. Suddenly a door hidden within the paneled wall of the bedroom opened, and the king, dressed in a quilted blue velvet chamber robe, stepped through into the chamber. Startled, Heartha dropped the hairbrush, which clattered to the floor.

"And whom have we here, sweetheart?" said the king with a smile. He was being his most charming.

Blaze arose and curtsied. "This is Heartha, my tiring woman, my lord king."

Heartha, regaining her wits, curtsied low before Henry.

"And have you been with your mistress long, Heartha?" asked the king.

"Since she was wed with my lord Edmund, sire," said Heartha. "I was born at RiversEdge."

The king drew a small gold ring from his little finger, and held it out to the servant. "Take this small token of my thanks for your loyal service to Lady Wyndham, Heartha. I know that you will continue to care well for her."

Heartha's mouth fell open with her surprise, and only when Blaze sharply poked her did she reach out, and curtsying once again, take the gold ring from the king. "Oh, thank you, your grace! Be sure I will continue my good care of my lady," she babbled as she backed from the room.

"You have quite taken her breath away." Blaze smiled. " 'Twas a kind thing to do, my lord. She will remember it always, and someday tell her grandchildren that the king actually spoke with her, and gave her the ring from his finger."

"She has children?" he asked.

"Several, but she is widowed, and they grown and serving the Wyndhams also."

"Let me look at you," said Henry, and set her back from him. Slowly his blue eyes moved over her form, and then he said, "The gown is most provocative, madam. Walk about the room for me," and when she did, he smiled broadly. "I can see your beautiful bare legs when you walk."

"The garment is a gift from my sister," said Blaze.

"The lovely Lady FitzHugh knows well how to gild the lily," the king remarked, "but I can see the gown does not please you."

"Perhaps, sire, I find the gown a bit too obvious," Blaze said quietly. She was no longer quite so afraid of the man before her. Only the feelings he engendered within her were frightening.

The king reached out, and with a deliberate motion tore the black silk gown from her, and flung the pieces into the fire, where they disappeared with a quick *hisssss*. Blaze, shocked, nonetheless moved not a muscle.

The king studied her for what seemed a long time, and then he said,

"This was how I longed to see you, as God made you in nature's estate, and I am not disappointed." He drew her across the room to set her before the pier glass. Standing behind her, he slipped his arms about her so that he might cup her breasts within his hands. The weight of the warm flesh against his palms was almost unbearably sensuous.

"What magnificent tits you possess, madam," he murmured, and bending down, placed a kiss upon her rounded shoulder. His thumbs encircled her nipples in a leisurely fashion.

Blaze sighed deeply, and as she did so, she felt a familiar languor spreading through her limbs. What was it that he did to her to arouse such feelings within her body? She had no love for him. He was her king. He had threatened her child's welfare unless she yielded her body to him. He had forced her cruelly, and yet at his touch her body was afire. Did all women behave so? She leaned back against the king, and her round breasts pushed themselves forward within his tender grasp. Through half-closed eyes she saw him smile.

"So, sweetheart, you begin to feel desire already, do you?" His lips began an exploration of the curve of her slender throat, lingering at the soft junction between neck and shoulder. "Ah, lovey, you set my heart afire!" Turning her about, he lifted her up into his arms, and carrying her across the bedchamber, he laid her gently upon the large bed.

Blaze lay quietly watching the king as he first removed his quilted robe, and then his white silk nightshirt. Her eyes widened at his nudity. If her body was beautiful to his eyes, then his was magnificent in hers. His shoulders were wide and well-proportioned. His chest was broad, and covered in a mat of tight reddish-gold curls. It tapered down to a neat waist, and slim hips. His legs were long and very shapely. They, too, were covered in red-gold hair. At the junction of his belly and his thighs was a triangle of auburn-gold curls from which jutted his manhood. Seeing the weapon that had earlier probed her flesh, she was amazed at its size, and that he had been able to enter her at all.

He laughed at her look, amused by her silence. "Aye, sweetheart, here is the big boy that earlier played havoc within your sweet sheath! Look on him, and know that he is well-rested and once again hungry for the taste of your body. He'll not be so quick now, either, for his earlier bout with you has but whetted his prodigious appetite." The king flung himself down upon the bed, and pulled her atop him so that she was looking down into his face, the nipples of her sensitive breasts brushing against the stiff curls upon his chest. "Now kiss me, my little country girl," he begged her. "I long for your pretty lips."

She bent, her mouth closed over his in a shy kiss. She had never been atop a man, and her cheeks grew warm with the thoughts her position aroused in her. He kissed her back, his lips demanding, his tongue pressing into her mouth to tease her so she was assailed by feelings of both passion and of guilt. He felt her hesitation.

"Nay, sweetheart," he whispered against her mouth, "don't go away from me. Do you not know that I love you, Blaze?" Gently he rolled her over onto her back, and his eyes looked into hers. "Your king loves you, my pretty little country girl. He lays his heart at your feet. Would you scorn him, lovey? Could you be that cruel?"

"Sire, it is your poor wife I feel guilt over," Blaze said, not quite daring to believe the wonderfully romantic words he had just uttered. Did she dare believe him, or was it merely something a man said to coax a reluctant lover? Her lack of experience was so damned regrettable!

"Darling Blaze," the king said, "I have no wife. My own clerics assure me that the marriage performed between me and the Princess of Aragon all those years ago was not lawful in God's eyes because she had been wed to my brother, Arthur. That is why God has denied me living legitimate sons. My *marriage* has been a terrible sin, and in fact it was no real marriage. My sons by Bessie Blount and Mary Boleyn are but God's way of showing me that with a lawful wife I may have the sons I so deeply desire.

"You, my darling, are widowed, and I a bachelor whose legal rights will soon be confirmed by the pope. I know it! We may love each other freely, Blaze! Do not deny me your heart any longer, lovey, for you will break mine if you do!"

"Oh, Hal!" she cried, knowing that this was madness, but unable to resist him. "Love me, my lord king! Love me!" She would regret this, instinct warned her. He would betray her in the end, yet she had been so damnably lonely since Edmund's death, and she frankly admitted to herself that she had missed the pleasures of a man and a woman. The king was not to be denied. Why should she not enjoy it? No one in the court thought the worse of her for it. Indeed she was constantly being congratulated for her wonderful coup in gaining the king's attentions.

Realizing his victory, Henry Tudor covered her face with his excited kisses. His head moved to her breasts, where he tasted and loved first one round globe, and then the other. His teeth tenderly bit at the soft flesh, sending pins and needles of delight through her whole body. He sucked vigorously upon the nipples, causing her to sob with her pleasure. His knee pressed a message between her thighs, and they fell open before him. Fitting himself between her legs, he guided his great manhood to the mark, thrusting into her in one long, smooth movement that caused her to cry out in pleasured pain. Slowly he withdrew himself from her, and then even more slowly he reinserted himself. Each slow withdrawal became like an agony for her; and each time he drove back into her he seemed to push more deeply inside her.

A sound very like a whimper came from her throat, and her nails raked down his strong, broad back. Her hips thrust fiercely back up at him each time he filled her full of himself, and reaching her first crisis of passion, she cried aloud, digging her nails even more deeply into his muscled flesh.

"So," the king growled into her ear, pleased, "my little country kitten has sharp claws. Then she must like my fucking! Tell me, sweetheart! You do like it, don't you?"

"Aye! Aye!" she panted. "Ohh, my Hal! Do not cease this wondrous torture! Do not cease it, I beg of you!"

The more he gave, the more she seemed to desire. At last, he thought, he had found a woman whose passion matched his! He would not have believed it possible before tonight that this sweet little country innocent was, beneath her demure manner, a raging tigress. Fiercely he pumped her until finally with a gasp she swooned beneath him, and he poured himself into her parched garden.

The color had drained from her face, but as he lay panting his own exhaustion, it slowly returned. Rising from the bed, the king moved across the room to a table which held a decanter of strong red wine. Pouring out two gobletfuls, he returned to the warmth of the bed, drawing the covers over them both. Gently he drew her into his embrace, cradling her within the curve of an arm, putting a goblet to her lips, encouraging her to drink. Half-coughing, she swallowed the heady wine, finding it an excellent restorative. Sure of her comfort now, he quaffed his own wine down in three gulps.

"You have pleased me, Blaze," he said finally. "You have greatly pleased your king."

"You have pleased me also, my lord," she said.

He laughed, realizing that no woman had ever, ever said such a thing to him. He had always assumed of course that he had pleased his women, but none before this one had openly admitted to it. "You are a breath of fresh air in my life, Blaze Wyndham. I have never loved anyone quite like you in my whole life."

There it was again! That word. *Love.* How easily he used it, and yet did he really mean it? What difference did it make? She was his mistress for better or worse until he decided otherwise, and despite her country naiveté, Blaze knew that he would eventually discard her. Even if the church did actually dissolve his marriage to the queen, Henry Tudor would not rewed with the daughter of a poor baronet from Herefordshire despite her fecundity. He would marry a princess.

The king dozed, his leonine head upon her shoulder. Beneath the kingly strength was a boy. She saw it now in his face, all naked and unguarded in sleep. She felt almost maternal toward him, and smiled to herself in the dimness of the firelit room. He did not make love like a boy, of that she was certain despite her previous lack of experience. It was a loyal subject's duty to serve the king, she thought, and so she would serve him with her body in her way as long as it pleased him.

He said that he loved her, and she supposed that in his own fashion he did, or at least he believed that he did. Henry Tudor was not a mean man, and so she knew that one day when he was through with her he would provide for her in some fashion. He would probably choose a husband for her, and unless the man were a beast, she would obediently remarry, for she understood now that a woman needed a man's protection to survive in this world. Until then she was safe in the king's arms, and more important, Nyssa was safe. At least in that she had not failed Edmund.

Chapter 10

The summer progress had begun, and the court moved from Greenwich to nearby Eltham. Like Greenwich, Eltham was set within the green confines of a great parkland. Here their days were spent in hunting and hawking, playing at bowls upon the green, shooting at archery butts. The king amused himself by teaching Blaze to shoot, and to his amazement her eye was quite accurate.

"By God, sweetheart," he told her approvingly one warm summer's afternoon, "I shall enlist you in the ranks should ever war break out."

The weather was so lovely that they frequently stayed out-of-doors until long after dark. There were picnics, and dancing, and boating upon a lake that was situated within the royal park. The king often retired early those summer evenings, for he found he was not easily tiring of his new mistress, and he remained fascinated that her appetite for passion was as large as his. Yet there was nothing unwholesome in her attitude.

The Quiet Mistress. 'Twas a phrase that Cardinal Wolsey coined to describe Blaze, and the nickname stuck. Unlike her predecessors, Elizabeth Blount and Mary Boleyn, Blaze Wyndham did not use her place in the king's bed for a power base. There were those who thought her a fool not to gain every advantage she could during her tenure as the king's favorite. They could not understand a woman who would not take such a golden opportunity to help advance her family and friends, as was certainly only natural. A few, men like Thomas More, understood that the beautiful young widow had not sought the king's attention, and though she served the king in her sensual capacity, she preferred to do it with as much dignity and modesty as was possible for a lady in her position. It was certain that she made no enemies, and even those who thought her a fool for her apparent lack of ambition were won over by her sweetness, her good manners, her clever wit, and her charm.

The court moved again, this time to Richmond Palace in Surrey. Sheen Manor had once been located on the site of what was now Richmond Palace. When the king had been a lad of seven, Sheen had burned to the ground one Christmas season when the royal family had been in residence. King Henry VII had rebuilt it within two years, renaming it Richmond to remind him of the earldom which had been his title before he overcame King Richard III and took England's crown for himself.

Richmond was a large Gothic residence built about a paved court. The royal apartments were in the privy lodging, which was decorated with fourteen turrets and had more windows than Blaze had ever seen in one building. The court arrived at Richmond to find that Queen Catherine and Princess Mary were in residence.

Blaze was embarrassed. Henry's reassurances regarding his marital state had salved her conscience until now. The king could not ask the queen to leave lest he appear mean-spirited, and besides, he loved his daughter, whom he had not seen in some time now. Blaze's apartment at Richmond was therefore placed at a discreet distance from both the queen's and the king's.

Catherine of Aragon was forty years old, and the toll of her years of futile childbearing showed cruelly upon her once pretty face, which stared out upon the world from beneath her heavy architectural headdress. Though she wore the most rich-looking and elegant clothing that Blaze had ever seen, her small stature and her plumpness rendered them wretchedly unfashionable. She was sallow of complexion and dark-eyed, and Blaze noted that the king did not speak to her at all when they sat side by side at the high board.

Blaze now sat with her sister and brother-in-law at meals, and Bliss was not silent on the subject of what she considered the queen's interference. "The old crow," she muttered one evening as they ate. "Just look at her sitting so smugly by his side. It is only a matter of time until she is cast away entirely, and yet she sits there pretending that all is as it once was."

"Hush, Bliss, do not be cruel. The queen loves the king. Can you not see it?"

"You love the king too!" whispered Bliss.

"I have not the right to love him, whatever my feelings toward him may be," replied Blaze.

Love. No, she did not love him. At least not in the way in which she had loved Edmund Wyndham. Her adoring and gentle husband who had loved her with tenderness was nothing at all like this all-powerful monarch who loved her with such a wild and frenzied passion. His great and deep desire still frightened her a little.

She had grown to like him, however. Henry Tudor was a man for pillow talk, and she had learned all about the childhood in which he had been but second best to his favored elder brother, Arthur, Prince of Wales. He spoke of how, believing it was his dying father's wish, he had married the Princess of Aragon. He spoke of the pain they had both endured at the loss of their son, the six-week-old Prince of Wales, and the string of stillbirths and miscarriages that had followed. "All sons," the king lamented. It was then he realized, he told her, that God was displeased with him, and sure enough his bishops had shown him a biblical passage that said a man who took his brother's wife to wife did an unclean thing. Suddenly, he explained, he knew in his heart that his marriage was in reality no marriage.

Blaze had listened as he unburdened himself to her of these and other sundry thoughts. He had asked her in his turn many questions, and she had told him of her happy childhood at Ashby of her family with its eight daughters and three sons, her wonderful marriage to Edmund Wyndham, of Nyssa, and of the loss of her infant son when her husband had died.

"So your mother has borne eleven children, and lost not one," the king said admiringly. "What fine stock you come from, my little country girl! Would I could make you my wife, and we breed up a large family of sons and daughters."

"You must wed a princess, Hal," she told him, showing him that she truly understood her position in his life.

The summer progress moved on to Hampton Court. Built by Cardinal Wolsey, and furnished magnificently, it now belonged to the king. Though the cardinal struggled to resolve the king's marital difficulties, the bureaucracy of the papacy moved slowly, and in an effort to placate his king, and forestall his fall from favor, which was lobbied for by many, the cardinal had parted with his home just a month ago. They stayed but a week, and moved on to Windsor.

The king did not like Windsor but it fell along his route to Woodstock where he intended going to hunt. Woodstock was small and rustic, and there would not be room for the entire court, most of which along with the queen would be left behind at Windsor. The night before their departure from Windsor, for Blaze was to go with the king, the king's mistress was bearded by his daughter in a passageway. Blaze curtsied to the nine-year-old Princess Mary, and stepped aside, believing the child and her attendants wished to pass. The girl, like her mother, was of sallow complexion with dark eyes, but her auburn hair was lovely, Blaze thought.

The princess stared at Blaze with open hostility. "My governess says that you are a bad woman," the child said fiercely. "You have stolen my father's love from my mother, and you sleep in his bed, which is against God's law! For that you will burn in hellfire!"

Blaze gasped. There was nothing she could say to defend herself from the child, who then stalked past, her attendants smiling smugly at the blushing countess. In the banquet hall that night, however, a page came to tell Blaze that the queen desired her presence. Even Bliss whitened at the news. There was nothing the young widowed dowager Countess of Langford could do but follow the boy to where the queen sat with her ladies. Blaze curtsied low, her head bowed to hide her flaming cheeks.

"You may rise, Lady Wyndham," said the queen, and Blaze stood to look into the face of the scorned Catherine. The queen smiled a small smile. "I understand that my daughter, the Princess Mary, showed an extreme lack of good manners and want of delicacy toward you this afternoon, Lady Wyndham. For that she has been punished. I hope you will forgive her. Mary is young. She adores her father, and she does not understand him as we do."

"Forgive me, madam," said Blaze softly. "I mean you no harm."

"I know that," replied the queen. "You are not like the others, Lady Wyndham. I know all about you, in fact. I am not yet as helpless as some would believe. I know my husband, and the things he does to gain his way. Be careful. You are a good woman, I know. Do not let him hurt you, as he has so many others. You may go now."

Blaze curtsied once again, and made her way back to where Bliss was awaiting her.

"What did the old crow want?" demanded Bliss.

Blaze shook her head. "Poor lady," she said.

"What did the Princess of Aragon desire of you this evening, my little country girl?" the king demanded of her bluntly later on.

"If I tell you," replied Blaze, "you must not be angry, my Hal. 'Twas nothing serious, and my heart goes out to the poor lady, who has certainly behaved toward me with great generosity."

"I promise then," he said, putting an arm about her.

"Your daughter called me a 'bad woman' early this afternoon. The queen apologized for her, and said that the princess had been punished for her behavior. She said that Mary's excuse was that she loves you."

"The little wench grows more like her mother every day. I should remove her from Catherine's influence, and the influence of her priests, lest they spoil the child if it has not already been done." He pulled her into his lap and kissed her, his hand fumbling with her plump breasts. "Put them both from your mind, Blaze," he told her. "I would make love to you. There is something special that I would teach you tonight."

"What is that, my lord?" she asked him.

They were naked within his chamber, and standing, he tipped her gently from his lap. "I would have you kneel before me, sweetheart," and when she had obediently complied, he said, "Now take my big boy in your pretty little hands, and place it within your mouth. Suckle upon it even as I suckle upon your beautiful breasts."

"Hal," she pleaded with him, "I dare not do such a thing! Surely 'tis not right!"

"*Obey me!*" he snapped. "*Immediately!*" His voice was hard and cruel, and grasping her by the hair with one hand, his other lifted his half-hardened manhood and forced it toward her reluctant lips.

Blaze knew she must obey him. Closing her eyes so she need not look upon her shame, she parted her lips and took him within her mouth.

The king groaned, but the sound was one of pleasure. "Suckle upon it," he said more gently. "Play with it, using your sweet tongue . . . ahh, yes! Yes!"

She obeyed him, at first unwillingly, but then Blaze found there was a certain naughtiness about what they did that excited her greatly. When the king bid her cease, and laid her back upon the bed to repay her in kind, she gasped with her own pleasure. Never had she imagined that such a thing was possible. His flickering, probing tongue did for her even what his great manhood did. She was totally amazed.

In the morning it was raining, and it continued to rain for the next few days without ceasing. The king was irritated. "We will return to Greenwich," he finally decided. "Woodstock in the pouring rain is unbearable, for it is a simple lodge. We shall hunt there in the autumn instead."

The entire court gratefully returned to Greenwich, although the queen was sent to stay at Eltham. It was September, and Mistress Anne Boleyn came back to court. The sister of Mary Boleyn, she had been sent down from court to her home at Hever Castle in Kent the year before for her bad behavior. Anne Boleyn was nothing at all like her elder sister, for where Mary was round and plump, Anne was slender almost to the point of thinness. Mary was an English rose with fair skin, warm brown eyes, and chestnut-blond hair. Anne's complexion was somewhat sallow, her long straight hair black as a raven's wing, her eyes like onyx. Mary Boleyn was sweet of face, but her younger sister had the sharp features of a little cat. Mary Boleyn was liked for her charming, almost childish good nature. Anne was not well-liked, for she was thought to be overproud, and she had a nasty temper.

"An ugly crow! A nightbird," Cardinal Wolsey called her, and Anne Boleyn marked him down as an enemy upon whom she would have her eventual revenge.

The Duke of Norfolk looked upon his young relative, and considered best how he might use her to his own advantage. Then he decided it was better to watch and wait before making that critical decision, or before allying himself openly with the wench.

Henry Tudor found himself quite unwillingly fascinated by Mistress Boleyn. She was no beauty, but she was quick of wit, which he counted an equal virtue. The king contemplated the possibility of bedding his former mistress's little sister, and found that the sheer peversity of the idea appealed to him. What if he could get a son on her as well? It was an amusing thought, but alas Mistress Boleyn had a suitor in the presence of young Lord Percy. The church was being very difficult in the matter of the Princess of Aragon, and he had a lovely mistress of whom he was still quite fond.

Yet as he watched Mistress Boleyn making her way through his court, always gowned in the most elegant fashions, and surrounded by a group of amusing young people including Henry Norris, Henry Percy, and her brother, George Boleyn, he was more drawn to her than he would have liked to be. More drawn than he had ever been to any woman, and this caused the king to feel guilt about Blaze, and guilt was not a feeling Henry Tudor enjoyed. Still, he could not be angry at Blaze, for his little country girl was not simply a perfect mistress—the most perfect he had ever had—but she had become his friend and confidante as well. How could he be so mean-spirited as to cast her off so he might pursue Mistress Anne Boleyn? Then it came to the king that what he needed was to find a husband for Blaze so she would not be left helpless to the lechers and roués of his court. He put his mind to it, but he could think of no one worthy enough.

"What am I to do, Will Somers?" he asked his fool, who was no fool at all, but the only other real confidant in his life.

"You must cage your lust, Hal," replied Will, "lest it devour you alive. Lady Wyndham deserves only the kindest treatment from you, and to do otherwise would bring shame upon your name."

"But I can find none I consider good enough to be her husband, Will. I would not have her unhappy because my fancy turns elsewhere," the king replied.

"Perhaps you should look to someone closer rather than farther from the lady in question," the fool said.

"What kind of a riddle do you riddle me now?" laughed the king, cuffing Will Somers a playful blow.

"I hear on the autumn breezes that the Earl of Langford has come to court this day."

"The Earl of Langford?"

"Aye, Hal! The nephew and heir of your little country girl's late husband. He seeks an appointment with you, but being of no import, your secretary has put him off, and so he must wait. 'Tis said he has no wife, nor any contract to wed a wife. Could this not be the answer to your very difficult dilemma?" The fool cocked his head to one side, bright-eyed.

"Are you suggesting, Will, that I should wed her to the Earl of Langford?" said the king.

"It is a possible solution to your problem, Hal," Will Somers replied.

"She detests Anthony Wyndham, my friend."

"Why, Hal? Can you tell me why?"

"She holds him responsible for the death of her husband, who was the earl's uncle. Then, too, the shock of her husband's sudden demise caused her to miscarry of their son and heir. She bears Anthony Wyndham a great grudge, Will."

"What is the truth of the matter, Hal? Is her complaint a just one, or merely the desperation of a grief-stricken woman?" the fool asked.

"From the facts I have gathered, *and* I have sought the truth of the matter, for I will have no murderer, even a highborn one, go unpunished in my kingdom, Blaze's charges stem from her anger and her sorrow. There is no merit in what she says."

"Then," said the fool wisely, "is it possible her antipathy toward Lord Anthony is in reality an unknown passion toward the gentleman? Hate, they say, is but one side of the coin. Love, Hal, is, however, the other."

The king pondered his fool's words for several long minutes, and then he said, "Most marriages are those that are arranged between two people by others. The bride and the groom do not always begin as lovers, but living together teaches people the value of compromise, does it not, Will? If I wed Lady Wyndham to the Earl of Langford, she would return to a home she loves, and to her daughter. The child's fortune would be well-managed, for the earl is not just known to Blaze, he is a blood relation to her little girl."

"You can also offer her an alternative that is no real alternative. Tell her you would have her do this, but if she is truly opposed to it, that you will choose another husband for her. She dislikes young Thomas Seymour greatly, I believe," chuckled the fool. "I do not think she could choose him over even Lord Wyndham."

The king smiled admiringly at Will Somers. "I think, Will, that you have missed your calling. You are clever enough to be a man of the government."

"Nay, Hal," came the dry reply, "I am not, thank God, enough of a fool for that!"

The king roared with laughter. "You are right, my Will! You are far too wise, I fear!"

"Then you will see Lord Wyndham, my lord Henry?"

"Aye, but we shall not make it an official meeting. Do you know where he is staying at Greenwich?"

"Nay, Hal, but I can find him."

"Do so then, and fetch him to me as quickly as you can. We will see what the earl wants of me, and whether in exchange for it he can be persuaded to marry my sweet and lovely Blaze so that I may be free to pursue the fascinating Mistress Anne Boleyn."

"If that be your desire, Hal, then perhaps I do you a disservice in helping you to dispose of Lady Wyndham," said Will Somers seriously.

"Ahh, Will, not you too? What is it about Mistress Anne that turns people so quickly against her?"

"I am but a fool, my lord," replied Will Somers, "but have eyes. The lady is not as simple a creature as she would have you believe. She will not succumb as her sister did, for I can see in her character that she is a woman of determination who desires far more from life. There has been no gossip from France about her lack of morals as there was with Mistress Mary, whom King Francis called his hackney. This lady is surely a virgin, and even you cannot force a wellborn virgin, Hal. Her price will be high indeed, and you may find that you are not ready or able to pay it, my good lord."

"I mean to have her, Will," said the king. "Whatever it takes to gain Mistress Anne Boleyn for my own, I will gladly pay the price!"

Will Somers shook his head. He was extremely fond of the king, but sometimes Henry thought more with his cock than he did his very facile brain. Women were his greatest weakness, and if he were not careful, they would surely be his downfall. He bowed himself from the king's presence, and went to find the Earl of Langford.

After an hour he finally located Anthony Wyndham, who sat dicing and drinking with a group of young courtiers in a remote alcove. "My lord earl?"

Anthony Wyndham looked up. He did not recognize Will Somers, for the young man had only come to court at Twelfth Night, as had Blaze. "Aye, I am Lord Wyndham," Anthony replied.

"I am Will Somers, my lord, the king's fool. It has come to his majesty's ears that you sought to gain an audience with him, and knowing that you have come from so far, the king grants you his time. If you will come with me, I will take you to him."

"But the king's secretary said—" began Tony.

"The king's secretary is a greater fool than even I am, my lord. I hope you are not." And turning, he began to walk quickly away.

Anthony Wyndham grabbed up his winnings and followed after Will Somers, who led him through the corridors of Greenwich Palace and into the king's privy chamber by means of a secret entrance, thereby avoiding the royal antechamber with all its gentlemen and its sharp-eyed gossips.

The king turned at the sound of their entry, and smiling, held out his hand. "Anthony Wyndham, it is good to see you back with us once more. You sought to see me, I have learned. What is it that you would have of me, my lord earl? Will, pour us some Rhenish! Come, Tony, let us sit down."

"My lord, I find myself in a rather delicate position, for since arriving at court this morning, and requesting an audience of you, I have learned things that could render my quest useless, and I certainly have no desire to offend you, my lord," Anthony said carefully.

Will Somers handed the wine goblets to the two men, and settled himself upon his stool by the king's knee. The king was not quick enough to pick it up, for Hal, God bless him, was too self-involved, but he would wager a gold rose noble that the Earl of Langford's business had to do with Blaze Wyndham.

"Your tact and your candor do you credit, my lord," replied the king. "Tell me why you have come, and I shall promise you not to be offended by your honesty."

"How can we be offended by that which we hardly recognize, Hal?" teased Will in an effort to lighten the situation, and help the earl.

The king's laughter rumbled good-naturedly about the chamber, and he took a deep sip of his wine. "True, fool," he said, and turning to Anthony ordered him, "Say on, my lord earl!"

"You must surely know, my lord," began Anthony, "that I inherited my title from my dearly beloved uncle, Edmund Wyndham. Edmund and I were but four years apart in age, and as he was orphaned of a mother at his birth, he was raised by his half-sister, my own mother. After my birth we were raised together, and were more like brothers than an uncle and his nephew.

"Last autumn I left the court to see to my own lands, which border on

Edmund's. I stayed with him and his wife at their home, RiversEdge. My uncle and I spent several days hunting, and then the day before I was to leave Edmund suggested that, it being a dank and cold day, we stay at home. I, foolishly, teased him into hunting. As we returned home late that afternoon we were deep in conversation, and totally unprepared for the stag that leapt forth without warning from the forest. The dogs went berserk, and both of our mounts reared, but Edmund could not regain control of his horse quickly enough. He was thrown from its back. I jumped from my own beast and went to my cousin. He was dying, my lord, but by some incredible strength of will he lived a few minutes longer.

"I knelt by his side, my lord, hating myself as I saw the very life ebbing away in his eyes, and remembering my taunts of the morning that had brought us to this pass. Edmund's lips moved, and putting my ear to them, I heard him say, *Marry my widow, Tony. Protect her, and my children.* Then he was gone, my lord.

"We brought his body home to RiversEdge, and the ensuing shock of losing her husband caused his wife to miscarry of their son. After the funeral she begged my leave to take her daughter and visit her parents for several months to recover from her sorrow. I had not been able to bring myself to tell her of her husband's dying words, for in her grief she rightly held me accountable for Edmund's death, and it seemed an indelicate thing to do. I felt that when she returned to RiversEdge would be the proper time to tell her.

"A week after Easter I traveled to Ashby to escort my uncle's widow and daughter home. You can imagine my surprise when I found little Nyssa in her grandparents' care, and her mother gone those four months past to court. Lady Morgan persuaded me, however, that her eldest daughter was better off at court easing her sorrow than she was in Hereford. I told her of Edmund's words, and she then begged me to leave her daughter at court until the autumn, when Blaze's period of mourning would be fully satisfied.

"I thought to come up to court now to reacquaint myself with the lady, to tell her of Edmund's wishes, and to court her preparatory to our marriage, which can take place after the thirty-first of October, which is the first anniversary of Edmund's death. I arrived at court but this morning to quickly learn that my uncle's widow, whom I promised to make my wife, is, ahhh, greatly in your majesty's favor, and hence my dilemma, sire, as you can surely see," Anthony finished.

The king appeared to be lost in thought, and then he said, "Perhaps 'tis not such a dilemma, Lord Wyndham. We are two gentlemen, and so

I will not mince words with you, or leave you in doubt as to the position Blaze holds in my life. Since the first of May she has been my mistress. Her loyalty to me is without question, and she is well-liked here at court. Nonetheless, I am not a man to deny the dying wishes of one of my subjects. How could I face my God with so large a sin upon my soul? Then, too," and here the king smiled a smile that said, *this is just between us men*, "I am not like ordinary men, and my kingly appetite cannot be satisfied by even so charming a lady as Blaze Wyndham.

"You will keep your promise to your late uncle, *and* you will please me greatly by marrying the lady when her period of mourning is finished. Let me assure you that her character is of the finest, for in her early months here at court her reputation for chastity was legend. She even needed a bit of persuading to see her duty toward her king. Like my mother, and my grandmother, Blaze Wyndham is a good woman. She will make you a fine wife, and if you will but give me the time to tell her, you will have my leave to court her. I will speak with her tonight, but until that time I would prefer that you remained out of sight. Will will take you to a comfortable room, and everything you need will be provided. That room will be yours until you wed the lady. Your wedding I will shortly decree, and you will be married here at Greenwich, lest the lady escape you again."

Anthony Wyndham was astounded by this turn of events. He could think of nothing to say, and so rising from his chair he stammered his thanks, and followed Will Somers from the king's privy chamber. The king's fool led him to a small, comfortably furnished chamber with a view of the Fountain Court, and a little fireplace that was already blazing merrily. There was but a small bed within the room, several chairs, and a table upon which were set a decanter of wine and two goblets.

"No one will disturb you here, my lord Wyndham," said Will Somers. "You will be brought food, and I shall come when the king has given me his permission to release you." The fool bowed politely, and departed the room.

Tony laughed softly to himself. What an incredible day it had been, he thought, and laughed again. Going to the table, he poured himself out some wine, and drinking it half down, sat himself by the fire. He had to be stark raving mad. He had just told the king the most incredible lie, and Henry Tudor had accepted it without so much as a query. He had lied to his king, and for what? For a woman with whom he had been in love from the day he had first seen her. For a woman who hated him, and took the first opportunity to run from him. For a woman who had used her body to gain power and position. For a woman whose purported grief had lasted no more than six months, if that!

His uncle had died the moment his body had hit the ground on that terrible day almost a year ago. There was no dying request made, nor a promise given. Yet he had said it with such conviction that the king had accepted it as truth. He almost had himself. He was amazed at what he had done. Amazed that even after knowing the kind of woman Blaze Wyndham really was, that he had still lied in order to gain her for himself. And he had succeeded! Dear God, he had certainly succeeded. Now he must wed with her even if he did not want her.

Did he still want her? He wasn't really certain. The thought of Blaze in the arms of another man, even if that man be his king, was an extremely unsettling thought. The thought of Blaze in the king's bed was a worse one. It did not disturb him that she had been Edmund's wife so much as it disturbed him that she was Henry Tudor's mistress. He had no intention of turning a blind eye like Lord Tailboys or Master Carey so that the king might swive his wife once he was wed to her. Nay! Marry her he would here at Greenwich, and with the king's blessing, but they would start for RiversEdge that same day! That permission he would gain from the king before the match was officially struck.

He laughed once more. There is no room for bargaining left, Tony, he told himself. The match is already officially struck, and 'tis you who did it, not Henry Tudor! Rising, he walked across the room, and pulling his boots off, lay down upon the bed. In his eagerness to see Blaze once again he had ridden hard from Hereford over the last several days, and he was now suddenly very, very tired. He slept so soundly that he did not even hear the young serving girl who tiptoed into the chamber to place a tray of cold meats, bread, and cheese upon the table.

It rained that night, and the king, sitting back upon his hips atop his beautiful mistress, fondled her breasts thoughtfully. His hardness throbbed its lustful message within her warm body, and he knew that he would miss her. Blaze Wyndham was a strangely wise and loving woman. He had never been more content than when he was with her. She was not a wickedly clever or seriously complex woman as he sensed Mistress Anne Boleyn was. Blaze had given him no pain, nor, he believed, had their relationship continued, would she ever have given him pain. It was a great pity that with her family's reputation for healthy babies he could not wed with her himself. She would have made him a good queen, a good mother for his unborn sons. God's will was often puzzling.

She sensed his detachment from her, and considered what it could mean. She had seen him casting what he believed to be secret glances in the direction of Mistress Anne Boleyn. She did not mind if he grew tired of her, she thought, but dear heaven, not that cat-faced bitch with her wicked tongue! It had already come to Blaze's ears that Mistress Anne upon hearing Blaze referred to as *The Quiet Mistress* had said, "She is not so much quiet perhaps as she is *dull*, my lords." Nay, Mistress Boleyn was not the kind of woman that Hal needed.

"What is it, my lord?" she asked him, looking straight at him.

He immediately focused upon her, and bending forward, kissed her lips. "Let us finish this sweet business first, my little country girl," he said, "and then we shall talk." For a few moments he teased her nipples, knowing how their delightful sensitivity roused her. Then he began to pump her fiercely as he had never done before, hammering into her soft core with an almost maddened frenzy of rising passion. Leaning even farther forward upon her, he pinioned her arms above her head, and his mouth ground down almost cruelly upon hers.

He was the most wonderful lover, she thought, knowing precisely how to arouse her to meet his own desires. He had taught her things between a man and a woman that she had never believed possible in her wildest imagination; and though he had always been strong, and maintained a mastery over her, never since that first day had he been cruel to her. Tonight she seemed to soar beneath his tutelage until finally they were both sated, and lay companionably together catching their breaths.

He took her hand in his, and turning it, placed a kiss upon the soft palm. "I have arranged for you to be married," he said bluntly, and she gasped at the thunderbolt he had just hurled at her.

"*Who?*" She managed to force the word from between her lips.

"Anthony Wyndham," he said, and braced himself for the storm he knew would follow.

"*Anthony Wyndham?*" She pulled her hand from his, and sitting up upon her haunches, she looked into his face. "Dear God, what have I done to displease you that you would wed me to the man who murdered Edmund?" The tears began to slip down her rosy cheeks, and he felt guilty, for he hated to make a woman weep.

"Anthony Wyndham did not murder his uncle, Blaze. I have personally overseen to the investigation into that matter. Surely you are still not angry with him?"

"*Angry with him?* I despise him!"

"Nonetheless he promised your husband, who died within his arms, that he would wed you and protect your children," said the king. "He has arrived at court this day, and told me all. How can I deny your husband's dying request? How can you?"

"I have *never* heard this before," Blaze said suspiciously. "I do not believe him!"

"Why would he lie about such a thing, Blaze? He told me that he could not bring himself to tell you of his promise to your husband because of your great grief with your double loss. He planned to tell you in the spring, but when he came to Ashby you were not there, and your mother persuaded him to let you stay here at court until the autumn, when your mourning would officially be over."

"It is September sixteenth, my lord," Blaze said, and then she cried out, "Ohh, how heartless he is! He has come on September sixteenth! Do you know what this day is? It would have been the fourth anniversary of my wedding to Edmund Wyndham!"

"I do not think he even considered it, Blaze," said the king gently.

"Edmund will be dead a year on All Hallows' Eve," she said sadly.

"You will be married in my own chapel on the fifth of November," the king said quietly. "I will give the bride away myself. I promised Anthony Wyndham that I would tell you this evening, which, sweetheart, must be our last together. Tomorrow you will receive the Earl of Langford as your intended husband and your devoted suitor. I shall not make him a cuckold, for he is, I know, a proud man."

"I will not wed him," Blaze said stubbornly. "I will not!"

"Then," said Henry Tudor, "you will wed Thomas Seymour, but you will wed someone on the fifth of November, my little country girl," and the king's voice was equally stubborn.

"You would not give me to Thomas Seymour? That cockscomb who will brag all about the court of his prowess over you each time he fucks me!"

The king had not considered that, and so he decided that to continue the threat of Thomas Seymour would be both unbelievable and foolish. "I had not considered that, lovey," he admitted. "However, I will accept no disobedience from you, Blaze. You will wed Anthony Wyndham! Now, come," he said, pulling her back into his arms, "let us make the most of the time we have left together."

"*I do not believe it!*" shrieked Bliss upon learning her sister's news the following morning. "The king has cast you off? It is that Boleyn bitch! I know it! They say she is a damn witch, and this surely smacks of witchcraft!"

"God's foot, Bliss! Watch your waspish tongue!" Owen FitzHugh warned his beautiful wife.

"We are in our own chambers!" Bliss snapped back. "Am I not allowed to speak my mind in private?"

"Not in the king's house!" returned her husband. "You have been at court long enough to know the walls have ears!" He turned to his sister-in-law. "This will be for the better, I know it, Blaze."

"I did not love him, Owen, and so my heart is not broken. I always knew that one day I would be *pensioned* in this fashion, but Anthony Wyndham? That is where the trouble lies for me. I still see Edmund's broken body in my dreams, and the blue face of my tiny swaddled son. Then, too, I worry for Hal's sake, for Bliss is right. My lord's thoughts stray toward Mistress Anne, and I fear no good will come of it for the king. You see, Owen, I know better than most that Hal is but a man like any other man. I will agree that he needs a wife to give him his desired sons, and although Mistress Anne will go the same way his sister and I have in the end, I fear she will hurt him before it is all over."

Owen nodded, suddenly seeing in Blaze what it was that had so pleased the king. There was a pure sweetness in her that existed in few women, and she was certainly not the fool that so many believed her to be. "He will miss you," the Earl of Marwood said. "In the dark of night he will awaken, and reach for you, and he will miss you."

"What of Anthony Wyndham?" demanded Bliss. "What if what he told the king is true? Surely he would not lie to the king!"

"That troubles me too," admitted Blaze. "What reason would he have for lying, and since I can think of none, then I must conclude therefore that he is telling the truth. I do not find it very flattering that he beards Hal and gets his permission to wed with me merely out of a sense of duty. Oh, damn the bastard!"

There was a knock upon the chamber door, and Betty, answering it, admitted Anthony Wyndham. Owen FitzHugh stepped forward, his hand outstretched.

"It is good to see you, Tony. I understand from Blaze that we are to be related by marriage."

Anthony Wyndham's eyes swept the room, finding her. For a moment he could not speak. He had forgotten how beautiful she was, but seeing her standing there in her mauve silk gown, her honey-colored curls loose about her plump shoulders, reminded him sharply. Her eyes, however, were icy with their disdain. So she was not happy about this turn of events. She obviously liked being the royal whore, he thought, and anger welled up within him.

"Greetings, madam," he said. "The king has obviously told you of our upcoming nuptials." His voice was cold, and Bliss found herself shivering openly.

"Last night as we sported ourselves," replied Blaze unkindly, seeing his look, and recognizing it as contempt. "The date has been set for November fifth, if you did not know." She glared at him defiantly. How dare he judge her! How could he know what it was like to be a woman, helpless before a king's power?

"So the king informed me this morning, madam. He also informed me that your intimate association is now finished. I assume that you remember how a Countess of Langford conducts herself?"

"As well as I remember how Edmund died," she replied in a deceptively sweet voice.

"Let us have some wine to toast this event," said Owen FitzHugh, and he valiantly attempted to ease what was obviously a tense situation, particularly seeing that his wife was totally nonplussed by the open warfare that had broken out between Blaze and Tony.

"There is nothing to celebrate," said Blaze angrily, and she swept past them out of the room.

Bliss, never at a loss for words, could only stare after her elder sister.

Owen FitzHugh calmly poured three goblets of dark, rich wine and handed them around. Then raising his own cup he said, "You'll find that Morgan women are as hot-tempered as they are hot-blooded, Tony, but at no time are they ever dull to be wed to, my friend!"

"Owen!" Bliss had recovered, and glowered at her husband. "What a thing to say about my sister and me."

"I speak only the truth," teased the Earl of Marwood, and Anthony Wyndham found himself suddenly smiling.

"Do you beat Bliss often?" he inquired politely, but his blue eyes were warm and twinkling.

How very handsome he is, thought Bliss, seeing those eyes now in a different light.

"Nay," replied Owen. "I do not beat her at all, for I have a far sweeter way of moderating her behavior, do I not, my adorable one?"

"And I oversee his behavior the exact same way," said Bliss in honeyed tones, "do I not, my lord?"

Tony laughed now, and said ruefully, "I doubt that Blaze and I shall ever find the happiness that you two have."

"Then why do you claim her?" asked Owen FitzHugh.

"Because he loves her!" crowed Bliss. "Oh, you do, don't you, Tony?" In the space of a brief moment she had seen the vulnerability on his face when he spoke of Blaze.

"Aye, I love her. I always have," came the quiet reply.

"Which was why you could never see Delight," Bliss continued, and then, "Oh! poor Delight! She will be heartbroken when she learns that you are marrying Blaze, or does she already know?"

He shook his head in the negative, and Owen said, " 'Twill be the best thing that could happen to Delight. She has been mooning about Ashby for two years. Now, perhaps, she will look to some of the young men who have been trying without success to court her."

"Oh, Owen, you do not understand Delight! For men everything is so black-and-white," said Bliss in an exasperated tone. "You have surely been wed with me long enough to·know that is not so."

"With you, my darling Bliss, nothing is ever certain," said Owen FitzHugh.

"Neither is it with Blaze," replied Bliss, looking to her future brother-in-law. "You will have to meet with her on some common ground, Tony. You cannot go battling to the altar."

At the mention of Blaze and their situation his eyes clouded once more. He was now publicly committed to her, and he wondered if he might not live to regret his impetuosity. He had deliberately pledged himself to a virago who obviously hated him. What hope could he have of their happiness under those circumstances? Still, he had to try to bring her to reason. In a few short weeks they would be condemned to spend the rest of their lives together. The thought was a most sobering one, and he recklessly drank his wine down in two gulps.

Life at court had not changed, he found. There were factions everywhere, and right now those factions were attempting to reassess the king's position in relation to Lady Blaze Wyndham, particularly since the king had that very day publicly announced the betrothal of Anthony Wyndham, the Earl of Langford, to his dearly beloved friend, Lady Blaze Wyndham. Was the king planning to use Tony Wyndham to father for an expected bastard? Lady Wyndham had but one servant, a stubborn red-cheeked countrywoman who could not be bribed, and so no one could be certain if the slender Blaze was or was not with child.

It was obvious that the king was not in any way angry with Blaze Wyndham, for his manner toward her was most jovial and kind. She was therefore not out of his favor, particularly as she remained in her apartments directly over the king's. That gave rise to additional rumors, these of a more salacious nature suggesting that the king and the earl were sharing Lady Wyndham's favors.

Then, of course, there was the possibility that the king had found another lady to pursue. It did not take the sharp eyes and the sharper tongues long to discover that Mistress Anne Boleyn was suddenly being singled out for royal favor as Lady Wyndham was being eased out of it with her upcoming marriage. It was truly a most exciting autumn! On one side of the coin was the king coyly attempting to court a new ladylove. On the other was his previous inamorata publicly squabbling with her betrothed husband, much to the delight of the court.

"Can you limit your shows of temper to our private times, my lord?" snapped Blaze when Anthony had escorted her to her apartments one evening.

"I will confine my shows of temper when you behave as you should, madam," he snapped at her.

"Lord Neville and I were but speaking. We were in public where we could be seen by all. What did you think he would do under such circumstances?"

"Lord Neville was openly staring down your gown," raged Tony. "In another minute his hand would have been on your breast, and he would have been tumbling you in the open for all to see!"

Blaze slapped him furiously. "How dare you!" she shrieked. "I have never behaved like a common drab in the past, and I am not behaving as such now. You, however, are behaving like a fool!"

"I see," he said coolly. "Playing the whore for a king is different from playing the whore for just a simple peer!"

Blaze whitened outwardly though inwardly fierce rage pumped through her veins. "You know nothing, my lord," she said. "*Nothing!* If, however, you think me such a whore, why do you even disturb yourself by wedding with me? Surely some whey-faced and unsullied virgin would suit you better!"

"Perhaps you are right," he shouted at her, "but I gave my promise to Edmund, and I have always been a man of my word! I will wed you, Blaze, and then I will take you home to RiversEdge where you will behave as my wife should behave, and bear my children so that the Wyndhams do not die out."

Furious, she backed away from him. "I bore a son for the Wyndhams once. You killed him!" Her hand found a porcelain bowl of potpourri, and grasping it she threw it at his head with all her might.

He ducked, and the bowl, spewing its contents of dried flower petals and fragrant spices, scattered all over the room. Threateningly he stepped toward her, his face a mask of black anger.

"Go ahead," she taunted him. "Beat me, if you dare! The king is still not so enamored of Mistress Anne that I cannot bring his wrath down on your damned head! Wherever you mark me I shall show him! He has always loved my fine white skin, and it distressed him whenever I sported a bruise. Touch me, and he will know of it, I swear it you!"

"You damned bitch!" he growled at her, and turning, flung himself from the room, hearing her mocking laughter, hearing her shout after him, *"Coward!"*

The king called her to him the next day, and seating her upon his lap within his privy chamber, he said, "You are causing a scandal with your constant battles, my little country girl. You cannot continue to openly disagree on every matter with our good Tony. There are those who say I am forcing you to this match, and such chatter hurts me, for you know I do this only so that you will be safe and content in your home with your little daughter once more. You are really not meant for the court, Blaze Wyndham, and once you are wed you are to go home again. Do you understand what I have told you?"

"I understand more than you believe I do, my Hal," she said, and her lower lip quivered as her eyes filled with hot tears.

"I have loved you, Blaze," the king said softly, "but you must never make the mistake of presuming upon that love. As I have warned you often enough before, I am not a simple man. *I am the king!* Do you now understand what it is I am saying, sweetheart?"

Mutely Blaze nodded, and was then sent from his presence. She understood. Oh, yes, she understood quite well. As Bliss had said those weeks before, the king had cast her off. He had seen her provided for with a suitable husband, and now he was washing his hands of her so he might concentrate his efforts upon his pursuit of Mistress Anne, the cat-faced bitch! As long as Blaze would behave herself she would have the king's friendship, but Henry Tudor had all but bluntly told her that if her public disagreements with Anthony Wyndham did not cease, she would have his enmity.

Fleeing to her apartments she locked herself in her bedchamber much to Heartha's distress. She needed to think. She needed to be alone. Really alone. For almost a year now the fires of her anger over Edmund's untimely death had burned hot within her. Though with the passing of time she had come to realize that Anthony Wyndham was not really to blame, she had not been able to openly release him from his culpability in the matter, but now she had to if there was to be any peace between them. Henry Tudor had virtually insisted that there must be.

She had loved Edmund Wyndham with the first love of an innocent girl. Had he lived she knew that she would have loved him for the rest of her life. He had given her everything she had ever wanted, and more. His devotion. A sweet love. His name. Little Nyssa. RiversEdge. She had never dreamed that such happiness could exist between two people as had existed between them, and then he was gone from her life as suddenly as he had entered it.

As for the king, she had not willingly sought to catch his attention, yet with Henry Tudor she had found a different sort of love. She quickly learned how his royal upbringing had molded him into the powerful, volatile, brilliant monarch that he was. Henry needed a gentle woman who would allow him to lead her, and with him she had found real passion. Few, if any—the Princess of Aragon, Will Somers, herself—saw the unsure and uncertain boy beneath Hal's bluff nature. The boy who needed the comfort and reassurance that only a soft-spoken woman could offer. Aye, the king had needed her, though he would never have admitted to it. She wondered who would minister to those particular needs now. Certainly not Mistress Anne Boleyn with her French manners and her grand pretensions.

What was left? What kind of love could Anthony Wyndham possibly offer her? Certainly she could not go back in time and give him what she had given Edmund. Nor could he be to her the man that Henry Tudor was, nor would she want him to be. She shook her head ruefully. Why was she even considering love where Tony was concerned? He did not love her, and she doubted that he ever would. He would marry her because of a promise that he had made a dying Edmund. She had come to believe that, because there was certainly no reason for him to have said such a thing if it wasn't so.

There would be no love between them; but then, what *would* there be between them? She was not so silly as not to realize that true love within a marriage was a rare thing. Most people married for other considerations, such as property, children, familial duties of some sort. How on earth did they manage to live in peace together, feeling nothing for one another? She had been so fortunate her entire life, for her own parents loved one another, and she had loved Edmund, and her sisters had found love with their mates. They were, she knew, all the exception to the rule.

Without love what was there? Friendship? Respect? A mere toleration of one's mate? He did not love her. Did he love any other woman? Did he have some rustic little mistress who had already borne him children? She did not know, for she had to admit to herself that she did not really know Anthony Wyndham. Still, if she could manage to forgive him Edmund's death, perhaps they might build something on that. She had to try. She couldn't go on being angry, wanting to stick a knife into his black heart! In just a few days' time he would be her husband, and they would leave Greenwich and the court. She would not have the king to run to anymore in her pique. She smiled ruefully. She did not have the king anymore at all now. He had told her so only a short while ago. She must make peace with herself. *She must!*

"M'lady! M'lady!" Heartha was rapping upon her bedchamber door. "M'lady! Betty says that Mistress Bliss needs you right away!"

Blaze unlocked the door to the room and hurried out. "Where is my sister?" she asked Bliss's tiring woman.

"She's in her apartments, and she's very sick, m'lady! Ohhh, she's very sick indeed, poor lady!"

Bliss was as white as a sheet. She had already vomited twice into a silver basin, and was looking dreadfully drained. "I feel awful!" she wailed. " 'Tis the second time this week that this has happened. What is the matter with me? No! Not that gown, you stupid girl! Did I not say it was too tight the last time I wore it? Ohh, Blaze! I feel wretched!"

"When was your last flux, Bliss?" demanded her sister.

"What has that got to do with anything? You know how irregular I have always been. It is the one great difference between Blythe and myself."

"When?"

"Three, four months ago. I don't remember!"

"You are breeding," said Blaze matter-of-factly.

"Oh, no!" shrieked Bliss. "I cannot be! Owen always said that we might stay at court as long as we had no children, but once the babies came, I must remain at home!"

"You are long overdue a child," said Blaze. "Blythe has two, and is expecting another. I bore Edmund two. It is time, Bliss. Besides, if you give Owen a few sons and daughters, I will wager he will let you return to your wonderful court. He doesn't like the quiet life in the country any more than you do, and you will not let him get away without you, of that I am quite certain," laughed Blaze.

"Indeed I will not," said Bliss firmly. "If I must stay in the country, then so will Owen FitzHugh stay too!"

"Why are we going to the country?" demanded Owen, who had entered his wife's chamber with Tony and heard but the last of the conversation.

"Because I am going to have a baby," said Bliss without any preamble.

"*A baby!*" The Earl of Marwood's face almost split with his delighted smile. "We are having a baby, madam? This is wonderful! This is marvelous!" Then he considered. "But why must I leave court if you are having a baby?"

"Because, sir, I shall not leave court unless you leave," said Bliss sweetly.

"The court is no place for a baby!" Owen insisted.

"I agree," replied his wife, "but I cannot be happy away from you, my lord, and if I am to successfully bear your son, then I must be happy, must I not? To be happy I must have you by my side at all times, and not playing the bachelor to all the lightskirts here at Greenwich while I, full of your seed, grow plump as a shoat deep in the country!"

"Now, Bliss, my darling . . ." began Owen FitzHugh.

"Now, Owen, my love . . ." returned Bliss.

Blaze moved silently across the chamber, and taking Tony by the hand, drew him from the room. "They are going to fight," she said softly, and then with some humor, "And we do not need lessons in fighting, my lord, do we?"

"Nay, madam, in that sport we are most proficient."

"I would say that in that sport we excel, sir," she replied. "Perhaps it is time we tried to mend our differences."

"And how do you propose, madam, that we do that?" he asked her.

"I am not certain, my lord, but I know we cannot bring our differences back to RiversEdge. I would not have Nyssa distressed by our anger with one another."

"You have thought little of your daughter since you left her those nine months ago," he taunted her.

"She is safe with my parents," Blaze said through gritted teeth. *I will not fight with him*, she silently vowed.

"Nyssa is at RiversEdge, where she belongs," he answered.

"You took *my* daughter? How dare you?" Blaze was furious, but mindful of the fact that they were on public view, she kept her voice low.

"Nyssa is a Wyndham, madam, and she belongs at RiversEdge. It is her home, and Edmund would want her there."

"I would have brought her back," Blaze said, keeping her voice even. "I, better than you, know what her father would want, my lord. She was content at Ashby with my baby brothers for companions. She was safe at Ashby with her grandmother, whose experience with children cannot be questioned."

"She is in her own home, and under my mother's care," he answered her, surprised that she was not shrieking at him by now.

"You had not the right to order Nyssa removed from my mother's care, my lord."

"I am the Earl of Langford, Blaze. The welfare of my predecessor's child is, of course, my concern."

"I will not argue further with you, sir," said Blaze. "Nyssa is safe, but in future remember that I am her parent, not you."

"I shall remember it, madam, as long as you do," he replied, and Blaze bit back an angry retort.

Over the next few days, as the date of their wedding drew nearer, Blaze concentrated upon keeping her temper where Anthony Wyndham was concerned. It was not easy. It seemed the more she attempted to find a common ground upon which they might build some sort of relationship, the harder he seemed to work at being deliberately aggravating. The king, however, was most pleased with her. He took her aside one afternoon to stroll with her in the picture gallery as he told her so.

"We are pleased, sweetheart, at your good behavior."

"I have always tried to please, your majesty," said Blaze demurely.

Henry Tudor chuckled, and the sound held more meaning than anything he might have said. She had never not pleased him, he thought, even in the beginning when she attempted resisting him.

From a corner of the picture gallery Mistress Anne Boleyn bit her lip in vexation at the sight of Lady Wyndham, her little hand upon the king's arm, laughing up into his face. From another end of the gallery the Earl of Langford watched them come, and wondered if the king was already making him a cuckold. He felt his anger rising.

On November 5th, 1525, Lady Blaze Wyndham, widow, was married in the King's Chapel at Greenwich Palace by Cardinal Wolsey himself, to Anthony Wyndham, bachelor, the Earl of Langford. The bride wore a gown of rich tawny orange velvet that was heavily embroidered with gold, pearls, and topaz about the bodice, sleeves, and underskirt, which was of the same color. The ruffled cuffs and neckline ruffle of her chemise were of gold lace. Her honey-colored hair was parted in the center, drawn back over her ears, and set prettily into a soft French knot at the nape of her neck. It was looped with pearls, and there were pearls and a chain of topaz about her neck, and pearls in her ears. The bridegroom was more than her equal in his wedding suit of black velvet, its doublet heavy with pearls and gold, his heavy gold chain, each square section set with a fat baroque pearl, his knee-length velvet gown both lined and edged in sable.

The king gave the bride away, a fact which no one dared to laugh publicly about, but privately there were many wry jokes made. The Earl and

Countess of Marwood attended the couple, which was only proper since they were related to the bride. The wedding was celebrated first thing in the morning, and afterward the king hosted a breakfast. There were many healths drunk to the couple, and then prior to their departure they were given a final blessing by Cardinal Wolsey.

"Let us hope their marriage lasts longer than the cardinal will," murmured Mistress Anne Boleyn to her brother, George.

"The king is not yours yet, *petite soeur*," George Boleyn whispered back.

Anne Boleyn smiled her little smile. "He will be," she said softly. "Oh, yes, brother George, he will be. Particularly now that I have rid him of the good and sweet Lady Wyndham."

"You need not have bothered with so elaborate a plot if you simply wished to follow in sister Mary's footsteps," mocked George Boleyn.

"I have not preserved my maidenhead all these years to play the whore like our sister," snapped Mistress Anne.

"You do not mean to be the king's mistress?" George Boleyn was surprised.

"*His mistress?* God's foot, nay! I most certainly do not mean to ever be *any* man's mistress!"

"What then, Anne?" demanded George Boleyn.

"I mean to be his wife, George," said Anne Boleyn. "*I mean to be queen!* It is for this that I have rid the king of Blaze Wyndham!"

George Boleyn threw back his head and laughed aloud. "By God, Annie, you are a rare one!" he chortled.

"Indeed, brother, I am," Mistress Anne agreed, and then without even seeming to look, she reached up and neatly caught the bride's bouquet that Blaze had just thrown. Coyly she cradled it in her hands, and pressed her face to it, inhaling its sweet fragrance of violets and late roses.

Unable to contain his mirth, George Boleyn laughed all the harder.

Part Four

RiversEdge

Autumn 1525–May 1527

Chapter 11

❧

They left Greenwich Palace in midmorning in a party of four carriages. Two of the vehicles carried baggage and servants, but in the first and second coaches rode the earls of Langford and Marwood and their wives. The little convoy was escorted by close to two dozen armed riders. They swung wide, avoiding the city of London, and thereby saving themselves at least half a day's travel. They would travel together most of the way, separating only five miles from the boundaries of the estate lands, when Owen and Bliss would turn slightly west for Marwood Hall.

The Langford traveling coach was a large and comfortable one with fine padded seats of soft, well-tanned leather and real glass windows that could be raised and lowered. There was plenty of leg room for Tony, who stood six feet in height, to stretch himself. The coach was wide enough so they might sit side by side and still have room between them. The interior of the coach was padded in a like manner to the seats, and bolted into either side of the vehicle wall by the seats were small silver sconces holding two candles each.

Blaze had changed into a traveling gown of rich dark green velvet with a cloak trimmed in gray rabbit fur. The day was cool, but windless and sunny. Here and there along their route brightly colored leaves still clung to the trees. The horses moved along at an even and easy pace. Anthony had sent to RiversEdge for additional animals so the teams might be changed each day, and so that spare horses would be available should one go lame. It would be several days before they arrived at their destination, and arrangements had been already made at the best inns along the road.

They could not seem to find much conversation between them.

"You are as lovely a bride today as you were the first time, Blaze," Anthony said awkwardly.

Was it really necessary for him to remind her of Edmund? she thought, and then she realized that he had meant his words to be a compliment. He had probably remembered too late that to mention her first marriage was hurtful to her. "Thank you, my lord," she managed to reply. "You were as handsome a groom as I can ever remember seeing. Several of the ladies looked quite disconsolate."

Neither of them could think of anything else to say, and so they rode in silence as the miles faded away behind them. At last he said, "Are you warm enough, Blaze?" and she nodded in the affirmative. Silence again. Finally when he could stand it no longer he signaled his coachman to halt and said to her, "I think, with your permission, of course, madam, that I shall ride for a while."

"Of course, my lord," she agreed, and he scrambled from the coach as, behind him, she was forced to smile at his haste to escape her. At least, she considered wryly, they were not fighting. Then her amusement faded. Was this what it was going to be like for the rest of their lives? How could they build anything on the yawning emptiness of the gulf that seemed to separate them? The coach began its forward passage once more, and Blaze closed her eyes in an attempt to prevent the tears pricking at her eyelids from escaping down her cheeks.

There had been a basket of food put into the coach with them before they left Greenwich Palace, but though the hours slipped quickly by, Blaze found she was not really hungry. Neither, it seemed, was Anthony; except for a brief stop to rest the horses and relieve themselves, they took no time to eat. Shortly before the final and last light of the day faded away on the western horizon they stopped at a comfortable and welcoming inn called The Swan. She was well chilled by now, and she found the inside of the inn warm and inviting. Bliss, however, was practically pea green in color.

"She has been ill ever since this afternoon," explained Owen, looking both distressed and uncomfortable.

"I shall never live to reach Marwood Hall," Bliss pronounced dramatically.

"You are expecting a baby, Bliss, not suffering from a wasting sickness," Blaze answered her sister, and then looked to Owen. "What have you done for her?" she demanded.

"*Done?* What should I have done? I have been trying to comfort her these several hours past since we stopped to rest the horses," Owen said. "At one point she vomited in my new velvet cap, and I was forced to hurl it from the carriage," he finished in an aggravated tone. "It had ostrich tips."

Blaze burst into laughter at the thought of Bliss emptying the contents of her last meal at Greenwich into her husband's fine new cap. Only the outraged stares of the Earl and Countess of Marwood brought her humor to a halt. She turned to the innkeeper's wife. "Elixir of peppermint in hot water for Lady FitzHugh, please." Blaze next directed her attention to Owen. "Ride with Tony tomorrow, and Bliss shall ride with me in my coach. You meant well, but commiserating with your wife over her queasiness was the wrong thing to do. It only increased Bliss's attention to her problem, which in turn exacerbated her difficulties. She needed diversion, not sympathy, Owen, but I will care for her myself on the morrow. Now, Bliss, I shall choose a light supper for you."

"I cannot eat," moaned Bliss.

"Indeed you can, and you must for the child's sake."

The innkeeper's wife offered Bliss a goblet upon a tray, and Bliss weakly lifted it to her lips to sip delicately. "There, dearie," the innkeeper's wife said kindly. " 'Tis better now, ain't it?"

Feeling her rolling belly beginning to settle, Bliss nodded. "It is better," she admitted.

"Bring Lady FitzHugh a plate with two slices of capon, from the breast only. A small slice of ham, not fatty though. A slice of fresh bread with honey, and a small goblet of sweet wine," said Blaze.

"And for the gentlemen, m'lady?" said the innkeeper's wife, who recognized authority when she saw it.

"Capon, ham, beef, meat pies, cheese, soup, fruit, bread, ale, and wine. Whatever you have that will fill them up." Blaze smiled.

Anthony checked upon the horses, and ordered the innkeeper to see to the comfort of their escort. The two young couples ate their supper together quietly, although by meal's end Bliss was obviously quite recovered. For a while they sat by the fire roasting apples, but finally acknowledging their journey on the morrow, they departed for their rooms. Heartha had had her supper with Bliss's Betty, and was awaiting her mistress. Anthony discreetly waited outside while his bride was readied for bed.

"A fine place for a wedding night," grumbled Heartha. "Some tumbledown inn in the middle of nowhere."

Blaze said nothing. She was tired, and in no mood to argue with her tiring woman. Besides, she knew what was to come, although she doubted that her bridegroom would be happy about it.

"What's this?" Heartha looked outraged. "I put in your new pale violet nightrail, m'lady, not this plain thing! Who has been playing tricks on me?"

"I removed the violet gown, and packed it in one of the trunks," said

Blaze. "It was much too flimsy to wear in a draughty inn without a fireplace to keep the room warm."

"Your husband is supposed to keep you warm," huffed Heartha, her visions of romance destroyed by the bride'e herself.

"My *husband*"—God, how strange that word sounded suddenly—"will want to get some rest, as we must arise early to continue our journey," Blaze replied. Freed of her gown and her petticoats, she washed herself in the little basin of warm water that Heartha had provided. Then, removing her chemise she took the plain white silk nightrail with its long sleeves and its high neck from her servant, and slipped it over her head. "Where is my nightcap?" she asked.

With an audible sniff of disapproval Heartha found the required item, and handed it to her mistress. Then, grumbling beneath her breath she sat Blaze down, and brushed out her long hair. When she had finished Blaze tied the charming little silk cap with its pink ribbons beneath her chin, and climbed into bed. "You can tell Lord Wyndham that he may enter now, Heartha, and then find your own bed. Good night," said Blaze sweetly.

Anthony Wyndham closed the door behind his wife's servant, and adjusting his eyes to the dimness of the room with its one chamberstick, he finally saw her awaiting him in their bed. "You are a most fetching sight, madam," he said, and began to strip off his own garments. Here was the only compensation he would get from this marriage, and he would wager that Henry Tudor had taught her some clever little tricks to please a man. There was at least that benefit to be had from marrying the king's mistress.

"A moment, my lord," she said, and he immediately knew that the tone of her voice boded no good.

"What is it, madam?"

"There will be no intimacy between us for the time being," she said quietly.

"*Indeed?*" He could feel a faint throb behind his temples just beginning. "Perhaps you will enlighten me as to why there will be no intimacy between us for the *time being*. Do you have your flux at this time?"

"No, my lord, I do not!" she said, unable to keep the snappishness from her voice, feeling the warmth in her cheeks.

"Then mayhap you will tell me, madam, why it is you are proposing to deny me my rights as your husband?" He crossed the room to sit down upon the bed. "Are you afraid of me, Blaze?" His voice had gentled.

"Afraid of you?" She barked a laugh. "No, my lord, I am not in the least afraid of you. Tell me, though. Am I not expected to produce an heir for you, for the Langford earldom, as quickly as possible?"

"Aye, you are!" was his blunt answer.

"Then, my lord, if you would be certain that the son I eventually bear you is yours, and not Henry Tudor's, you will restrain your passions for me for the next three months. I will have no doubts about my child's paternity, my lord. I will not have you flinging any such doubts in my face ever. There will be no uncertainty with our first child as there was with Mary Boleyn's."

"I had not thought of it," he said in a tone that surprised her in its reasonableness. "Do you think you might be carrying a royal bastard, Blaze?"

"I do not know," she said simply, thinking how easy this lie was to tell him. She had no intention of spreading her legs to satisfy his lusts, *or* his curiosity as to what she had learned in the king's bed. At least not this night. Not any night until there was something more than anger and suspicion between them. "I have heard it said that when in doubt over a matter such as this, it is better to wait three full months before coupling again. The women of my family have an irregular flux, and so I cannot be certain of my condition, but I would not deliberately foist a bastard, even a royal bastard, upon the Wyndhams, Tony. Whatever our differences may be, I think you know that my loyalty to the Langford earldom is unquestioned."

"Aye," he admitted, knowing even as he did so that he was also agreeing to restrain his natural desires. "Why the hell did you not wait to wed with me then, Blaze?" he demanded of her.

"You will remember, my lord, that it was the king himself who set our wedding day, not I," she said primly.

"Aye," he grumbled. "The king set our wedding day, and set it as quickly as he dared so that he might chase after Mistress Anne Boleyn. He would give no thought to our comforts, would he? Did you see the bitch catch your wedding bouquet, Blaze, and the coy smile upon her face when she did? God, the thing flew to her hand as if directed by witchcraft!"

"Poor Hal," said Blaze softly.

"*Poor Hal?* What of poor Tony, who must now sleep upon the cold floor in a room without a fireplace?"

Blaze could not help the giggle that escaped her. He looked so genuinely forlorn. "If you can promise me that you will keep your baser nature under strong control," she said, flipping the comforter back, "I shall keep mine under as tight a rein, my lord, and we may share this bed."

"Agreed!" he said, and immediately climbed in next to her. "Good night, madam." Turning away from her he worked his way beneath the covers.

"Good night, my lord," she returned, and blew out the chamberstick.

Within a short time she heard him breathing evenly, and the tension relaxed from her body. She snuggled down beneath the coverlet, and sighed softly. There was something so comforting about the bulk of a man's body next to one. Oh, Edmund, she thought as she had thought so many times over the last year. Why did you have to die? I liked our life together. It was simple and peaceful, and I felt safe. Most of all I felt loved. I suppose that you would approve of Tony, yet God help me there is nothing between us. I could not bear the thought of creating a child with a man for whom I have no feelings. Children should come of love between a man and a woman. Perhaps that is why I never conceived a child with the king. Oh, what shall I do, Edmund? I have but three months' grace. After that I cannot deny Tony that which is his by both God's law and the king's law. With these troubling thoughts swirling about her head Blaze finally fell into a restless sleep.

He awakened before first light, hearing the faint stirrings of the innkeeper and his staff in the taproom below, hearing the soft nickering of the horses in the stables. Gingerly he stretched his long body, easing the kinks from his limbs, turning slowly to see her sleeping beside him, her face invisible to him in the gray darkness, her body a shapeless lump beneath the coverlet. *His wife.* His wife, Blaze. Blaze Wyndham was his wife. He had gained his heart's desire, yet in doing so he seemed to have gained nothing at all. Quietly he slipped from the bed, and relieving himself first in the chamber pot, he quickly dressed, for the air this morning was frosty. The sky was beginning to lighten, and turning, he could now see her.

She looked so innocent and sweet in sleep. How hard it was to equate his sleeping wife with the ambitious woman who had been the king's whore. Still, even knowing it, he had wanted her for his wife. How fortunate it had been that the king was tiring of Blaze when he arrived at court to claim her, else he would have never been able to wed her. Her honey-colored hair was tousled about her face, and spread over the pillows. God, she was so fair! How could any man, even a king, tire of such loveliness?

Reaching out, he touched her shoulder, and shook her gently. "Wake up, Blaze. It is morning, and we must go soon."

She was instantly awake, and nodded silently to him.

"Shall I send Heartha to you?"

"Please, my lord, if you would."

They ate a breakfast of baked apples with clotted cream, ham, hard-boiled eggs, and a cottage loaf fresh from the oven with melted butter and plum jam. Blaze prescribed a small goblet of brown ale for her sister, and then made Bliss walk a goodly mile in the crisp morning air before she would allow her sibling to get into their coach.

"The trouble with you is that you indulge yourself too much," she gently scolded Bliss.

"But I am having a baby," Bliss protested.

"Which is a natural event in the life of a young married woman," laughed Blaze. "You have been at court so long that you have become confused as to what is natural and what is not. You have been getting sick because you eat too many rich foods. Look how you protested this morning that the eggs were but plain and hard-boiled, and not poached and covered in some thick sauce of marsala wine and cream. Simple foods are best. Surely you do not want to get fat, Bliss. If you continue as you have, you will be a plump little partridge after the child comes, and you will never be able to get back into your court finery."

"You certainly know how to threaten me," grumbled Bliss, "but you have been with child twice. I suppose you know what you are talking about."

Blaze's violet-blue eyes twinkled. "Aye, Bliss, I do. You had best heed me, else Owen's roving eye stray to a more slender female."

"*Never!* The rogue is so enamored of me that no woman could ever take my place," Bliss declared. "Nonetheless I shall watch my diet, as you suggest, as I do not choose to be plump." Her eyes narrowed speculatively. "Enough of me, sister. What of you? Was Tony as good a lover as the king?"

"I have no idea if Tony is a good lover," said Blaze calmly.

Bliss's mouth fell open, and she stared at her elder sister in complete surprise. "What!" Then, recovering, she demanded, "Tell me what happened! Tell me at once!"

Well, thought Blaze, amused, Bliss will not have time to be ill today. "There is nothing mysterious or terrible. I have asked my husband to wait three months before coupling with me because I would be absolutely certain that I do not carry the king's child. Remember poor Mary Boleyn. The child came in six months after her wedding to Master William Carey, and the king would not acknowledge it formally as his own, even though he said privately that it probably was. I could hardly allow such a thing to happen to me. There'll be no bastards in the Langford earldom."

"Are you with child?" demanded Bliss shrewdly. "You are not, are you, Blaze?"

"Remember the irregular flux of the Morgan women," Blaze answered.

"Which only Delight and I seem to have," Bliss reminded her. "Why did you lie to Tony?"

"I am not of a mind to lie with Tony right now, sister. I am tired of having to spread my legs at my *master's* will. The king blackmailed me to it, and then when he tired of me he married me off to Tony, who thinks because he is my husband, swiving me is his natural-born right whether he cares for me or no. Would you really enjoy serving the needs of a man you did not know or like, Bliss? Be honest with yourself, would you?"

"Nay," said Bliss slowly, "I would not."

"Then have some sympathy for me, dearest. I need some time for myself, *and* to get to know Anthony Wyndham. I do not really know him, Bliss. Perhaps living with him will help me to put aside my anger. There should be something between us even if it is nothing more than respect and friendship. It is hard for me to go back to RiversEdge and know that Edmund is no longer there, that it is Anthony who is now my husband, and the man who will share the bed where Edmund and I once loved. Where Nyssa was created and born. Where her brother died."

Bliss nodded her head slowly. "I had not thought of those things," she said, and then, "You are a very brave woman, Blaze! I had not thought of it until now, but you are."

Blaze laughed. She could never remember Bliss having ever offered her a spontaneous compliment such as she had just given her elder sister. "I am not brave, Bliss," she said. "I simply do what I must do to survive, and I always will."

Several days later the sisters waved farewell to each other from their coaches as the vehicles turned away in different directions. Shortly afterward the Earl of Langford's carriage rolled through the villages of Wyeton and Michaelschurch and down the hill road to where RiversEdge stood.

"God's foot!" Blaze said without thinking and using the king's favorite oath. "It is good to be home again!"

Anthony could not help but smile at her. "It *is* good to be home," he agreed.

Lady Dorothy Wyndham flew from the house to greet them, barely waiting for Blaze to climb from the coach so she might hug her. "Oh, my dear Blaze, how good it is to have you home again! RiversEdge has not been the same without you, but oh, I understood why you left! Still, memories are not easily escaped from, especially happy ones. I know that my brother would be glad you have come home."

"As I know, Mother, that he would be equally happy to learn that Blaze has become my wife. We were married at Greenwich by Cardinal Wolsey five days ago," said Anthony quietly.

"What?" His mother was astounded.

"In the king's own royal chapel, and the bride was given away by Henry Tudor himself," Anthony finished.

Dorothy Wyndham burst into tears.

"God have mercy, Doro, are you that disappointed to have me as your daughter-in-law?" Blaze asked.

"Oh, Blaze," the good lady sobbed, "nothing could make me happier! *Nothing!*" she declared, and hugged the younger woman once again. "Now I know that this family shall not die out."

"Dearest Doro, there is something that you must know," Blaze began, but she was interrupted by her husband.

"Later, my angel," Tony said lightly, but she saw the warning in his eyes. "Let us go inside the house, for it is chilly outside here."

They entered into the house, and Dorothy Wyndham brought them to the Great Hall, where the fireplaces were burning brightly. Blaze's eye scanned the hall, and then lightened as she saw her daughter.

"Doro! That cannot be Nyssa!" she exclaimed.

Dorothy Wyndham nodded.

"She has grown tremendously. I cannot believe it! Oh, she looks so like her father!"

At that moment the little girl in her dark velvet skirts saw them, and detaching herself from her companion, raced directly across the Great Hall. "Papa!" she cried as, ignoring Blaze, she dashed into Anthony's arms. "Papa is home!" she said as he swept her up into his arms. "What did you bring me, Papa? What?"

"I have brought you your mother, Nyssa," said Anthony. "Is that not a fine present?"

Nyssa Wyndham turned in his arms and stared down her small aristocratic nose at Blaze. There was absolutely no recognition in the violet-blue eyes which were so like her mother's. Then she turned back to Tony, saying, "I do not like her. Send her away, Papa. I like Henriette better. I want Henriette to be my mama!"

Blaze felt as if she had been hit hard, and mutely she turned questioningly to Doro.

Her mother-in-law patted her arm. "You have been away so long, Blaze," she said by way of explanation. "Little children forget quickly. In a few days all will be well between you."

"Why does she call Anthony Papa?" Blaze asked.

"From the moment he and I came to Ashby to get you, and you were not there, Nyssa insisted upon calling him Papa. Nothing any of us said could sway her," Doro replied apologetically. "She does not remember Edmund now, and means no disrespect."

Blaze nodded.

"I want Henriette! I want Henriette!" sang Nyssa infuriatingly.

"Who is this Henriette who has usurped my position?" demanded Blaze. "Where are my daughter's nursemaids, Maisie and Polly?"

Maisie and her assistant hurried forward, bobbing curtsies. "Welcome home, m'lady," they chorused.

"Take Lady Nyssa," Blaze ordered them.

"No!" shrieked Nyssa. "No! No! No! I want my maaaamaaaa!"

"I am your mama, Nyssa Wyndham," said Blaze, taking her child from her husband's arms.

"No! Henriette is my mama! I want Henriette!" She squirmed wildly in Blaze's arms, seeking to evade her mother's grasp.

Blaze passed the screaming child to Maisie, but Nyssa kicked out, catching the poor servant in the shoulder with her little foot, and causing the woman to howl with her hurt. Instinctively Blaze sat down, and turning her unruly child over her knee, lifted her little skirts and paddled her bottom several strokes. Nyssa roared her outrage, for she was more angry than hurt. Blaze knew now that in leaving her child she had done her a great disservice. The little girl was totally out of control, for it was obvious from the horrified faces about them that no one had ever dared to discipline Lady Nyssa Wyndham.

Before anyone might speak, Blaze made her position quite clear to them all. Setting her daughter on her feet in front of her, she said furiously, "Nyssa Catherine Wyndham, be silent!"

Surprised at the harsh tone directed at her, the little girl grew quiet, and glowered up at the pretty lady who had just spanked her. Her eyes were wet with her tears, but their angry glare was mutinous.

"Now, Nyssa Catherine Wyndham, you will listen to me. I am your mother, and I have been at court serving the king. I have come home now, and I expect you to behave properly not only to those who are your equals, but to those who serve you as well. You are to apologize to poor Maisie, whom you have injured in your bad temper. Then you are to go to your room, where you will be served bread and milk for your supper. You are to say your rosary three times, and tomorrow you will come to me and apologize for your dreadful behavior. I will then give you a final penance. Now, say 'Yes, Mama,' and then give your good nights to your father and Grandmama Doro."

"Yes, Mama."

"Where is your curtsy, Nyssa?" Blaze said severely, and thought of her own mother.

Scowling, Nyssa curtsied to her, and then bidding Anthony and Doro lavishly affectionate good nights, she departed the Great Hall clutching at her nursemaid's hand and casting a last scornful look at her mother as they exited the room.

"I have returned just in time," said Blaze quietly.

"No one has been able to do anything with her," Doro explained, "for she has a fearful temper."

"Bliss was like that," Blaze said.

"Then," continued Doro, "Henriette arrived, and she seems to be able to control her better than anyone else. Frankly we have let her, for it is better than constantly fighting with the child. Nyssa can disrupt the entire household when she chooses."

"She will not do it ever again," said Blaze ominously. "Who, Doro, is this Henriette?"

"I am, madam." A slender and extremely sweet-faced young girl stepped forward and curtsied politely to Blaze and Anthony.

"This is Mistress Henriette Wyndham," explained Doro. "She is the only child of Richard's younger brother, Henry, whose wife was a French-woman. Henriette is now orphaned, and it was her father's dying wish that she come to us for protection. She arrived from France the day after you left, Anthony."

"You are most welcome to RiversEdge, Cousin Henriette," said the earl. "I hope that you will be happy with us."

"Ohh, how could I not be happy in such a beautiful place!" exclaimed Henriette, clasping her two hands together in rapture as she beamed ingenuously at Tony. "Ohh, thank you, my lord, for taking me in! Had your mother not had such a generous heart, I do not know where I would have gone."

"I am surprised that your father did not make proper plans for you, Mademoiselle Henriette," said Blaze curiously.

"Alas!" sighed the young girl. "My papa left many debts. Had he not warned me to secrete my mother's jewelry in my skirt hem, I should not have even had the means for my servant, Cecile, and myself to travel here to England." Her amber-colored eyes grew teary. "I was forced to sell almost everything, madam, for our passage."

"Poor child!" sympathized Doro. "Then she had to buy a cart and horse in order to get here from the coast. They were three days without food when they finally arrived!" She turned to Blaze. "Henry was the younger son. Their father wanted him to go into the church, but he would not, and was disowned. Richard was nonetheless fond of him, and occasionally would hear from him. He married a Frenchwoman who was some upper servant attached to the French court. When Richard and I went to *The Field of the Cloth of Gold* in France with the court several years ago, we saw them. She died shortly afterward, and Henriette tells me that he died this past summer."

"It was plague," the young girl said. "The boil beneath his arm would not burst, and they always die when that happens. They would not let me bury him, but took his body away in the death cart."

"Poor child!" Doro said once again.

"How old are you, Mademoiselle Henriette?" Blaze asked.

"Seventeen, madam," came the soft reply.

"We shall have to find you a husband," said Blaze sweetly. "As you are the same age as my little sister Delight, I shall invite Delight to Rivers-Edge so you may have a companion," Blaze finished.

"You are so kind, *madame la comtesse*," replied Henriette, but her golden-amber eyes were looking to Anthony, who was now speaking with his mother.

Blaze's eyes narrowed as she studied the girl. She had a little oval face, very French in appearance. There was not the slightest evidence that she was a Wyndham. Her features were sharp, a slender nose, a narrow little mouth. Her hair was but shoulder-length, a mass of soft dark curls. She played the innocent, and yet Blaze thought there was something a little too calculated, a bit too knowing about the girl. Still, she could hardly toss a relation of her husband's, even one she suspected was not quite the innocent she claimed to be, out into a friendless world. Aye! A suitable husband, *and* the sooner the better!

Later, as she and Doro sat before a fireplace in the smaller family hall, her mother-in-law said, "You do not really mean to invite Delight to RiversEdge. Finding that Tony has finally married will but break her heart once more."

"Delight is seventeen, Doro. It is time that she grew up. Anthony rejected her three years ago, and yet she moons her life away dreaming that one day he will come to Ashby and carry her off on his white horse. Bliss and I have discussed it. It is time for Delight to face life as it really is, and not how she would have it. I shall send a messenger to my parents tomorrow telling them of my marriage to your son, of our new relation, and then I shall invite Delight to RiversEdge. If she can but see Tony and me as husband and wife, then perhaps she will finally admit to herself that he is lost to her. Only then will my parents be able to find her a husband, for they have not been able to bear the thought of forcing her to some marriage or other. Delight has always been the odd one out in our little group. Although nearer in age to the twins and me, she really has no one, for we married young and went off, leaving her with nobody to talk to. Larke and Linnette are a full four years Delight's junior, and extremely clannish. Perhaps having Mademoiselle Henriette for a companion will also help to cheer her."

"You may be right," agreed Dorothy Wyndham, "and Henriette needs a friend her age. I do not like that servant of hers. There is something un-wholesome about the woman, but of course I cannot send her away. She is old and she is all the poor child has left from her past."

"You are certain that she is Henry Wyndham's child?" Blaze queried.

"Aye, Henriette was with her parents at *The Field of the Cloth of Gold*, a little girl, only just eleven that June first. I could not forget that funny little French face. Only her hair is dark like the Wyndhams', but then her mother's hair was dark too. Henriette's mother was one of the French queen's personal serving women, some nobleman's by-blow by a shop-keeper's daughter, Henry told us. She was a quiet woman. I do not think I spoke more than twice to her. My French is not very good, and Henri-ette's mother spoke no English."

"Yet Henriette's English is quite good," Blaze noted. "Almost accent-less, I might add."

"I commented on that when she arrived, and she told me that her fa-ther insisted that she be bilingual. I think Henry meant her for a decent marriage if he could but find the means to dower her. Her mother had some little bits of jewelry, gifts I suppose from her mistress, that the girl used to make her way here to us, but there was nothing else."

"How did Henry Wyndham live?" Blaze asked curiously.

Doro smiled. "Mostly by his wits, his charm, and his sword, Richard told me. It broke my father-in-law's heart, for he had intended that Henry be a bishop one day, but there was too much of the world in Henry, and he had no intention of giving it up. Richard's father finally disowned him in hopes of bringing him to his senses. Instead, Henry went to France."

Blaze nodded. "Well," she said, "we shall have to find someone suit-able for Henriette to wed. Edmund dowered my sisters generously, and so I will certainly see that Tony dowers Henriette as well. I would see her gone as quickly as possible."

"*Blaze!*" Dorothy Wyndham was surprised by her daughter-in-law's hard attitude.

"Doro, I have lived at the court of Henry Tudor for almost a year. It is a very sophisticated court, and I have met all sorts of people. Mademoiselle Henriette is not quite the innocent she pretends to be. Perhaps you do not see it, for you are a good and loving lady, and certainly Tony does not see it, for he is a man, and the girl simpers and fawns on him, inflaming his masculine ego. I, however, see it. She has already exercised an influence on my daughter that I do not approve of, and so I would have her gone as quickly as possible. There is nothing wrong in that. I wish her no harm. I just wish her gone from my house."

"I cannot fault you for that, Blaze," replied Doro. "Perhaps the girl is a bit more knowledgeable than she would have us know, but mayhap she feared our rejection if we did not think her the helpless innocent. I cannot blame her for that. She really did not know us well enough to be certain. Let us give her the benefit of the doubt for poor Henry's sake."

"Very well, Doro, but at the same time let us seek for a man to marry her," said Blaze.

"What of your marriage to Tony?" asked Doro. "I did not know when Tony left for court that he intended to wed with you. I am most vexed that you married at Greenwich instead of coming home where I and your family might share in the happy event." The older woman smiled at Blaze to show her that she was not really angry, simply disappointed.

Blaze took a deep breath. "There is something that you should know, Doro," she said. "I would not feel right keeping it from you," and she went on to explain to Edmund's sister how the king, using Nyssa, had blackmailed her into his bed. How she had, nonetheless, grown fond of him, for he was really a lonely man. How, just as Henry was trying to decide how to get rid of her, for his affections were straying in the direction of Mistress Anne Boleyn, Anthony had arrived at court and explained to Henry that he had promised the dying Edmund that he would take his widow for his wife to protect both her and the children.

"So he told the king *that*, did he?" said Doro.

"Aye, and so the king insisted we be married, thus solving his problem, and allowing Tony to keep his promise to Edmund," finished Blaze, who had not noticed the tone of Dorothy Wyndham's voice.

"So you are married," said Doro quietly, "but do you love my son, Blaze?"

Blaze shook her head. "Do not think badly of me, Doro. I still love Edmund. I think I always will, but I would be a good and faithful wife to

Tony, I swear it! I am trying very hard to overcome my rancor toward him."

Doro patted her daughter-in-law's hand. "Do not worry, my dear," she said. "You have only done what you had to do, and I know you will try to make Tony happy. He loves you."

"Oh, no, Doro, he certainly does not love me. He married me because he loved Edmund, and he promised him that he would do so. Anthony is an honorable man, but love has nothing to do with our marriage."

Dorothy Wyndham held her tongue. She knew that her son loved Blaze with all his heart. Loved her enough to tell the king that outrageous and incredible lie about a deathbed promise that she knew never existed. Yet Blaze suspected it not, and before Doro said anything to her about it, she would talk with her son. As for Tony, he did not realize that Blaze had only gone to Henry Tudor's bed in order to protect her child from being taken away. That knowledge was also not hers to impart, and so she must remain silent there also. She approved of Blaze's decision not to cohabit with her husband for three months so that when an heir was born for Langford there could be no mistaking his parentage. Three months was time enough for her son and new daughter-in-law to settle their differences, and possibly to even learn to love each other a little.

Blaze settled back into RiversEdge, and after a week it was as if she had never been gone. The household ran smoothly, and Tony spent most of his days out riding the estate lands with his bailiff, making certain that his people were settling in for the coming winter, that roofs and chimneys were in good repair, that the granary was safe from pillaging rodents. There seemed to be more deer this year than he had ever seen, and so Tony gave the head of each family belonging to his estates the right to take one deer. It was an incredible gift, and if he was thanked once, he was thanked a thousand times as he rode through his villages.

"Long life, and many sons to yer lordship," the goodwives called after him, and he grinned to himself. There was little chance of any sons, let alone many sons, until that damned three-month waiting period Blaze had ordained was over. That her decision was an intelligent and correct one did not console him.

Lady Nyssa Catherine Wyndham came to accept her mother's presence, although she was not an easy child under any circumstances. With Blaze's return, however, discipline reentered Nyssa's life. She did not like it, but she was wise enough not to show her displeasure in front of her mother, who did not hesitate to administer her an immediate sharp slap for her transgressions. Her first penance involved embroidery of a linen napkin to be used by Father Martin in the communion service. Her first efforts were met with disdain by her mother, who, ripping out the sloppy stitches, told her to do it over again. Nyssa glowered at Blaze angrily.

"Do you want me to show you how?" Blaze offered.

"Henriette showed me," came the surly reply.

"Yet you did it badly. Perhaps Henriette does not sew well. It is not easy to learn, Nyssa. I know I always had trouble. Your aunts Bliss and Blythe are ever so much better than I am, and faster too."

"They are?" Nyssa was interested.

"Aye."

"Then perhaps my aunts should show me, madam," was the child's quick reply.

She was clever, thought Blaze. Her father's daughter without a doubt. "Not this time, but if they come at Christmastime then I shall ask them. Today, however, you must learn from me, for I am here and they are not."

"Show me then . . . Mama," Nyssa said.

"Hold your needle so," Blaze said, showing her. "Good, child, now make your stitch."

"Look!" Nyssa cried excitedly. "It is much nicer than before, Mama!"

"Aye," replied Blaze. "If you do it that way, I will not have to reject your cloth when you are finished."

Dorothy Wyndham smiled as she watched the mother and daughter, their heads bent close together. Blaze was beginning to win Nyssa back to her. If only Anthony could win Blaze over as easily as she was bringing her daughter around. Their exaggerated politeness to one another was beginning to wear on her nerves. She would have even preferred that they fight. At least Blaze and Tony would have been showing some emotion toward one another, thought Doro.

Delight Morgan arrived at RiversEdge. Doro had not seen her in some time, and was startled at the beauty Delight had become. Unlike her elder sister, who was petite like their mother and other sisters, Delight was tall like her father, and slender. She had perfectly proportioned features, and an exquisitely lovely body. Though she greeted Tony warmly, she was less than cordial to her elder sibling.

"How could you marry him!" she demanded of Blaze when they were finally alone. "Knowing that I loved him, how could you do it? Is being the Countess of Langford so important to you that you had to wed your husband's heir? You don't love him! How could you? You don't even know him!"

It was no time to be gentle, Blaze realized. "I did not choose to wed him, Delight. It was an arrangement made by Tony and the king. It was Edmund's dying request that Tony marry me."

"You might have released him from Edmund's request, Blaze!"

"Why?" said Blaze cruelly. "The king was tiring of me, and 'tis custom with discarded mistresses to marry them off. I should just as soon be wed with someone I know and like, as to some stranger. Besides, Anthony does not love you, Delight."

"He had not even the time to learn to know me," the girl cried. "*You* saw to that! You lured him to court and stole him from me!"

"God's foot, Delight! I cannot believe that you *really* believe that tale, even in your secret heart of hearts. If I had wanted to *lure* Anthony, I should not have bothered to go up to court with Bliss and Owen. I might have stayed right here at RiversEdge and captured him even sooner. Anthony is not in love with you, Delight. He never has been, and God only knows you have tried hard enough to gain his love and his attention. He is not the man for you, sister. Admit to that fact, and get on with your life!"

"Anthony is really in love with me, Blaze. 'Tis you who had best face facts!" Delight asserted firmly. "I have come to RiversEdge to take him from you, and I will!"

"I am going to have to send her home to Ashby immediately," Blaze told Doro as she recounted her talk with her younger sister. "I had hoped seeing Anthony and me together might convince her, but she seems unable to accept anything except what she chooses to believe. I think this passion she has for Anthony has unhinged her, Doro."

"No," replied Dorothy Wyndham. "Let her stay but a bit longer, Blaze. Perhaps Henriette's company will aid her pained spirit. It might also help if you and Tony appeared a bit more loving toward one another. You are polite to each other, but despite your bond of marriage, you seem totally uninvolved with one another. Remember that Delight saw you with Edmund, and she remembers it well. If you would like, I shall speak to Tony about it too."

Blaze felt herself flushing with embarrassment, but she managed to nod. How ridiculous that her mother-in-law must speak with her husband about such a matter, but she knew that Doro was right. Delight was behaving in a stubborn and an irrational manner. She needed more convincing. She must be forced to face the truth, for despite Doro's reassurances, it was obvious to Blaze that her younger sister was tottering on the brink of madness.

It was early evening, and having overseen her household successfully, Blaze stood by the fireplace in the family hall staring into the fire. She watched as a log collapsed, sending a shower of orange sparks up the chimney. When his hand fell upon her shoulder she did not start, but turning her head, looked up at him. He smiled softly at her, and then to her surprise he bent his head, gently touching her lips with his.

"Your sister is watching," he murmured against her mouth.

"Doro spoke to you?" Why was her heart beating so quickly? she wondered.

He pressed little kisses along her upper lip. "Aye, in her motherly way she reminded me that I had never kissed you. Do you realize that, my angel? I have never kissed you until this moment."

Surely it was the warmth of the fire that made her cheeks so warm, Blaze considered as his arm slipped about her waist. "We did not kiss at our wedding, did we?" she noted.

"The king kissed you most heartily," he remembered, "but I did not. I realize that it is yet two months before we dare share a bed, my angel, but surely such pleasantries as these must not be denied us." He kissed her lightly once again.

"Tony—" she began.

He put a finger to her lips to silence her. "Blaze, you do not love me, I know it. Still, we must eventually join our bodies to produce the next generation of Wyndhams. I would not make love to a stranger. I am not a man to make love coldly and without tenderness. Perhaps you will never really forgive me my part in Edmund's death, unintentioned as it was, but do not hate me, I beg of you. I do not want our children born of hate, my angel. Can you understand that?"

She put her hand up to touch his face in a gentle gesture. "Aye, my lord, I understand, and I agree. Anthony Wyndham, I beg your pardon, for I have wronged you. You were not responsible for Edmund's death. Oh, you teased him to hunt that day, 'tis certain, but Edmund was a strong man. He went because he wanted to go, and your taunts offered him the excuse he sought to avoid his half-promise to me. As for our son, it was my anger, I am certain, that pushed his tiny body from my womb, and nothing else. I am to blame there, and not you.

"I do not promise that I will ever love you, my lord, but I will cease warring with you. Perhaps if we take the time to know one another we will find that we can love each other, if only a little bit. Surely that is better than the anger and misunderstanding that has been between us."

"And in finding each other," he answered her, "mayhap we can help little Delight to face life as it is." His beautiful light blue eyes held a warmth she had never seen before, and Blaze found it not displeasing.

"Does she still watch us?"

"Nay, my angel, she was gone after our first kiss," he said.

She felt a sudden pleasure in his words. He had kissed her for Delight's benefit, and yet he had kissed her again several times afterward because it pleased him. He had even stayed speaking quietly to her of working out their differences, *and* it had been for them that he had done it, not for Delight. Had she misjudged him? Had her hate blinded her to the man he really was? He was, after all, Edmund's nephew.

It was a quiet Christmas at RiversEdge. Both Bliss and Blythe preferred not to travel in their conditions, and a series of early and heavy snows had decided Lord Morgan and his family to remain at Ashby. Delight cared not, however, for she and Henriette Wyndham had become close friends.

"I do not care if I ever see Ashby again," she declared at supper on Christmas Night.

"You cannot remain here forever," Blaze reminded her. "In the spring Tony and I intend seeking candidates for Henriette's hand in marriage. She will be eighteen on June first and you will be eighteen on the seventh of June. You are both growing a bit long in the tooth to be wed. When I was your age I already had Nyssa."

"And the year after, you were the king's whore," said Delight, and Henriette giggled. "How Tony could honor Edmund's request when you had so shamefully dishonored Edmund's memory and the Wyndham name is hard for me to understand."

Blaze was too shocked to even speak, as was Doro, but Anthony Wyndham leapt to his feet, his anger all too apparent. "Go to your room, Delight!" he thundered. "You are not to be allowed out until I give my permission. How dare you speak to my wife in such a fashion, and in front of our daughter?" he demanded.

Delight jumped up sobbing. "I understand, Tony," she wept. "You were forced to the altar. I understand, and I forgive you." Then, turning, she fled the little family hall where they were gathered.

Henriette stood up, and with a curtsy to her elders she said, "I will go with her, and attempt to calm her. *Pauvre* Delight! Her heart is broken." She hurried after her friend while behind her Blaze and Doro looked at each other in despair.

Henriette easily caught up with Delight, and linking her arm with her friend's, she chided her, "You are a fool, Delight, to so openly quarrel with your sister. Her kindness and her patience with you make you look all the worse for your tantrums. Have I not warned you, *chérie?*"

"He loves me, and not her," sobbed Delight. "I cannot bear to see him unhappy. I should be the one he kisses by the fireplace! I should be the one he beds with! I should be the one who has his children! Not her! Not Blaze! Anthony is the only man I have ever loved, Henriette! Why should she have him and not I?"

"In time, *chérie*," murmured Henriette. "In time you will have your Anthony, and I shall help you, I promise you!"

"Why will you help me?" demanded the weeping Delight.

"Because you are my very best friend in all the world, Delight Morgan, that is why!" said Henriette with such great conviction that innocent Delight believed her, and allowed her to put her to bed.

"I shall never sleep," complained Delight.

"Yes you will, for I shall give you a special draught," said Henriette, and pulling her little purse from her waistband, she dropped a pinch of powder into a small goblet of wine, and encouraged Delight to drink it all down. Within minutes the overwrought girl was asleep.

Henriette looked down upon Delight scornfully. What a fool the girl was! The little idiot had convinced herself that Cousin Anthony had wed with his Blaze simply as a duty, yet Henriette could see that nothing was further from the truth. Anthony Wyndham was in love with his wife, and if she was not in love with him now, she would eventually be. Henriette hurried to her own room next door.

"What was all the shouting in the hall?" demanded Cecile. She spoke in French, for her English was poor.

"It was Delight, *grand-mère*, baiting her sister again. Cousin Anthony sent her from the hall. I have put the little silly to bed."

"Be careful, *chérie!* You must not call me *grand-mère* lest someone over-hear you. As long as these English believe that I am your servant, and that I speak no English, they feel free to chatter in front of me. I can learn much for you."

Henriette hugged the elderly woman. "Do not fear, *grand-mère*. I gave Delight a sleeping potion to calm her, and everyone else is still in the hall." She settled herself on the bed with her skirts tucked beneath her. "They spoke again of marrying me off tonight, *grand-mère*. Cousin Blaze says that Delight and I are getting a bit old to find husbands, and come the spring they will find us each a mate." She laughed. "Beautiful Blaze, who is so sure of herself and her life. How I hate her! How I hate her for being married to Anthony when I had planned to wed with him myself. Is that not what Papa wanted for me, *grand-mère*?"

"*Oui, oui*," replied the old woman, "but it cannot be now, *ma petite*. You are fortunate that Madame Blaze was willing to keep you here, and is willing to see you dowered and wed well. She is not stupid, *ma petite*. She has been a powerful king's mistress after all. Be grateful she has not seen through you."

"Do you think I shall wed with some English country squire when I have been promised a nobleman all my life? I intend being Madame la Comtesse de Langford, *grand-mère*!"

"*Zut alors*, Henriette! And what of Madame Blaze?"

"She will die," said Henriette.

"And Mademoiselle Delight?"

" 'Tis she who will murder her sister, and then in remorse over her wicked deed, kill herself. Then only I shall be left, *ma chère grand-mère*. I shall be here to comfort my poor cousin Anthony, to oversee that little brat Nyssa, who calls him Papa, to wed with him when his mourning is over."

"And how will you get Mademoiselle Delight to do your bidding, *ma petite*?" demanded Cecile.

"I must move slowly, and carefully," said Henriette thoughtfully. "Delight must be driven far enough that she will not panic at the last moment and foil my plans. That would not do at all, *grand-mère*. Trust me. I learned much at the court of the King François. I know just what to do."

The old Frenchwoman nodded her head as her granddaughter spoke. Her own husband had been an Italian from the court at Firenze, where he was an apothecary. He had taught both his wife and his daughter all of his knowledge of poisons and potions. It was this skill that had gained Henriette's mother her place with the French queen, who was constantly slipping love potions into her husband's wine in hopes of retaining his passion. Both Henriette's grandmother and mother had passed on their skills to her in hopes that she would one day be given a place in some important household. Henry Wyndham, however, had had other plans for his pretty little daughter.

"You will be a lady, my little Henriette," he told her over and over again as she grew up. "One day I will see that you marry a fine English lord, and then your papa can go home to live out his old age in style."

When she had just turned eleven she had gone with her parents to the meeting of the two great kings, François and Henry, that was called *The Field of the Cloth of Gold*. There, by chance, her father had met his brother and his brother's wife. Henry Wyndham had not seen his family in many years, but there was no animosity between the brothers. She remembered that her uncle, Lord Richard, had given her sugarplums and a silver piece. She remembered him bemoaning his son's wifeless state.

Afterward her father said to her, "If Anthony Wyndham is not wed by the time you are old enough, then by God, I shall match you with your cousin, *ma petite!*"

She had never forgotten his words, and when she had arrived at RiversEdge she had been more than pleased to learn that her cousin was still without a wife. Though she was shocked when he returned two months later from Greenwich with a bride, she had hidden her deep disappointment very well. No one, not even Madame Blaze, suspected her. The coming of Delight Morgan with her stubborn passion for Anthony Wyndham was a wonderful piece of luck. She would use that silly and bitter young girl to rid her of her rival, and then she would take Anthony for her very own.

During the long winter she would play upon Delight's jealousy. Carefully. Oh, so carefully. She would rouse the innocent girl's desires and natural lust for Anthony. She would drive her gently to the very brink, and then . . . Henriette laughed.

"I shall make a most elegant *comtesse, grand-mère,* shall I not? Then I will go to court and surprise my old friend Mademoiselle Boleyn! She will be very surprised to see us, will she not?"

The old woman cackled. "Indeed she will, *ma petite!* Poor King Henry Tudor. He will not rid himself of Mistress Anne Boleyn as easily as he has rid himself of his other *amours.* She means to have it all, that one!"

"The king wants to fuck her, *grand-mère,* but I know Anne well enough to tell you that though his desires strain his codpiece to the breaking point, he will not get his royal cock into Mademoiselle Boleyn's sweet hole until he has made her his wife! She is a proud little bitch."

" 'Tis a shame that you were not so scrupulous in your behavior, *ma petite,* as Mademoiselle Boleyn, else your papa would not have died of those fearsome wounds he gained defending your honor. An honor that was long lost, Henriette."

"Papa would have never found out about Monsieur le Duc but that Mademoiselle d'Aumont coveted him also." She shrugged. "I did not ask him to defend me. Besides, *grand-mère,* you know that I love to fuck."

"Aye, child," was the answer, "but you must be careful here, else you are discovered, and your plans fail."

Chapter 12

❧

The new year of Our Lord, 1526, had begun. The snows of December showed no signs of abating as the cold January days passed. Nyssa had celebrated her third birthday on the last day of December. Though her temper showed no signs of easing, she had now completely accepted Blaze once more as her mother. Under her mother's tutelage her stitchery had improved tremendously, and the little girl was extremely proud of her accomplishment.

"I believe she will sew as well as Bliss and Blythe," chuckled Blaze to Tony one evening as they sat before the fire in her dayroom. "It is very embarrassing to have such a small child outstrip you."

He laughed back at her, and reaching out, took her hand in his. "She imitates you, you know," he told her. "She watches you very carefully, and then tries to mimic what you do. The way you stand, for instance, when you are giving the maids orders. I saw Nyssa set herself just like that the other day, and give orders to Polly."

"The little imp!" said Blaze, not knowing whether to be angry or whether to laugh.

"She admires you tremendously," Tony continued. "From the moment you returned home and had to upend her and paddle her bottom. I thought you were wrong at the time, but it turned out that you were right, Blaze."

"Children need boundaries, Tony. Without them they are apt to run wild and frightened. As long as children know what is expected of them, it is easier for them to behave. My mother raised us that way. When you took Nyssa from Ashby and brought her home, you let her run wild, and she grew afraid. Her temper was the result, and I will have to work long and hard to improve that, but how could you know? You are a man."

"A man who counts the days until the fifth of February," he said quietly. Then, raising her hand to his lips, he kissed it.

Startled, Blaze looked up at him, her eyes widening in her surprise. "Anthony . . ." Her voice caught.

"You do not hate me any longer, Blaze. I know it."

"But I do not love you, my lord."

"Did you love Henry Tudor?" he asked her.

"I was the king's whore," she said quietly, "but I am your wife. Even you know the difference."

"Yet you deny me that which you so freely gave the king," he answered her.

Blaze sighed deeply. She did not hate Anthony any longer, but she also did not know how she felt about him. She was no silly girl to grow indignant at his unspoken accusations. If she was to be happy with him, she would have to tell him the truth. "You are mistaken, Tony. I gave nothing freely to the king. Henry Tudor takes what he wants, be it a woman or an estate. My chaste behavior is what attracted his attention, and so he marked me for his own as a hunter marks a doe.

"He made it quite clear that on the first of May I would become his ladylove. He had me moved from my little chamber in the Marwood apartments to a large apartment set over his royal chambers. There was an inner staircase, hidden from public view, that allowed him to move back and forth in private between the two places. I wanted none of it. Neither the king, nor his spacious apartments, nor the supposed *honor* of being a royal mistress."

"Then why did you simply not leave the court and come home?" Tony asked her.

Blaze laughed. "It is so simple for men, is it not?" she gently mocked him. "I wanted to do just that, but how could I deny my king? I was no virgin with a maidenhead to protect. Besides, he threatened to take Nyssa away from me and give her custody and that of RiversEdge to Thomas Seymour, who had tried and failed in his seduction of me. I do not like the Seymours. They are very ambitious people, and I feared for both Nyssa and her estates. I had no powerful allies to protect me. As long as I obeyed the king's commands, Nyssa was safe and remained where she belonged."

Anthony was shocked, for he admired the king. Still, as he thought on it, it was not so surprising. Henry Tudor was a most ruthless man when he chose to be. "Blaze," he said, "I am so sorry! You were alone, and you were helpless. As Edmund's heir I should have been there to help you!"

"I ran from your kindness and help," she said truthfully, "but let me finish. Even so, I resisted the king as best I could, putting off the inevitable, hoping he would lose interest. On May Day, however, the king grew impatient for the night to come, and in early afternoon dragged me off in full sight of the court to his privy chamber. Then he forced me over a library table, and lifting my skirts, took me then and there. After that I did not resist him. What purpose would there have been in it? As long as I was his loving and gentle *sweetheart*, the king was content, and my child was safe from the Seymours.

"Strangely, I grew to like Hal over the months that I served his pleasures. He is a cruel man, yet there is great kindness in him. He is amusing and educated. He has great wit and even greater charm. Except for our first encounter, he was kind and thoughtful of me; but never, Anthony, *never* did I aspire to the position in which I found myself." Then she laughed softly, realizing the double entendre of her words. "I think," she amended, "that you know what it is I am trying to say to you, Tony. I did not seek to be the king's mistress, and offered a choice, I would have declined the honor."

He nodded. "I see now that I have been a fool," he admitted. "I believed that you had gone to court, and having attracted the king's attentions, were pleased with your place in life. How could I have been so blind? You would have never done such a thing, and yet I was so quick to think the worst when I arrived at court and learned your place in the king's life."

"I am not surprised," she answered him. "The morality of those who live at court is far different from those of us who live quietly by simpler values in our country homes. You had been at court, and you knew its values. You judged me by those values. Bliss was always remonstrating with me for not enjoying my place, for she was convinced that I should adore living atop the pinnacle of power. She never really understood my unhappiness with my situation. Still, I never used my place in the king's mercurial affections to gain either wealth or power for my family. There were many that called me the fool for it. I was known as *The Quiet Mistress*." She smiled.

"Why did you not use your position in Henry's life to benefit your family, Blaze?" He was curious, for her behavior was indeed a most unconventional one.

"I did not seek to be the king's mistress, Anthony, but to have used my body as a weapon once I was his mistress only to gain riches and power for my family seemed to me a dishonorable thing to do, even under those circumstances," Blaze told him.

"I have been a fool," he answered her, realizing now how he had wronged her.

"Perhaps we have both been foolish," she said.

"Do you think you can forgive me, Blaze, for believing that you had chosen to live the life you lived at court?"

"There is nothing to forgive, Tony. As I have said, you but judged me by the values of the court. You did not know me well enough to make any other judgment."

"But you were Edmund's wife," he protested, convinced of his error.

"I was Edmund's wife, but I was not Edmund. Edmund was like a brother to you, and you knew him as well as you knew yourself. You have never really known me. There is nothing to forgive. Let us put the past behind us, Anthony. It is not important. What is important is the here and the now."

"Begin anew, Blaze? Is that what you would have us do?" His look was a serious one.

"Aye, Tony. Begin anew. Do you think we might?" Her voice had grown wistful.

His heart was hammering wildly. *Begin again!* She was trying her very best to make her peace with him. To really settle all the anger and misunderstanding that had been between them. He loved her now more than he had ever loved her, and he longed to tell her so, yet he dared not. She was only half-right when she said he did not know her. He had fallen in love with her the moment he had seen her lovely face and form. He had watched her secretly when she had been Edmund's wife, and he had believed her to be perfect. How he had envied his uncle then!

When Edmund had died, Anthony had known that he could never allow Blaze to wed with anyone other than himself. He had planned a scenario in his mind in which he would court and win her after her mourning was over. Her flight to court and away from everything she had ever known and loved had confused him. When he learned of her place in the king's affections everything he had always believed about her had been destroyed, and he had been angered at what he believed was his own stupidity.

Now he was learning the real truth about Blaze. She was not the perfect woman, as he had once thought. A perfect woman was one that was made of marble, that had no warmth or feeling in her at all. There was no such thing as a perfect woman, any more than there was such a thing as a perfect man. Blaze was real! She was alive, and warm, and giving. Her heart was so great that she had even been able to forgive the king his treatment of her, and find something good within Henry's royal soul. God, how he had misjudged her, and now she was asking him to begin once more!

"Aye," he told her, "we can begin again, my angel!"

Then suddenly, to his great surprise, Blaze took his face between her two small hands and kissed him. His head reeled at the warm touch of her lips upon his, and he wanted to clasp her tightly within his arms, but dared he? Not yet. He would not have her believe that his interest in her was only in bedding her, for it was not.

"To seal the bargain between us," she said as she drew away, and her eyes smiled into his.

"Let me love you just a little more," he begged her, all his good intentions dissolving.

She was tempted. Dear heaven, she was tempted. He was really a kind and gentle man, so much like Edmund, and yet he was different. She needed to be loved again by a man who truly cared for her, but she did not think he did. He was simply a man, and men needed the pleasure of a woman's body in order to be happy. She had denied him that pleasure for two months, but she would stick to her original bargain with him. She shook her head. "We are too old, and too experienced in the arts of passion, my lord, to play at children's games. Let us know one another a little better before we embark upon a voyage of sensuality."

"What would you know of me, madam?" he demanded. "I would have you learn it quickly, for what I seek to know of you, you would deny me for your lack of knowledge about me," he teased her.

Blaze burst out laughing. "I have already learned one thing about you, my lord. You have a sharp wit."

"And you have been known to have a sharp tongue, madam," he quipped at her.

"I think the court lost a valuable courtier in you, Anthony Wyndham," she told him.

"I am no courtier, my angel. I am happiest living here in the country with you, Nyssa, and my mother. I long for the day when we shall have a houseful of children to love and to raise, even as your parents have. I seek no glory, nor honors, Blaze Wyndham. I seek your heart and the happiness we shall one day, God willing, make between us. Now, kiss me again, madam. I promise you that I shall restrain my baser nature, but only if you kiss me!"

Leaning toward him, she placed her mouth on his once more, but this time his arms enclosed her in a gentle embrace, drawing her across the settle upon which they were sitting. Gently he ran his tongue across her lips, and they parted themselves for him. Delicately he explored the honeyed grotto of her mouth, and she trembled ever so faintly as his tongue at last made contact with hers. Like two spears of fire their tongues danced and wove about each other, slowly stroking their passions.

I must stop this. The thought fuzzily entered her mind. *I must!* Yet she could not seem to muster the willpower that she needed to demand that he cease his kisses. They were such wonderful kisses, warm and tender, filling her veins with a voluptuous sweetness that seemed to throb throughout her whole being.

His fingers found the laces to her bodice, and he skillfully and quickly undid them, ignoring her sudden little cry of protest. "Nay, sweetheart, I am in control," he whispered to her. "Let me! Please, let me!"

A single hand cupped a soft breast, and Blaze felt herself close to tears. It had been so long since she had been touched with such gentleness. It was almost unbearable. Tenderly he fondled the perfumed globe, unable to take his eyes off the delicate ivory flesh with its tight coral tip that almost vibrated beneath his touch. He could feel his own vaunted control beginning to slip away, and then he saw the crystalline tears slipping from beneath her closed eyelids to pearl upon her cheeks.

"Oh, my angel," he said, "do not weep! You must not weep!" With supreme effort he restored her dress to its proper mode and cradled her in his arms. "Oh, Blaze, my adorable wife, do not weep. I have ceased, and I will not touch you again until you are ready."

Her quiet tears suddenly stopped, and opening her eyes, Blaze looked at him, saying, "Oh, Tony, do not be such a great fool! I weep because of the wonderful pleasure you have given me, not because you have violated my sensibilities!"

"*What?* Do you say that I made you happy then, my angel?"

"Aye, my lord, you did. Yet I worry now to wonder what sort of woman I am that enjoys the lovemaking of a stranger."

"Dammit, Blaze, I am not a stranger! I am your husband! We have known one another since you were fifteen, and you are now twenty! Would you know what kind of woman you are, my angel, then I shall tell you. You are a warm and a loving woman. Do you think that Edmund did not brag of your loving nature to me, for he did. He could not believe his good fortune, for though his first wife was sweet and she loved him, she was cold in the marriage bed. You were not, and he could not resist sharing that knowledge with me."

"I did not think that men spoke of such things except when discussing *other* women," she exclaimed.

"Do not women discuss the men with whom they make love, my angel?" and he laughed when she blushed.

Suddenly a friendship blossomed between them, a friendship that was more than evident to all who saw them together now. Though Blaze worried about her enjoyment of the more carnal side of their budding relationship, she worked hard to put it from her mind, for she was too busy discovering more and more that she liked about the man who was now her husband.

Dorothy Wyndham continued to light her candles in the family chapel, thanking the Blessed Mother to whom she had been fervently praying that Blaze and Anthony would settle their differences, that Blaze would learn to love her son, and that Tony would finally have the courage to tell his wife that he had always loved her, that his story of Edmund's dying request had been just that: a story. Her prayers seemed to be answered in part at least. In time, perhaps, all of her prayers would be answered.

Seeing that her sister and Anthony seemed to be happy ate like a canker in Delight Morgan's breast. She was forced to remain at Rivers-Edge because the heavy winter snows had made the roads virtually impassable. When Anthony's mother suggested that perhaps she would like to go across the river to visit with Blythe, Henriette had cried and begged that her *dearest* and *only* friend in the whole world not be sent away. Blaze had given in, for the two girls kept virtually to themselves, thereby giving her less trouble. Besides, she would not wish the sad and embittered Delight upon sweet Blythe now in the last months of her third pregnancy.

One day when the sun shone for the first time in many days, and the air was softly warm for winter, the two girls, arm in arm, strolled about the January barren gardens. Henriette had learned that Delight was still a virgin, albeit a curious virgin. Delight had shared with her the stories of her little sister Vanora's spyings from the stable lofts when she was just a wee girl. The way in which she related the tales told the wily Henriette that Delight's virginity was a frustration to her, and the French girl suspected she could use Delight's weakness to her own advantage.

"Did you ever watch the servants fucking from Vanora's loft?" Henriette asked innocently.

"Ohh, no," Delight said with a blush that turned her cheeks a fiery red.

"Would you like to see a man and woman doing *that?*" Mademoiselle

Henriette tempted her friend. "Doing what you so very much want Tony to do with you?"

"Oh, no," whispered Delight. "I would be afraid to watch someone doing *that*. What if I got caught?"

"You'll never know just what to imagine or how delicious lovemaking really is unless you either see someone else do it or you do it yourself," taunted Henriette. "As I know you would save your virginity for Anthony alone, the only other alternative open to you is to watch the act. You would not get caught if you watched a friend, Delight. *If you watched me!*" Her little French face was alight with her mischief.

"*You?*" Delight was not certain if Henriette was serious or if she were making mock of her.

"*Oui, chérie*, me! Alas, I was raised at the French court, and a girl has little chance of keeping her virginity much past the age of twelve there. I have found that I have a taste for passion, *chérie*."

"But if you are not a virgin," gasped the shocked Delight, "will your bridegroom not be angry?"

"He will never know," laughed Henriette. "Men are rarely that discerning. All a girl need do is struggle and cry a lot on her wedding night, and then later when her bridegroom is asleep, smear a chicken's bladder of blood on the sheets and her thighs for her proud and unsuspecting husband to find the next morning! It is so simple, *ma petite* Delight. So tell me now, would you like to see me fuck?"

Delight's beautiful eyes were wide. "Who would you do it with?" she whispered.

Henriette giggled. "Come along," she said, "and while you are watching me, just imagine it is you with your beloved Tony!" Taking her companion by the hand again, the French girl led Delight to the stables.

For a moment Delight hesitated, but Henriette laughed again, and pulled her into the dim barns where the estate horses were stabled. It took a moment for their eyes to adjust to the pale light, but when it had, Delight could see no one at all in sight. Still, she followed after Henriette, who seemed to know her way about the place quite well. They moved to the rear of the buildings, and as they did, there suddenly appeared before them a tall young stableman.

"*Bonjour*, Johnny," murmured Henriette. "Are you feeling as randy as milord earl's stallion today? I hope so, *chéri*, for I am like a little mare in her first heat!"

"Then I won't disappoint you, mistress," replied the stableman. "Who's yer friend?"

" 'Tis the countess's sister, and she wants to watch us fuck, Johnny. You will not mind, *chéri*, will you?"

The stablehand smiled broadly, showing surprisingly even teeth. "Nay, mistress, I will not mind. Maybe she'd even like a little taste herself of Johnny's big pecker, eh?"

"Nay, *chéri*," cautioned Henriette. "My friend is not ready to give up her virtue yet. She will just watch us to see how it is done." They had reached the back of the stables, where a large empty stall filled with straw awaited them. "You can stand here in the doorway and watch us, Delight," said Henriette. "Be certain to warn us if anyone comes this way. We would not want anyone else to know our little secret, would we? Madame Blaze would be certain to send you home and away from your Tony if we were caught, and then he could not do to you what Johnny is going to do to me now."

Delight nodded, a shiver of fear running down her spine. In the back of her mind was the thought that Henriette was a very bad girl, and that neither of them should be here. Then the thought of Anthony Wyndham crossed her mind, and she focused her eyes on the couple in the stall box. The stableman had already unlaced and removed Henriette's bodice. He had pulled her chemise down to her waist so that her big breasts were bare. Now he groveled on his knees in the stall before her, his head moving swiftly and he nuzzled, sucked, licked, and kissed at the ample bosom before him. Henriette looked down on him scornfully, and then she looked up to smile conspiratorially at Delight. Soon the stableman's hands slipped beneath the girl's dress, and then he pulled her down into the straw upon her back, pushing her heavy skirts up and baring her to the waist. To Delight's surprise, Henriette had a triangle of dark curls between her legs. Kneeling between those outspread limbs, the stableman straightened himself back up, fumbled with his breeches, and suddenly Delight saw his organ—a great and long affair with a purplish head.

She gasped with shock, for she had never expected that a manhood could be that big. The stableman heard her startled sound, and turning about for just a moment, grinned, pleased at her. Delight blushed, to his vast amusement, but then Henriette was hissing, "Put it in me, you vain bastard! Put it in me!" With a shrug of apparent regret Johnny turned back to his partner and thrust himself into her body. Fiercely he jammed himself in and out of her body, and beneath him Henriette began to squirm and moan once more. Delight could not take her eyes off the spectacle before her. Her vision glazed and she saw, not Henriette and her brawny stableman, but herself and Anthony locked in passion's embrace.

Delight's legs grew wobbly, and she clung hard to the stall door to keep herself from falling. Her breathing grew harsh, and she moaned so softly that only she herself could actually distinguish the words. *"Anthony! Oh, yes, my darling! Yes! Yes! Love me! Love me!"* Only Henriette's little shriek of satisfaction brought Delight back to reality.

The French girl smiled, and rolling her lover off her, stretched languidly before getting up to readjust her clothing and dress herself. When she had finished, she stepped over her still-fallen lover, and linking her arm in Delight's, drew her back out from the dark stable, saying in the most conversational tone, "There, *chérie*, was that not exciting? Did you imagine yourself and your wonderful Tony the very same way?"

Delight flushed. "Aye," she admitted. "I did, Henriette."

The French girl laughed low. "The real act is ever so much better than the imaginary one, Delight, but in time you will find that out."

"When, Henriette?" demanded the overwrought girl. *"When?"*

"You must not be in too much of a hurry, *chérie*," replied Henriette. "In the spring we will make a plan, I promise you, dearest Delight. Until then you may watch me whenever I amuse myself with my Johnny. Have you ever let a man touch you, Delight? I will wager you have not, for you are an overly chaste little thing."

"Never," came the expected reply. "I save myself for Anthony."

"Next time you come to watch Johnny and me, let him play a little with your pretty titties, Delight. You will still be a virgin, but it will give you great pleasure. You can close your eyes and pretend that he is your Anthony," Henriette said.

"I do not know if I should," Delight murmured.

"We will speak about it again when the time comes," replied Henriette sweetly. "I am your best friend, and I want you to be happy, *chérie*."

February came, and Blaze knew that she could no longer deny her husband her bed. She was growing to like Tony more each day, but she did not feel for him what she had felt for Edmund. How could she? Still, her duty as the Countess of Langford was to supply an heir for the Wyndhams. She would couple with Tony if only for Edmund's sake. He had so desperately sought an heir. If she and Tony had a son, she would name him for her first husband. She knew that Anthony would not mind.

On the morning of the fifth of February she had Heartha wash her honey-colored hair and perfume it with her violet fragrance. If he remembered the date, he discreetly said nothing. After the evening meal was over Blaze arose from her place saying, "I will leave you now, my lord, for I wish a bath before retiring."

"I shall join you in an hour," he said without even looking at her.

So he had remembered! She had half-hoped that he wouldn't, and yet she had hoped that he would. He had been gently courting her over the last few weeks, and she had to admit, albeit guiltily, to enjoying his kisses. Arriving in her apartments, Blaze was surprised to find that her tub was already set up, and filled with steaming violet-scented water.

"You are amazing!" she praised Heartha.

"Humphhh," came the sharp reply. " 'Tis the fifth of February, is it not?" She undid Blaze's bodice and helped her from her skirts.

"Aye," said Blaze slowly as she stepped from her petticoats. "What has that got to do with my tub?"

"Is not tonight the night that you will finally allow your husband into your bed?" demanded Heartha.

Blaze laughed. There was simply no use denying anything to Heartha. Heartha knew all her secrets. "I had to be certain that I was not carrying the king's child," she explained to her tiring woman. "I want no bastards for Langford." She unrolled her stockings and allowed Heartha to pull them off.

"I understood that," said Heartha. "Now, get into that tub, m'lady, before you catch your death!"

Blaze climbed into the tub and sighed as the warm water eased away her busy day. "Let me be awhile," she said.

"Not tonight, m'lady," came the quick retort. "You'll not keep him waiting any longer than is necessary. Langford needs an heir!"

Blaze shook her head. It was obvious that she was going to get no rest from either the family or her servants until she had produced a son for the Wyndhams. She sat quietly while Heartha scrubbed her skin until it was glowing, and then ordered her from the great oak tub. When she had been dried thoroughly and dusted with fragrant powder, Heartha slipped the violet-colored silk nightrail she had originally chosen for Blaze's wedding night over her mistress's head.

"No nightcap!" she ordered in a tone so fierce that Blaze did not dare to question her. "Now, into the bed with you, m'lady! Nay, wait!"

"What is it, Heartha?" Blaze demanded, beginning to become annoyed.

"Take the gown off, m'lady," and before Blaze might protest, the tiring woman pulled her arms up and drew the silk over her head. "There is no need in wasting this lovely gown, m'lady," she told her astounded mistress. "An eager man would only rip it off you, and Lord Tony loves you greatly. Into bed with you!"

Shaking her head, Blaze climbed into her bed. She did not know whether to laugh or to scold her tiring woman for her presumption. Having draped a lacy little shawl about her lady's shoulders, Heartha bobbed a curtsy, and was gone before Blaze could make up her mind in the matter. She heard the footmen removing the tub from her dressing room, and then all was quiet. A chamberstick burned on either side of the bed, and the room was delightfully warm with the fine fire that burned in the fireplace. She was nervous, and yet she was not. After all, she was no virgin, and yet she could not help but wonder if they would please each other.

Lord Tony loves you greatly. Dear Heartha, who still believed in the fairy tales she had once told her children, and was now telling her grandchildren. Tony loved RiversEdge and the Langford earldom even as she did, and it was for this that they would produce children. Tony had married her because he had promised Edmund, but how could dear Heartha know this? What did it matter? she thought. This was her life, and it was not an unhappy one.

She dozed lightly, awakening to the sound of the door that connected his bedchamber with hers as it swung open. God's foot! How long had it been since she had heard that sound? She opened her eyes to see him coming toward the bed. He was stark naked, and his body was magnificent.

"Stand a moment in the firelight, my lord," she asked him softly, and when he did, she said, "You are so beautiful, Tony! Never have I seen such a beautiful body upon a man." Even in the dimness of the chamber she could see the light flush that stained his cheeks, and Blaze bit her lip to keep from laughter.

"Madam, you embarrass me," he said softly.

"Why? Because I praise your body?" She threw back the coverlet and stepped from the bed. Proudly she walked toward him. "You may praise mine if it pleases you, my lord."

They stood staring at one another, she with a faint smile upon her face. He was very straight, she thought, his broad shoulders and wide chest very much like Edmund's. At first he could not take his eyes from her beautiful globe-shaped breasts. How many times had he caressed them over the last few weeks, and yet seeing them now, perfect adornments to her exquisite nudity, was almost more than he could bear. He felt a tightening in the region of his hard, flat belly. She felt an answering ripple of excitement in the pit of her softly rounded belly. Her pretty little Venus mons was properly denuded and plumply pink, but from his groin a mass of tight dark curls sprang. His manhood was beginning to arouse itself, the sight of her loveliness being a heady one.

"You are the most beautiful woman I have ever known," he said simply.

"Dare I ask just how many it is that you have known, my lord?" she teased him.

"You may not, Blaze Wyndham. The answer would surely only serve to increase your natural feminine vanity."

She laughed. The sound was a sensual, throaty one that set his heart to racing and his pulses pounding. Reaching out, he slipped an arm about her slender waist and drew her to him. Blaze looked up into his face, and was shocked by the love she saw in it. No! No! she thought. This cannot be! He cannot love me! He cannot! I do not love him! I do not! Irrational with her sudden panic, she placed the palms of her hands flat upon his chest to push him away.

Anthony immediately saw the change that swept over her features. "What is it, my angel?" he asked her gently.

"Do you love me?" she asked of him brokenly.

"I have always loved you, Blaze," he answered her honestly.

"No, no, you cannot love me," she began to sob. "Oh, Tony, it is not right that you love me. I do not love you, and I do not know if I ever can. When Edmund died, my heart was buried with him!" she wept against his hard shoulder.

"Perhaps that is so," he agreed, "or perhaps you just believe it to be so, Blaze. Nevertheless, I cannot help loving you. I have loved you from the first moment I saw you, even knowing that you were to be my uncle's wife, but in my heart I ached for your love. Why do you think I could find no woman to suit me when I went to court? Why do you think I could not bring myself to arrange a match with your sister Delight?

"There was never any hope of your being my wife. Yet I knew that I could never be happy with another woman. I vowed to myself that I would never wed. I would leave Riverside and all I possessed to Nyssa, making her a great heiress. It was the only way in which I might offer my love without offending either you or my uncle. Then Edmund was killed."

"He must have known of your feelings for me," Blaze said low. "How like him to ask you to wed with me to protect me and Nyssa, yet at the same time manage to give you your happiness. In his last moments he thought of us all."

He had to tell her the whole truth. He would have no more lies between them. "Edmund died instantly, Blaze. He did not have time to ask me anything, let alone exact a deathbed promise from me."

"But you told the king . . ." she began.

"I would have sworn it before God himself to gain you for my wife!" Anthony declared.

The fierce reality of what he was saying burst inside her brain, and she cried out, "Oh, villain! Oh, brute, to do this to me! To love me so greatly when I cannot love you. To tell me so! Ohh, I shall never forgive you, Tony! Never!" and she burst into racking sobs of despair.

"Do not weep, Blaze," he begged her. "Do not weep, my darling wife. I shall teach you to love me! I vow it!" and he held her tightly in his arms, letting her vent her terrible grief. He would have given his life to have avoided causing her any sort of pain, but tonight at their real beginning as man and wife he wanted the truth between them.

Blaze wept on. She did not think she could bear the terrible pain of what he had just told her. He loved her! *He loved her!* He had lied to the king in his bold attempt to have her for himself. Had not Henry been tiring of her, and his interest drifting in another direction, Anthony might have incurred the king's undying wrath. He might have endangered his very life! He had done it for her. All for her! Yet she did not love him, and she could not be certain that she would ever feel anything more for him than what she felt now. But what did she feel for him now? She could not be certain anymore. This startling revelation had left her totally and utterly confused. She should be glad that he loved her, yet she felt guilty for her own lack of feelings toward him.

"Damn you, Tony!" she managed to sob. "Damn you! Damn you! Damn you!" and she began to beat upon his chest in a frenzy.

He could not understand why she was angry at him. Had he not just admitted his love for her? Had he not just admitted the dangerous and daring deception that he had effected in order to make her his wife? He had believed that this truthful admission would somehow change everything. That she might even admit a love for him. What a fool he had been! Her overtures of friendship had been nothing more than a sham. He had been right all along. She probably wept because he had taken her away from court and a life she actually had been enjoying. Lies! Lies! All her sweet explanations had been nothing more than lies!

Catching her by the shoulders, he looked down into her face, ignoring, or perhaps not even seeing, the bleakness of her look. "If this is some ruse, madam, to avoid further your wifely duties to this family, you have failed in your intent. You will begin accepting your responsibilities to the Langford earldom this very night!" His voice was icy, and devoid of kindness.

Her hand flew to her mouth for a moment, and then lowering it, she said low, "You would force me, even as the king forced me?" Her look was hollow.

"A husband does not force a wife," he replied. "A wife belongs to her husband. She is his to do with as he wills, Blaze. Did my uncle never teach you that?"

"How do you dare to even mention Edmund in the same breath as you voice your intent to rape me?"

"*Rape you?*" His voice was indignant. "A husband cannot rape his wife. She is his property, both body and soul."

Blaze said nothing to him, but turning, she walked to the bed, and laying herself upon it, spread herself wide. "If I fought you I could not win," she said in a voice devoid of emotion. "Have your will of me, my lord, but you will have no pleasure of it."

All the hot desire that had been building in his body was suddenly and totally gone from him. He looked at his manhood, a small and shrunken thing now. He looked to her, lying coldly and without welcome upon her bed.

His first instinct was to call her the bitch he thought she was, and leave her. Then sanity prevailed. In his disappointment over her reaction to his admission of love he was again, he knew, misinterpreting her.

She had not lied to him. She had told him the truth, and as she had spoken, he had instinctively known it. If he left her now, if he did not try to repair the damage between them, he knew that he could lose her forever. He would be patient even in his angry and great disappointment. Some little warning voice deep within him admonished him that he must be.

Walking over to the side of the bed, he said, "Cover yourself, my angel," and when she had obeyed him he sat down beside her. "Blaze, hear me out, I beg of you. When you wed with Edmund you did not know him, nor he you. Yet you both learned to love one another. Have you forgotten that? Such a love is a great blessing. In many marriages there is no love, none at all, nor is there even friendship or respect to bind the couple together. Yet I have always believed, much to my mother's amusement, that there should be love within a marriage. I have admitted my love for you as you have admitted the truth of your life at court. We chose to have no barriers between us, yet suddenly you seek to erect yet another one even as we have struck down the others. Do not do this to us, my angel.

"I love you, yet you say you do not love me. Still, you do not hate me. I had begun to believe that you were even beginning to like me perhaps.

It is upon this strong, but small foundation that we should build. I can. Can you?"

A little tear rolled down her pale cheek. "You offer me so much, Anthony, for I know the great value of love. I am ashamed that I can offer you so little in return for your love. If you still want me knowing even that, then I am yours." There was such sadness in her voice that he almost wept himself.

Instead he drew back the coverlet and the perfumed sheets, and slid beneath them. "I am beginning to get chilled," he said softly, and he reached out to draw her into his arms. "Come and warm me, my angel."

She lay quietly within his embrace, thinking that her body was probably even colder than his right now. He held her gently, so gently that she felt, not his captive, but rather something cherished and protected. He made no other move to touch her, and gradually as the warmth seeped back into their bodies, husband and wife relaxed and fell asleep. They slept half the night through, awakening when a large log within the fireplace fell noisily in a shower of sparks.

Rising reluctantly from the bed, Anthony padded across the bedchamber to add another large piece of wood to the fire, stubbing his toe in the process. "God's foot!" he swore irritably.

"What has happened, my lord?"

"I have stubbed my toe," he grumbled.

"Would you have me kiss it, and make it all better?" he heard her gently tease. Sleep had definitely improved her disposition.

"Would you?" he demanded of her. "Or perhaps I might interest you in other parts of my anatomy that would benefit from kissing."

Blaze laughed softly. "My lord!" she cried, pretending shock. Sleep had also restored her common sense. This was her husband, and love him or not, they owed a duty to the Langford earldom. She was fortunate in that he loved her. He would not be an unpleasant lover, for he would be seeking to please her.

Anthony slipped back into the bed, and catching her boldly, began to fondle her plump breasts. "God," he half-groaned against her mouth. "Here are the sweetest little fruits ever created, my angel!" And he kissed her deeply.

Love him or no, she had to admit to enjoying the delicious sensation of his hands upon her flesh. She might have felt guilty, but that she remembered the king's words comparing a woman's body to a fine instrument. She believed that she would find Anthony as skilled a player upon that instrument as was Henry Tudor. He seemed to be in no hurry to have her, and she sighed and stretched with pleasure as he caressed her.

Her soft flesh grew taut and firm beneath his stroking hands. His fingers encircled each now-firm breast, sliding leisurely over the swell of its top, moving around the side, cupping the fullness from beneath, smoothing back up sleek warmth once again. It was an exercise that he did not easily tire of, but finally he began to amuse himself with the nipples, catching at the tight little coral buds between his thumb and his forefinger, drawing them out as he gently pinched them. At last his dark head lowered itself, and his warm mouth closed over a nipple. Sensuously his tongue flickered around and about the sentient little tip, and Blaze murmured with soft little sighs of contentment that set his pulse racing.

As he loved the soft ivory globes of her breasts, she found herself unable to keep from caressing him. Her supple fingers moved over his head, entwining themselves in his night-black hair, enjoying the silky feel of it. Her hands fondled the back of his neck, and swept over his smooth, muscled shoulders, digging her nails lightly into the hard flesh.

The touch of her hands aroused him deeply, and he heard himself groan, "Sweet, sweet," as he transferred himself to her other nipple, while beneath him his wife sighed, obviously satisfied with his attentions. He loved her without haste, amazed by his own self-discipline, for he had desired her for so very long. Still, he would have her remember always the way it was the first time between them. Relinquishing her nipple, he moved his head slowly downward over the silky flesh of her torso and belly. He could feel the delicate pulsing of the blood as it coursed through her veins beneath his cheek. He pressed little kisses upon the rounded, perfumed flesh.

Deep within her, Blaze could feel the quivering, although she did not know if it was visible to him. Would he dare? Would he dare to love her in *that* way on this their first encounter? She thought that a man who could lie successfully to a powerful king would dare anything. His head moved lower, and he was kissing her thighs with the same little soft kisses that he had laid upon her belly. His lips coaxed her limbs apart; his fingers gently opened her as one might open a delicate shell; and Blaze found that she could hardly breathe for the excitement that coursed through her body. His tongue touched her, finding immediately with unerring accuracy that tiny little pearl of her womanhood, and Blaze found herself crying out with her pleasure as he loved her until she was so filled with that special and sensual joy that she wept as it receded, leaving her feeling bereft and alone.

But she was not alone. His body covered hers for the first time, and she took the weight of him upon her thighs as he slowly and gently pressed into her, drawing forth another cry from her straining throat. He filled her with his throbbing weapon, burying it deep inside her sweet warmth. Blaze reached up and clasped his body to her, feeling her breasts being crushed against his smooth chest. He caught her face between his two hands, and kissed her until she was breathless and her lips felt bruised and tingling. She fiercely returned his kisses, giving no quarter, receiving none. Suddenly he began to move upon her, thrusting into her with passionate vigor, drawing back almost to complete withdrawal, thrusting back hard again.

Blaze cried out once more. Cried with her pleasure, yet wept her despair to feel her crisis approaching, yet when it came she was ready for it. She soared like one of her hunting birds from the falconry. Soared straight and true into the burning blue of the heavens until she thought she could go no higher, only to discover that beyond the blue lay a new zone of fiery gold. Uncaring of anything, she hurled herself toward certain destruction, and she cared not, because it was too wonderful. The pleasure burst over her like honeyed wine, and at the same time she heard him cry aloud with satisfaction as his own passion exploded.

They lay wet and chilled and gasping amid a tangle of bedclothes. They shuddered in unison with the receding wave, and then Anthony reached out and took her hand in his. Tenderly he kissed it. There were no words necessary between them now. Within minutes he was asleep, turning onto his side and sighing softly. Blaze smiled to herself, and then the smile faded. He had given her such pleasure, and he loved her. How could she not love him back?—yet she did not. It was sad, and in time he would certainly hate her for it. What kind of woman was she? She who had always believed herself so giving suddenly found that she was taking more, and it disturbed her.

She drew the coverlet up and over them, appreciating as she did the taut curve of his buttocks. He really was a handsome man, and they would make beautiful babies together. Nay, she thought then. Babies come from love, and without it we have no chance of having children. Oh, Edmund! Help me! Must I stop loving you in order to love Tony? I cannot! I simply cannot! Yet I must. I must let you go, but I do not know how. She sighed deeply, and to her great surprise, he suddenly rolled back over and pulled her into his arms.

"You think far too much for a woman," he said quietly, but there was a hint of amusement in his voice. "Go to sleep, Blaze. Go to sleep safe in the knowledge that I love you; and whether you believe it or not, I promise you that one day you will love me."

Would she? she wondered as she snuggled gratefully against him. Would she really? For a brief moment she felt a glimmer of hope.

Chapter 13

❦

*I*n mid-March the spring came quite abruptly and the roads, which a mere fortnight ago had been made impassable by the snows, were quite suddenly free of snow and awash with mud. Lord Morgan came from Ashby to escort Delight home. He was engaged in negotiations with an Irish lord who wanted an English wife of good stock for his heir. The Irish lord and his son would be coming from Ireland in May to meet Delight. There was to be no more nonsense tolerated in Delight's case. She would be married this summer, if not to the Irish suitor, then to another suitor with whom she could be matched. Delight would be eighteen on the seventh of June, and she was too old now to be allowed her childish whims and crotchets.

Delight pouted prettily at her father, and begged, "Please, Papa! Let me stay at RiversEdge until after Easter." She did not protest the proposed marriage. Why anger her father whining about a proposed Irish marriage that would never be, especially when she wanted a favor from him?

"Oh, please, m'lord Morgan," Henriette echoed Delight's plea. "Please let Delight stay until Easter. I shall be so very lonely without her!"

Robert Morgan did not understand his sweet Delight's friendship with this French girl. There was something about Henriette Wyndham that troubled him, although he could not quite put his finger on what it was. Still, Delight had not howled with outrage at the news of a proposed marriage. If her previous closeness to Blaze seemed gone, and her attitude toward her eldest sister cool, her friendship with the Wyndham cousin had obviously matured her, and her stay at RiversEdge this winter had not been for naught.

"If it is all right with you, Blaze," Lord Morgan said, "then I will let Delight stay a few more weeks."

"Ohh, please, Madame Blaze," Henriette pleaded, *"please!"*

"Of course Delight may stay," said Blaze, who actually wished nothing more than to send her younger sister home as quickly as possible. "Mayhap when she goes you will let our Henriette visit."

"Indeed yes!" said Robert Morgan with false joviality. "After Delight's match has been settled we shall be happy to have Mistress Henriette come for a visit." But not before, he silently vowed to himself. I would not put it past that young vixen to steal the Irish lordling that I have found for my daughter!

They had no sooner waved her father farewell than Delight was demanding from her friend, "What plan have you made, Henriette? I have but a few weeks left, and then I shall find myself wed with some strange and wild Irishman. My father will not let me get away this time, I know it! He means to marry me off for certain!" Her voice was high-pitched, and her eyes had a haunted look about them.

"Come, *chérie*, come." Henriette caught at Delight's hand and hurried her into the stables. "You must not get yourself all excited, and fret. Let us find my Johnny, and he will soothe us both."

"I do not know if I should," Delight considered.

"You have said that every time since the first time you let him play with your titties. Why do you fret, *chérie*? Your virginity is as intact as the day you were born. Of course it does not have to be if you do not want it to, *chérie*. Johnny is like a good stud stallion. He can be put to several mares in an afternoon, and still gallop off in fine form."

"No," said Delight. "I am not as confident as you in my ability to pretend a virginity that does not exist. I will keep my innocence until I wed Tony."

They had reached the isolated stall in the rear of the earl's stables, to find the stableman already awaiting them. "Saw you coming," he said by way of explanation, and grabbing at Delight, he shoved his hand into her bodice.

For a brief moment she allowed him the liberty, and then she pushed him away, exclaiming, "You will tear my gown, you great oaf. You stink of onions, and besides, you are bruising me!" Turning to Henriette, she snapped, "When you have finished sporting yourself, I will be in the gardens. Have a plan for me or I shall tell my sister of your behavior with this rustic." Then she stamped away.

The stableman grinned after her. She was a spitfire, that one, even if she was half-mad. He would enjoy spitting her on his big cock, but he knew if he did, she would cry rape, and he could find himself at the end of the executioner's rope. No woman was worth a man's life.

"What are you looking at, you great beast?" The French whore was glowering at him.

"Nothing, lovey," he said, and yanked her, giggling, down into the straw.

Delight paced the gardens, where small primroses in their cheerful pinks and yellows brightened the landscape. The lawns were turning a soft green, and at its edge the River Wye flowed blue and free of ice. How much longer was she to bear it? How much longer could she watch Blaze and Anthony together? Of late Blaze was changing before her very eyes. Becoming softer, casting long, thoughtful glances at Tony.

Her poor Tony. Forced into a marriage with a woman he did not love or want. Forced to accept the king's leavings. *But soon.* Soon she would rid him of his royal castoff, of the woman who stood between them. Soon it would be Delight who sat beside Anthony at the high board in the hall. Soon it would be Delight who slept in the countess's apartments, and bore the precious and long-awaited Langford heirs. She would give him the especial gift of her virginity, and from her chaste love for him would come the next generation of Wyndhams.

"You must not look like such a thundercloud, Delight," warned Henriette, rejoining her friend.

"Have you a plan?" demanded Delight. She had better, or as God is my judge, I will tell Tony about her lewd behavior! Once I am married to him, she must go if she has not already been married off to some poor unsuspecting soul.

"But, of course, *cherie*. I have had it in my mind for weeks, but now is the time to put it into effect," responded Henriette. Delight was nearing the breaking point, she could easily see.

"What is it?"

"You are to make your sister a very special gift, Delight. A gift to thank her for her kindness to you these past months."

"What kind of a gift?" Delight said suspiciously. Was Henriette playing some sort of trick on her?

"A nightrail of the finest and the sheerest silk. There are several bolts of just such fabric in the storage rooms. We will choose the color that is the most flattering to Madame Blaze, and I will even help you with it. My embroidery was much in demand amongst the queen's ladies. When the gown is finished it shall be impregnated with a special poison that I know how to make. When your sister wears the garment, the poison will be absorbed by her skin. She will die. The death will appear to be a natural one, and voilà! M'lord Anthony is yours!"

The first thing that struck Delight about Henriette's plan was that it was so simple. She was not shocked at the idea of killing her sister. In her half-mad mind her own need for Anthony far outweighed her basic morality. Then a thought came to her. "If we treat the gown with your poison, what is to prevent the poison from killing us when we give Blaze the gown?" she said.

"I will make us a special hand lotion that, when dried upon our hands, will protect us from the poison in the handling of the nightrail. We must, however, wash our hands immediately afterward."

"Let us begin today," said Delight. "It will take several weeks after I choose the fabric to design and cut it, sew it, and prepare it properly. We will have just barely enough time, Henriette."

"That is why I will help you, *chérie*, so that you may finish in time. You will present your gift to Madame Blaze the day that you leave. That way you will be gone long before she dies. I will see that she wears the gown that very night, or the next. You can trust me, *chérie*, in this as you have trusted me in *other* things." Henriette smiled conspiratorially at Delight, but the girl's mind was already far away imagining her wedding day to Anthony Wyndham.

The days melted into weeks, and the spring deepened. Palm Sunday came, and then Easter. In the waning days of the Lenten season Delight and Henriette had worked diligently upon the gift for Blaze. Heads together in the family hall as they sewed, they had made a pretty picture, but they would show their work to no one.

"It is to be a surprise!" said Henriette.

"A surprise for my sister," Delight told Lady Dorothy. "She has been so kind to me despite my behavior toward her. I do not know if I am quite ready to forgive her for stealing Anthony away from me, but I would have no more animosity between us now that my parents are to arrange a match for me that will take me from England. I may never see my family once I am married. I would not leave with hard feelings between Blaze and myself."

The words were those of a reasonable woman, but Delight's eyes told a different story. Still, Lady Dorothy could not fault the girl, but she had an uncomfortable feeling each time she saw Delight and Henriette giggling together. Henriette Wyndham. The wench was a far slyer puss than Lady Dorothy had first seen. Blaze had been right. Marriage would be the only solution, and, Doro thought, to an older man who would not be so taken in by the girl that he would not beat her when she needed it, and Lady Dorothy suspected she needed it very much.

Now with Easter past, the day for Delight's departure came, and Lord Morgan arrived to collect his daughter. Everything was in readiness. Delight's trunks were packed and loaded into the baggage cart. As for Delight, she had declined a carriage, preferring to ride by her father's side. The good-byes were said all around, and, the sun barely up, father and daughter prepared to leave.

"I have a gift for you," Delight said to Blaze. "I know that we have been much estranged these past months, but my anger is cooling, and I would not wed in a foreign land while there is bitterness between us. I have worked these past weeks to make you a special night garment. Henriette has helped me with the embroidery. She will bring my gift to you tonight. Wear it in happiness, and think of me when you do," finished Delight, and then she hugged her sister, her smile bright, but the smile did not extend to her eyes.

It had been decided by the two conspirators at the last minute that Henriette would bring Blaze the gown that night, as Delight was truly afraid of touching it now that it had been impregnated with the French girl's poison. Henriette realized that to argue with Delight in this would only be to arouse her suspicions. Delight had worried about the possibility of Tony being poisoned, but Henriette assured her friend that she would slip a sleeping draft into Anthony's wine cup that evening, and he would appear to be drunk. He would seem so drunk that he would be put into his own bed, and awaken in the morning to the sad news of his wife's sudden passing.

Blaze hugged her younger sister lovingly. "Dear heart," she said, "I have never wanted you angry with me. I am sorry that you could not have your life as you would have wanted it. Give the young Irish lordling a chance, Delight. The Irish are a charming race, I am told."

Delight lastly hugged Henriette, and as the two girls parted, a look shot between them that made Lady Dorothy wonder what it was that they had been up to, and why it was worrying her so.

Lord Morgan and Delight rode from RiversEdge through the two villages of Michaelschurch and Wyeton. The Langford ferry took them easily and swiftly across the river, and they moved off at a leisurely pace until the river disappeared behind a hill. The road to Ashby stretched before them, winding through the sprouting fields of barley and hops; past the orchards now so heavily abloom with pink-and-white apple blossoms that the portent of a bumper crop was already in evidence; past meadows filled with frisky young lambs who scampered wildly about, bumping heads and madly chasing one another; past ponds ruled over by regal white swans who swam proudly in formation with their newly hatched young. The day was incredibly fair, the sky a bright and cloudless blue.

Lord Morgan had assumed that his daughter would be sad at leaving RiversEdge yet her countenance was a pleasing one—nay, it was almost merry. "Are you glad to be returning home, Delight, or do you smile because of Blaze's happy news?" he asked her.

Delight turned her head to him, caution and curiosity both upon her face now. "What *happy* news?" she demanded.

"Ahh," he answered her, "I had thought that Blaze might have told you, but perhaps she chose to wait until you had been betrothed, and now I have spoilt it."

"*What happy news?*" Delight repeated, her voice now holding a note of nervousness.

"Blaze and Anthony are expecting their first child sometime in the late autumn. She tells me she feels the same way that she felt carrying her little son that died, and so she is certain she carries a boy. Is that not happy news? Anthony is ecstatic with happiness!"

At her father's words sanity burst like a bubble in Delight's brain. In but a few seconds all her hate for Blaze was destroyed, and the full realization of what she had planned rose up to overwhelm her like a powerful wave. With a shriek she cried, "Dear God, what have I done?" and fell from her horse to the ground senseless.

Lord Morgan leapt from his own mount while calling the little traveling party to a halt. Kneeling by his daughter's side, he ascertained that there were no broken bones, but try as he might, he was not able to arouse her from her stupor. He moved her out of the sun to a place beneath a shade tree. Finally, when an hour had gone by, Delight began to show signs of regaining consciousness. Lord Morgan forced some strong wine from his traveling pouch between her lips, and she managed to swallow it. Slowly the color began to return to her pale face, and she opened her eyes.

"What have you done, Delight?" her father asked quietly. "You *must* tell me what you have done."

"Tony doesn't love her," Delight whispered. "He does not! He only wed her because he promised Edmund, and the king made him do so when he tired of Blaze as his mistress."

"Anthony loves Blaze very much, Delight," said her father gently. "Why do you not see it, child? I am going to tell you something that even the king does not know. Edmund exacted no promise from Tony. Edmund was killed instantly. Anthony, however, has loved Blaze from the moment he first saw her. When his uncle died he saw his opportunity to finally marry her himself. Eventually his aspirations were realized because he boldly went to the king and dared to tell him that false tale of a dying man's wish. Who was to say he was lying? That is why he could never settle his heart upon another woman, Delight. *Even you.*"

Delight began to weep piteously.

"You must tell me what you have done, my child. You must tell me quickly if your act has endangered any member of our family," Lord Morgan persisted.

"I have conspired to murder my sister," Delight sobbed. "Dear Lord Christ! I have attempted murder!"

Robert Morgan felt as if a cold hand was clutching at his heart. His younger daughter was tottering dangerously between sanity and total madness. He could not drive her the wrong way lest he lose both Blaze and Delight. "Tell me, Delight," he said softly, "tell me how you have planned to kill Blaze."

"The night garment that I made, Papa," Delight said, and he could see she was making a strong effort to hold on. "My farewell gift to Blaze, Papa. It is treated with a special poison, and if Blaze wears it she will die by morning."

"Where is the gown, Delight?"

"Henriette has it in her chamber. She will give it to Blaze tonight. Do you not remember, Papa, that I told Blaze so?"

"Tell me how you got such a poison, Delight," said her father, already suspecting the answer.

"Henriette, Papa. She made it with the help of her servant, Cecile. Henriette is a bad girl, Papa. She fucks with one of the stablemen, Johnny, in a back stall in the stables."

"How do you know this, child?" He was horrified by the French girl's consummate evil. Why had no one caught her? She was obviously quite a clever bitch.

"Henriette lets me watch her," came the terrible reply. "She said if I watched, I would know what Anthony would do to me one day when I was his wife."

Pray God, thought Lord Morgan, that Mademoiselle Henriette had not corrupted Delight any further, but he had to ask. "Did the stableman ever . . . ?" He hesitated, ashamed to have to ask his daughter the question, but Delight fortunately spared him.

"Oh, no, Papa! I never fucked with anyone. I swear it! I am saving my virginity for my husband," she said primly, not telling him how the servant had fondled her, however, for she could see the deep distress etched into his handsome face. Poor Papa. He was such a good man.

Lord Morgan pressed a little more wine upon his daughter, and said, "I must return to RiversEdge, my child, and put an end to this affair."

"Ohh, Papa! I shall die if Blaze and Anthony know what I have done! They will hate me! They will never forgive me, and I am really so sorry! I do not want to hurt Blaze anymore! If I had only known that Anthony really loved her, I swear I would not have done it!"

"Do not fret, my daughter. I will try to do what must be done without your sister learning of your foolishness. Do you feel well enough to ride now?"

"Aye." She nodded.

"Good," he replied. "You are to go on to Ashby. We are almost halfway there. I will ride back, not upon the road, but cross-country, for it is faster. I will go to Lord Kingsley's home, for I can reach it far more quickly cross-country than I can the earl's ferry crossing. Nicholas will see me across the Wye to RiversEdge. I will be there before nightfall, and I will correct this matter. You must tell me, though, what the nightrail looks like, for the French bitch may try to foil my intent."

"It is pale mauve silk, Papa, and we embroidered violets upon the bodice and sleeves in a lavender silk thread. I chose the color because there was just enough material in the bolt for my purposes, but none extra. When Blaze puts it on, the poison will begin to be absorbed into her skin, and once it all is, the gown is safe for unshielded hands to touch again. Henriette has a special hand cream to keep her safe tonight."

He nodded. "Get on your horse, child," he said, helping her to mount again. "I have not much time, but do not fear, I will be in time!"

They had been stopped almost two hours now, and, his horse well-rested, Lord Morgan set off for his Kingsley son-in-law's home. He paced his mount carefully, for he knew the importance of reaching his destination quickly and safely. God forbid his animal put his foot into a rabbit hole and leave him helpless. It was with great relief, and a prayer of thanks, that he finally reached Kirkwood. Dismounting, he hurried into the house to Nicholas Kingsley. To his relief, Blythe was nowhere to be seen as his son-in-law hurried into the library to greet him.

"Warn your servants not to mention my being here," he told Nicholas. "Not even Blythe." Then Lord Morgan went on to explain the situation. He concluded by saying, "Blaze must not know."

"And Anthony?" asked Nicholas.

"I have no choice but to tell him, for his French cousin must die else she attempt once again to harm my daughters. I do not believe that she merely aided Delight in this scheme. I believe she plotted it, using my child's unrequited love for Tony. I think that she meant to have him for herself. I cannot leave her alive under the circumstances, and if I am to kill her, Anthony must understand why."

Nicholas Kingsley nodded. "Let us go," he said. "The sun must not set upon this woman lest the powers of darkness aid her in escaping our justice."

The two men hurried from the house and down to the riverbank, where Lord Kingsley's barge awaited them. The river was calm in the late-afternoon sun, and they were quickly rowed across. The two men walked swiftly up the lawns of RiversEdge and into the house.

"Find the earl and bring him to us in his library," said Lord Morgan. "No one else is to know that we are here. Do you understand?"

The servant nodded, and exited the room. In a very few minutes Anthony Wyndham entered the room, a surprised look upon his face. "What is it?" he asked. "Robert, why have you returned? Is everything all right?"

"Sit down, Tony," said Lord Morgan, "but first tell me, where is Blaze?"

"Counting linens with my mother. Why?"

"What I have to tell you is a horrifying tale, but you must not interrupt me until I have finished."

"Very well," replied the earl to his father-in-law. "Say on, Rob."

Quickly Lord Morgan explained the reason for his return to RiversEdge and as he spoke, the earl's face grew more somber with every passing minute. A bevy of emotions passed across his face. Anger. Sorrow. Compassion. When Robert Morgan had finally finished telling him what poor Delight had related to him in her remorse, he could but shake his head.

"The French bitch must be destroyed, Tony," said Lord Morgan. "She cannot be allowed to harm Blaze or your child. There is Nyssa also to consider. Did she not attempt to subvert my granddaughter before you and Blaze returned from court last autumn? She is a dangerous creature, Tony. She cannot be allowed to go free."

"What would you do to her?"

"Make her wear the same night garment that she planned for Blaze to wear tonight. If she has not lied to Delight, the poison will be absorbed into her skin, killing her, and it will appear that she died a sudden but natural death."

"And the servant?"

"The woman is involved too, but I cannot justify the taking of her life.

Pack her off to France with a small pension. She dare not speak of what she knows lest she implicate herself."

Anthony Wyndham nodded. "Let us do it now," he said. "Henriette is in her chamber. Let us hope in the ensuing distress of her death no one, including Blaze, will think to ask about Delight's parting gift, and where it is."

His two companions nodded in agreement, and the three men, after ascertaining that no one would see them, hurried from the library up a back staircase to the floor housing the family's bedchambers. The wide hallway with its afternoon sunlight was deserted. Blaze and Doro were in another part of the house, and Nyssa was out-of-doors in the stableyard learning to ride her new pony. The earl led Lord Morgan and Lord Kingsley to his cousin's chamber, and the three men entered into the room without knocking.

Henriette Wyndham did not at first hear her visitors, for she was busily grinding something into a fine powder with her mortar and pestle, and her concentration was intense. Suddenly sensing that she was not alone, she whirled about, surprise suffusing her lovely features.

"Tony," she said, and then, seeing Lord Morgan and another gentleman, her face hardened. "So, the little madwoman could not keep her secret long enough to attain her heart's desire," Henriette noted, and her voice dripped scorn.

"It was not Delight's idea at all, was it?" asked Lord Morgan.

"Of course not," came the bold reply. "Do you think the little simpleton could be as clever as I?"

Robert Morgan smiled coldly. "No, Delight is not clever, for she tends to think with her heart. You, however, have no heart, do you, Mademoiselle Henriette?"

The French girl laughed delightedly, as if pleased with his discovery.

"And it was not my daughter who was to benefit by this murder, was it, mademoiselle?" continued Lord Morgan. "You would have concocted a way to expose her, and then you planned to snap up the grieving widower, n'est-ce pas, mademoiselle?"

"How is it," Henriette asked him, "that you are so clever, and your daughters, at least the two I have met, are so stupid?"

"Perhaps it is because they are pure of heart, mademoiselle," Lord Morgan replied.

"You will want the garment, I suppose?" Henriette said.

Lord Morgan smiled a savage smile. "No," he answered her. "I do not need it. You see, mademoiselle, I think that you are too dangerous a woman to continue living. If we saw you incarcerated in a convent, you might escape. If we returned you to France, you might attempt to reenter England. We can hardly wed you to a decent man, given your propensity for stablemen. Besides, you might decide to conveniently widow yourself in a similar fashion as you thought to rid yourself of my daughter. It has, therefore, been decided that you will suffer the same fate you proposed for her."

"*No!*" Henriette Wyndham hissed the word in almost reptilian fashion. "You cannot do this! You cannot! *Anthony!*" she appealed to him. "We are cousins!"

" 'Tis a pity, madam, that you did not remember that when you prepared your little scheme to murder my wife and our unborn child," he replied coldly. "Fetch the garment, Henriette, and put it on."

Henriette's eyes rolled in her head with her fright. "*Grand-mère Cecile, aidez moi, je tu prie!*"

From a corner by the fireplace where she had silently viewed and heard all, the old woman arose. She spoke the same French dialect that her granddaughter had spoken. "Do as they say, my child, and without further delay. There is an antidote to your poison that I have never told you. I had already prepared it in case the wrong person touched the gown, for we could not have had that happen, could we? As soon as they leave I will give it to you, and then we will escape this place. Madame Blaze is counting linens with Madame Dorothy and Heartha. It will be easy to steal some of her jewelry. We will have enough to live on the rest of our lives. We will go home to France, *ma petite. Vite, vite,* now! Do as you have been ordered."

As the old woman spoke, a look had passed between Lord Morgan and his sons-in-law. Henriette and her grandmother were not aware that the three knew enough of the French language to have understood even Cecile's dialect. They watched now as the false servant, covering her hands in the special lotion, brought forth the deadly garment. It was exactly as Delight had described it, and Robert Morgan was satisfied.

"Very well," Henriette said in what she hoped passed for a cowed voice, "I will don the gown, but may I first say my prayers? If I am to die, at least let me make my peace with God."

"The nightrail first," said Lord Morgan stonily. "Then you may pray, but I suspect it is the Devil you call upon, and not God."

Henriette sent him a venomous look. "Leave me then," she said.

"Nay," said Anthony. "We will remain here until the deed is done."

With a shrug to indicate that she did not care, Henriette unbuttoned her bodice and pulled it off. Next she loosened the waistband of her skirts, and stepped from them as they fell with her petticoats to the floor. Casually she unrolled her stockings, and kicking her shoes off, pulled them from her feet. Finally she drew her chemise over her head and tossed it aside. She posed naked before them, thrusting her large cone-shaped breasts forward, fondling them with her hands until the nipples were no more than big sharp points. Fascinated, the three men watched as her hands smoothed over her torso and downward, the tips of her fingers coming to rest amid the dark triangle of curls of her Venus mons. Henriette's eyes closed for a minute, and from between her pouting red lips came a sound that was almost like a deep purr.

Then opening her amber eyes wide she murmured, "Come now, *monseigneurs*, would you really destroy such loveliness as this? Tell me, have you ever shared a woman, the three of you? I have more than enough to go around. You could have me one at a time, or I have even been known to take three men at once. One of you in my burning sheath, which even now aches to be stuffed with a hard and throbbing cock such as I know you each possess. One of you in my ass, for my French and Italian lovers schooled me well in that particular perversion. The third in my little mouth, but do not be fooled, for I am able to swallow the largest cock after I have tongued it to pleasure. Surely you cannot refuse such an offer as I am now making you? Do you not want me? Men have killed for my favors." Her little tongue ran rapidly over her red lips.

They stared at her as they might have stared at some particularly loathsome reptile or beast. Each of them felt a lustful response to her words, yet none of them would have accepted her wicked offer. She was the most tantalizingly evil woman that they had ever encountered, and with a singularity of mind they realized that there could be very little sin in ridding the world of such a creature.

"Put the gown on, you vile bitch!" growled Anthony. "When I think that I gave you a home, and allowed you to associate with my wife and mother, I shudder."

With Cecile's help Henriette put the gown on, and seeing it, Lord Morgan thought that it was exquisite, particularly the embroidery. It had been a beautiful but deadly trap. "Say your prayers, mademoiselle," he ordered her, and Henriette knelt piously for as long as she dared before rising.

"Now lie upon your bed," Anthony ordered her, and turning to the startled Cecile, who had expected that the men would leave now, he said, "Tie your mistress to the bed with these ropes," and he handed the old woman four short lengths of strong rope.

Suddenly afraid, Cecile obeyed him, not daring to even try to thwart him, for he checked the knots of each binding as she tied it. When she had finished she was made to return to her corner, where she intended to sit until they left her, that she might supply her granddaughter with the antidote to the poisoned gown.

Lord Morgan, however, spoke up. "I will stay until the bitch dies," he said quietly. "You two take the old woman where she will not be heard or found, and lock her up until mademoiselle is lifeless."

"Rob—" began the Earl of Langford, but his father-in-law interrupted him.

"Nay, Tony. It is enough I have put on your conscience and Nick's this day. The rest is mine to bear, and I shall. Go now."

"Anthony, I beg of you," pleaded Henriette from her place upon the bed, "let me have the comfort of my servant at least in the moment of my dying! Do not be so cruel as to let me die with the pitiless eyes of this monster watching over me!"

Anthony Wyndham walked to the bedside and stared icily down at Henriette. "Listen to me, *cousin,* and hear me well. We all understood what it was you said to your *grand-mère* but moments ago. I have no intention of leaving her here to give you an antidote, free you, steal my wife's jewelry, and then help you escape retribution for your wicked deeds. If you have not said your prayers, if that sham of motionings and mumblings upon your prie-dieu was no more than that, then now is the time for you to make your peace with God." Then, turning away from her, he departed the room with Lord Kingsley, hustling the protesting old woman between them, while behind them Henriette Wyndham shrieked curses upon them all.

"Rob is a brave man," Nicholas Kingsley said quietly.

"Aye, I should not really have enjoyed being closeted with that hell-cat in her death throes," admitted Tony.

They forced their captive up the stairs into a tiny room in an unused tower room at the very top of the house. "Monsieurs, monsieurs," whined Cecile, "what is to become of me? You would not kill an innocent old woman surely." Her wrinkled face was a mask of fear.

Anthony laughed harshly. "*Innocent?* Not you, madam! Who taught that viper you nurtured her little trade in poisons? Did you seek to thwart her when she lured my poor misguided sister-in-law into her web of deception? You are as guilty as she, but you are more fortunate, for none of us could pass a judgment upon you. Of the two, your crime was lesser. How long will the poison take to kill her?"

"Three hours at the most, my lord," quavered Cecile.

"When we are certain that she is dead, you will be released from this room. You will find Henriette, and you will bleat your terrible news to the household. Henriette will be buried in the family vault, her crimes against the Wyndhams unknown. You, madam, will then be returned to France with a small pension in gold. Say one word of what has passed here today before you leave RiversEdge, and after denying it, I will see you killed. Speak one word of it when you reach France again, and I shall know also. As you know, my wife stands high in King Henry's favor, and the king is ever in contact with his fellow monarch, the French François. Dare to tell what has happened here today once you are in France, and I will see you burned as a witch. Do I make myself clear, madam?"

She nodded. "If your uncle Henry had been as you, *monseigneur*, what he could not have done! What we would not have had! Alas, he was but a dreamer and a fool. I comprehend your words, *monseigneur*, and I will obey."

"Practical old bitch," remarked Nicholas Kingsley when they had locked her behind a stout door of solid oak and returned to the earl's library. "I doubt she'll shed any tears for Henriette. Do you think she really is the girl's grandmother?"

"Probably. Her mother's mother, for Henriette showed us a miniature of my uncle Henry and her mother. Now that I think back on it, there is a pronounced resemblance between the old lady and Henriette's mother."

The two men waited for Lord Morgan to come to them and tell them that the French girl was dead. While they waited, they played chess, and got just a little drunk with Anthony's good red burgundy. Suddenly the door opened, and Blaze stepped into the room.

"Nick! Why did no one tell me that you were here? Is everything all right at Kirkwood?"

"Just came to play a little chess and have a friendly drink with Tony," Lord Kingsley said.

"How is my sister?"

"Blythe is in excellent health. Having babies agrees with her," he told her.

Blaze laughed. God bless men, she thought. For them it is all so simple. "And how is our new nephew?" she inquired.

Edmund John Kingsley had been born on the twenty-fifth day of February, and named after his late uncle, the Earl of Langford.

"Were it not for Edmund's kindness and generosity," Blythe had declared, "I should have never had a dowry, but worse, I should have never met my Nicholas!"

"My dear," her husband had responded gallantly, "I would have had you without a dowry."

"The young fellow is doing quite well," answered Lord Kingsley in reply to Blaze's question. He was enormously proud of his daughter and two sons.

"Then having gained all your news, Nick, I shall leave you both to your game, and that fine French burgundy. Tony, where is Henriette? I have not seen her since Delight left this morning."

"I saw Cecile just as Nick arrived, and she mentioned that my cousin had a headache and would spend her afternoon resting."

"Henriette always manages to disappear or become indisposed when there is work to be done," grumbled Blaze. "I doubt she was so fine a lady at the French court as she would have us believe. Your mother and I could have used her help with the linens, but no matter. She will only whine and fuss if I arouse her, so she is best left to her bed."

"Do not tire yourself, my angel," Tony cautioned her.

"I will not," she promised him, and smiling at them both, she departed, closing the door behind her.

"You do not think she will change her mind and go to fetch your cousin, do you?" Nicholas Kingsley asked nervously.

"Nay," said Anthony. "Henriette does cause a great to-do when asked to do what she considers menial chores. Blaze has no patience with her, and is actually happy for the excuse to leave her in peace."

They continued their game, to be interrupted a half-hour later when Lord Morgan entered the library, quickly shutting the door firmly behind him. The two younger men looked up questioningly.

"She is quite dead," said Robert Morgan. "To be certain, when her breathing stopped, I pricked her sharply on the bare sole of her foot, but she moved not. God, how she curst us after you left, and in the foulest language that I have ever heard. Then she seemed to accept her fate, and spoke not again. I think the silence was worse. I untied her before I left her bedchamber, and burnt the ropes in the fireplace. Then I placed a coverlet over her so she would look more natural. I was frankly quite afraid to touch her lest I draw some of the poison to myself," he finished.

"Let the old woman risk the handling of her for her burial," said Anthony.

The other men nodded, and then Lord Morgan said, "I must get back across the river, gentlemen. There is at least an hour of daylight left to me, and with the moon tonight my way will be quite clear. I had best get home and reassure Delight that her sister is all right. Her state of mind is very fragile right now."

"Do you still intend to match her with the Irish lad?" Tony asked.

"I think so. Once Delight is assured that her attempt on Blaze's life came to naught, *and* I can tell her that no one else knows but the three of us, *and* that you, Anthony, forgive her, I believe that her recovery will be guaranteed. The Irish suitor will be a good diversion for her. I am almost certain now that I will make the match unless the lad turns out to be feebleminded or cruel. I believe it is best if Delight's married life be far from you and Blaze, Anthony. It will not be easy for her to look on you both for some time without feeling some sort of guilt. The farther away she is, the easier it will be for her to forget all of this; the less chance she will have of constantly confronting her guilt; and there will be more opportunity for her to heal herself."

"You are a wise father, Rob," said Anthony, and the two men embraced one another. Then the earl moved to touch one of the beautiful linenfold panels that made up his library's wall, and the wall swung open, to his two companions' great surprise. "This passage will take you down to the boat quay without being seen," he said. "I think it best you use it today."

Lord Kingsley and Lord Morgan nodded, and without another word, went through into the passage, each holding lighted tapers that they had taken from the sconces on the wall. The earl quickly closed the hidden door behind them, and going to the windows that overlooked the river, he watched until several minutes later he saw his brother-in-law's barge pull away from the landing and make for his own on the opposite shore. Anthony Wyndham turned and hurried back up the stairs of his house to the unused tower room where they had earlier incarcerated the old Frenchwoman. Unlocking the door, he motioned her out into the hallway. Together they descended back down to the level upon which the family bedchambers were located, and entered into Henriette's room.

The French girl lay upon the bed, deceptively innocent-looking in death. Her eyes were open wide and sightless. The earl dug deep into his doublet and brought forth two copper coins, which the old woman placed upon her granddaughter's eyelids as she drew them closed. There was not a mark upon the already stiffening body, and Henriette's death appeared to be a natural one. Cecile drew her granddaughter's arms down, and crossed them over the girl's breasts.

"Take that damned hellish garment off her and burn it now," said Anthony. "I would be certain that it is destroyed."

Silently the old woman ripped the gown from the dead girl and dumped it on the smoldering red coals. The silk immediately caught fire, and within minutes was burnt to black ashes.

"You will prepare her for her burial," said the earl. "I want no one else touching the body."

Cecile nodded. "She can hurt no one now, *monseigneur*. Once absorbed into her system through her skin, the poison is harmless to everyone but its victim."

He watched her as she wrapped Henriette in another chamber robe, and then he said, "I am going back down to my library, Cecile. In five minutes you will come screaming from this chamber to announce my cousin's death. Play your part well, old woman, and after Henriette is buried amongst the other Wyndhams with an honor she neither had nor deserves, you will find yourself on your way back to France with your gold, and able to live out your wretched life quite comfortably. Do you understand me, or shall I say it in French?"

Cecile smiled, baring half-toothed gums. "I understand, my lord earl, quite well, for my English has improved immeasurably during my stay here. It is not necessary to speak my own tongue to me. I will play my part well. My daughter, her husband, and my grandchild are all dead. I have no one left but myself to care for me. My lord earl's gold will give me a little cottage in Brittany, and I shall not go hungry even in the hard times."

Anthony left the old woman, and returned to his library to await her display. As he seated himself by the fire, the tension of the last hours drained from his body, and for a moment he felt quite weak. He had come so close to losing Blaze that the knowledge of it caused him a sharp physical pain deep in his chest. Only Delight's true and real love for her sister, and the decency that Robert Morgan and his wife had taught her, surfacing at the last moment, had saved his wife. Had saved their unborn child. He had come so close to losing them both, but Blaze would never know. She must never know the depths to which her unfortunate younger sister had been driven. She must never know that there were women such as Henriette in the world, wreaking their havoc in their selfish quest for that which they did not deserve.

How sad they were, those women, and men too, who did not realize that family was all. That without family there was nothing. No love. No friendships. No security of knowing that you were not really alone. No meaning to life. No reason for going forward. A person might want to be alone sometimes, thought Anthony Wyndham, but how good a thing it was when such a time passed to be able to walk into one's own hall to be greeted by those who loved you. The Henriettes of this world did not understand that and sought for other riches, but family was the greatest wealth of all.

But for a twist of fate he might have lost his, and Anthony Wyndham silently thanked God that he had not. It was at that moment that a piercing shriek of anguish rang throughout his house, and rising from his chair, the earl prepared himself to be surprised and shocked by the news he would shortly hear.

Chapter 14

*L*ord Morgan reached Ashby in midevening, to find his wife anxiously awaiting him. "Where is Delight?" he asked her.

"What is the matter?" Rosemary Morgan demanded. "Delight arrived, greeted me wanly, and then locked herself in her room. She will not speak with me, nor would she join the family for the evening meal. Vanora was heartbroken, for she has so looked forward to Delight's return."

"Let me speak with Delight first, my dear, and then I will reassure you, I promise. Everything is all right. You must trust me," he soothed her.

Lady Morgan nodded, and waved her husband up the staircase to their daughter's room.

"Delight, it is Papa. Everything is all right. Let me in, for I must speak with you." He stood in the dark silence of the upper hall, and then to his deep relief he heard the lock turning in the door, which then swung open.

"*Blaze?*" Delight rasped.

Lord Morgan gently pushed his daughter back into her bedchamber and closed the door behind them. "Sit down, Delight," he ordered her, and she sat upon her bed. "Blaze is fine. She will never know what happened, nor your part in it."

"Does Anthony know?"

"Aye, and Nick Kingsley too."

"Ohh, God! I shall never be able to face either of them again," moaned Delight, stricken.

"Tony forgives you, Delight. He understands that you were driven half-mad by your deep love for him. Nicholas understands too. Both of these men know the depths to which love can drive one. This was not your fault, Delight. Not really. You have not the capacity for evil that Mademoiselle Henriette had. It was she who encouraged you to your

266

wickedness. You were like soft clay in her evil hands, and she used you for her own purposes."

"Oh, no, Papa! Henriette is my friend. She had nothing to gain by Blaze's death. I was the one who had everything to gain!" Delight protested.

"Listen to me, child," said Lord Morgan. "Henriette Wyndham led you like a lamb to the slaughter. She planned for you to take the blame for the murder of your sister, and then she intended luring Tony into marriage. She did not, I suspect, know when she came from France that he was in love with Blaze, and would marry her. She planned to marry him herself, and when she found him with a loved wife, she plotted to use you to gain her own ends. She will not trouble you any longer, however, for she is dead. Put this all from your mind, my child, and concentrate upon rebuilding your own life."

"Henriette is dead?" Delight looked shocked. "Papa! What happened?"

"The Frenchwoman was an evil creature, Delight. She could not be left alive lest she attempt once again to harm Blaze and her unborn child. Do you understand that?"

Delight nodded. "But how?"

"The nightrail," he said quietly. "It is a secret you must share with Tony, Nick, and myself."

Delight was very pale. "So then," she said, "it is truly over. I will pray for Henriette."

"Aye, you should," he agreed with her. "She was a wicked woman for one so very young. Your forgiveness and prayers may help her. Now, Delight, go to sleep. It has been a long and terrible day for us all."

"Not yet, Papa. Tell me of the Irish lord and his son. I need something of my own to think upon lest my memories arise to assail me."

Aye, she did, he thought, and so he stayed, tucking her into the large bed she had once shared with her sisters, seating himself next to her. "There is not a great deal that I can tell you, my dear. The family name is O'Brian. Not the great lords of Thomond, but distant cousins nonetheless. Our own Father John has a nephew who is also a priest. You will remember that Father John's mother is Irish, and his nephew, the son of his mother's brother, one Father Kevin by name, is the priest in the household of the O'Brians of Killaloe. He and his uncle correspond, and it was through Father Kevin that we first received the tentative offer of a possible match between the O'Brians' son, who is just your age, and one of my daughters."

"But why have you chosen me, Papa? Both Larke and Linnette are old enough to wed."

"But you are my oldest unmarried daughter, Delight. Besides, you know that I must see Larke and Linnette wed to brothers who are hopefully as close as your sisters are. They could never survive without one another, I fear. Delight, I will not mince words with you. There is no more time left to cater to your whims. You will be eighteen in another few weeks. Unless the young Irishman and his family prove highly unsuitable, I intend making this match. Surely you understand now that Anthony Wyndham can never be yours. Unless you seek to enter holy orders, you must have a husband."

Delight sighed deeply. "I am not fit to be a nun, Papa, nor do I have the desire to be one. I know now that Tony really does love Blaze. Even if she had died, he would have not wed with me. I will not fight you, Papa, on this match you propose."

Robert Morgan patted his daughter's hand. "There is one other thing, Delight. I must tell your mother of what has passed."

Delight nodded in agreement. "I know, Papa. You have never kept anything from Mama, nor has she kept anything from you. She will not hate me, do you think?"

"Nay, Delight, she will not hate you," he answered her, and arising, he bent back down to place a kiss upon her cheek. "Go to sleep now, my child. Your nightmare is over."

Lord Morgan left his daughter's bedchamber, and seeking his own, found his wife awaiting him. As gently as possible he told her their daughter's tragic tale, and Rosemary Morgan's tender heart broke with Delight's pain and hurt.

"My poor child," she wept softly upon her husband's shoulder. "I must go to her!"

"Aye," he agreed. "I think that it would ease her conscience to know that you are not angered with her."

Lady Morgan left her husband, and hurried to Delight's bedchamber. "Are you awake, child?" she asked as she entered.

"Aye, Mama."

Rosemary Morgan enfolded Delight into her arms, and the girl burst into healing tears as she clung to her mother's neck. "Thank God," the good lady said. "You need to cry, my daughter, but rest assured that I love you."

When finally Delight's sobs had subsided, her mother settled her back upon her pillows, and smoothing her forehead with a gentle hand, she left her to return to her husband. Delight felt that a great weight had suddenly been lifted from her shoulders. With a little sigh she closed her swollen eyes and slipped into sleep.

Delight turned eighteen on the seventh of June. She had grown into a tall and slender girl whose long, dark, chestnut-colored hair and deep blue eyes only served to highlight the paleness of her creamy skin. Within the close and loving circle of her family her confidence had returned. Though she had been greatly matured by her experience, there were tiny glimpses of her former merry self. She was not the girl she had once been, but neither was she yet a woman by any means. A fact brought strongly home to her a few days after her birthday, when she once again found herself behind the great hedge near the front of the house with Larke and Linnette, who were fourteen, Vanora, who was twelve, and Glenna, now ten. They were spying upon a visitor who was just arriving at the house. For a brief instant she was hurtled back in time, and she remembered the day that Edmund Wyndham had ridden up to Ashby thereby changing all their lives forever.

"Who is he?" the twins queried in unison.

"He cannot be very important," Vanora noted.

"Why do you say that, sister?" asked Glenna.

"He has no great retinue with him," replied Vanora wisely.

"Perhaps he is Delight's suitor," answered Glenna.

"I think not," said Delight. "There is but one man, and Lord O'Brian is coming with his son."

"There are two riders," said Glenna.

"One is obviously a servant, you silly," Vanora chided her little sister.

"Well, I did not know, Mistress Wisdom!" snapped Glenna with spirit. "How is it that you are so well-informed?"

"You have but to compare his clothing with the other man's garb," was the smug reply.

Delight smiled to herself. Nothing, it seemed, changed. "I think," she said, "if we want our answers as to who he is, and for what purpose this gentleman has come, then we had best go into the house. Perhaps he is someone with twin sons for Larke and Linnette," she teased, and the twin sisters giggled.

They waited until the gentleman had entered Ashby, and then, trailing out from behind the hedge, they hurried toward the house. The other rider, now dismounted, stood before the house holding the reins of the two horses. He was not a very large man, and he was extremely wiry to boot, but he had the merriest twinkle in his eye that they had ever seen. Grinning boldly at them, he tipped his cap as they moved by him.

"Good day to yese, pretty ladies," he said.

Delight tilted her head politely as she had seen Blaze so often do. The twins giggled, Glenna flushed at having been called a "pretty lady," and Vanora demanded, "What kind of an accent is *that?*"

"Vanora, your manners!" Delight admonished, pushing her younger sister into the house.

"Well, how am I to ever know anything if I cannot ask questions and get answers?" said Vanora, her tone offended.

Rosemary Morgan hurried forward. "Quickly, Delight! Upstairs! You must change your gown. Lord O'Brian is here!"

"I was right! I was right!" cried Glenna, dancing about.

"Oh, be silent, you smug little toad!" snapped Vanora.

Glenna made a face at her sister, and then scampered off squealing as Vanora chased after her, eager to render a harsh judgment upon her little sister.

"Vanora grows more like Bliss every day," chuckled Delight.

"And Glenna is more like Vanora at that age as well." Their mother smiled as they moved up the stairs.

"Where is Lord O'Brian's son, Mama? I thought he was to come with his father so we might get to know one another."

"I know nothing," replied Lady Rosemary. "All I can tell you is that your father introduced us, and then told me to fetch you as quickly as possible." Lady Morgan helped her daughter change from her simple house garb into a more elegant gown. Carefully she laced her daughter's bodice of rose-colored silk with its delicate pearled embroidery. The overskirt and underskirt of the gown were of the same rich color, although the underskirt had been lightly embroidered with seed-pearl daisies and small butterflies.

Delight caught up her hairbrush and ran it through her tangled curls, but as she made to put her hair up, her mother stopped her.

"Leave it loose. I know you would appear sophisticated, but it is better you not seem any older than you are, lest Lord O'Brian think we seek to foist an elderly crone upon him."

Delight made a little moue with her mouth. "You make my situation seem so desperate, Mama."

"Need I remind you of your age, daughter?" came the sharp reply.

Delight said nothing more, instead putting small pearl earbobs in her ears and looping a beautiful rope of pearls about her neck. These were gifts from Blaze and Tony sent to Ashby for her birthday, and Delight felt almost guilty in the face of their generosity, but as she had no other jewelry of value that would impress Lord O'Brian, she wore the pearls.

Lady Rosemary hummed her approval of her daughter's appearance, and escorted her back downstairs to Rob's library. Delight had become quite the beauty, though she would never tell her daughters that they were, lest vanity obscure their common sense. Entering the library, the two women curtsied to the two men already within.

Lord Morgan came forward and took Delight by the hand. "This is my daughter Delight, my lord."

He arose from his chair, a big-boned tall man with the fierce look of a highwayman to him. His hair was blacker than any she had ever seen, even Tony's. The oval-shaped eyes glinted green as he coolly assessed her, as if assessing the finer points upon a blooded horse.

Delight felt herself flushing beneath his scrutiny. His look made her feel as if she were some slave girl, naked and upon the block for all to see. Furious, she glared at him.

Lord O'Brian chuckled. "She's got spirit," he said in the most beautiful voice that Delight had ever heard. It was deep, yet both rich and musical at the same time.

"She is a well-mannered and well-behaved girl, my lord," responded Robert Morgan.

"The hell she is, and so much the better!" came the reply. "I want no milk-and-water miss mothering the next generation of O'Brians!"

Lady Rosemary gasped at the frankness of his words, but Delight stamped her foot with outrage.

"And what makes you think I want to mother any generation of O'Brians?" she demanded.

Lord O'Brian burst out laughing at her words, but when he had recovered himself he looked straight at Delight and said, "Because you are eighteen, wench, and this may be your last chance for a decent match!"

"Go to the devil, you great Irish oaf! I would sooner die an old maid than marry any son of yours!" snapped Delight.

"I'll take her." Lord O' Brian grinned, turning to Robert Morgan.

"You'll take me?" Delight screeched, outraged. "Are you deaf, man, that you did not hear me? I'll wed no son of yours!"

Rosemary Morgan could not move. What was Delight doing? She was driving away the only good chance that they could possibly have now to gain her a husband.

"Nay," said Lord O'Brian, "you'll wed not my son, for the damned fool went and got himself killed in a cattle raid last month. You'll wed me, my fine-tempered girl, for he was the only heir I had left, and I need sons!"

At last Delight was stunned into silence. Marry this big, fierce man? It was the last thing that had ever entered her mind, for she had expected for a husband a boy her own age.

"Lord O'Brian's son has, as he has stated, been killed. He has, nonetheless, come to us to propose that he wed Delight in his son's place. I see no reason not to consent to this match, provided, of course, Delight, that you can refrain from killing the man until you have given him at least several sons," said Lord Morgan, his eyes brimming with amusement.

Delight could only stare for a moment.

"What, wench, does the news overwhelm you that much?" taunted Lord O'Brian.

Delight immediately recovered at his mockery. "Nay, my lord," she replied sweetly. "It was just that I had prepared myself to wed with a young man, not an old one."

He chuckled. "I suspect you'll get a great deal more from me, wench, than you would have ever gotten from that bullying milksop I sired on my last wife," came the wicked answer.

"And just how many wives have you outlived, my lord?" Delight was not in the least fazed.

"You'll be my third, wench, and like the others, I'll soon have you purring like a kitten."

"Unlike the others, I'll long outlive you, my lord, and you had best beware, for this kitten has sharp claws."

Lord O'Brian laughed again, and then said to Lord Morgan, "Draw up the betrothal papers. I want this hot-tempered wench in my bed before the summer's out. In Ireland a man needs a wife like this one during the cold winter nights."

Rosemary Morgan had finally managed to recover herself. "If you do not need us any longer, my lord," she said to her husband, "then Delight and I will withdraw," and grasping her daughter's arm in a death grip, she practically dragged her from the library.

"I will *not* marry that overbearing, pompous oaf!" said Delight, pulling away from her mother.

"Your father has agreed to it," said Lady Rosemary.

"*I hate him!*" shouted Delight.

"You do not even know the man," her mother reasoned.

"I know all I need to know," raged Delight, and picking up her skirts, she ran from the house.

Rosemary Morgan looked after her, bemused. She had never seen any-one react so strongly to another person as Delight had reacted to Lord O'Brian. Turning about, she hurried back to her husband's library. She really must speak with him about this. Perhaps Delight had a point, but upon entering the room where the two men stood toasting each other with goblets of wine, she found herself quickly and completely charmed by the big Irishman.

"Lord O'Brian and I have agreed on terms, my dear. Delight's dowry is acceptable to him, and I will also include two of my good brood mares, for the O'Brians raise horses."

"Do not tell Delight that, my lord, I beg of you," pleaded his wife.

Lord O'Brian laughed. "Nay," he said, "I do not think the wench would like to know that part of her bride's price is two horses. If she should ever learn it, however, I should like to be the man to tell her," and he laughed again. "Where is she, by the way? I would drink a toast with her."

Lady Rosemary sighed. "If Delight is true to form, then she was headed for the orchards, my lord. Through the front door, and to the right."

"Thank you, madam," was the reply, and he bowed most elegantly to her before leaving the room.

When he had gone, Rosemary turned to her husband. "Rob, is this match a wise one? I do not want Delight unhappy."

"I think," responded her husband, "that Delight may be a far more fortunate girl than she realizes, my dear. Lord O'Brian is Tony's age, and although I was surprised to learn that his son had been killed, on reflection I believe that an older husband is a better thing for Delight. A boy might have bored her. I consider this God's will. She will marry, and live in Ireland far from the scene of her former heartbreak, for though Delight seems recovered, I think to remain so near her sister and Anthony would eventually bring her pain again. Should she have compared a young husband with Anthony, the boy would have certainly suffered by comparison, but Lord O'Brian is a man as Tony is. I think he will keep Delight far too busy to even remember her broken heart."

"When have you decided upon the wedding ceremony?"

"We'll have a formal betrothal ceremony in a few days, for the Irish enjoy the pomp and pageant of such things. The wedding will take place in late summer before the autumn storms make a crossing of the sea between England and Ireland an impossible thing. Lord O'Brian will have to return to Ireland after the betrothal, but he will be back in August."

"I only hope Delight will be happy, Rob," fretted Lady Morgan.

"She will have to make her own happiness, my dear," he said, "but Lord O'Brian is much taken with her. If she will only stop fighting him, there is a very good chance that she should be not just happy, but content."

At the moment, however, Delight was neither happy nor content. She had seen Lord O'Brian coming from the house and into the orchard, and now she attempted to hide from him amid the falling blossoms of the fragrant trees. He did not call to her, but he seemed to be walking straight toward her. Suddenly she lost sight of him, and forced from her hiding place behind a large tree, she peered about to see where he had gotten to, for he was simply nowhere to be found. Suddenly a pair of strong arms imprisoned her, turning her about, and Delight shrieked, only to have her mouth stopped by his.

She had never been kissed, and this was certainly not what she had expected at all. He totally possessed and overwhelmed her in a way she wasn't certain that she even liked. On the other hand, she found that she did not dislike it either. His hard mouth bore down on her soft lips, almost burning them, and setting her pulses to racing in a manner that she had never known. She was suddenly afire, and unable to help herself, she wrapped her arms about him as she kissed him back.

Finally, when it became clear that neither of them would be able to breathe if they did not part, he pulled his head away from hers, but he kept his arms about her. "By all that's holy, wench, you are my match, and that is for certain," he growled at her. "I came here expecting some milk-and-water pale English rose. I even considered telling your father that since Desmond was dead there could be no uniting of our families, but the voice within warned me not to, and so I listened as I have always listened. And what have I found, eh, wench? A hot-tempered, hot-blooded vixen with an improbable name who, from the looks of her, will breed me up strong Celtic sons for Ireland. It took only a moment, but I knew I wanted you!"

In his passion Lord O'Brian had let his grip upon the girl loosen, and pulling away from him suddenly, Delight hit him a blow that might have staggered a lesser man.

"What the hell was that for, wench?" demanded the Irishman.

"You kissed me!"

"You kissed me back," he said.

"I didn't!" she denied.

"You did, wench," he teased. "You kissed me with a passion that you are too innocent to even understand, and I'll wager your pulses were racing when you did." He laughed at her guilty flush and continued. "I kissed you, wench, and I intend to keep on kissing you, and in time I'll be doing other things to you. Things that will make you weak with pleasure, and leave you begging me for more even as I will want more of you. I want to kiss your lovely body, and caress your pretty breasts. I want to teach you how to touch a man and make him content even as my touching of you will make you content." His arms snaked out, and he pulled her back against him. Delight attempted to struggle, but his grip tightened until she thought she would faint, and so she ceased her futile resistance. "I want to fill you full of me, Delight Morgan, and give you my sons and daughters." His lips brushed tantalizingly against hers. "I want to love you even as you want to love me."

"I don't want to love you!" Delight protested. "I do not even know you, my lord!"

"Cormac, wench! My name is Cormac. Aye, you know me! You know me well. I am the faceless man who has haunted your dreams since you grew old enough to have such dreams. I am the one who has caused you to awaken in the night aching with a feeling you have never understood until now. I am yours, wench, and you are O'Brian's Delight. Thus it was always meant to be, and it will be!"

She couldn't move. She was simply mesmerized by the beautiful voice that said such outrageous things to her, and the green eyes that glittered so dangerously as they devoured her. She did not quite understand what was happening to her. Up until a month ago she had thought herself in love with Anthony Wyndham. She had been in love with him since she had first seen him when she was only thirteen. She had just begun to accept the fact that Tony was Blaze's and would never be hers. Yet suddenly this wild man was sweeping into her life, saying incredible things to her, words that were touching her as no man's words had ever touched her. How could he have known of the faceless man in her dreams whom even she had dared not acknowledge aloud to herself?

"I will not be yours," she whispered.

"Oh, aye, wench, you will be," he promised her. "No one, even a stubborn little English girl, can fight the fate that's been ordained for her." He loosened his grip on her. "Now, run along, wench, and consider the things that I've said to you."

Delight did not wait to hear any more. She fled him, his mocking laughter echoing in her ears. Were her parents mad, matching her with this wild Irishman? Surely they would not do it! Particularly when they saw him for what he really was, but to Delight's great annoyance they didn't. Cormac O'Brian charmed everyone at Ashby, from the lowliest to the highest. Her sisters were in love with him, including Larke and Linnette, who, for the first time in their young lives, got into an argument with one another over who would sit next to Lord O'Brian at the table. Since Delight had been placed at his right, there was but one other place available. Lady Morgan finally solved the problem by asking her eldest son, Gavin, to sit by her daughter's husband-to-be.

With a smug and mischievous grin at his sisters, Gavin took the prized place. He had already told Delight that he thought the Irishman a grand fellow. Even the little children, three-year-old Hal and his twin brother, Tom, liked Lord O'Brian. He seemed able to sit for hours by the fire, the two small boys snuggled deep in his lap, telling them wonderful and outrageous tales of Ireland that left them wide-eyed and admiring.

In a rare moment of quiet shared with Cormac O'Brian, Delight asked him, "Why is it that no one else can see you as I do?"

"Because, wench, they are not afraid of me as you are," he answered her.

"I am most certainly not afraid of you!" Delight told him emphatically. "Why should I be?"

"Because you are independent. Because you are a virgin, and virgins always believe that to be loved is to be possessed. You do not want anyone to possess you, but believe me, wench, when a man and a woman love one another, the possession is mutual. There is no winning in love, only sharing. You will understand that one day soon, and then you will not be afraid of me."

His words left her thoughtful, even if she did not really totally understand him. Mad! The man was simply mad. Her parents were matching her with a madman, and there was nothing that she could do about it.

The day chosen for their betrothal was the twenty-first of June. Blaze and Tony sent their best wishes, but the Earl of Langford would not allow his wife to travel in her newly announced condition. Delight was secretly relieved, for she was not yet quite up to facing Blaze and her husband. Still, she smiled to think of Blaze's outrage at being told she must remain at RiversEdge and miss the family event. Bliss, of course, was near her time. There was absolutely no question of her coming. She and Owen also sent gifts and good wishes to the couple.

Blythe, however, came with Nicholas and their children. "I could not let this happy day go by and not be with you, dearest," the gentle Lady Kingsley declared as she hugged her sibling. "I know that Bliss and Blaze are very disappointed not to be able to be with you in this joyous moment."

Cormac O'Brian's eyes warmed at the sight of the fair and beautiful Blythe, her two elder children clinging to her skirts, baby Edmund in her arms.

"There are two like that?" he asked Lord Morgan.

Robert Morgan smiled. "Aye, her identical twin is the Countess of Marwood, but more fiery of temperament. Blythe is my lamb. I've no other like her."

"I'd not complain of daughters if Delight gave me some like that," Lord O'Brian said admiringly.

The bride-to-be wore a gown of pale cream-colored silk, its bodice decorated with tiny seed pearls and gold threads, as was the panel of its underskirt which showed. Her upper puffed sleeves were slashed to show pearl-dotted lace beneath, which fell into cuffs as they emerged from beneath the narrower lower sleeve of her gown. In her ears and about her neck were her pearls. Her loose dark hair was crowned with a wreath of daisies and ivy.

Cormac O'Brian was dressed in dark green velvets and silks. Though his clothes gave him the thin veneer of civilization, there was still a savagery about him that was both intriguing and fascinating. About his neck he wore a heavy gold chain from which hung a great round medallion upon which was the raised figure of a falcon in flight.

They stood side by side within the family chapel while Father John spoke the ancient words of the betrothal ceremony which, in effect, caused them to pledge themselves formally, one to the other, and to agree upon their intent to marry. Cormac O'Brian then pushed the betrothal ring upon Delight's finger. She stared down at the beautiful circle of Irish red-gold which was carved all around with tiny forget-me-nots studded with tiny blue sapphires.

A formal betrothal ceremony was a serious and binding thing, which in many places was considered more important than the marriage ceremony itself. There was no going back now. The marriage agreement was then signed by the bride's father, her intended husband, and the bride herself. Lord O'Brian was then instructed by the priest to give Delight the betrothal kiss, which he did, in a most chaste manner, thus finalizing the vows made between them, and ending the ceremony.

"Now," said Lord Morgan, "let us celebrate this happy event!" and with his wife he led them all back to the Great Hall of Ashby, where a feast awaited them. They had scarcely sat down to table when a messenger wearing the Earl of Marwood's badge rushed into the hall and ran up to Lord Morgan who waved his permission to the servant to speak.

"The young countess has gone into labor, my lord, and she begs that her mother and father attend her immediately. His lordship agrees with her ladyship, and also begs that you both come."

"Trust Bliss to take the attention away from Delight at her own betrothal feast. She has always had a flair for the dramatic," said Vanora primly.

"Vanora, have some charity for your sister," scolded Lady Rosemary. "You do not know what it is like to give birth to a child."

"Neither Blaze nor Blythe whined for you, Mama, when they first gave birth," noted Vanora.

"Nevertheless, I was with them both. A woman in labor with her first child wants the company of the other, more experienced women in her family. You will too one day. Blythe is here with us, and Blaze cannot travel." She arose from the table. "I must go to Bliss immediately, although it will be hours before she has her child. Still, she needs the reassurance of her family about her. Rob, see to the horses, for we will have to ride. The coach will take too long."

"I am going with you, Mama," said Blythe. "I cannot be away from Bliss at such a time. My lord," she said, turning to her husband, "will you see the children safely home, and then join me?"

"Go along, sweetheart," he told her. "Tell Owen I shall soon be with him, and we will all get drunk together."

"Oh, Delight," said Lady Morgan, "I am so sorry that your day has been spoilt, but you and Cormac must continue to host your feast." She hugged her daughter, and then hurried off to seek her traveling-cloak.

Blythe went with her, and Lord Morgan, with a hurried apology to his daughter and Lord O'Brian, quickly followed. For a long moment the hall was silent in the wake of their departure, and then Vanora said, "When are you going to cut the betrothal cake, Delight? I am fair starved to taste it!"

"So am I," replied Lord O'Brian, "but I think Delight's lips are probably far sweeter."

"My lord, behave yourself!" snapped Delight.

"Why, wench, if I behaved myself I should not be half the grand fellow that Gavin says I am," Cormac O'Brian teased, and snatching up his goblet, he arose. "A toast, my lords and my ladies! A toast to the loveliest bride a man could ever have! A toast to O'Brian's Delight!"

"A toast!" cried the remaining guests, rising and raising their own goblets while Delight blushed, half-irritated, half-pleased by his words.

And while the merriment continued in the Great Hall of Ashby, Lord

Morgan's little party rode out for Marwood Hall. It was a ride of several hours' length, and sometimes they kept to the high road, but at other times they scorned it, riding cross-country, always taking the most direct route, until finally in the late afternoon they arrived. The women, almost falling from their horses, hurried on wobbly legs into the house, to be greeted by Owen FitzHugh, who was looking gaunt and haggard.

"I will never do this to her again," he declared dramatically. "My God, how she is suffering!"

"When did her pains begin, Owen?" Lady Rosemary asked him.

"Not until midmorning, *belle-mère*," he answered her.

"But your messenger arrived at Ashby at midmorning," she answered, puzzled.

"Her waters broke at dawn," he said, "and she insisted then and there that I send for you."

"Ahhhh," replied Lady Morgan understandingly. "Take me to her, Owen."

He led them to Bliss's apartments, where the expectant mother was found sitting up in her bed eating sugarplums and drinking wine. "Ohhhhh, Owen!" Bliss cried dramatically when she spied her husband, "I feel so dreadful!"

"And no wonder!" snapped her mother, coming into the room. "Stop eating those sweetmeats, and put that wine down, you little idiot! When did you ever see me eating and drinking in the midst of labor? You are going to be as sick as a pig, Bliss, and 'twill serve you right!" scolded the good lady, snatching the goblet from her daughter and sweeping up the dish of candies.

"But, Mama," wailed Bliss, "it keeps me from thinking about my pain!"

"You are supposed to think on your pain. How else is your child to be born if you do not consider on your pain? I do not think, however, that you are in that much pain if you can eat and drink sitting up. When was the last time you felt a spasm?"

"A little while ago," said Bliss vaguely, but then she gasped with surprise as a very sharp pain knifed through her vitals. "Ohhhh!" she shrieked. "Here is another one, and sooner than the last, Mama!"

"I am astounded," replied her mother dryly, "for I would not have been surprised if you had rendered my grandchild in his cups with all your wine! Where is the birthing table? Is no one in this house properly prepared for Marwood's heir?"

Lady Morgan took immediate charge. She sent her son-in-law off with her amused husband, who cast her a fond look as he escorted Owen

FitzHugh away from the scene of activity. Her orders quickly rang out, and Marwood Hall's servants, used to their more lackadaisical mistress, scurried to and fro obeying Lady Morgan's recognized voice of authority. Under her mother's guidance Bliss got down to the serious business of having her child. Her labor quickly progressed stage by stage until shortly after ten o'clock in the evening she brought forth her son, and as the infant's howls rang through the house, Owen FitzHugh burst into his wife's chamber to find his exhausted but happy wife cradling their child, a look upon her face that he had never seen before.

"Is he not wonderful?" she cooed at her husband. "Is not my little Owen a fine baby boy?"

The Earl of Marwood knelt hollow-eyed by his wife's bedside. "I will never do this to you again, sweetheart," he vowed to her.

Bliss looked down on him as if he had gone stark raving mad. "God's foot, Owen! I've had a baby, 'tis all, not endured the Holy Inquisition! Little Owen is only the first. I want a houseful like him!"

"But what about the court?" he asked her, confused. "Do you not wish to return to court, sweetheart?"

"Oh, there is time enough for that," she answered him airily, "but first I want to raise my children."

Rosemary Morgan was still laughing about that two days later when they returned to Ashby. "Did you see the look upon his face," she asked her husband for the hundredth time, "when she said she wanted a houseful of children?"

"Motherhood is a potent emotion," chuckled Lord Morgan, "but you have been a shining example for our daughters, my dear. In the end the acorn does not fall far from the oak."

"Delight will be so excited to know that she is to be little Owen's godmother. I am glad we sent the children a message of Bliss's safe delivery. At least they did not have to wait until we returned home to know their sister and her son were all right. Now I can concentrate properly upon Delight's wedding. Unless there has been some difficulty with Blaze's confinement, you must convince Anthony to allow her to come, for I would not have her the only one of my children absent on such a particularly happy occasion."

"I will do my best, my dear," her husband replied, "for I agree that upon such a happy day we should all be together once again."

Lord and Lady Morgan and their escort reached their home shortly after sunset. It had been a lovely spring day for a ride, even as long a one as they had just completed. They were anxious to be home, for Lord Morgan had three mares in foal near their time, and his wife was concerned about their two youngest sons who had been sniffly. There was also something to be said about the comfort of one's own bed. Entering the house, they were greeted by Vanora.

"Lord O'Brian has kidnapped Delight," she announced without any preamble.

For a moment her parents looked uncomprehendingly at Vanora, but she did not bother to repeat her words, for she knew that they were not deaf.

Finally Lord Morgan said, "What do you mean that Lord O'Brian has kidnapped Delight, Vanora?"

"They were gone the morning after the betrothal, even before the messenger arrived from Marwood Hall to tell us of Bliss's son. They have not been back since, and there is a letter in your library for you."

"That does not mean that he has kidnapped her, Vanora," said Lady Morgan. "Wherever do you get such fanciful ideas from in the first place?"

Vanora looked mightily offended, but she could not respond sharply to her mother as she might have to her siblings. "Mama," she said frostily, "what am I to think when Lord O'Brian comes from the house carrying a struggling, muffled body over his shoulder, which he slings onto one of the two mares that you promised him, Papa? What am I to think when he, his servant, the muffled body, and the two mares go off? What am I to think when Delight is no longer here afterward?"

"You actually saw all of that?" her father said.

"Aye, Papa, I did. The bedchamber was stuffy, and as it was dawn, I saw no harm in opening the window, which as you know overlooks the front of the house. Lord O'Brian even saw me. He grinned, and he waved farewell to me."

"Oh, Rob!" cried Lady Morgan. "I feared that this match was a mistake."

"Let us see what the letter says before we render too quick a judgment," answered her husband as he hurried into his library. There the letter sat, just as Vanora had said, upon his desk. Slowly he picked it up and broke the thick wax seal. Carefully he unfolded the heavy vellum and lowered his eyes to peruse its message. He read:

Robert, I can stay no longer away from my lands. In Ireland a man who stays too long off his lands may return to find he has none. I have taken Delight with me, as she is my betrothed wife. I will wed with her on the date agreed upon by us, but 'tis better we wed in Ireland. The late-

*August seas are chancy at best, and I fear a storm would prevent me
from reaching England, which would mean I should have to wait almost
a year to claim my wench. Come if you can. I promise to cherish her.*

> *Your ever grateful son-in-law,*
> *Cormac, Lord O'Brian of Killaloe.*

"Oh, Rob, what is it?" begged Rosemary Morgan.

Lord Morgan looked up from the message. His fine blue eyes were bright with their amusement. "Well, my dear, I suppose one might say that Lord O'Brian did indeed kidnap our daughter, since Delight did depart under some duress. He has taken her back to Ireland to wed, as he feels it is dangerous for him to be off his lands for so long, particularly, I suspect, as he has no sons right now. The Irish are an opportunistic race. We are invited to come to the wedding if we can."

"Ohh, my poor Delight," wailed Rosemary Morgan "and in her fragile condition too!"

Lord Morgan was forced to laugh. "Delight is about as fragile as a rock, my dear. Cormac O'Brian is an honorable man. I have no fears that he will marry her. Father John will keep us informed through the letters that he and Father Kevin exchange."

"He had no right to steal our daughter!" Lady Morgan was now indignant.

"Our daughter, *but* his betrothed wife," reminded her husband. "Perhaps you will think me mad, my dear, but I think it is the best thing that could have happened to Delight. He has yanked her away from everything that is familiar, and forced her into a different world from the one that we know. Delight is a strong girl. She has to be, to have survived what she has survived. Now she must be strong for herself, and she will be, my dear. She will be!"

"I think that it is heavenly," murmured Vanora, her dark eyes dreamy. "Imagine having a man so in love with you that he cannot wait until your wedding day, but must steal you away instead."

"How old are you now, Vanora?" asked her father thoughtfully.

"Twelve, my lord, this February past," she answered him.

"Time to be considering a husband for you, I think, my daughter," replied Lord Morgan.

"I shall choose my own husband," said Vanora stubbornly.

He smiled down at her. "Perhaps you will, little one. Perhaps you will. Run along now, and tell the others that your mother and I have come home. We will see them all in the chapel for vespers shortly."

Vanora curtsied to her parents and ran off.

"Well now," said Lord Morgan, sounding extremely pleased with himself, "we can truly count ourselves quite fortunate, my dear, can we not?" He smiled broadly at his wife.

"I do not understand you, Rob. Delight has been kidnapped by her betrothed husband, and you consider us fortunate?"

"One must look at the larger picture, my dear," he told her, and when she looked puzzled he said, "Four are wed, *and* but four to go!"

Chapter 15

Lord Morgan rode to see his three married daughters several weeks later that he might explain to them that there would be no wedding at Ashby come August.

"You do not seem unduly distressed," remarked Bliss as she nursed her greedy son.

"I am not," her father said. "Cormac O'Brian is the man for Delight, whether she has the sense to admit it or not."

"Ohhh," said Bliss. "You make him seem quite fascinating, Papa. I am sorry I did not get to meet him."

At Kirkwood the gentle Blythe smiled at her father's news. "Delight," she said, almost repeating his very words to his wife, "will survive quite nicely, and before it is all over with, poor Cormac O'Brian will find himself her slave. He was quite obviously mad for her, Papa."

Lord Morgan left his horse with the Kingsleys, and took their barge across the Wye to RiversEdge. There he encountered his eldest daughter dozing upon the green lawns beneath a tree in the late July sunshine. He looked down upon her, and he smiled. Blaze had surely grown even lovelier over the years, and being with child obviously agreed with her, for she had a glow about her that he had not seen before.

Kneeling down, he gently shook her awake. "Blaze. It is Papa, my dear. Wake up."

She stirred, yawned, and then with a sigh she opened her violet-blue eyes. "Papa?"

" 'Twas such a fine day, I came for a visit. I was with Blythe earlier, and yesterday I went to Marwood Hall to see how my new grandson is doing."

"Mama?"

"Fine, but still somewhat in shock. Lord O'Brian has taken Delight back to Ireland with him."

Her look both surprised and startled, Blaze sat up, brushing a lock of her honey-colored hair aside as she did. "What? Why on earth would they go to Ireland with the wedding so close? Will they be able to be back in time?"

"There will be no wedding here in England. It is to be celebrated in Ireland. Lord O'Brian could not stay away from his lands any longer for fear of encroachment by his neighbors, and he worried that late-summer storms could prevent his claiming Delight in August. He did not want to wait until next year. They were gone when we returned from little Owen's birth."

"I am quite surprised that Delight would go with him without waiting for you and Mama to return," said Blaze.

"Vanora says that Lord O'Brian forcibly kidnapped your sister," came the amused reply, and then Lord Morgan went on to explain to his oldest child what Vanora had seen.

Seeing her father's amusement as he told his tale, Blaze could not help but smile. "You are not saddened by this turn of events, are you, Papa?" she said.

"I am saddened that a looked-forward-to family event will not be, my dearest, but I know that Delight is going to be very happy when she ceases being very angry," their father wisely noted.

"Now," teased Tony that night as he and Blaze curled together in their bed, "I shall not have to fight with you about traveling in your maternal condition."

"Then I shall have to find something else for us to fight about, my lord," she taunted him back.

She felt him push her hair off her neck, and then his warm lips pressed a series of little kisses upon the sensitive skin. Drawing her back against him, he sought for, and found, a plump breast, which he fondled. She murmured and purred as he touched her, grinding her bottom against him until finally, carefully arranging her legs as she lay upon her side, he was able to enter into her, thrusting with long yet gentle strokes until they both found sweet fulfillment. "You are such a randy fellow," she mocked him afterward. "What will happen when we can no longer do this? And we cannot much longer. I want no harm to come to this child."

"Neither do I, my angel," he whispered back, wondering if she would ever love him.

The summer passed, and the Countess of Langford ripened with her child even as the apples in their orchards ripened. It was a happy summer. Doro grew plump with her contentment of family life, and Nyssa, nearing her fourth birthday, seemed to lose her baby looks. Bliss and Owen came from Marwood Hall to show off their healthy young heir. Blythe, Nicholas, and their offspring came from across the river to visit. They spread cloths upon the lawns and picnicked. The three sisters, their colorful skirts spread out about them like the petals on a flower; the men, their formal attire put aside, and sleeves rolled up as they played at bowls; the children, scampering about barefoot, and wading in the shallows of the Wye.

"I have the latest news from court," said Bliss. "Adela keeps me well-informed in her letters, one of which came just before we departed home for this visit."

"How is the king?" asked Blaze.

"Desperate, my dear, simply desperate!" crowed Bliss. "The queen has rejoined him and now refuses to retire from the court. The king is forever moving about without informing her, in his efforts to court Mistress Boleyn, but the queen always catches up to him within a day or two. Adela says they are exhausted with all the traveling."

The sisters laughed as each thought about the situation. It really was quite ludicrous, and secretly Bliss and Blaze were relieved to be in their own homes, and not dashing about on the summer progress as the king attempted to escape from the queen so he might pursue his little *amour*.

"Why will the queen not retire if Hal wishes her to?" wondered Blaze aloud.

"She has taken the most strong dislike to Mistress Boleyn," came Bliss's reply.

" 'Twould not be a hard thing to do," remarked Blaze. "Mistress Anne is a most infuriating chit who has the habit of putting herself quite above her station."

"She is of good stock, sister," said Bliss. "Her mother was the daughter of Thomas Howard, the Earl of Surrey. As for Sir Thomas Boleyn, her father, his mother was Margaret Butler, daughter of the Earl of Ormonde."

"But Sir Thomas's father was a London cloth merchant," Blaze replied. "Mistress Anne is all Boleyn, for she is as ambitious as her antecedents who, in two generations, have gone from trading in the London marts to a castle at Hever."

"We were poor once too," reminded Blythe. "Remember, Blaze, that had not Edmund married you and dowered us, we should all still be at Ashby without our husbands and children. Even Father should not have been able to regain some prosperity raising horses without Edmund's aid. There is nothing wrong with ambition, sister."

"It is not so much Boleyn ambition that bothers me as Mistress Anne herself. The king needs a kinder and more biddable companion."

"Such as the queen?" asked Blythe. She did not approve of the king's efforts to put aside his wife.

"Nay, Blythe," replied Blaze, who knew her sister's feelings on the subject quite well. "The queen is not an easy woman, which is where the problem lies. There is a precedent for a king to put aside a barren wife. Queen Catherine could easily step aside so that the king might marry a young wife on which to get his legitimate sons. She will not, and hence, we have the problem."

"Certainly she will not," noted Bliss, "if she thinks that she will be replaced by Mistress Boleyn. For a daughter of Castile's queen and Aragon's king to give way for the daughter of a Kentish knight is not within the queen's character."

"Nor should it be," said Blaze. "As much as I would have the king divorced and remarried, he must remarry in a dynastically correct fashion. A princess of France, or one from the German or northern kingdoms, but certainly not Anne Boleyn."

"What other news from court?" demanded Blythe.

"It all revolves around the king's great matter." Bliss laughed. "Mistress Boleyn, it is said, has not yet yielded her virtue to the king, and he suffers greatly."

"He would, for his appetite is great for female flesh," said Blaze. "Poor Hal! Whatever I may think of Mistress Anne, I must agree she is chaste, unlike merry Mistress Mary."

"She wields her chastity like a weapon," chuckled Bliss, "dangling her virginity like some great prize before the king's twitching nose. In the end he'll grow tired of having naught of her, however, and then 'twill be farewell to Mistress Anne Boleyn. She'll not even get herself a husband for her trouble. Perhaps a few baubles, but nothing more."

"Nyssa," called Blaze, "you and Mary Rose are to stop teasing Robert this instant! What scamps they are," she laughed at her sisters.

The autumn came, and with it the harvests. On All Hallows' Eve day Anthony ordered a Mass for the soul of his uncle, now gone two years. Great with her child, Blaze, nevertheless, insisted on attending, pulling herself up slowly from her knees after she had prayed. Something had changed, she thought. Edmund had always seemed so close to her, and yet now, to her growing horror, she could scarcely remember his face.

Afterward, she almost ran to the family picture gallery to stare into his portrait, grateful that she had it, but as she stared she faced seriously for the very first time that Edmund Wyndham was really gone from her. He would never return. She found herself crying, and then she felt Anthony's arms go comfortingly about her. He said not a thing, nor did he even turn her about so she might weep upon his chest. He simply held her, and raising her eyes up to Edmund's portrait, Blaze said her final farewell to the gentle, loving man who had been her first husband. Her tears ceased as suddenly as they had begun, and wiping the evidence from her cheeks with the heel of her palm, she turned to face Anthony.

With one tender finger he brushed away a single rebellious tear that had dared to streak down her face. "What now, madam?" he asked her gently.

A sudden spasm crossed Blaze's face as she looked up at him, and with a weak laugh she said, "What next, my lord? The birth of our son, I believe."

"Can you walk?" he asked her anxiously, and she nodded. He helped her to her apartments, and called for his mother to come. "Do you want your own mother? I will send for her if you do."

"It is too late in the day, my lord. Let us instead send a messenger tomorrow announcing our son's birth."

"You are so certain," he laughed.

"This time I am," she agreed.

"Go, my lord, go!" Heartha shooed him from the chamber. "This is woman's work. You did your part those nine months back," and she cackled her laughter.

Anthony had not long to wait. He went to the family hall, and calling a servant to him, sent the man across the river to fetch Blythe. He knew how much having someone of her own meant to Blaze. Then he poured himself a goblet of Rhenish. Nyssa wandered into the hall full of self-importance.

"My mama is having a baby," she announced to him. "She is having it this very minute."

"I know," he said.

"Will the baby like me, do you think, Papa?" Nyssa cocked her head even as he had seen Blaze cock her head a thousand times.

"I am sure the baby will like you, Nyssa."

"If I do not like the baby, Papa, can we send it away?"

"Nay, sweeting, but you will like the baby, I promise."

"Will you still love me even though there is a new baby, Papa?" She stood by his knee looking up at him with Edmund's face, and Blaze's eyes.

"I will love you both, Nyssa. There is enough love in my heart to love a hundred babies, and still not take a bit of my love away from you. I love your mama, and yet I love you too," he explained.

Nyssa nodded. "Will Mama have four babies? Fluff, my cat, had four babies this summer."

"Sometimes a woman will birth two children at once. Your own grandmother Rosemary has done so four times, but I think your mama will have but one child this time."

Nyssa stayed talking with him for a few more minutes, and then suddenly his mother was calling his name. He looked up to see her standing there smiling and holding a swaddled bundle.

"My lord," she said, "here is your son." She bent and lifted the coverlet from the baby's head.

"My God." He breathed as he looked down into a replica of his own face.

"He looks like you, Papa," cried Nyssa, standing on tiptoes to peer down at her half-brother. "I like him!"

The baby took that moment to open his eyes, and a look not unlike a tiny smile touched his mouth.

"He likes me too!" Nyssa said excitedly. "Oh, Papa! The baby likes me too!"

"So he does, sweeting, so he does," Anthony said, feeling close to tears. Then he looked at his mother. "Blaze?"

"Never have I seen such an easy birth as she had. She is fine, and asks if you would approve her choice for your son's name. She would call him Philip Anthony Edmund Nicholas. She says he should have his own name to answer to, and not someone else's."

"Aye," he said, "she is right, Mother, and I shall go and tell her so this minute!" With a final look at his son he raced from the family hall. He had not been certain earlier if she had been grieving for Edmund or bidding him farewell. Now he knew! But did she love him? God, how he wanted her to love him with all her heart as she had once loved Edmund. As he loved her. Possessing her body was not enough. He wanted her love!

"My lord, behave yourself!" the startled Heartha admonished him as he raced into his wife's bedchamber to find Blaze sitting up, drinking from a goblet.

"You have seen the baby?" she queried him.

"Aye! He's a fine lad, Blaze! Thank you! At last Langford has its heir."

"And you approve his name?"

"I thought you meant to call him after Edmund," he queried her.

"Blythe has just named her son Edmund, and besides, as I told Doro, this boy should have his own name. Not yours, nor Edmund's, and God knows this country does not need another Henry! Let him be our Philip, my lord."

" 'Tis a good name, my angel."

The bedchamber door opened, and Blythe peeped around it to be waved into the room. She came smiling and saying, "Here I am sent for because you have gone into labor, and I arrive to find my godson already birthed! What will you name him?"

"His name is Philip," said Anthony.

"Lord Philip Wyndham. It has a good ring to it," said Blythe.

The baby was christened the next day, with Blythe and Nicholas standing as his godparents even as messengers were dispatched from RiversEdge to the various family members about the countryside announcing his birth.

"We should best send a messenger to the king," said Blaze quietly. "He would want to share in our good fortune."

Anthony nodded, and it was done.

The baby thrived, and Blaze quickly recovered from the easy birth of her son. Nyssa was fascinated with the infant. She was constantly begging to be allowed to help with him. It was decided that the entire family would gather at RiversEdge for the holiday season, for Blaze would not hear of them doing anything else. They had not celebrated the Twelve Days of Christmas together in several years. A messenger arrived from the king just before New Year's. He brought a velvet-lined box holding a dozen silver goblets engraved with the Langford crest, a royal gift for the baby.

Blaze was pleased by the king's generosity, but Bliss pithily noted, "You earned them!"

For a moment Blaze stared at her sister in astonishment, but then she was forced to laugh. "I suppose I did," she said.

"I think her worth far more than just a dozen silver goblets," Tony teased his wife.

"Well, at least no one will say he is the king's son," retorted Bliss. "He is far more generous to his bastards than that," and the whole family laughed at her wry, yet truthful observation.

Winter came, and the landscape lay quiet beneath a mantle of white, the trees black and stark against a pearl-gray sky. Still it was not an overly harsh winter, and when the snows had melted, revealing the brown earth of very early spring, there were still stores enough in the granary to feed the peoples of the Langford earldom.

The days grew warmer. The newly turned red-brown earth sprouted with its first green, and Blaze took her children into the flowering orchards to enjoy the fragrant apple trees. Nyssa ran about filled with excitement at being allowed to go barefoot for the first time this year. Her mother sat beneath a large old tree enjoying the *hummm* of the bees amid the blossoms, watching Philip, who could now roll over, sit up, and was seriously contemplating crawling. At this moment, however, Philip slept, his thumb tucked firmly in his small pink mouth. Then Blaze saw her husband coming through the orchard. With him was another man. A man who wore royal livery, and Anthony did not look very pleased.

"Papa! Papa!" called Nyssa, spying him. "Here we are!"

"Lady Wyndham," said the king's man, "I have a message for you from the king. I am to await your reply."

Blaze struggled to her feet, and took the parchment from the messenger. Breaking the seal, she read the brief message:

To Blaze Wyndham, Countess of Langford, from Henry Rex:
Come to me as quickly as you can. I need your aid in a most delicate matter.

Blaze handed her husband the king's letter. Reading it over quickly, he swore softly. "Damn him! What can he want with you now? You are mine!"

"We are the king's loyal subjects first and foremost, my lord," she reminded him with a flick of her eyes toward the waiting royal servant. Royal servants were such notorious gossips. "I must obey this royal summons, and you know it." She turned to the messenger. "Where is the king now?" she asked him.

"At Greenwich, m'lady."

"You are to return to the king, and tell him that I will need a few days to prepare my family for my absence, but then I shall come to him with all good haste. It is late. You will stay the night, of course."

"Thank you, m'lady," replied the messenger.

They fought. For the next few days the house rang with their constant battle over the king's summons.

"I forbid you to go!" Anthony shouted for what surely must have been the hundredth time. "I absolutely forbid it!"

"Why do you make foolish pronouncements that you know you cannot enforce?" Blaze demanded of him. "Would you bring the king's wrath down upon this house? Remember that Langford was given to this family by a Henry. It could just as easily be taken away by another Henry!"

"How do you think I feel, having my wife summoned to that satyr's bed?" he raged.

"You think he summons me to his bed?" Blaze burst out laughing. "Believe me, Tony, swiving me is the furthest thing from the king's mind. He is far too busy in his pursuit of Mistress Boleyn. I do not know why he desires my presence, but it is not to make me his mistress once again. Of that I am certain!"

"Then why does he send for you, Blaze?"

"I shall not know that until I go, shall I?" she replied with what he felt was infuriating logic.

"Let me go with you," he insisted, as he had been insisting for the past few days.

"You have not been invited, my lord, and besides, you are needed here. It is spring, and there is much work for you. The shepherds will be beginning the lamb count in another day or so, and a decision must be made whether to plant barley or rye in the western portion of the estate fields. You are the Earl of Langford, Anthony, and you are needed here. It is tradition that we run our own estates," she told him.

She made him feel like such a small boy. Edmund had taught her well. Sometimes he felt she was more a part of Langford than he was. If only he did not love her so very much. If only she loved him. Perhaps then he would not be so fearful of her leaving, but he could not prevent her. The king had called, and she must go, and so he saw her off, albeit reluctantly, the following morning.

It rained almost the entire journey, and the roads grew worse each day. Gooey brown mud clung to the wheels of her coach, making the going almost impossible. It took two days longer to reach her destination than she had anticipated. She and Heartha sat together in the carriage as it slogged its way along the high road. Although she had never thought that she would be glad to see Greenwich again, she found that she was. To her vast amusement, the sun peeped through the clouds as they arrived, and she said to her tiring woman, "Undoubtedly at the king's request. Hal does hate the rainy days so."

To her great surprise she was led by the king's majordomo to the apartments that had once been hers. She felt uneasy even being here, and to be placed in such familiar surroundings gave her the feeling that perhaps nothing had really changed. Perhaps there was no Anthony, no

Nyssa and Philip. Even Heartha was grumbling beneath her breath about it.

A very young royal page arrived. "My lady Wyndham?" he inquired in a piping voice. Blaze smiled and nodded at the boy. "The king sends his greetings, and asks that after you have refreshed yourself from your travels, you join him in his privy chamber. He suggests that you use the inner staircase."

"Tell the king that I shall be with him in but one half of an hour," Blaze replied.

The boy bowed and departed.

"Such goings-on I don't know, m'lady. You should be home, and not back in this place. Having to turn the baby over to a wet nurse, and travel with your poor breasts all bound up to stop your milk," Heartha fussed irritably.

"I know, Heartha, I know," soothed Blaze. "But the king must really need me to have called me from all that I love best. I thought that you liked the king."

"Then was then, but this is now," answered the tiring woman. "You are a Wyndham of Langford, and at RiversEdge is where you belong, not here at Greenwich. 'Tis your husband you should be waiting on and not the king, I'm thinking!"

Blaze gently cajoled her servant, and water was brought for her to wash away the evidence of her travels. She changed from her traveling gown of plain black into a court gown of scarlet silk whose underskirt was embroidered with black silk and gold-thread hummingbirds and small sparkling garnets. Her lovely honey-colored hair was neatly fixed into a French knot that Heartha dressed with fresh red roses. She wore garnets in her ears, and a long, wonderful rope of jets and pearls.

With a final pat to her coif Blaze slipped through the hidden door and descended the narrow inner staircase. Reaching the bottom, she put her hand out, feeling for the doorknob, for she had no candle. Her fingers closed around it, and turning it, she stepped into the king's privy chamber. The page whom she had earlier spoken with leapt to his feet from a stool by the fire where he had been catching a moment's rest, and hurried out into the king's anteroom. Blaze waited patiently, and then suddenly Henry Tudor was there, filling the doorway first, and finally the entire room, with his presence. He closed the door behind him, and Blaze swept him a graceful curtsy.

"So, my little country girl, you have answered my summons, have you?" he said as he raised her up.

"Could I have refused you, sire?" she asked him. "You did not make that clear in your communiqué. Had you, I should have far rather stayed at RiversEdge."

"It is so great a trial I have visited upon you, madam?" the king demanded.

"Aye," she said blandly, "it is, Hal. For one thing, I have been forced to stop nursing my son because I am here, and he is there."

"For that great injustice I tender my apologies to my lord Philip Wyndham," the king said, his eyes twinkling. "I know how grievous an injury I have done him."

Blaze laughed. "My lord, this is serious!" she scolded. "I have fought bitterly with my husband, who is convinced that you have summoned me in order to seduce me again. I have had to reassure him that your majesty is far too honorable a man to even consider such a thing."

"Madam, you wound me!" the king protested, and then he caught her in his arms. Quickly he kissed her pretty lips, and fondled her breasts. "Not even a small seduction, Blaze?"

She shook him off. "Nay, Hal, not the tiniest!" she replied sternly.

"Do you love your husband then, my little country girl?"

For a moment his question took her unawares, and then the truth burst upon her with such startling clarity that she did not understand why she had not known it before. "Aye, Hal," she said. "I do love my husband. I love him very much!"

The king stared at her shrewdly, and saw the look of dawning realization in her eyes. "I think, Blaze," he said, "that you owe me more now than you did when you first walked into this room."

"Aye, Hal, I think you speak the truth," she admitted slowly.

"Then surely now you will aid me, for only you, I believe, can help me in this matter." He led her to a chair, and seated her, placing himself in a chair opposite her.

"Tell me, Hal, how I may help you, though I cannot imagine how a simple countrywoman could be of help to so great a king."

"You know," the king began, "that I have sought quietly for several years now to dissolve my marriage in order that I might seek a younger and more fecund wife."

Blaze nodded. "There is precedent for such an act, my lord."

"Aye, there is, and yet the pope has niggled and naggled until I am half-mad with the worry that I should die in the night, and England be ruled by a half-grown girl child. She would have to marry, and I do not believe our good Englishmen would be content beneath the rule of the foreign prince who would be her husband. It could be the Wars of the Roses all over again, Blaze!

"Several weeks ago Gabriel de Grammot, the Bishop of Tarbes, came from France to discuss the possibility of a marriage between François's second son, the Duc d'Orléans, and my daughter, Mary. I had thought the negotiations going well, and then it was that the bishop brought up the possibility that my daughter might not be my true daughter because my marriage is not a true marriage. He cited texts of Leviticus. *Thou shalt not uncover the nakedness of thy brother's wife: it is thy brother's nakedness;* and *If a man shall take his brother's wife, it is an impurity: he hath uncovered his brother's nakedness; they shall be childless.*

"If the French ambassador would consider the possibility that my marriage to the queen not be a true one, then I am in reality a bachelor after all, am I not? The dispensation issued by the then pope must surely be invalid. I must seek not a divorce, but an annulment. Catherine, however, will listen to none of it. She stubbornly maintains that our marriage is valid, and as long as her nephew, the Holy Roman Emperor, has the pope holed up in his Vatican, I will get no fair judgment. Catherine must agree to step aside, and that is why I have sent for you.

"I want you to go to her. She is here at the moment. You must prevail upon her as a woman to release me from this unclean sham she calls a marriage. I will have no legitimate sons until I can be free of that woman!"

"Sire!" Blaze was both astounded and shocked. "You have sent the highest lords in your kingdom to reason with the queen. She will not give way before the most clever and reasonable of arguments. The cardinal himself has spoken with her, and he has gotten nowhere. Why do you think that the queen would listen to me? I was your mistress, Hal! An offense to her! I am an unimportant woman of no great family. How can you, therefore, send me to her? *How?*"

The king leaned forward in his chair. "My little country girl, you are my last hope for an equitable settlement with Catherine. If you cannot convince her, then it is war between us, and I swear to you on the body of Christ crucified that I shall win that war! Catherine likes you, Blaze. You are not like Bessie or merry Mary. She liked you enough to punish our daughter when she was rude to you. She has even mentioned you on several occasions with kindness. If there is the smallest chance that she might listen to you, I must take that chance. That is why you must speak to her for me."

"My lord, she will not see me. I am nobody."

"She will see you because I ask her to see you," the king replied.

"Oh, Hal! Hal!" Blaze said softly. "After this there can be no debts between us! Whether I succeed or fail the account between us is clear."

He nodded. "Agreed, madam. Do this for me, and I will not trouble you again."

"Are you so in love then, my lord?" Blaze said quietly.

He flushed beneath her gaze. *The king flushed!* "Is it so obvious then?"

"To me, but then you are my friend, Hal."

"She is the most virtuous of women, Blaze. I would not dishonor my Nan. She will one day be the mother of England's king."

"*You would marry her?*" Blaze was shocked. "Oh, Hal, such a thing is not right! You should have a princess for a wife!"

"An ancestor of mine, Edward, who was known as the Black Prince, had for his wife Joan, called the Fair Maid. She, too, came from Kent," said the king, ignoring her. Perhaps he had not even heard her at all. "Good English stock," said the king. "That is what I need in a wife. Good, strong English stock!"

They spoke together for a while longer, and then the king dismissed her. Blaze hurried back up the inner staircase to her own apartments. She did not know whether to be angry or to be sad. The king had tricked her, although she did not think he had meant to do such a thing. Still, how could she speak to the queen, importuning her to release the king from their marriage, or was it really a marriage? She was no cleric to know such things. True, she believed the king should have a wife who could give him sons, and poor Catherine was past childbearing. But how could she beg the queen to let the king go, knowing that it was Mistress Boleyn with whom the king intended replacing the queen?

Reentering her apartment, she exited the bedchamber to find Heartha in the dayroom with a page in the livery of Cardinal Wolsey.

"Ahhh, you are awake then, my lady," said Heartha.

Blaze feigned a small yawn and a stretch. "Aye, my nap did me good after all our travels." She turned her attention to the boy. "You wish to see me?"

The page bowed politely to her. "My master, the cardinal, begs that you wait upon him at your convenience, my lady Wyndham."

"Take me to him now then," Blaze said, wondering when she was going to be left in peace.

The boy led her through corridors she had never known existed, let alone ever seen in her months at Greenwich. He seemed to be avoiding the more public routes. Indeed, he brought her into the cardinal's privy chamber through a door she did not see until after he had opened it.

"Go in, my lady. His grace will be with you shortly." Blaze entered the small paneled room. There were but two places to sit, small tapestried chairs before the fire. She sat down. She was cold suddenly, and so she held her hands out before the crackling fire, starting as she heard a hard voice beside her.

"Such little hands, madam, in which to put England's future." He lowered his bulk into the other chair, waving a hand at her and saying, "No, madam, do not rise. We are to be quite informal here." Cardinal Wolsey stared frankly at her; his gaze half-speculative, half-admiring. "You are lovely close-up," he said. "I have only seen you from a distance in the past."

"How may I serve you, your grace?" Blaze asked him quietly. In all her time at court he had never so much as glanced her way, she thought. Why now?

"You have been with the king," he stated. She said nothing. He smiled, but his eyes were somewhat haunted, Blaze thought. Not the eyes of a secure and powerful man. "You need violate no confidence with me, madam. I know why the king has sent for you. He wishes you to plead his case with the queen, does he not?"

"I do not understand why," Blaze said, neither admitting nor denying anything to the cardinal.

"Because his lust for Tom Boleyn's young bitch is eating him alive," the cardinal said bluntly. "He cannot force himself upon a nobly born virgin, and he has convinced himself, therefore, that she must be his wife. What think you of that, my lady Wyndham?"

"I think, your grace, that though the king certainly needs a young wife to give England sons, he should marry in France, or the German or northern states."

The cardinal nodded. "There, madam, we are agreed. Proud Catherine of Aragon will not give way to Anne Boleyn."

"But what is it you want of me, your grace?" Blaze demanded.

"Your answer to my question, my lady Wyndham, tells me that you cannot be happy with the task that the king has set you. It tells me that though you will obey the king, you cannot put your whole heart into his request, knowing that it is Mistress Boleyn he seeks to queen."

Blaze said nothing, but her expression told Cardinal Wolsey that he was yet a keen judge of character. This was no bubble-headed former mistress, but a woman of principles upon whom both he and the king could rely.

"Listen to me, madam," he said. "The king may think that he is in love with Mistress Anne. He may think that he seeks to make her his wife. He may even believe it at this time, but it will never happen. I tell you now that Anne Boleyn will *never* sit upon England's throne as its queen, nor will a child of her body and the king's ever rule England. The people will not have it!

"The king must be freed from the barren Catherine, and he must re-marry, but I promise you that it will be to a princess of the blood royal, and not the daughter of some Kentish knight. Do you understand me, madam? You may do the king's errand with a good heart, although I seriously doubt that your words will have any effect at all upon that impossible woman. Still, you may try, and try your best, for eventually the king will be freed of her, and he will wed a proper wife. This is all that I would say to you." He held out his hand, and Blaze, kneeling, kissed his ring of office. "The boy will see you safely back to your own apartments, madam," said the cardinal, arising from his seat.

She had no sooner reentered her apartments than another pageboy arrived upon the scene, and without bowing to her said in a strident young voice, "The lady Anne says you are to attend to her at once!"

Blaze felt her temper flare. "Sirrah!" she said in a harsh tone. "Where are your manners? I did not see you bow to me. I am the Countess of Langford, and I am used to far better manners than you have just shown me. Who is this *Lady Anne* who demands my presence? Only the queen or the king's sisters may demand my presence, and none of them are called by the name Anne."

The page flushed with embarrassment, and attempting to mend his fences, began again. "My lady Wyndham," he said, bowing deeply, "my mistress, the lady Anne Boleyn, requests that you attend her immediately."

"Tell your mistress that I have just arrived after a horrendous journey from Herefordshire. I am far too exhausted to speak with anyone at the moment. Tell her that I hope that I shall see her on the morrow," Blaze concluded. She had had enough. First the king, and then the cardinal, and now that upstart bitch!

"Well, boy?" demanded Heartha. "What are you standing there for yet? Be about your business!"

When the boy scampered out, Blaze turned to her servant and said, "I want a hot bath, and I want it now! No more cardinals, and no more kings, Heartha! Just a bath."

"They are bringing the water in even as we speak, my lady," chuckled Heartha. "That big old tub was exactly where we left it. I do not think anyone has used these apartments since you were last here."

Blaze shortly found herself ensconced within her tub, the warm, oily water with its violet fragrance soothing her weary and travel-exhausted body. "Leave me in peace," she told her tiring woman. "Do you realize that this is the first time in months that I have been really alone? It seems a pity that I had to come to Greenwich to find a little peace."

Heartha chuckled. "When we are at home, you take all your responsibilities too much to heart, my lady. You must make a little time for yourself. We certainly cannot keep coming to Greenwich!"

Blaze smiled as the door shut, and lying back in the delicious bath, she closed her eyes. It was the first moment she had had to think since she arrived at Greenwich. It was the first time she had had to consider her words to the king in answer to his question of her.

Do you love your husband then, my little country girl?

And she had answered him that she did. That she loved him very much. It was the truth, she realized. She loved Anthony Wyndham. Not, perhaps, with the young love that she had given to Edmund. That would always be his alone. The love she felt for Tony was something that she had nurtured and that had grown slowly over the short months of their union, and she had never even known it. She wished that she could finish bathing, and get right back into her coach so she might go home and tell him. Tell him that she loved him, loved him and no one else!

Suddenly outside in the dayroom there came the sounds of shrieking and screaming and great protest. The door to her bedchamber flew open, and Anne Boleyn burst into the room, Heartha behind her. "How dare you refuse my summons, madam!" she shouted at Blaze. Her beautiful long black hair swirled about her. She was garbed all in yellow.

For a brief moment Blaze was totally nonplussed, and then in a flash of inspiration she considered what Bliss would do in such a situation. The answer came quickly. She eyed the Boleyn girl in a leisurely fashion, and feigning a yawn, drawled, "You should not wear that shade of yellow, Mistress Boleyn. It makes your skin quite sallow."

Anne Boleyn's cheeks darkened with her anger, and her black eyes were filled with hate. "One day I will be your queen," she said in a low and even tone. "You would do best not to rouse my ire, madam!"

"You would do best not to publicly boast of a position to which though you may aspire, you do not yet possess, Mistress Boleyn," Blaze warned her.

"I called you to my presence, madam!"

"I chose not to come," replied Blaze. "Who are you to demand my attendance? I have just this afternoon arrived after a long journey. I am tired, and filthy, and I wished to bathe in peace."

"You were with the king! Do not deny it! I have my ways of knowing such things!" Anne stormed.

"Aye," said Blaze. "I was with the king." She took the bar of violet-scented soap that Heartha had left for her, and began to soap her arms.

Mistress Boleyn's dark eyes narrowed into slits and she almost hissed, "Do not think that you can trip lightly back to court and into the king's good graces once again, madam. He is mine! *Mine!*"

"I did not come of my own volition, Mistress Boleyn," said Blaze sweetly.

"What do you mean?" The Boleyn's tone was not quite as sure of itself now.

Blaze laughed, enjoying the girl's discomfort, and allowed her to consider the worst before she said, "The king sent for me, and being the loyal servant of his majesty that I am, I came to find my lovely old apartments freshened and awaiting me." Having washed her arms and shoulders, she now began to soap her legs, humming, as she did, the latest popular ditty.

Anne Boleyn shrieked, her voice rising into a screech of pure anger, *"You cannot have him back!"*

"My dear," said Blaze, "do you think to rule the king? It is what he wants, and not what either you or I want. You had best understand that."

"I will not let you have him!" The Boleyn's eyes were almost bugging from her head in her rage. Anger did nothing for her looks.

Blaze considered for a moment, and decided that she really was enjoying herself. Slowly she arose from her tub and stepped out onto the rug. The oily water sluiced down her body, giving it a particularly lush sheen in the golden firelight. Her breasts were fuller than they had ever been. Her belly was prettily rounded. Her limbs pleasing in form. Lifting her arms, she undid her hair, and the honey-colored mass tumbled about her shoulders. A drop of water glittered and hung from one of Blaze's nipples. Casually she flicked it off, and looking up, stared directly at the other girl.

"Can you offer the king what I offer him?" she murmured huskily with devastating effect, and then she laughed again at her opponent's look.

Mistress Anne could do naught but stare, and she opened her mouth as if to speak, but no words came forth.

"Get you gone from my chambers, Mistress Anne Boleyn," said Blaze haughtily. "You are not welcome here, and it may be that I am expecting a guest."

To her surprise the girl turned abruptly about and ran from her apartments, sobbing.

"Why, m'lady, I have never seen you behave in such a fashion before, not that the little bitch did not deserve it, uppity creature that she is. Leading her on like that, and making her believe that the king was eager to be your lover once again! For shame, m'lady!" But Heartha was hard-pressed to hold back her laughter. "She's got ambitions, that one, and what big ones they are," Heartha went on as she dried Blaze off. "You've made a bad enemy in her though, m'lady."

"I will not be here long enough for her to even consider it," Blaze said quietly. "The jest of the whole matter is, however, Heartha, that the king has sent for me to try to reason with the queen to release him because he believes that he wants to wed with that strumpet."

Heartha shook her head. "I'm a simple woman, m'lady. I do not think that however long I serve the gentry, I will come to understand them."

Blaze laughed. "I am not certain that I understand either, Heartha," she said, "but as the king's loyal subject I cannot help but do his bidding."

Chapter 16

❦

$\mathscr{I}$t was several days before Blaze was able to obtain an audience with the queen. Seeing her back at Greenwich, alone and without her husband, and living in her royal apartments, confused the members of the court. Her presence gave rise to much gossip, particularly when Mistress Boleyn was seen to sulk within her own little room, avoiding the king. Blaze, however, said nothing that either stemmed the rumors or confirmed them. As for Henry, he seemed glad to have the lovely Countess of Langford about once more, joking openly with her, and insisting she sit by his side one evening during a musical. No one could understand what was happening, although there was a great deal of speculation. Had Lady Wyndham been recalled to her former place? Was Mistress Boleyn already being replaced in the king's fickle affections?

Finally the queen's chamberlain set the time for Blaze's private audience with Catherine. It was to be the following morning in the hour immediately after the queen had heard the Mass.

"Good!" Blaze said to Heartha. "We can leave afterward, and still have practically a full day for travel. With all this sun the last two days, the roads have surely dried. We will certainly get home quicker than we came. I doubt that it will take me very long to report on my interview to the king."

Blaze chose with much care the clothing that she would wear. Although she was not a noblewoman of great family, she must still show Catherine that her coming on the king's behalf was not meant as an insult, but rather an honor. Her gown was made of a golden-brown velvet, its bodice very heavily embroidered with a design of gold and pearls, its upper sleeves slashed to show cloth of gold beneath. The fitted lower sleeves were also heavily embroidered, and from beneath them emerged soft cream lace which fell over her wrists. The underskirt of the gown was made of cream-colored silk brocade, its plainness a severe contrast to the overskirt despite the rich material.

The neckline of the dress was square and very low, as the fashion dictated. About her neck Blaze wore a gold necklace that lay flat at the base of her throat, and from which hung an oval-shaped jeweled medallion. Her second necklace was a long strand of matched pearls that hung gracefully below her bosom. In her ears were fat baroque pearls, and upon her hands she sported several fine rings in addition to her wedding band.

Her hair had been parted in the center, and drawn back over her ears to be fixed in a French knot at the back of her neck, and held neatly within a golden caul that was decorated with pearls. From the dainty gold *cordelière* attached to her girdle hung a delicate, small round gold mirror studded with pearls. Blaze stared at herself in the pier glass and was satisfied. The gown was one she had never gotten to wear when she had been at court last as the king's mistress. Thank God the fashions had not changed.

"Is everything all packed, Heartha?" she asked her tiring woman for the tenth time since she had arisen that morning. "The coach is ready, and the escort also?"

"Aye, m'lady. All is in readiness. We'll be on our way as soon as you've completed your business here. I'm just as anxious as you are to be home again."

Home. RiversEdge. God, yes, she was anxious to be home! Anxious to tell Anthony that she did love him. That she loved him with all her heart, and that she never wanted to be separated from him again. How could she have been so damned blind? How could he be so incredibly patient? Even after Philip had been born she had not been able to admit the truth to herself. She had not been able to say the words to him that he so desperately wanted to hear. How her callousness must have hurt him. She did not deserve him! He was the dearest and best man in the whole world, and she was going to spend the rest of her life making it up to him. All that she need do was speak with the queen, speak with the king, and then she was free. Free to go home to RiversEdge and her wonderful husband!

Shortly before the appointed hour the queen's page came to fetch her, and brought her to the queen's apartments. The antechamber in which she was left to wait was a lovely room with windows looking over the green lawns that fell away to the river. She was alone in the room, and very uncomfortable. Then at last one of the queen's ladies-in-waiting, Lady Essex, came to fetch her. Her smile of greeting was a pleasant one, but there was no cordiality about it.

"You are to come with me, Lady Wyndham," she said.

Blaze followed her into the queen's dayroom, where the other of the queen's ladies-in-waiting, ladies of the bedchamber, and the maids of honor were clustered. Some were sewing while others worked upon a tapestry depicting the coronation of the Blessed Virgin. One woman read to the group from a book of pious meditations, while another girl played softly upon the virginals. Several of the women were simply talking, but they all looked up with curious eyes as Blaze was escorted into their midst.

These were women she did not know. Most she had only seen at a distance, and all knew of her past relationship to the king. A few nodded politely to her, for they understood that she was not the queen's enemy. Others stared in a hostile manner, for they were extremely loyal to the queen, and suspicious of her presence. The younger maids of honor in the group looked at her, openly curious, for a king's mistress, though honored by the king's friends, was considered a bad woman by the queen's adherents. The maids of honor could not remember ever having seen a really bad woman before. Secretly they considered Blaze a great disappointment for she did not look wicked at all.

"The queen will see you in her privy chamber, Lady Wyndham," said Lady Essex, and she opened a door for Blaze to go through. Blaze took a deep breath and walked through into the small room. It was a square chamber whose walls were prettily paneled. A small bow window looked out upon the river, and in the fireplace a large fire burned, for the queen was always cold at Greenwich.

Catherine sat now by that fireplace in a high-backed tapestried oak chair with beautifully carved arms that was not unlike a throne. She wore a gown of black velvet whose low, squared neckline was heavily encrusted with a band of pearls, and jet and gold beads. The sleeves of her gown were full to the wrist and not slashed, but whereas the upper half of the sleeve was of black velvet, the lower part of the sleeve was of a rich gold brocade from which peeped fine lace at the wrist. She wore no jewelry upon her hands but her marriage ring, but about her neck were magnificent pearls and a second gold necklace from which hung a crucifix of rubies and pearls. Centered upon her bodice was a beautiful brooch of gold and rubies. Her hair was hidden beneath a richly adorned architectural headdress resembling a diamond that was studded with rubies and pearls, and to which was attached a black silk veil that flowed down the queen's back.

Blaze curtsied low to Catherine.

"You may arise, Lady Wyndham," came a deep male voice.

Startled, she stood, to see a tall, thin man in priest's garb standing next to the queen. He had a narrow ascetic face and black eyes that seemed to bore right into her.

"I am Father Jorge de Atheca, the queen's confessor, Lady Wyndham. Before you speak with the queen I must know whether you have made your confession regarding your previous adultery with the king, *and* if you have paid the full penance for your sin."

"Aye, Father, I have," Blaze answered, feeling very uncomfortable, which was, she thought, exactly how she was expected to feel. "I could not wed with my husband with the weight of my guilt upon me," she finished, knowing it was just the sort of thing the priest wanted to hear.

He nodded, a small frosty smile touching his lips. "Now, madam, I ask you to swear upon this relic of the true cross," and he held out a silver crucifix to her into which was embedded a splinter of dark wood, "that the answers you will give me to my next questions are the truth. Do you swear?"

Blaze kissed the crucifix, wondering what was so important that she must swear such an oath, yet she could not refuse.

"I swear," she said.

"Is your son the king's bastard?" the priest demanded bluntly.

The look on Blaze's face was first shock, which was quickly followed by outrage. *"No!"* she snapped, and then her temper spilled over. Priest or no, he had no right to insult her. "How dare you ask me such a question, Father? Both my husbands have been earls of Langford, and I have too much love and respect for them to foist a bastard upon the Wyndhams."

"Even a royal bastard?" the priest inquired slyly.

"Especially a royal bastard!" she shot back.

"Your son's birthdate?" he demanded.

"All Hallows' Eve of last year, and he was christened the following afternoon upon All Saints' Day. You have but to look in the parish records. Do you think a priest would falsify such records? If you think that Philip is the king's son, which he is not, then I carried him at least twelve months. Have you ever heard of a woman who carried her unborn child for *that* length of time?" Blaze was furious now. "I did not even sleep with my husband for three months after our marriage, to be certain that there would be no doubts to our child's legitimacy when we were finally blest with an heir!" she blurted out.

"Enough!" The queen had finally spoken.

The priest bowed, and stepped back into the shadows by her side once more, but Blaze could see his eyes glowing with the light of a fanatic as he looked at her.

"You may be seated, Lady Wyndham," the queen said, motioning her to a high-backed stool opposite her. "So your son's name is Philip? I have a nephew named Philip. Is he your first child?"

"Nay, madam. I have a daughter by my first husband. Her name is Nyssa Catherine Mary Wyndham."

"How is it that you came to marry two earls of Langford?" asked the queen.

"Anthony, who is my second husband, was the nephew of Edmund, my first husband. Just before Edmund died he requested that Anthony wed me to protect me and our daughter. As my second husband had no other match arranged, he agreed to his uncle's dying request. A dispensation was arranged by our priest through Cardinal Wolsey, my lady."

"Was your first husband very old? I expect he was, that his nephew was old enough to become your husband."

"There were but four years between the two men. They were more like brothers, madam."

"Where is your home?"

"In Herefordshire, madam, on the banks of the Wye River. It is very peaceful and very beautiful."

"Do you love your husband, Lady Wyndham?" the queen said.

"Oh, yes, madam!" Blaze answered with feeling.

"Then I am curious as to why you have left a husband that you love, your two children, and your beautiful and peaceful home upon the banks of the River Wye. I am curious as to why my husband, the king, should have insisted that I speak with you; and certainly as to why you have returned to court," said Catherine.

"I returned to court, madam, at the king's specific request. I should not have come otherwise."

The queen nodded. "Say on then, Lady Wyndham," she said.

"The king has asked me to intercede for him with you, though I have told him that it is not my place, madam. He said that he thought you liked me, for during my time I was not forward in my behavior. He believes that you will at least hear me out, that perhaps my woman's words will move you."

Catherine's lips had compressed themselves into a narrow, tight line. For a moment she closed her eyes, and Blaze thought she saw a spasm of pain cross the queen's features.

"You do not have to hear this, majesty," hissed the priest from his place at her side. "Send the bold creature away. Her presumption is not to be tolerated."

"Where is your charity, Father Jorge?" asked the queen, who had reopened her eyes. "Lady Wyndham has been practically dragged from her home and family to be thrust into the midst of something that does not concern her. Yet if I do not hear her out, my husband will complain loudly and publicly about my unreasonableness. Lady Wyndham, I give you leave to plead your case for the king, though it will do you little good. This country's greatest lords have come to me on bended knee to plead the king's case. I have listened to them also with courtesy. What harm is there in hearing one more plea, although I doubt you can bring anything new to this matter."

"Madam," began Blaze, "you know better than any other that the king must have an heir." She was beginning to see how Catherine's obdurate behavior was driving Hal to his wits' end.

"I have given the king an heir in the person of our daughter, the princess Mary," replied Catherine serenely. Her whole attitude was that of a woman who believed in the rightness of her cause.

"The king must have a son, madam. Can you give him a son?"

"I gave him three sons, and two other daughters," the queen said. "Is it my fault that God took them from us? I am but a humble servant of God. As such, I cannot interpret his motives!"

"Nevertheless, the king has no legitimate son, and he must. The princess Mary cannot rule England alone. She must have a husband, and of necessity, that husband must come from another land. Our people will not accept a foreign prince as their king. They will not, madam. Therefore, the king must have a legitimate son to follow him as England's ruler. How can you deny him that if you truly love him as you say you do?" Blaze said gently.

"My mother was Queen of Castile in her own right!" cried Catherine.

"Yet she wed with the King of Aragon, and together they strove to forge Spain into one land, madam. Neither was truly foreign to the other. It is different here in England. England is one land which is ruled by King Henry Tudor, who has no son to follow him. What will become of my country, madam, if that happens? The people, the high lords, they will not accept a foreign prince as their king, even if he is wed to your daughter. There will be civil war again, as there was in the time of my parents' parents. This is the legacy your daughter will bring to England. Is that what you truly desire, madam?"

"What would you have me do, Lady Wyndham? I cannot deny my marriage to the king."

"But you could step aside, madam, even as St. Joan of Valois stepped aside for Anne of Brittany in the reign of the twelfth Louis of France. That childless queen made a great sacrifice, for she loved her lord even as I know you love the king. Yet, madam, she put aside her own feelings, her own desires that France might have an heir, for the widowed Duchess of Brittany was a proven breeder of healthy children."

The queen was rather fascinated by Blaze's knowledge, for she knew the young Countess of Langford to be, as indeed the king had called her, a little country girl. Catherine would have been surprised if there were even many amongst her own women who had such a grasp of history, particularly the history of another land. "How came you by your knowledge of these facts?" she asked Blaze.

"My first husband, Edmund Wyndham, may God assoil his dear soul, found it amusing to teach me. I knew little but how to cipher, read, and do simple mathematics when I became his wife. We had an elderly cousin at Ashby, my childhood home, who had taught at Oxford. He felt that he repaid my father's kindness in giving him a home in his old age by pounding some learning into us. When I wed with Edmund he taught me further, madam."

"What?" asked the queen.

"Latin, for I knew only church Latin. Greek. Higher mathematics, philosophy, French, history."

"And you liked your lessons?"

"Aye, madam! There is so much to know, and so little time in which to learn it," replied Blaze.

"Poor Henry," said the queen. "He knew you not at all, did he, Lady Wyndham? He saw only your youth, your lovely body, and your honey-colored hair. Henry is most fond of honey-colored hair. If I were ever to step aside from my place, it would only be for someone like you. You are not an ambitious woman, rather you are gentle and good. Aye, despite your adultery with my husband, I do believe you to be a good woman. Alas, you have not the family to be a king's wife; but had you, you would have made a good mate for the king. You have charm, wit, and intelligence. These are the things that Henry values.

"It cannot, however, be. You are a happily married woman, and I do not intend stepping aside, Lady Wyndham. I am no Saint Joan of Valois. She had no children, nor was she ever with child. I have borne my lord six children, though only my Mary has lived. First the king would divorce me, and now he says our marriage is no marriage. That he has sinned in taking his brother's wife as his wife, and that is why our children died. Yet he knows that though I was wed with Prince Arthur, our marriage was never consummated. He knows that I came to him a maid. My marriage to Arthur Tudor was a marriage in name only. That poor boy was far too sickly to do naught but brag about that which he could not accomplish. He died shortly after our marriage.

"What will happen to my daughter, Lady Wyndham, if I step aside, or if the king is successful in his attempt to annul our marriage? Will she still be the princess Mary, or perhaps only the lady Mary? What will her chances for a decent marriage be under the cloud of a suspicious birth? You are the mother of a daughter, Lady Wyndham. Would you want this kind of fate for your child?"

"Madam, your daughter's fate rests not in my hands. These are things that you must speak with the king about. It is not my concern," Blaze told the queen.

"And neither is what they now refer to as 'The King's Great Matter,' yet here you are before me, Lady Wyndham."

"Only because the king asked it of me, majesty. I would not presume otherwise, and I think you know that."

"You care for my husband," the queen said. It was a statement of fact, and not a question.

"Aye, I do, madam. You know I did not aspire to the position to which I was raised. You know that I never used my short term of power to enrich myself or my family. I will not grieve your delicate sensibilities with a pure rendition of the truth, but I sought to avoid the honor foisted upon me. I fought against it so hard that the first time your husband took me it was by force."

The queen went pale.

"Still, madam, I quickly grew to understand the man we call our king. I found that I actually liked him, for though he be stubborn, there is much goodness in him. The people love him, madam. We all love him. Though what he has asked of me is foolish, I understand his deep and growing desperation. Surely you do too? The king must have an heir. You are past your childbearing. Oh, dear madam, you must step aside so the king can take a young wife."

"Never, as long as there is breath in my body, will I give way my place to that strumpet Nan Boleyn!" the queen suddenly snarled, her fine dark eyes flashing; and Blaze saw that though Catherine be worn with her many years of unsuccessful childbearing and royal intrigues, she was yet the daughter of Isabella, the warrior queen of Castile. There was still much fight left within her.

"Surely the king will not wed the daughter of a mere Kentish knight, madam. He merely seeks to make her his mistress, as her elder sister was his mistress. It is the kind of perversity that occasionally appeals to the king. She is a little more clever and able to hold him off longer, because of her maiden state, but he will soon tire of her games and look elsewhere for easier prey should she not yield herself to him."

"So think you, madam, but I do not," the queen replied.

"So thinks the cardinal, madam," Blaze said.

"Ahh, yes, I had heard that you had seen that wily old fox," Catherine remarked.

"The cardinal says that he does not believe for a minute that the king seriously contemplates marrying Mistress Boleyn. Any other marriage would be with a French princess or possibly a German princess. The people would not allow the king, despite their love for him, to marry with *that* girl."

"Lady Wyndham," the queen said, "you know my husband. You have said yourself that he is a stubborn man. There is little in this court that I do not know about. My husband has worked himself into a fine froth with the thought that a good English wife is the answer to his problems. The cardinal grows old. He is sickly. He has made enough enemies during his tenure in office to assure that he will not die a peaceful death. He has soothed my husband's vanity by giving him Hampton Court when Henry grew disquieted with John Skelton's little ditty. Surely you remember it?"

Blaze smiled, for she did indeed. Henry had been furious, and as a consequence the cardinal had had no choice but to give the king the beautiful home that he had built for himself.

> *Why come ye not to court?*
> *To which court?*
> *To the king's court,*
> *Or to Hampton Court*
> *Nay, to the king's court.*
> *The King's court*
> *Should have the excellence;*
> *But Hampton Court*
> *Hath the eminence.*

"Aye," Blaze said, "I remember that little ditty well. I had just come to court myself."

"The cardinal's days are numbered, Lady Wyndham, which is sad, for though he be a proud prelate, he has always and ever been a loyal and hardworking servant of the king. His judgment now, however, is clouded by his desire for a French marriage. I stand in his way, and will, therefore, eventually be responsible for his downfall."

"You know this, and yet you will do nothing to help him, madam?"

"If I step aside, if I admit that my marriage to the king is not a true marriage, Henry will marry with Mistress Boleyn at the first opportunity, even as he married with me in secret six weeks after his ascension to England's throne. Even then there was talk of sending me back to Spain, and wedding Henry to a French princess. He, however, took it in his head that he must make good the betrothal vows made between us when he was but a lad of twelve and I a maid of eighteen. He loved me then, even as I have always loved him. I will not give way my place as queen of this land, as mother of its heiress, the Princess of Wales, so that Nan Boleyn may rule in my place. So that Nan Boleyn's sons follow Henry! Never! Never! Never!"

"Madam, what will happen to you if you do not give way to the king's wishes? What will happen to the princess Mary? I know only too well the folly of refusing the king," Blaze said softly.

"I can only keep to my position, and pray that the king's eyes will be opened to the follies that he commits. If God answers my prayers, then the king will be turned from his wickedness. I will put my trust in God as I have always put my trust in him," replied the queen.

"Alas, madam, all your prayers will not give England the prince it needs. Only another wife for the king can do that," answered Blaze sadly. There was to be no turning the queen, but then she had known that before she had even entered this room. She thought now that perhaps the king had known it too, but he had tried just once more.

"Your daughter, Lady Wyndham, how old is she?" the queen said.

"She will be five on the last day of the year, madam," Blaze replied.

The queen drew a small ring from her finger and handed it to Blaze. It was a gold ring with an oval-shaped ruby surrounded by little pearls. "This is for your daughter, madam. A child who bears both my name and that of my daughter should have something to remember us by," she said.

The interview was over. Blaze slipped from the high-backed stool onto her knees and kissed the queen's outstretched hand. It was soft, and white and plump. "Thank you, madam. My child will cherish this token of your favor." Then she rose to her feet. "And I thank you for so graciously hearing me out."

The queen nodded. "Father Jorge," she said, "have Mistress Jane show Lady Wyndham back to her apartments."

"Aye, my lady," the priest said, and Blaze followed him back out into the queen's dayroom. "Mistress Jane! You are to show Lady Wyndham back to her own apartments."

A young lady-in-waiting came forward. She was of middling height and modest demeanor. "If you will follow me, Lady Wyndham," she said in a gentle voice. She had large dark eyes, and her best feature, Blaze considered, was her soft brown hair, for she was certainly no great beauty with her prim little mouth, receding chin, and somewhat large nose. Someone's sister, or niece, or a northern heiress with nothing but her wealth to recommend her, Blaze thought, who had been endorsed for her honored position by an important relative here at court. Yet, there was something familiar about her, although Blaze knew she had never seen the girl ever before. Of whom did she remind her?

They reached Blaze's apartments, and the girl curtsied to her politely.

"Thank you, Mistress . . . ?" Blaze looked to the girl.

"Seymour, Lady Wyndham. My name is Jane Seymour."

"You are Tom Seymour's sister."

The girl smiled almost mischievously. "You remember him? He will be so pleased!"

"Pray do not say so," Blaze importuned Mistress Seymour.

Now Jane Seymour laughed. "You were the first girl who ever refused my brother's advances. He thinks himself quite the fine fellow, Lady Wyndham. When you hit him several years ago he had to consider that perhaps he was not the fine fellow he thought he was. I believe you did him a favor, my lady." Jane Seymour curtsied prettily to Blaze, and turning, moved back down the corridor away from her.

"You were gone so long I thought you had been clapped into the dungeons of the Tower, m'lady," said Heartha. "The king has twice sent a messenger, and I expect another will be arriving shortly. I hope you will not be as long with him as you were with the queen. I am anxious to depart this place."

"Is the coach loaded and ready?"

"Aye, m'lady, it is!"

Blaze washed her face and hands in a basin of warmed water that Heartha placed out for her, and carefully replaced several tendrils of her hair that had escaped her caul. She daubed her favorite violet fragrance at her pulse points, and then stared at herself in the pier glass. She was a beautiful woman. More beautiful than the queen, and certainly more beautiful than Mistress Boleyn, although she had to admit that the Boleyn girl had an exotic fascination to her that would have intrigued the king, whose tastes usually ran to women more blond than brunette. Both Bessie Blount and Mary Boleyn Carey were blonds.

"The king's page is here," said Heartha, and the boy stepped into the bedchamber.

"We are to go by means of the inner passage, madam," the lad told her.

Blaze nodded, and silently opened the hidden door in the paneling. With the lad lighting her way, they descended the narrow staircase and entered the king's privy chamber. The boy immediately passed through the room and out of it, leaving Blaze with the king. She curtsied, and then looked curiously, for the king's fool, Will Somers, was also in the room.

"You may speak, my little country girl. Will is my good friend, and privy to all that happens to me."

"Hal, I am sorry," Blaze said, "but the queen will not give way her place to another. I sat with her for almost an hour. I pleaded with her, citing Joan of Valois's sacrifice, but she said that she is no saint, and that Joan was a maid without children, whereas she has given you six children."

"Of whom but one lives, and that a puling girl!" the king spat. "God has taken my sons from me for the sin of my union with my brother's wife. Why will Catherine not understand that?"

"She says she is God's servant, and is incapable of interpreting his will."

"Aurrgh!" the king cried as if in pain. "She understands! She understands too well! She but plays the fool, but she is not a fool. She does it to annoy me! Oh, Blaze! What am I to do? I must have a legitimate son! *I must!* Catherine does this from her own bitterness. She knows I am able to sire sons who live on the bodies of other women. She is angered that she cannot bear me sons that live, and this is her revenge upon me, but it is not my fault that she has this weakness of body. It is not!"

"Oh, Hal," she said, and took him in her arms to comfort him. "Whenever you have wanted something, you have wanted it immediately. This will take some time, and you must accept that. You, better than I, should know that the wheels of power grind slowly."

"But what if I die, Blaze?" he asked her in a tone of voice she had never heard him use before. It was an almost fearful tone.

"You will not die, my lord," she said, speaking to him firmly, as she spoke to Nyssa when she had terrorized herself with some imagined fear. "You will live to father sons for England upon a new young queen, Hal. The Tudors will not die with you. Oh, no, Hal! Not with you."

"Until now," said Will Somers from his stool by the fire, "I had thought myself to be your only true friend, my lord. I see now that you have two real friends upon whom you can count."

"*Can I count upon you, my little country girl?*" the king queried her anxiously.

"Always, my lord!" she answered him. "I will always be your majesty's most loyal servant."

"Provided," the king, now recovering, teased her, "that I do not tempt you to overcome your principles."

"Exactly, sire!" she answered him quickly. "You see, you are my friend also, for you understand me, Hal."

The king smiled down at her. "You will want to go home now, my little country girl. I can see it in those wonderful violet-blue eyes of yours. You are anxious to shake the dust of Greenwich from your heels, and hurry back to your Anthony."

"And to my babies too, Hal," she said, returning his smile.

"Kiss me good-bye then, Blaze Wyndham," he said quietly.

She tipped her head up to his, placing her arms about his neck as she did so. His mouth, warm and, as always, sensuous, closed over hers, evoking memories she had thought long forgotten. He drew her against him, prolonging the embrace, and it was just at that minute the door to the king's privy chamber slammed open and closed.

A scream of pure outrage pierced her consciousness, and she heard the half-hysterical voice of Anne Boleyn. "Villain! Oh, you are such a great villain!"

The king released Blaze and roared, "How dare you enter this room without my permission, Nan!"

Blaze turned about to see Anne Boleyn in her favorite pale yellow, her young face a mask of jealous fury.

"Aye, I dare, Henry! I should dare anything to keep you for myself, for I love you, and well you know it! Still, you cannot be at peace with yourself unless you are fondling some low strumpet! Can you not wait until we are wed? Must you recall your past *amours* to court, and parade them before me until I am half-mad with my pain?"

"Nan! For shame that you should think such things. Lady Wyndham came to court at my request to intercede with the queen for me, for Catherine has always liked her. I hoped that perhaps if another woman spoke with Catherine she could be made to see reason. Lady Wyndham has done us a favor in coming, even if Catherine will not listen to her any more than she will to me, and to all the others who have spoken to her."

"I know the kind of favors Lady Wyndham does for you, Henry," Anne

Boleyn hissed. "The kind my sister, Mary, did for you both before and after her marriage to poor hapless Will Carey. The kind of favors Bessie Blount did before and after her marriage to Gilbert Tailboys, mad old Lord Kyme's son! She spreads her legs and takes your cock into her! Do not think to mislead me, for I am not a fool!"

Before the king might remonstrate further with Mistress Boleyn, Blaze stepped forward, and with her small open palm slapped the hysterical girl across the face.

Anne gasped, and sputtered, and then screamed at the king, "She has slapped me! Your whore has slapped me!"

Blaze slapped Anne Boleyn a second time. "If you continue to call me names, Mistress Boleyn, I shall continue to slap you. How dare you speak of me in such terms. I am the Countess of Langford, and as such, your superior in rank. I am loyal to my king, but faithful to my husband, Mistress Boleyn. All is precisely as the king has told you. Do you dare to doubt the king's words?"

"Come, sweetheart," the king said, opening his arms to Mistress Boleyn, and she flung herself into them, sobbing. "There, lovey, there. You have no cause to be jealous. I could have no better nor truer friend than Blaze Wyndham, and neither could you." He stroked her long dark hair.

"I th-thought you had brought h-her back to court to b-be your mistress, Henry," wept Anne Boleyn. "She as much as said so the other n-night."

"The other night?" The king looked curiously to Blaze.

"Mistress Boleyn paid me a visit while I was in my bath," responded the Countess of Langford. "She obviously misunderstood all that I said, putting her own interpretation upon my words." Blaze's eyes were twinkling, and the king could not help the chuckle that escaped his lips.

"I would know about this visit you paid Lady Wyndham, Nan," the king said, releasing her from his embrace.

Anne Boleyn did not tell the king that she had rudely sent for Blaze, who had refused to come. Instead she said, "I visited Lady Wyndham when she was in her bath. She said you had sent for her."

"I did," replied the king.

"But she did not tell me why," protested Mistress Boleyn.

"You did not ask me," answered Blaze. "You were too busy, my dear, accusing me of all sorts of naughtiness. I decided that you must have a lesson in good manners."

"Good manners?" Mistress Boleyn was outraged. "You stood naked before me and asked me whether I could give the king what you could give him!"

Henry Tudor burst into laughter, and his great guffaws rumbled all about his privy chamber. The picture Anne's words evoked were deliciously provocative, and his eyes misted with remembrance. "For shame, my little country girl," he scolded her. Then he said, "I did not know you had such deviltry in you, Blaze."

"I but thought what my sister Bliss would do, sire."

He nodded. "Lady FitzHugh was always one for high spirits, as I remember."

For a moment there was a short silence between them. Anne Boleyn had slipped back into the king's embrace, and stood, his arm about her, half-turned toward Blaze. There was a more contented expression on her face now, and the small light of triumph in her eyes.

"If your majesty has no further need for me then," said Blaze, breaking the stillness, "I will retire. I am anxious, as you know, to be on my way home to Herefordshire."

The king held out his hand to her, and taking it, Blaze kissed it. Then she swept him a graceful curtsy.

"Farewell, my little country girl," the king said, "and God speed you safely home to RiversEdge."

"Farewell, Hal," Blaze said, and then she withdrew from the king's privy chamber, exiting through the private staircase, to the amazement of Mistress Boleyn, who had not known that such an exit existed.

When the door had closed behind her, Anne Boleyn said, "I want those apartments for myself, Henry."

"Not yet, my dear," he told her. "You have not earned them. Do you know where the door opens above? It opens out into the bedchamber. You are not ready for that yet, Nan, or are you?"

"Your mistress I will never be, Henry," Anne Boleyn said boldly, "and your wife I cannot be until you have freed yourself from the Spaniard."

"Then," replied the king, "those apartments above my own cannot be yours, can they, Nan?"

With a hiss of annoyance she pulled out of his embrace and ran from the room.

"Methinks you will not win over the lady Anne without a band of gold," Will Somers said thoughtfully. "Are you willing to pay the price, sire?"

"Good English stock, Will! She is good English stock, and I need her to get sons for England!" the king answered.

"Perhaps it is the wrong mare you have set out into another stallion's pasture, my lord," observed Will, "but what is done is done. God save England!"

"He will," said the king. "Of that I am most assuredly certain, my good friend and confidant. Has God not finally opened my eyes to my great sin with the Princess of Aragon? Time, Will! My little country girl is sensible and wise. It will take time to unravel this coil, but in the end I will have my way, and England will have its princes at long last! God will indeed save England!

Chapter 17

$\mathscr{B}$laze hurried from the king's presence up the steps of the private staircase that led to her bedchamber.

"Are we free to go?" Heartha asked as her mistress stepped through the door into the room.

"Aye! Are my traveling garments ready?"

Heartha offered her lady a jaundiced look as if to say: When did I not have everything in order when it was needed? Then she helped Blaze from her elegant court gown, and into a simpler traveling gown of mulberry-colored silk with a matching cloak that had a gold-and-garnet closure. As Blaze put the finishing touches on her toilet, her tiring woman finished the packing, and then ordered the palace maidservants to help her get the remaining luggage to her lady's coach.

"If you have attended to your own needs, Heartha, await me in the coach. I will be directly there."

"Very good, m'lady," responded Heartha as she herded the others from the apartment with their burdens.

Blaze walked slowly through the rooms that she had once inhabited as the king's mistress. There had not been time for a proper farewell when she had been wed to Anthony. Wherever she went, part of her would always be here at Greenwich, here in these rooms where she had shared so many hours with England's king. She looked out over the Thames River, wide here, and with a view of the royal shipyards across the water on the opposite bank. The Thames was so different from her beautiful and pastoral River Wye. It had a great vibrancy to it. It was the path that led to England's very heart, the city of London, and up its tidal waters the world sailed to pay its homage to Henry Tudor, the handsomest prince in Christendom.

She turned from the view with a soft sigh, her glance passing through the open door back into the bedchamber with its enormous bed. How many hours had she spent there entertaining the royal satyr with his voracious appetite for passion? God, how frightened she had been in the beginning, and then she had discovered that ancient truth known to all women since the beginning of time. She had learned that every man is simply a man; a creature with the desperate need for love and tenderness and reassurance. Men might love in different ways, but their need was always the same. Having learned that, she was no longer afraid.

"Do you relive the scene of your former triumphs, if indeed they may be called that, Lady Wyndham?" came Anne Boleyn's scornful young voice.

Blaze turned slowly to see the girl standing there, her graceful flowing sleeves skillfully concealing the sixth finger upon one of her long, beautiful hands. The finger was whispered by some to be a witch's mark, although no one would say such a thing aloud or publicly. "There is no triumph between lovers, Mistress Boleyn. What is between lovers is something equally shared, but you could not know that, could you, my dear?"

"I will never give myself lightly as did you and Bessie Blount and my foolish sister, who still weeps, when she thinks no one knows, for her great royal lover," spat Mistress Boleyn.

"Dear child—" began Blaze, but Anne Boleyn interrupted her.

"I am no child! I am nineteen, but two years your junior, my lady Wyndham."

"You are a child in the knowledge of love, Mistress Boleyn," Blaze said, "and you had best listen to what I have to say. I cannot speak for your sister or Lady Tailboys, but understand one thing. I did not give myself lightly to the king. I did not give myself to him at all. Hal has much good in him, but be careful how hard you drive him, for this king can also be a most ruthless man. I shall be blunt with you, Mistress Boleyn. The first time the king had me it was by force, not by consent. Oh, it is true that I had no precious maidenhead to protect, being a widow, but do not think that that will protect you if you push the royal stallion into too great a fit of heat."

Anne Boleyn's sallow complexion had paled. "You speak treason," she whispered.

"Nonsense." Blaze laughed. "I speak the truth, and if you are wise you will heed what I have said to you. Now, let me pass, Mistress Boleyn. My carriage awaits me, and I have a journey of several days before I will reach my beloved husband and children."

"When I am queen here," said Anne Boleyn, recovering her shock at Blaze's words, "you will not be welcome at court, my lady Wyndham."

"Nevertheless, Mistress Boleyn, be advised that I shall come whenever my lord, the king, calls me. I am the king's most loyal servant first and foremost. So I have told my husband, and so I tell you," Blaze said quietly. Then, brushing the slender girl aside, she moved past her out into the corridor.

As she exited the palace out into the courtyard, Heartha came hurrying forward, saying, "I was about to come and seek you, my lady. What has kept you so long? The horses are anxious in their harness. It is as if they know we are going home."

"A last-minute good-bye, Heartha," Blaze said, and climbed into her coach.

It was late May. The day was one of perfect and stunning beauty. The sun shone bright, and was warm upon the shining flanks of the horses. There was not a cloud to mar the pristine beauty of the blue sky. They rode with the carriage windows lowered, for although it was fair, the roads had had enough rain that spring not to be dusty yet. Upon the high box the Earl of Langford's coachman sat with his assistant, handling the reins for the four horses with great skill. They had an escort of ten armed riders, for a total of twelve men in case of an emergency.

The coach avoided the city of London, taking instead the western road. They traveled at a steady pace, and although Blaze was anxious to reach her home, she insisted that the horses be rested regularly during the day, for they had no extras should an animal be injured. By early afternoon of the first day Blaze was bored with sitting in the bouncing coach, and chose instead to ride her saddle horse, which was tied behind the vehicle. They stopped that night at The Red Rose, an excellent inn of good repute. Blaze was glad that she had so large an armed escort, for despite the inn's reputation as a safe place for a lady of good family and character to stop, it became necessary for the Countess of Langford's men to remove a drunken nobleman who, having seen Blaze when she arrived, was so taken by her beauty that he attempted to batter his way into her rooms.

The poor innkeeper was beside himself with dismay. "My lady, I cannot apologize enough," he said. "This is a respectable inn. The man was a stranger, and one cannot always tell, despite fine dressing and ready gold in the pocket. Please forgive this terrible incident!"

Blaze calmed him, more amused than annoyed. It was rather reassuring to one's ego to elicit that much passion on the part of a stranger with whom one had not even exchanged a single word or glance.

Heartha was outraged enough for them both. "Respectable inn! So says that fat toad of an innkeeper!" she fumed. "He should have known, for the man was surely drunk before he even arrived here, but our host, I fear, saw the gleam of his gold before he saw the disgraceful condition of that randy lordling who insulted you with his attentions!"

In midafternoon of the following day one of the carriage horses threw a shoe, and they were forced to slow their pace as they sought a village with a smithy. Heartha was quiet and unusually irritable by turns when they finally stopped. They were fortunate in that the little village in which they found themselves had a small, clean inn. It was only a country place, and rarely, if ever, did it see elegant visitors except in incidents similar to Blaze's own. It was called The Three Ducks, and indeed there were three ducks swimming in a pond behind the inn.

The landlord hurried forward on Blaze's arrival, wiping his worn hands upon his apron, and bowing. "Welcome, m'lady. 'Tis a simple house I own, and I cannot offer you a private room, for alas, I have none. I've no other guests at the moment, the men being in the fields, so 'twill be private-like for your ladyship."

Blaze smiled, and the innkeeper was instantly her slave. "Have you some good cider?" she asked him. "I have a taste for cider. As for my men, give them what they wan to ease their thirst. The sun is warm today." She turned to her tiring woman. "Heartha? What will you have?"

"Brown ale," came the reply. "I've a terrible thirst, my lady. The coach is stuffy despite the open windows."

"Poor Heartha," Blaze sympathized as the innkeeper hurried off to bring their refreshments. "Knowing how you dislike riding, I did not bring a horse for you."

"Just as well," Heartha muttered. "Traveling offers one little choice when it comes to discomforts. I would as lief stay home, my lady."

"I do not think we will be doing much traveling when we return home," Blaze said with a smile. "I am of a mind to give Nyssa and wee Philip some brothers and sisters."

"And about time too," was Heartha's opinion.

The coach horse was reshod, and they were on their way once more. Blaze enjoyed riding in the warm late spring sunshine, for the countryside was particularly lovely. Everything seemed so very green, and although the orchards were past their blossoming now, the fields were bright with poppies and daisies and purple gorse that so resembled bell heather. On the edge of a stand of tall beeches Blaze spotted a clump of graceful pink foxglove with its spotted throat, and near some rocks she was certain she saw bright yellow rock-rose. The lambs in the fields were not quite so babyish-looking now, but there were new calves to be seen here and there, and an occasional colt kicking its heels for the pure joy of being alive.

Home. She was going home to RiversEdge. Home to Anthony. Home to the man she loved. She wanted to get there as quickly as possible so she might tell him that she loved him. How could she have been so foolish? So blind? So stubborn? She had borne his son, and she had never told him that she loved him. She hadn't even known it until the king had forced her to face the truth. Or had she? Had she known it deep within her secret heart all along, but just been too obstinate to admit it to herself, too self-willed to admit it to him? She had never thought herself a headstrong person, but then she had learned a great deal about herself over the last few years, and this divulgence was obviously just one more revelation.

Their stop at the blacksmith's had put them behind their schedule, and it was necessary to ride until just past dark, when they arrived at The King's Arms, the inn where they were to spend the night. Blaze dismounted her horse, and walked over to the coach, where one of her men was opening the door for Heartha, but when she did not appear, he looked into the carriage, only to recoil in horror.

"What is it?" Blaze demanded. "Where is Heartha?"

The man-at-arms could only point, and going to the coach, Blaze looked in to see her servant crumpled in a heap on the floor. She was alive, however, for Blaze could hear her raspy breathing.

"Get her out of there," Blaze commanded her men. "She is ill!"

"Nay, my lady, I'll not touch her! She's got the sweating sickness!" He slowly backed away to where the rest of the men stood.

"The sweating sickness!" A cold chill ran up Blaze's spine. "How do you know that? You are no physician!"

"Everybody knows what the sweating sickness looks like, my lady! 'Twas just beginning at Greenwich when we left. Half the kitchen servants was down with it. I thought we got away in time." He crossed himself.

At that point the innkeeper came out from the inn to welcome them, but seeing the confusion, he stopped and inquired, "What is wrong?"

"I am the Countess of Langford," Blaze said. "You are expecting me. My servant is ill, and I will need to get her inside."

"*Ill?*" The innkeeper shifted from one foot to the other. "Ill with what, my lady? I runs a public house, and must be careful."

"She's got the sweating sickness!" babbled the frightened man-at-arms.

Blaze shot him a furious look.

"*The sweating sickness?*" Now the innkeeper began backing away. "Begging yer pardon, my lady, I cannot allow you on my premises. Yer whole party is suspect. You could infect us all. Get you gone!"

The captain of the men-at-arms moved swiftly forward and grabbed the innkeeper by his scrawny neck, lifting him up off the ground so that his feet just dangled. "We'll not trespass upon your inn, you maggot, but you'll see that her ladyship and the men are fed. That the horses are fed and watered. Only then will we be on our way. Do you understand me, you runt of a weasel?"

"I'll need a basin and clean clothes and cold water," said Blaze, recovering from her initial shock.

"You heard her ladyship," snarled the captain ferociously, and he released the innkeeper, who, nodding his head rapidly, ran back into his inn. The captain of the men-at-arms then came forward, and reaching into the coach, lifted the unconscious woman up and laid her out upon a seat. "You should not get too close to her, my lady. The sweating sickness is contagious."

"Then I have already been exposed, Captain," Blaze said. "Who is closer to Heartha than I am? I will nurse her, but how can we get home quickly? No one will allow us to stop and rest, and the horses cannot be run without rest."

"I'll find us shelter, my lady, never fear," came the strong reply. "In the morning I will send two men to RiversEdge for help. It will take them a day to get there, and it will take another day for help to reach us, but it will."

"Send that fool with the loose tongue," Blaze ordered, "and when we get home, send him back to the fields."

The captain nodded. "Indeed, my lady, he did not react well under duress, and I agree with you, for I want no cowards with me in a tight spot."

"Just get us to shelter," said Blaze. "Then you and the others are to stay clear of Heartha and me. I do not want you infected."

"There is no cause to fear on my account, my lady. I had the sweating sickness when I was a lad of fourteen. Once you have had it, you do not get it again—if you recover from it," he told her. "There are certain to be others among the men who have had it and recovered too. Why not let us nurse your tiring woman?"

"Nay, Captain," said Blaze. "It is not meant that you nurse a woman, and besides, it is my responsibility as Heartha's mistress to see her safely through this illness. God and the Blessed Mother will protect me, never fear, for I do not."

The captain looked admiringly at her, and nodded his head, acceding to her wishes. His family had been part of Langford since the Wyndhams had been the lords of Langford. He was proud that this woman was his countess. Proud that her sons, who would surely be strong as she was strong, would inherit the lands of Langford.

The innkeeper's servants brought them food. Capons hot from the spit, beef, and ham and mutton. They brought bread and cheese, and ale and wine both. There was even a basket of early strawberries for Blaze, a peace offering of sorts from the justifiably frightened host of The King's Arms, who, nevertheless, regretted having to turn away so prestigious a guest.

After they had eaten, the captain came to Blaze and told her, "The innkeeper, is, of course, terrified, but he says there is an old barn in which he stores hay for the horses that come and go here, just a half mile or so down the road, my lady. He offers to let us shelter there until Heartha is well enough to travel. I've given him the silver we would have paid him for the night's lodging, and he has agreed to see that we are supplied with food. I think we have no choice, and I apologize for the roughness of the accommodation, my lady."

Blaze laughed weakly. "We will have a roof over our heads, Captain, and for that I am grateful. I have seen the inside of a barn before, you know, but what of water?"

"There is a well in the barnyard that the innkeeper swears is potable."

"Let us go then, Captain. I want to get Heartha as comfortable as possible as quickly as possible."

The barn was small, but sound. Heartha was carried from the carriage by two others of the men-at-arms who had recovered from the sweating sickness at various times during their lives. Of the twelve men with Blaze, five had not had the sickness, and these men Blaze ordered to return to RiversEdge to lessen the danger of their contamination. This was not a gift she wished to bring her people from court, and then there were her children. They were so little, both of them, and she shuddered to think of her infant son contracting such an illness, let alone her only legacy from Edmund, their daughter, Nyssa.

"Send the man to me who will be carrying the message tomorrow," said Blaze before she entered the barn, and when he came she told him,

"You are to tell the earl that the children must be moved to Riverside with Lady Dorothy until this is all over. Do you understand?"

"Aye, my lady!" the man answered her.

She felt better then, for although Blaze had never seen the sweating sickness in her life, she knew how virulent it could be. There was scarce a village in England that had not suffered from this strange disease, which had first appeared during the reign of Hal's father, the late king. Ashby, because of its very isolation, had escaped the scourge in the years that it had appeared, but the Morgans had heard of it, as had all Englishmen.

Blaze went into the barn, where poor Heartha had been placed by the men upon a pile of fragrant hay over which the servant's cloak had been spread. Blaze took off her own cloak, and asking one of the men to bring her a bucket of cold water, knelt down next to her servant.

"You'll need some help getting her out of her clothes," said the captain, kneeling next to her.

Together they worked to get Heartha's bodice, heavy skirts, and several voluminous petticoats off her. Blaze pulled her servant's shoes from her feet, but left the stockings and chemise on.

"Take her cap off, and loosen her hair out so the sweat will not be contained, my lady. I always remember my old mother saying that the sweat should not be contained. She always said the more a body sweat, the better, for all the poisons were washed away then."

"Thank you," said Blaze, and did as he had bid her.

"We will take turns watching her, my lady," said the captain. "Go and rest now, for you look tired with your day's ride."

"No," said Blaze. "I will watch until I feel the need for sleep. Heartha is my friend, Captain. I cannot desert her, for she has never deserted me."

The captain nodded, and leaving her, went to the opposite side of the little barn, where the other men, having stabled the horses, had now rolled themselves into their cloaks to sleep. Only the five who had not ever had the illness slept outside, including the coachman's assistant.

Blaze sat pensively sponging her tiring woman with cool water on cloths she had gotten from the innkeeper. Poor Heartha was simply burning up with her fever, and despite all that Blaze could do, the fever seemed not to abate. Still Blaze tried, dipping and wringing the cloths until the water was finally cloudy, the salt of the sick woman's sweat which ran in rivulets down her body, soaking her chemise, soaking her cloak beneath her. Heartha began to shiver uncontrollably after several hours had passed, and Blaze covered the poor woman with her own cloak, but she could not stop the racking shudders that tore through the servant's body. So it went through the night, until finally Blaze saw light coming through the cracks in the barn walls and knew that morning had come. Heartha was still alive, but seemed no better at all.

"Why did you not call me, my lady?" The captain was at her side, his tone accusatory. "If anything had happened to you, the earl would have my life."

Blaze smiled at him. "I am not tired," she said.

"Nonetheless," he replied, "you must rest. It is just dawn, and our messengers are ready to depart even now."

"They must eat," Blaze fretted.

"There was food left from last night that we brought with us, my lady. The men have that. They will not suffer. I will watch for you now and care for your woman, but you must rest." He put his cloak around her, and pointed her toward a deserted section of the barn.

She did not argue with him, for she suddenly realized that despite her brave words, she was indeed tired. How fortunate for her that the captain was wise enough to see it since she was not. Gratefully she lay down, pulling his cloak around her, and was instantly asleep. She did not know how long she had slept, but no sooner had she awakened than one of the men was bringing her bread and cheese and a chicken's leg with some wine. The captain had obviously kept a good watch. She ate, chewing slowly and giving herself time to clear her head. When she had finished she slipped from the barn to find a hidden place where she might relieve herself. It was late afternoon, and the day was as beautiful as the two before it had been.

Returning to the barn, she found the captain still sitting with Heartha. "How is she?" Blaze asked, looking down at her servant, who appeared no better.

"Still alive, but then she's a tough old bird, my lady. I think she may survive this, for she's lasted this long, that's a good sign."

"Go and eat," she told him. I will watch her now." As the captain moved off, Blaze sat down again next to Heartha. The servant was less restless than she had been the night before, but Blaze did not know whether this was a good sign or not. Although she was still dripping with sweat, it did not seem to Blaze to be as heavy a flow of moisture as the previous day, and her shaking head had stopped for the time being.

Dear Heartha! Her tiring woman, aye, but her friend and her confidante ever since Blaze had come to RiversEdge. Dear Heartha, with her maternal wisdom, who could always sort out any situation no matter how difficult it seemed. She could not die! She must not die! Blaze had released her tenacious hold upon Edmund Wyndham's memory, but she was loath to release one of her two remaining links to Edmund and her past.

Blessed Jesu, she silently prayed. *You really have no use for my Heartha, but I do.* Were such prayers heard? Blaze wondered. *Blessed Mary, pray for my Heartha.* She dipped one of the cloths into the bucket of cool water and wringing it out, laid it on the older woman's forehead. Heartha lay still and pale, her breathing labored and harsh. Soon Heartha began to shake violently again, and it took two of the men-at-arms to hold her to prevent her from injuring herself. Blaze had to bite her lip until it bled to keep herself from weeping with her frustration. It seemed no matter what they did, Heartha remained exactly the same, unconscious, alternating between fits of sweating and fits of tremors. All they could do was sit by her, forcing liquid down her throat, and changing the cooling cloths as the monotonous hours crept by.

Night fell once again. The captain sent one of his men to relieve Blaze, and took her out into the warm evening twilight, where the scent of honeysuckle and woodbine was perfuming the air. Almost instantly her spirits were revived. It was such a beautiful evening. An evening for being alive! An evening that gave rise to the promise of a fairer tomorrow. Surely her prayers would be answered!

Servants came down the road from The King's Arms bearing food and a small cask of ale, which they immediately set into a cradle and broached for Blaze and her men. The captain settled his lady upon a three-legged stool he had found in the barn, and brought her a pewter plate containing a piece of rabbit pie, still hot and steaming from the inn's kitchen, oozing with rich brown gravy; a warm cottage loaf; a wedge of sharp, hard cheese; and a pewter goblet of tangy brown ale.

"There's more when you've finished that," the captain said with a smile.

Blaze thanked him, and began to eat, spooning the rabbit pie into her mouth rapidly as she discovered her hunger. She tore the cottage loaf apart, using some of it to sop up the warm gravy. The rest she saved to eat with her cheese. When she had finished every crumb upon her plate, she discovered that she was yet hungry, and getting up, wandered over to where the captain and his men sat. They gave her a piece of ham, and more bread and cheese, which she finished up. Finally sated, she found herself sleepy once more, and finding the captain said, "I will sleep until midnight, but you must wake me then, that I may sit with Heartha through the night. Promise me, Captain."

"I will wake you then, my lady," he said.

Blaze went back into the barn, and curling up in the captain's cloak, quickly fell asleep. She awoke instantly at the captain's touch on her shoulder, asking, "How is she?"

"There is no change, my lady," he said, "but each hour longer she lives is to the good. By tomorrow the earl and his men will reach us. As for Mistress Heartha, she will either be alive or dead, for the sickness rarely is longer than two days."

The night seemed to go so slowly. In the barn only the snores of the sleeping men and the rustlings of the rats in the straw seemed evidence of life. Blaze carefully nursed the small candles she had, which were her only source of light. She had to be so careful with them lest she set the barn with all its stored straw and hay afire. Heartha moaned now and then, but she seemed to have ceased her great thrashing. She still burned with fever, but the quantities of sweat that had previously poured from all her pores seemed to have eased to a mere dampness upon her skin.

Toward dawn Blaze struggled to keep her eyes open. Her huge supper had not set well upon her nervous stomach. Several times her head fell forward upon her chest, and twice she had to splash water from the bucket onto her face to keep herself awake. Finally, unable to help herself, she dozed, awakening with a start to the deathly silence of the barn, suddenly devoid of noise of any kind. Frightened, she reached out her hand to feel Heartha's forehead, for although she could see that the tiring woman was still breathing, her breathing was quiet.

"*M'lady?*" Heartha's voice! Considerably weakened, but Heartha's voice nonetheless, and her eyes were open! Open for the first time in several days. Open, and looking up at Blaze!

"Oh Heartha! You are alive!" Blaze cried joyously. "You are alive, and you have survived!"

Heartha somehow managed a wan smile at her mistress, and then, closing her eyes, she fell into a completely natural sleep.

"She'll make it now," said the captain, who was kneeling beside Blaze. "She just needs rest to gain her strength but the sweating sickness is gone from her, praise God!"

Blaze began to weep with relief, while the captain, rising to his feet, shifted uncomfortably from one foot to the other. Though his instinct bade him comfort her, for she was naught but a woman, his sense of propriety forbade such an intimacy, for she was his better. To his great relief, her tears were brief, as if she recognized his predicament.

"I am all right, Captain," she said, "but if you would have someone watch Heartha now, I need to get outdoors and clear my head." Without even waiting for his answer, she arose and moved out into the budding day.

To the east the dawn was even now breaking, and the horizon was stained with a vibrant red-orange that gave way to a swath of coral pink that was followed by a band of deep purple that ran into lavender and was edged in a ribbon of gold that seemed to run across the entire horizon. Blaze watched with pleasure as this wonderful display heralded the great red ball of the rising sun. Suddenly she became aware of two things. The birds were singing, and there was the distinct sound of hoofbeats on the western road. The hoofbeats of a large party of riders. Her heart began to hammer with excitement even as her husband and his men came into view.

"Captain!" she called excitedly. "Captain! The earl has come!"

The horsemen swept into the barnyard, and leaping from his horse, Anthony gathered Blaze up into his arms. "Thank God, you are safe!" He breathed. "Thank God!" and then he kissed her, to the cheers of his men. Then he asked, "Heartha?"

"The crisis has come and passed," Blaze said. "She will survive, the captain tells me. She is sleeping now."

"Good! We must get you both home, my angel."

"The children? You sent them to Riverside as I bade you? The danger is not over yet, Tony. Not until I am certain that we have brought no other contagion from Greenwich."

"They were gone with my mother within an hour of your message, Blaze. I value their lives every bit as much you do."

"Tony, there is so much I have to tell you," she said. "When I was at Greenwich—" she began, but he cut her off.

"Time to talk on it, madam, when we are home again. Heartha needs a more comfortable place to regain her strength than this barn, and you, I suspect, would like a bath. How near is this inn your messengers spoke of to me?"

"But down the road and around the bend," she answered.

"I shall send some of the men to purchase two additional teams of carriage horses. With four teams drawing the coach, we should be able to reach RiversEdge by midnight. See to Heartha now, that she is ready to travel, my angel."

He had seemed glad to see her. Even grateful that she was unharmed, yet suddenly his manner was brusque. Blaze turned away from her husband, and returning to the barn, gently woke Heartha.

"You must help me to get you back into your clothes, Heartha, for the earl has come to take us home," she said, and the tiring woman nodded. Together they managed to give Heartha some semblance of order in her dress.

"Thank you, my lady," said Heartha, her voice sounding a bit stronger than it had previously.

The extra horses were brought from The King's Arms and the eight beasts were harnessed to the vehicle, which was made ready for its departure. The captain carried the now conscious Heartha to the coach and settled her onto one of the seats. She was weak, but yet able to drink the egg beaten in wine that Blaze had also had her husband's men bring from the inn along with the additional teams. Other food had been brought, and the account settled with the innkeeper. The men ate heartily, but Blaze was still feeling queasy from her meal of the night before, and the thought of having to ride within the coach did not encourage her to add more food to that already souring in her stomach. Someone, however, had to sit with Heartha, and Blaze did not feel it fair to ask one of the captain's men, for they had been so helpful during the last two days.

Dutifully she climbed into her carriage to endure the long hours and many miles of the ride to RiversEdge. The coachman climbed upon the box, and with a lurch they were off. Anthony had hardly spoken to her. There was so much she had to say to him, yet he had not given her the chance. Suddenly it occurred to her that in reaching out to him for help she might have endangered him as well. She had no idea whether or not he had ever had the sweating sickness. What if in her need she had infected him, and he grew ill and died? The worry began to niggle at her as the carriage rumbled along the road. If only Anthony would call a halt to this journey so she might ask him. She shifted edgily in her seat. The coach, despite its lowered windows, was stifling. She felt a trickle down her back. Across from her seat, Heartha seemed not to mind it, snoring peacefully. Blaze loosened her laces so she might undo her bodice a little. There was no one to see, and she would correct her dress when they stopped.

Riding in the forefront of their party, Anthony silently thanked God that she was all right. When the messengers had arrived, he had been in terror that anything should happen to her. All he wanted to do now was get her home safely. Relentlessly he rode on, until finally his captain, drawing his own mount abreast of the earl's, called out to him over the thunder of the hoofbeats, "My lord, we must stop! The horses must be rested or they will not last."

The earl signaled his party to a halt, heeding the advice of his captain.

The men tumbled from their horses, relieved, while Anthony went to the coach to check on his wife and Heartha. Heartha was still sleeping, but Blaze, relacing her bodice, seemed restless and edgy.

"This coach is unbearable," she complained to him. "I am dying of the heat. Heartha is safe by herself for the next few hours. I want to ride, Tony!"

"You are not too tired?" he fretted, thinking that she really did look hot and flushed.

"Nay."

"I will have your horse brought then," he agreed. "Would you like some wine?" and he offered her some from the leather wine bottle that he carried.

Blaze drank several eager swallows, "I am so damned thirsty," she said as she handed it back to him. "You were right, earlier. I want a bath! A lovely cool bath, for it is much too warm for May."

They rested for close to an hour, allowing the horses to browse in the meadow that bordered the road. Heartha was awakened and fed some wine and a little bit of bread soaked in wine before she fell back into another restful sleep. The captain appointed one of the younger of his men to ride within the coach with the recovering tiring woman.

"She should have someone with her, my lady," he said, and Blaze thanked him.

Their journey began again, and at first the air upon her skin was refreshing, but as the afternoon faded into evening and the sun sank behind the hills, Blaze realized that she felt no cooler. If anything, she was growing warmer by the minute, and then suddenly she felt the moisture break as it ran down her back in several streams.

"Anthony!" She could barely hear her own voice over the pounding of the horses' hooves. "*Anthony!*" She was growing dizzy, and she couldn't seem to hang on to her reins. Blaze slumped forward onto her horse's neck, and the man riding behind her, seeing it, pushed his mount forward so he might signal the earl.

Anthony turned at the man's frantic signals, and seeing her barely able to hang on to her horse, he drew his own animal to a stop, leaning over to catch up her flapping reins so he might control her beast too. He leapt from his saddle only seconds before his wife fell from her horse, and catching her up in his arms, he cried frantically to her, "Blaze! Blaze! What is it, my angel?"

"Hot," she muttered, not even opening her eyes. "So very hot, Tony."

"My God," Anthony whispered. "She has the sweating sickness!"

"Let me take her and put her in the coach, my lord. You must not get infected!" the captain interjected.

"No," his master answered him. "I had the disease when I was a young man." He carried Blaze to the coach, and calling the young man-at-arms from the vehicle, he placed his wife upon the seat.

Their journey began again, but this time it was a desperate race to reach RiversEdge. Heartha had passed the crisis, and was now well on the road to recovery, but Blaze was only beginning to run her course of the illness. They had to get her home, where she could be nursed properly. The captain had sent two of his men ahead to alert the household staff of the latest developments, and of their needs.

The moon rose, lighting the road ahead for them as they traveled along. Finally the night landscape began to grow familiar, and at last they recognized that they were on Langford lands. They galloped through sleeping villages, hurrying to get their precious burden to safety, cutting over onto the shorter river road. The moon silvering the waters of the Wye gave the impression of great tranquillity, a peace broken only by the thunder of frantic hooves and the noise of the lumbering coach. At last the house itself came into view, the windows lit and awake as RiversEdge anxiously awaited their arrival.

Servants poured from the house as the vehicle clattered up to the front door. The doors of the carriage were pulled open before Anthony was even off his horse, gentle hands reaching in to lift their countess out of the coach; to help the weak and dazed Heartha. Blaze was quickly carried to her own bedchamber and laid tenderly upon her bed, which was already prepared for her. A bevy of maidservants scurried forth to remove her garments, to place her in a dry nightrail.

"The lasses will watch her ladyship around the clock, my lord," said Mistress Ellis, the housekeeper.

"No," said Tony, shaking his head. "I will care for her myself. I must!" He removed his traveling cloak and his doublet. "Bring me what I need, tell me what I must do, and allow only those who have had the disease into this apartment."

"My lord," Mistress Ellis admonished him, "it is not a man's place to nurse a sick woman."

He looked up at her, and his eyes were filled with such pain and fear that the housekeeper was startled. "She is my wife," he said simply, and drawing a chair up near the bedside, he sat down. She looked so small, he thought, looking at her lying there, and when her body began to be racked by tremors, he felt actual pain knifing through him. He remembered the sweating sickness from his youth, when both he and Edmund had contracted it. Neither of them had suffered greatly, and within a day, each had passed through his crisis; but he also remembered that there had been many deaths from the same epidemic that had struck them.

Blaze could not die. She could not! There was so much he had to tell her. So much that they had to do together. She was his very life. She was the heartbeat of Langford and its peoples. Surely God could not take her from him, from the children, from them all. Gently he mopped the perspiration that streamed down her face, and placed a fresh cool cloth upon her forehead.

Hot. Hot. Why was it so hot? she wondered. She could never remember a summer at Ashby being so hot. *Mama?* Where was her mama? Bliss! Blythe! Where is Mama? Probably taking care of her new baby. There was always a new baby. This one was called Delight. Father John had gotten so angry at Mama when she had told him the baby's new name. Mama had laughed, saying the baby would be baptized Mary Delight, as her other daughters were baptized Mary Blaze, Mary Bliss, and Mary Blythe, and the church would be satisfied. Mama said that Mary was the best of saints' names.

Hot. Hot. Would they ever find husbands? There was no gold for their dowries. Papa and Mama were worried. The squire's oldest son tried to kiss me in the orchard. I hit him. He will not dare to tell. Bliss says I am a fool, for if he'll take me without a dowry at least one of us will have a husband. I would sooner remain a maiden than marry the squire's son. Let Bliss have him, the slimy toad, but she will not, for she would climb higher.

I am to be wed! Oh, I am so afraid, but no one must see my fear. A countess does not show such emotions. I shall have to find a husband for her. I shall have to help them all. Ohhh! He is so handsome. If only my husband is as attractive, but nicer. Oh, please, Blessed Mother let my husband be kinder than Anthony Wyndham!

Edmund! Edmund! Dear God, how I love you! We have a daughter, though I'd as lief it been a son for Langford. Nyssa? You would call her Nyssa? Aye, lord, it is a good name! Edmund, I love you. Oh, Edmund, do not leave me! You cannot be dead! Not dead! Not dead! I hate you, Anthony! I hate you! You have killed my Edmund!

Oh, God, I am afraid! I am so afraid! Why do they bow and scrape to me simply because the king wishes to take me to his bed? I want to go home to RiversEdge, but I cannot. I should not have come here. Oh, God, I cannot cry out else I offend him. Please! Please do not force me! I do not want a lover. I do not! Oh, why do I feel such pleasure when I do not want to feel it? I do not understand. I do not understand.

Poor Hal. Being a king is not easy. Power, like everything else, has its price. Everybody wants something. Hal wants a son, but he cannot get one on the queen. He says he is not truly wed. I do not know. Poor Hal. Poor Hal. What will happen to me when he tires of me? I did not want this. I hate it! Poor Hal. Only Will, the fool, and I truly understand him.

Hot. Hot. Why am I so hot? I want to open my eyes, but I cannot. Help me, Tony! Help me!

Helplessly he watched her throughout the night as she poured sweat from every pore of her body. She burned with a terrible fever, and he could only try to aid her, placing and replacing cool cloths upon her forehead, forcing wine and chilled well water down her throat. She moaned incessantly, and moved restlessly upon her bed, and he could do naught.

In the morning two little maidservants entered the bedchamber, bringing with them fresh linens and instructions from Mistress Ellis that his lordship was to come and eat something while they changed her ladyship's bed and put a fresh gown upon her. Anthony rose stiffly, and with a worried look at his wife left the room. He was not gone long, however. Just long enough to ascertain that Heartha was awake and stronger. The tiring woman wept at learning that her mistress was even now in the throes of the illness.

"She should not have nursed me, my lord. I would have told her so, but that I could not! Oh, if she dies I shall never forgive myself!" Heartha declared.

"She could have contracted the disease from anyone at court, and not necessarily from you, Heartha. You must not blame yourself. Blaze will not die. *She cannot!* We all need her too much. Now, you must get well, for I shall need your help in the nursing of my wife."

"You are not nursing her yourself, my lord?" Heartha was as shocked as Mistress Ellis had been the day before.

Anthony smiled. "I must be with her," he said, and then he left his wife's servant, promising to see that she had the latest news on her lady's condition. He stopped in the kitchens to take a plate of cold meats, bread, and cheeses, then returned to Blaze's bedchamber, where the two maids had already changed the bedding and seen to dry attire for their mistress. With a curtsy they hurried from the room, leaving him alone with Blaze once more.

Slowly Anthony chewed his food, eating more from habit than any feeling of real need. He could taste nothing. Only the burning heat of the strong wine he drank made any impression upon him. She lay so still. So quiet now, and yet, taking the cloth from her forehead, he felt it, almost recoiling from the heat. She was so sick. Dear God, help her, he said silently. *Help her!* It was then that Blaze began to shake.

Hot. Oh, it was so hot! She was Anthony's wife now. Not Edmund's, but Anthony's. Anthony told the king a great lie in order to become her husband. He should not have lied to Hal, but how very convenient for the king that he did. Still, Hal must not know. He must not know that Anthony had lied. He lied because he loves me. He loves me! I do not love him. Oh, I should! He is so good to me. He is so good to Nyssa. Delight loves Anthony. Poor Delight. I would not hurt her, but I have. I don't love you, Tony. I don't! I don't! I do! Oh, yes, I do! I must not! I must be true to Edmund's memory. I will not tell, and no one will ever know. God will know. Oh, what will I do? The queen won't listen to me! Poor Hal! Oh, Poor Hal! Mistress Boleyn is a wicked creature. She would be the king's wife. Poor Hal! Poor, poor Hal!

The hours passed, and Blaze lay unconscious upon her bed, burning with fever one moment, then racked by fierce tremors that Anthony feared would pull her apart. Night came, and the earl left his wife's bedside to go once again in to Heartha to tell her that nothing had changed. He returned to find another plate of food on the table by his side. He ate listlessly, without appetite, leaving half the food upon the server.

Soak the cloth in water. Wring the cloth. Remove the warm cloth. Put a fresh one on her forehead. Drink, my angel. Put the goblet to her lips, and slowly drizzle the liquid down her throat. Drink, Blaze. You need the liquid. His eyes grew heavy, but he would let no one else watch until the danger was past. He struggled to keep awake, head falling forward, jerking with a start. Finally he could no longer help himself, and he dozed.

Hot. Hot. Would it ever be cool again? We have a son. Oh, he is so beautiful. I will call him Philip. Not Edmund, for Edmund is dead. Not Anthony, for I have my Anthony. Not Henry. Too many Henrys, and I will not have his parentage impugned by those fools who cannot count upon their fingers. Oh, Philip, I love you. How like your father you are. I love your father too, my little son, but dare I tell him? I have to leave you, my son. The king needs me. I am ever and always the king's most loyal servant. Poor Hal. How he suffers for lack of a son like my Philip. How he suffers for the love of Mistress Boleyn. He loves her. I know he does, but she will not admit to her own feelings. I think she loves him. She is so jealous. Poor Hal. He does not know she loves him.

Hot. Hot. It is not so hot now as it was before. I have been so hot for so long, it seems, but it is not so hot now. The king does not know he is loved. Anthony does not know that I love him. I must tell him that I love him, but we must get Heartha home. She has been so sick, my good Heartha. I must tell Anthony that I love him. I must tell him! I must! What if I die and he does not know that I loved him? I must tell him! Anthony! Anthony!

"*Anthony!*" Her voice was a raspy whisper. "*Anthony!*" Blaze opened her eyes to see him sitting by her side. There was a rough stubble of beard upon his face, his shirt was unbuttoned. He looked haggard and untidy. "*Anthony!*" she called him a third time.

He heard her voice. It penetrated deep into his sleeping consciousness, and he was suddenly awake. "*Blaze!*" He tore the damp cloth from her forehead and put his hand upon it. It was cool. *It was cool!* The fever was gone, and she had survived her crisis. "Oh, my angel, you will live! Thank God, you will live!"

"Anthony, I love you," she whispered. "*I love you!*"

He felt his eyes welling with tears, and embarrassed, he roughly brushed them away with the back of his hand. "You do not have to say that to me, my angel," he said softly.

"But I do! I love you! The king asked me if I loved you, and I realized that I did. Oh, Anthony, I have been such a fool! What sane woman would have a dead husband in place of a living one?" She reached out to take his hand in hers. "I love you, Lord Wyndham," she said.

Lifting her hand to his lips, he kissed it fervently. "And I love you, Blaze Wyndham. I have loved you from the first moment I ever saw you. How I curst the unkind fate that conspired to keep us apart! Now you are really mine. I will love you for the rest of my life, and beyond!" he declared. Slipping her hand from his she reached up to touch his face with a gentle pat. "No woman," she said quietly, her voice stronger, "has surely ever been as greatly blest as I have, Anthony. I have been loved by three men, and I have given my love in return; but never, my darling, have I received a greater love than that which you have given me. I shall thank God for you for the rest of my days."

"And I shall see that you do, madam," he teased her tenderly, "for I intend to be by your side for always."

"For always," she agreed. *For always!* Did that not have a fine ring to it?

Epilogue

GREENWICH

May 19, 1536

*B*laze stood in the king's privy chamber looking out upon the River Thames. Yesterday had been rainy and extremely windy, but today the sun shone brightly from a cloudless sky. Across the river the king's fleet bobbed in the gentle flow of the incoming tide. It seemed as if nothing had changed, Blaze thought, and yet everything had changed.

She had not been in this room, had not been to Greenwich in nine years, and oh, what had happened in that time. Breaking with the church in Rome, the king had finally been freed from Catherine of Aragon. He had married Anne Boleyn, and their only surviving child, the princess Elizabeth, had been born in the same year. The king was now forty-five, and still had no legitimate son. The tragedy was not just for Hal, but for England as well.

He had called for her once more. The royal messenger arriving like an unwelcome voice from the past less than a week ago. This time there had been no argument between herself and Anthony. He had known that she would go, but this time he came also. She had wanted him to come, for they had grown so together over the past years that to be apart was too painful. So, leaving their children in Lady Dorothy's care, they had come to Greenwich.

The king had changed. He was no longer quite so slender, but then, Blaze thought with a wry smile, neither was she. She was thirty years old now, with a marriageable thirteen-year-old daughter. There was a sadness, however, about Hal, and a new harshness about his mouth that had not been there before. She had curtsied low on their meeting this morning, and he had taken her into his arms and just held her for a long minute.

"How many sons do you have now, Blaze Wyndham?" he asked her.

339

"Four, my lord. Philip is now nine, Giles is six, Richard, who is four, and Edward, who is but a year old this April past."

"Your husband is fortunate in his wife and family," the king said, and she heard the sadness in his voice.

"Oh, Hal, I am so sorry!" she told him.

"Do not be!" he said fiercely. "You warned me! They all warned me of Anne, but I could not hear any of you, for I was blinded by my passion for her, may God help me!"

"She loves you," said Blaze. "I could see it even nine years ago. She was so afraid of losing you."

"*Love?*" the king roared. "The witch knows nothing of love. Of lust, aye! But nothing of love! Had she loved me, she would not have committed adultery with my friends, and involved herself in incest with her brother. Nay, Blaze. Anne did not love me."

He dared her to dispute him, but Blaze, who did not for one minute believe in any of Queen Anne's alleged crimes, realized that she must remain silent. Anne had failed in her primary duty to give the king a son, and now she would suffer for it. Rumor had it that the king had already picked himself another young flower of English nobility to make his wife. "I will not argue with you, Hal," she told him. "Only tell me why you have called me here."

"You and Will are my only real friends, Blaze," the king said.

"I tell him that Margot is his friend too," replied Will Somers, who was also with them. He stroked the small brown monkey that he cradled in his arms. Will had not changed. He was still lean and stooped, with his strangely young face that in a way resembled his pet's.

"Margot, as I recall," said Blaze, smiling, "bites."

"And has a great preference for royal fingers," muttered the king.

Suddenly through the open window there came the distinct low boom of a cannon from upriver. Both Blaze and Will crossed themselves, but the king's face was a blank, giving no hint about what he might have thought.

"It is done then," said Henry. "The witch is dead." He looked to Blaze. "I have brought you a long way simply to hold my hand in my hour of need, as you might do for one of your children. Thank you."

"I am, sire, ever your most loyal servant," Blaze answered him quietly.

The king smiled at her. "Aye, Blaze Wyndham, my little country girl, you are, are you not? Well, you are free to go now. Back to your husband, who is pacing so impatiently in my antechamber. Back to your beloved RiversEdge, which perhaps I shall even visit someday."

"And where will you go now, Hal?" she asked him.

"To Jane," he said simply. "It is not like the last time, is it? Catherine is dead these five months past, and now Anne. I am free to marry my gentle Jane. Surely God will smile upon this union, a true union, and we will have a son."

"Oh, Hal, how I pray for it," Blaze told him. "Jane Seymour is a good and sweet lady. You will be happy with her, I know it! God will indeed bless you with a son for England." Blaze curtsied low to him, and smiling, she backed from the king's privy chamber out into the other room where her husband eagerly awaited her.

Together Blaze and Anthony hurried from the palace down across the green lawns of Greenwich to where their barge was awaiting to take them upriver. They went hand in hand, laughing and talking happily to one another, totally unaware that the king was watching them from his windows as they went.

I have loved three women in my life, Henry Tudor thought. *Two are now dead. Blaze calls her gentle Jane, and indeed she is. I think I shall come to love her too.* He watched as Anthony helped Blaze down into their barge. He watched as the earl entered the barge himself, and it pulled away from the royal quay. Aye, the king thought again, *I have loved three women in my life. Two are dead. Farewell, my little country girl. Farewell!*

A Note from the Author

*H*enry Tudor was married to Jane Seymour on May 30, 1536, in a private ceremony which was held in the Queen's Closet at his palace of Whitehall. Anne Boleyn had been dead but eleven days. Queen Jane chose for her motto: *Bound to obey and serve*. This she did well, producing for Henry his only legitimate son, Edward, born on the twelfth of October 1537. Sadly, Jane Seymour died of a childbed fever some twelve days later, on October 24, 1537. Henry mourned her deeply.

Henry took three more wives in his efforts to secure the Tudor succession. Anne, a princess of the duchy of Cleves, whom he divorced immediately, to her great relief. Catherine Howard, a younger cousin of Anne Boleyn's, who, like her relative, was executed on the Tower green the thirteenth of February 1542. It was expected that the king, who was now over fifty, would remain a bachelor for the rest of his life, but he did not, marrying Catherine Parr, a widow, in 1543. The new queen, who was childless but had nursed two elderly husbands and raised their children, was the ideal mate for the king in his declining years.

Henry Tudor died on the twenty-eighth of January 1547. He was succeeded by his son, Edward VI, a boy of but nine. Ruled over by a series of "protectors," he died without issue on July 6, 1553, not quite sixteen years of age. Although the young king had attempted to alter the succession in favor of his cousin, Lady Jane Grey, English law prevailed and Catherine of Aragon's daughter, Mary, succeeded to the throne. Mary reigned five and a half troubled years, during which time she married her cousin, King Philip of Spain, and brought the Inquisition to England for a brief period, thereby gaining the enmity of her people. She, too, died without issue.

Cardinal Wolsey had said that Henry Tudor would never marry Anne Boleyn, and yet he had. He said that no child of Henry's and Anne's would rule England. Elizabeth Tudor, the only child of that unhappy mis-alliance, came into her inheritance on the seventeenth of November 1558. Since the death of her father she had faced many terrors, including the stigma of bastardy, the suspicions of her half-brother's protectors and her half-sister's advisers. She had survived the rigors of the Tower, coming perilously close to death on several occasions. She had lived in dishonored exile at Woodstock in her sister's reign. She survived it all.

Upon learning that she was Queen of England, she is reported to have said, "This is the Lord's doing; it is marvelous in our eyes." Anne Boleyn's daughter reigned over her people for forty-four years, giving her name to a golden age still hailed in history: *Elizabethan*. She died on March 24, 1603. She was England's greatest queen.

About the Author

Bertrice Small has written thirty novels of historical romance and three erotic novellas. She is a *New York Times* bestselling author and the recipient of numerous awards. In keeping with her profession, Bertrice Small lives in the oldest English-speaking town in the state of New York, founded in 1640. Her light-filled studio includes the paintings of her favorite cover artist, Elaine Duillo, and a large library—but no computer as she works on an IBM Quietwriter 7. Her longtime assistant, Judy Walker, types the final draft. Because she believes in happy endings, Bertrice Small has been married to the same man, her hero, George, for thirty-nine years. They have a son, Thomas, a daughter-in-law, Megan, and two adorable grandchildren, Chandler David and Cora Alexandra. Longtime readers will be happy to know that Nicki the Cockatiel flourishes along with his fellow housemates, Pookie, the long-haired greige and white, Honeybun, the petite orange lady cat with the cream-colored paws, and Finnegan, the black long-haired baby of the family, who is now three.